LORI G. ARMSTRONG

SNOW BLIND

PRESS

Medallion Press, Inc.
Printed in USA

Published 2008 by Medallion Press, Inc.

The MEDALLION PRESS LOGO
is a registered trademark of Medallion Press, Inc.

Typeset in Adobe Caslon Pro
Printed in the United States of America

ISBN: 9781933836591

10 9 8 7 6 5 4 3 2 1
First Edition

ACKNOWLEDGMENTS:

My family complains I usually thank them last, so I'm thanking them first: Lauren, Haley, Tessa— every damn day I'm so proud to be your mom. Mr. LGA—thanks for letting me live my dream; you're the biggest part of it.

For my Grandma, Mary Maxine Austin Knickrehm: yes, I believed you when you swore interesting things do happen at old folks' homes, and thank you for planting the germ of an idea in my head. I'm so lucky to have you in my life.

Thanks to Kerry Estevez of Medallion Press for bringing another Julie Collins book to the lineup; to my editor, Helen Rosburg, for 'getting' Julie's voice and letting me stay true to it; and to Adam Mock for another brilliant cover.

Again, a huge debt of gratitude to my invaluable crit partner, Mary LaHood, who's been with me on Julie's journey since day one, who never balks at my tight deadlines and keeps me honest.

Gracias to my fellow author and friend Mario Acevedo for the help with Spanish language phrases. Errors in translation belong to me.

I bow to the expertise of Jane Wipf Pfeifle—friend, attorney, judge, voracious reader, supermom, Jane-of-all-trades—my inside source on legal matters in the state of South Dakota: once again you rocked me with your generosity. Ditto to my buddy and author JD "Dusty" Rhoades for answering other lawyerly questions with good humor. Any mistakes are mine to bear.

A million thanks to Montana rancher Sarpy Sam (www.sarpysam. com) for helping with this greenhorn's questions. Your insight and knowledge of cattle and ranching in the modern day Wild West were amazingly helpful. Any inaccuracies fall squarely on my shoulders.

Dr. Doug Lyle, who never bats an eye when I pose very bizarre questions and is eager and prompt in his responses. Thank you, doc.

My fellow First Offenders, Alison Gaylin, Jeff Shelby and Karen Olson; for friendship above and beyond what we ever envisioned. Other writer friends who keep me sane, make me laugh, are great for a good cry or a good drunk, my biggest cheerleaders: Cat Cody, Toni McGee Causey, Mary Stella, Karen Hall.

Readers, fans, librarians, bookclubs, bookstores…thanks for the support; I am humbled and deeply grateful.

Found in the classified ads:

WANTED: Elderly Caretaker/Health-care Worker
HOURS: Variable, prefer full-time
DUTIES: All—from fixing meals to fixing the TV remote
QUALIFICATIONS:
1) Must be able to follow a strict medication schedule
2) Must be good at locating lost objects
3) Must listen without complaint
4) Must provide assistance with personal hygiene
PAY RATE: Volunteer

CHAPTER 1

"DIDJA EVER NOTICE OLD FOLKS' HOMES SMELL EXACTLY like funeral homes?"

Kevin's blistering look singed my eyelashes. "Maybe you could've said that a little louder, Julie."

"What?" I gestured to the chess-playing octogenarians in the glass-walled room beyond us. "It's not like anyone heard me. Most of them are deaf anyway."

He sighed.

"I'm just saying . . ."

"Enough. Stay back and let me handle this."

I hid my smile as he tromped to the receptionist's desk. Despite a friendship spanning two decades I found it easy to play him.

My triumph faded when I remembered why we were undercover at Prairie Gardens Assisted Living Facility. My best pal and business partner did his share of playing me, too.

Evidently my charm wasn't as pervasive as I'd imagined since he'd taken this case even after I'd argued against it.

Two days ago we found Amery Grayson dithering in the hallway leading to the offices of Wells/Collins Investigations. The bitterly cold month of February drags along like a three-legged dog in the private eye business, which was why Kevin quickly ushered the lovely Ms. Grayson into the conference room before she bolted.

I'd always pooh-poohed the iconic PI yarn where a beautiful, mysterious moll sauntered in, reeking of sex and turmoil. At first glance Amery's bloodshot eyes and trembling mouth evoked sympathy for whatever crisis marred her classic features. At second glance, Amery was all leg, all blonde, and all wet behind the ears.

Young and troubled. A bad combo.

A combo that kicked Kevin's protective instincts and his hormones into high gear, because the next thing I knew, I was fetching Kleenex, water, and smelling salts for Miz Amery while Kevin patted her hand and encouraged her to pour out her tale of woe.

Amery tearfully confided she'd never done anything like hiring a PI—she didn't know if we could help her, *blah blah blah*. Her spiel wasn't anything I hadn't heard a hundred times before. Somehow I managed to block out her simpering tone and focused on the issue: She feared someone was taking advantage of her grandfather.

Vernon Sloane resided at Prairie Gardens, an assisted living/retirement facility. The biggest issue in his life, besides being afflicted with the beginning stages of Alzheimer's disease, was the loss of his driver's license after he'd wrecked his car. A combative Vernon kept trying to sneak out of Prairie Gardens at all hours of the day and night, and Amery had received four phone calls in the last four months after Gramps had been caught wandering around outside the facility looking for his beloved classic Buick.

Which led Amery to the first problem: her concerns about the management team running the facility and the apparent passing off of nursing and security issues to volunteers.

Prairie Gardens boasted a new "in-reach program," Prime Time Friends, where volunteers visited residents at least once a week. Amery wondered why volunteers from an *in*-reach program would take an elderly man *out* on supervised, unnsanctioned outings. Why they'd encourage him to cancel doctor's appointments with the in-house physician and offer to drive Vernon to a specialist outside the facility.

The situation was getting progressively worse. The last time Amery visited her grandfather, he was more confused than usual, and he consistently called her by her dead mother's name, Susan. Amery discovered another problem while looking for her grandfather's missing medications. Crumpled up in his shaving kit

3

she'd found his quarterly bank statement. Vernon had withdrawn cash totaling more than thirty-five thousand dollars.

When Amery asked her grandfather about the missing money, he accused her—again referring to her as Susan—of stealing it from him.

Amery's hands were tied when it came to Vernon Sloane's financial affairs. Without guardianship she couldn't do anything to ensure her grandfather wasn't being bilked out of every penny of his meager retirement, or legally address his worsening health issues. She'd attempted to talk to the in-house physician, but he refused to tell her anything for fear of violating doctor/patient confidentiality. She'd spoken with the finance office at the retirement center, hoping they'd shed light on whether Vernon used the money to pay in advance for his long-term care. But without power of attorney, she was stonewalled.

Poor Amery was beside herself with worry and guilt.

I let Kevin murmur soothing words that would've choked me. He promised we'd look into the situation as he escorted her to her car.

My opinion differed from Kevin's. I figured Amery was jealous and angry her grandfather was spending her money and time with someone else, and therefore was trying to make problems. Kevin figured a couple of greedy people saw a confused old man and decided to take advantage, knowing Amery had no legal power to stop them.

So here we were trying to sort fact from fiction in an overheated, overdecorated reception area that reeked of sour unwashed bodies, tuna casserole, and Lysol antiseptic.

"Hey, sis." Kevin waved me over. "Dee is ready to give us a tour."

We'd decided to check out the facility by pretending to be looking for a place for our Aunt Rose. Hopefully we could wander around and ask the residents questions after the official tour ended, or else the idea was a total bust.

I smiled, thrusting out my hand. "Hi, Dee. I'm Kate Sawyer, Jack's sister."

Dee, a dowdy office drone with gooey eyes, wasn't the type of hard sell closer I'd expected. After she released my hand I withheld a shudder at her wimpy handshake.

"Nice to meet you, Kate. We're all set, so why don't you follow me?"

We stopped at a set of double steel doors. Dee ran her key card through an electronic reading mechanism bolted beside the door handle. The green light flashed and the locks clicked. A mechanical hum sounded. Very high tech.

Also very much like Martinez's various security setups.

Dee opened the metal doors and bustled down the long, empty hallway. She didn't bother to double check if the doors even latched behind us, say nothing of if they'd locked securely. Huh. Martinez had me so paranoid about security measures that I almost double checked the damn thing myself.

Kevin whispered in my ear, "Kate Sawyer? You've been watching way too many episodes of *Lost*, babe."

"Yeah? You started it, *Jack*."

"Your fantasy of becoming a Jack and Sawyer sandwich doesn't bother Martinez?"

"Nope. As a matter of fact he—"

"I thought we'd start in the wing with the private entrances." Dee spiraled around and walked backward while she lectured us. She pointed to the metal doors with a decent amount of blank wall space between each one. "These units are like condos. Residents have separate access to the outside and enjoy more autonomy than residents in the other wings."

"I'm assuming these residents aren't in need of daily assistance?"

"No. Actually, the residents must pass a physical to prove they're in decent health when they initially buy in."

My brain stumbled on the words *buy in*.

But Kevin's brain worked differently and he asked, "What do you mean by *initially*?"

"We are in the business of providing long-term care. If a healthy seventy-year-old man buys a private residence, but at some point needs to change to a unit where he's monitored either part-time or full-time, we can accommodate him almost immediately without a huge upheaval in the tenant's life."

Kevin flashed his teeth. "Kate and I are both hopelessly undereducated about the differences in the types of units Prairie Gardens offers. Would it be too much trouble to ask you to clarify them for us, please?"

Nice going, Kev.

"I'd be happy to," Dee trilled. "Our purpose here at Prairie Gardens is to provide the type of housing to suit anyone's needs. We have private residences like these." She made a sweeping Vanna White gesture. "However, the majority of our living spaces are devoted to individual apartments, the one bedroom/one bath, kitchen, and living room type efficiency units, with call buttons and twice daily check-ins.

"In the far south wing are the full-time care units for residents with terminal problems, and those are a basic hospital room with round-the-clock care from a twenty-four-hour nursing staff. And lastly, we have a wing devoted to temporary care, such as recovery from strokes or accidents, where the spouse or caretaker may live on the premises with the recovering party if he or she chooses to, and work in conjunction with the healthcare professionals. Some folks stay as little as four days, some as long as four weeks, but beyond that, they'll have to move to terminal care."

"Are all these buildings connected?"

"Yes, but only for selected staff. Residents cannot freely float from one unit to the next."

"And the 'buy in' factor? What exactly is that?"

Kevin asked.

"Somewhat like purchasing a house. The resident buys a unit, which includes all utilities and amenities of the facility—use of the pool, spa, weight room, activities, professional services, transportation, meals, medical staff—and they can live here in any of the three housing sections. Let's say health circumstances change, requiring a move from a private residence unit to a general care unit, or even to the acute care unit. That resident can stay until he or she passes on. If there's a surviving spouse, the same applies. Then the contract is fulfilled."

"And in the case of the private residences? Is ownership passed on to the surviving secondary family members?"

"No. Then the residence reverts back to us."

Whoa. That was just plain weird. I couldn't imagine shelling out a hundred grand and ending up with . . . nothing. Then again, the tenants were dead, so what did they care? And probably if their surviving children shoved them in a place like this in the first place, they shouldn't expect a windfall when Granny and Gramps kicked it anyway.

Cynical, Julie Ann.

"However, we understand that kind of cash outlay isn't possible for everyone, so we do rent the general units by the year, or by the month, or in the case of the temporary wing, by the week." Dee smiled at me. "Any idea of which type of unit your aunt would prefer?"

"Oh, our Aunt Rose is a social butterfly, so I imagine

she'd want an apartment right in the thick of things."

Dee's smile dimmed and the dollar signs in her eyes dulled. "Well, then, let's head over to that section of the complex, known around here as 'the hive.'" We exited the way we came in.

We hung a left at the front desk, passed through a set of double doors, and ended up at an unmanned kiosk. Eight long hallways spread out like a spider's legs. My gaze swung to the end of the first corridor. A single glass door marked the exit. It appeared to be a barred door, but I'd have to double check it to see if it was attached to some kind of alarm system, or if it was even locked. If not, that might be the reason Mr. Sloane was sneaking out so easily.

I squinted at the ceiling. Plenty of sprinkler heads but not a single security camera. Odd. Why wouldn't they monitor the hallways? Because people were paying to be here and didn't want to escape? Well, with the exception of Vernon Sloane.

It bothered me that the higher priced living area had better security.

Dee chatted amiably at Kevin. "Here's one of the efficiency units." She slid off a stretchy fuchsia plastic armband from around her wrist and rammed a big silver key in the lock. The door swung inward. A Renuzit air freshener couldn't mask the musty scent assaulting my nostrils.

The room was bare, save for the hideous orange plaid curtains covering the windows, and a frosted light fixture hanging from the ceiling. The kitchen was galley-style, located in a tiny alcove off to the left. A miniature breakfast bar separated the kitchen from the miniscule living room.

"Most of our residents are singles, widows or widowers. The bedroom and bathroom are through here." Dee took three steps and we followed her.

With no windows in the bedroom, the heavy floral wallpaper, the cloying scent of fake roses, and the low ceiling, I felt trapped inside an old-fashioned hatbox. To calm my nerves, I focused on the dusty ceiling fan while Kevin inspected the bathroom.

"As you can see, everything—the shower, the toilet, and the sink—are all handicapped accessible. Does your aunt have special needs?" Dee asked politely.

"No. She isn't as spry as she used to be. She relies pretty heavily on a cane. She's still too proud to admit she could use a walker."

"Understandable. But I do feel the need to warn you that we are a large facility, and fairly spread out, so she might need that walker."

"Thank you. We will need to take that into consideration before we make a decision."

"Any other questions about these units?"

Kevin shook his head. "We'd like to see the common rooms, if that's possible."

"I'll be happy to show you any place you like."

I bolted from the claustrophobic unit and started down the hallway at a good clip.

Kevin snagged my arm. "What is your problem?"

"The same one I had when we walked in," I hissed. "What the hell are we doing here? I don't want a fucking three-hour tour, Skipper. And if the empty hallways are any indication, chances are pretty high the Geritol set is napping and no one will talk to us anyway. This is pointless. Can we go now?"

"No. Amery paid the retainer up front, and near as I can figure, we still owe her two hours, so buck up, *sis*."

"I fucking hate you right now, *bro*."

Footsteps halted behind us and we spun in tandem toward Dee.

"Is there a problem?"

Kevin said, "No," the same time I said, "Yes."

Dee kept a polite mask as she waited for us to clarify.

"Could you point me to the nearest bathroom?"

"Certainly. Return to the main reception area and it's down the short corridor to your left. Can't miss it."

"Thanks."

"Would you like us to wait for you?"

"Not necessary. You two go on. I'll catch up."

Kevin glared at me; I resisted the urge to flip him off before I meandered away.

Might've been petty, but I took my own sweet time reaching the bathroom. I checked my makeup and my cell phone messages. When I couldn't justify hiding out in the crapper any longer, I sauntered to the receptionist's desk.

One plus-sized woman a decade older than me sat behind a gigantic monitor. Since she'd left the sliding glass partition open, she didn't bother to get up and acknowledge me; rather, she said loudly, "Something I can help you with?"

"My brother and I are taking a tour with Dee, and I wondered if you had a map of the facility?"

"They should be on the counter." She squinted and sighed. "Hang on. I see the clipboard. Looks like Dee moved them to her desk again." She rolled her chair back.

"No, I don't want to be a bother. I think I can reach it if you don't mind me hanging over the ledge."

"Go for it." She disappeared behind the monitor and I heard pecking noises from her keyboard again.

As I leaned across the counter, I noticed two manila folders on Dee's desk right beside the clipboard. One marked *PTF Schedules*; the other marked *Monthly Activity Sign-up Sheets*.

I shot a quick glance at the office worker. She wasn't paying attention to me. *Tsk-tsk.* I lifted the edge of the clipboard with my left hand, slid the folders underneath it with my right, and scooped up the whole pile.

A tiny shot of adrenaline worked free. Now this was the part I liked: snooping. Standing at the counter opening the files wasn't an option, so I moved to the seating area, keeping my back to the desk.

I flipped open the cover on the *Activity* file. My gaze

zeroed in on the volunteers' names. Five total. Millie Stephens. Bunny Jones. Margie Lessle. Dottie Rich. Luella Spotted Tail. Millie was listed as the bus driver/volunteer for the trip to the Rushmore Mall with Margie assisting. Bunny was conducting a memoir writing class in the common room with Dottie assisting.

More of the same. Busy. Busy.

Were these women on crack? Or just bored out of their freakin' minds?

Odd. Nothing listed for Luella Spotted Tail on the activity list.

I turned the map to the blank side and jotted down the info. After making sure no one was watching me, I switched to the *PTF* folder. The time sheets were organized by pod and room number; eight pods, ten rooms in each pod. Inside the individual hour boxes, from 9:00 to 3:00, Monday through Friday, were the volunteer's initials. I skimmed the sheet for Luella Spotted Tail. Luella was a busy woman. Her dance card was filled five out of five days, as she brightened elderly folks' lives.

But the majority of her time was blocked off for room 208 from 10:00 to 2:00 three days a week.

From a WTF standpoint, Luella only spent an hour with the other occupants of the room numbers on her list? One hour, once every two weeks? But lucky number 208 received twelve hours per week? Didn't someone in Administration find that strange and question her about it?

I scanned the time sheet for the previous month and found the identical schedule and no notation from Luella's supervisor—B. Boner—just a scrawled signature as final approval.

Although the name wasn't listed I knew who lived in room 208. I also realized that no other volunteer's initials were in any of the time boxes attributed to room 208. I thumbed through the remaining paperwork in the folder. On the last page marked *Extra*, at the top of the list, in roughly an hour, two full hours were blocked off as personal time for Luella Spotted Tail and Mr. Room 208—Vernon Sloane.

Guilt assailed me for my earlier dismissal of Amery's concerns. As far as I could tell, no other resident spent time away from Prairie Gardens with Luella on a regular basis.

A door slammed, startling me. I returned to the reception desk and poked my head through the partition.

"Thanks. I think I have a better handle on this place now. I'll just put this back"—and I purposely knocked the clipboard, the folders, and all the papers off Dee's desk right onto the floor. "Oh jeez. I'm so sorry; I'm such a klutz; let me come on back there and help you clean it up—"

"No unauthorized people in the office; it's against company policy," she snapped.

"I'm sorry."

She angrily hefted her girth out of the overtaxed office chair and lumbered to the jumbled mess.

Using the map, I trudged down the main hallway to the common rooms. I'd made it about ten steps when I heard a raspy voice behind me that sent chills up my spine.

"You'd be dangerous if you were half as sneaky as you think you are. I saw what you were doing. Give me a reason why I shouldn't turn you in, young lady."

CHAPTER 2

BUSTED. I EASED AROUND SLOWLY, AFRAID I'D FIND a battle-ax resembling my tenth-grade social studies teacher, Mrs. Bartelsby, itching to drag me back to the reception area to face the Muzak.

I looked down into a wheelchair at a shrunken woman, her thinning hair an unnatural shade of auburn, her watery blue eyes magnified by the thick lenses of her glasses. She wore a baggy gold lamé tank top, purple velour sweatpants, and Sponge Bob slippers. She'd gone braless. Her long, thin boobs rested on her skinny thighs as if waiting to be fashioned into balloon animals. I tried not to gawk at the droopy tubes or at the *Sex Kitten* tattoo melting down her right bicep.

"Hi there. I'm, umm—"

"Up to no good, aren't you?"

"Ah, no. Actually, I'm lost."

She snorted. "Actually, you have a map in your hand, which means you had no reason to paw through those private files."

Crap. "I didn't think anyone saw me."

"Why?" She waggled a bony finger around the vicinity of my belly button. Because this is an old folks' home? You see a sea of white hair and think we're all blind, deaf, and dumb? Oblivious to our surroundings?"

"No, ma'am."

She squinted at me. "What is your name?"

"It doesn't matter." I attempted to sidestep her; I'll be damned if she didn't maneuver her wheelchair like Earnhardt Jr. and run me into the wall.

"Don't you try to get around me. I'll ask you again: What is your name?"

Tired of being bullied by a woman half my size and three times my age, I leaned down until we were nose to nose. I smelled Emeraude perfume on her wrinkled skin and butterscotch candy on her breath. "You tell me yours and I'll tell you mine."

Those bug eyes blinked at me for a second before she sent me a sly smile. "Fine. I'm Betty Grable."

"And I'm Lauren Becall. Try again, *Betty*."

She smiled broadly—the grin of a woman proud to have all her own teeth. "Okay, I'm Reva Peterson."

"Nice to meet you, Reva. I'm Julie Collins."

The grip of her withered hand was surprisingly strong. "That isn't the name you gave to Dee."

Double crap. "You been spying on me, Reva?"

17

"Yep."

"Why? You the head of Security around here?"

"You're a real laugh riot. No, I'm keeping an eye on things because I have nothing better to do."

Great. Just my luck Prairie Gardens had their very own Miss Marple.

"So, unless you want me to turn you in, you'd better tell me exactly what you're up to." The wheels squeaked as she backed up. "Come on, I know a place where we can talk in private."

I was glad she hadn't ratted me out, so I followed her.

We ended up in a bare bones employee break room consisting of a card table circa 1970, two dilapidated chairs, a microwave, and a Coke machine. The angle of the room was cockeyed and doorless, providing an unobstructed view of the entire reception area. No wonder Reva knew what I'd been doing.

I flopped on a rickety folding chair.

Reva said, "Out with it."

"Why don't you get right to the point?"

"Don't see why I shouldn't. I'm old. I could die at any time."

"Well, there's that saying about curiosity . . ." My gaze landed on her *Sex Kitten* tattoo. Made me think of Martinez. Was I the only person in the world who wasn't inked?

"You're stalling."

"You weren't by chance a drill sergeant in your former life?"

"Nope. I spent forty-seven years as head librarian in the Gillette Public Library."

That explained it. "I'm assuming this will stay between us?"

She nodded.

"The truth is, I'm a private investigator."

"Really?"

"Really."

"Are you undercover? Like that woman on *Alias*?"

"Sort of, but without the cool clothes and awesome wigs."

"Do you have a hot partner like that Vaughn guy?"

"Yep." I grinned when her blue eyes widened behind her thick lenses. "My partner and I are checking out a couple of concerns a client has about a relative living here."

"Which resident?"

"I'm not at liberty to say."

"Shoot. That's no fun."

"Sorry. But you can answer a few general questions, right?"

"Be happy to."

"How long have you lived here?"

"Five years."

"Yeah? Been big changes since the new owners took over?"

Reva scowled. "Yes. They're bombarding us with people and visits and activities. Something going on all the time. They claim we need the mental stimulus."

She snorted. "Half the people in here only have half a working brain anyway, and that isn't because they're old in body."

"Meaning?"

"Who likes change? We're set in our ways. What's wrong with the way things were? Some of us like hiding out in our apartments entertaining ourselves."

"Then again, Reva, some of you skulk around the hallways making your own entertainment."

"True. But you wouldn't believe the shenanigans going on in the utility closet right after shift change." She offered me an impish smile. "Something to be said for access to unlimited Viagra."

"You talking about the employees?"

She shook her head. "The residents."

I did not want to think about prunish bodies slapping together. "I thought you were gonna say the volunteers. But I guess they gotta get their perks where they can since they're not getting paid."

"Who told you the volunteers weren't paid?"

That jarred me. "Doesn't the word *volunteer* mean 'work without compensation'?"

"You, me, and *Webster's Dictionary* are the only ones who seem to know that." Reva adjusted the gold chain holding her glasses. "These new owners started a senior group called Prime Time Friends. Notice I didn't say volunteer group. Their organization is run more like a hospice than Meals On Wheels."

"Hospice services aren't free."

"Neither are the visits from Prime Time Friends."

"So who's paying for the visits?"

"We all are."

"Individually? Like if you want someone to spend time with you alone, you pay for it?"

"Yes . . . and no."

I waited while she gathered her thoughts.

"Every resident is allotted two hours a month of personal time and two hours a month of activity time. If you want additional time with the friends, you pay extra. But collectively, when the new owners hired all new staff and started remodeling, they upped the rent, tacking on an 'activities and recreational improvement' fee."

"Jesus. Is that even legal?"

Reva harrumphed and tapped her foot. Sponge Bob's head bobbled. "Yes. Fair warning rate increase is perfectly legal. But when I looked up the statutes online, the language seemed vague when it comes to specifics governing assisted living facilities. The rules are much more rigid with traditional nursing homes."

No surprise Reva had researched the matter. Librarians lived for that stuff. "How much was the increase?"

"A hundred bucks straight across the board."

My stomach dropped. That'd be a huge financial hardship for residents on fixed incomes. It'd also be a huge chunk of cash for the organization. "No one questioned it?"

"A few did."

"What happened?"

"They got rid of them."

"You're kidding."

"No, I'm not." Reva counted off the infractions on her gnarled fingers. "Louise Ellis broke her hip and was transferred to acute care before she was shipped out. The staff counselor diagnosed Dan Reese as violent after he blew up about the increase so he had to move back in with his daughter. Jim Rea suffered a stroke and he's up at the VA."

Sounded like normal ailments for the elderly. Where was the conspiracy?

"Two others in wing C also left right away. The new residents don't question paying the extra hundred bucks. But you want know the worst thing?"

Not a rhetorical question so I couldn't shout *no*. Especially after I saw tears welling in Reva's buggy eyes.

"I feel sorry for the people who don't have a little financial cushion. I'm not talking about these folks giving up luxuries; I'm talking about them giving up necessities. They're either eating Meals On Wheels or not eating at all." She raised her moist eyes to mine. "Before you ask, no, they can't just up and move. Like me, most people in here don't have immediate family, so they're stuck."

The soda machine made a loud thump.

"Do these friends you've bought visit you on a daily basis?"

"Biweekly. We're assigned two friends and they

rotate. Of course, you have to take the good with the bad. Half the time I get Dottie, a cheerful do-gooder who treats me like an imbecile. Luella is better, but she should be since she's head of the program."

Casually I asked, "She is?"

"Yeah." The frown lines on Reva's face increased. "I thought it was strange at first, too. In my experience those administrative types don't get their hands dirty, yet Luella is here every day."

"I take it Luella is your favorite?"

"Mine. Not everyone else's."

My first thought was because she was Indian. Sad, but true. "Why is she your favorite?"

"She goes above and beyond."

"Meaning?"

"Oh, if she sees something in a magazine that might interest me, she'll bring it along. If I ask and give her cash, she'll pick me up a bottle of Jack Daniels without giving me a lecture on how dangerous drinking is at my age."

"You don't hop on the senior bus and go to the grocery store and all the other places?"

"No. I don't like being stuck in this wheelchair, but it does give me an excuse not to have to do those things. Doesn't get me out of the activities most times."

"What kind of activities?"

"Lectures about estate and funeral planning, wills, all that old folks' crap. Demonstrations on cooking for one. Those aren't bad. It's the craft ones I hate, making us decorate picture frames with beads and seashells like a bunch of kindergartners. Bah."

"Forced crafts? No wonder you sneak around. I would, too."

"Not a crafty person?"

I smiled coyly. "Not in the literal sense."

"Well, there's plenty of other crafty stuff going on around here to keep me occupied, not in the literal sense either."

"Prairie Gardens doesn't seem like a den of iniquity."

"It isn't. It's become a cave of apathy."

When she didn't clarify, I leaned closer. "Explain that remark, Reva."

"You wanna know why I've been roaming the hall-ways? Because the new punks they hired don't give a hoot about us. They're supposed to check on each unit twice a day. Half the time they don't bother to do it once. After what happened to my friend Nettie . . ."

"What?"

"She slipped getting out of the shower and hit her head on the toilet. By the time those minimum wage idiots found her the next morning? It was too late. She was dead. If they would've checked on her that night, like they were paid to, maybe . . ." Her chin wobbled and her glasses slipped down her nose.

I allowed her a minute to find her composure.

"I'm so sorry. Did Nettie's family know what really happened?" Neglect resulting in a fatal injury screamed lawsuit.

"Nettie didn't have family."

"No one?"

Her head snapped up. "No. Which was why I was so upset when I found out she'd . . ." Reva dabbed her eyes. "Too late at any rate. Things have changed for the worse. There's nothing anyone can do because most of us are stuck here until we die."

Wow. I had no idea what to say.

"So, I'm not surprised this place is under investigation."

"Does that mean you'll help me?"

She nodded. "I'll be discreet, since no one notices me."

I dug a business card out of my purse. "What's your room number in case I need to get in touch with you?"

"Four-oh-seven." The card disappeared in the side pocket of her wheelchair.

"Thanks."

"No, thank *you*. I look forward to seeing you again, PI girl."

"Same goes, spy girl."

Reva rolled down the maze of hallways and out of sight.

I exited the break room and turned the corner to see Kevin and Dee storming to me. Neither appeared very happy. I wasn't in a hurry to get my ass chewed so I stayed put.

Dee sent me a sour look. "We've been waiting for you for twenty minutes."

"I'm sorry. After I used the bathroom I stopped at the desk for a map and accidentally knocked over a stack of papers. After I made your office mate mad, I thought it'd be best for everyone if I hung out here until you showed up."

"I'm on a tight schedule today so we'll have to re-schedule your tour for another time."

"Jack can lead me back there for a quick run-through if you don't mind."

"I do mind." Her smile came off haughty, not apologetic. "We can't have people wandering around unattended. Against company policy and such."

I bit back the retort, *Except for letting the residents wander around unattended?*

Kevin smoothly inserted himself between us. "We understand." He clasped both of Dee's hands and mustered his Boy Scout smile. "Thank you so much for the tour. We'll be in touch about our decision."

"The pleasure was all mine." Dee put an extra swing in her abundant hips as she walked away, but Kevin wasn't paying attention.

He unhooked our winter gear from the coatrack. "Ready?"

"Yep." I buttoned up my coat and tugged on my Thinsulate gloves. That first punch of cold air seemed to crystallize my lungs.

Kevin didn't vocalize his anger until we were huddled in his Jeep. "What the hell were you doing, Jules? I didn't learn a goddamn thing while you were

26

screwing around. That woman watched me like I was a healthcare inspector."

"I wasn't screwing around." I unfolded the map I'd shoved in my jeans pocket and flipped it over, detailing what I'd found out from the files and from Reva.

When he didn't respond, I kept a stream-of-consciousness dialogue going, expecting some fact I missed would jump out at him.

"You wouldn't think Luella would want to spend so much time with Mr. Sloane, being she's the director and all. Yet, if he is paying her extra . . . oh, like 35K, I see why she'd do it."

No response.

Why didn't my information make him happy? "Wasn't that what Amery wanted us to find out?"

"We have a better idea of who is involved. And yes, there's definitely something going on, but without catching Luella cashing a check, or us breaking into the admin offices to track Vernon Sloane's payment records, I don't see how any of this will set Amery's mind at ease."

"We could sit tight until Luella shows up to take Vernon out and then follow them."

"To what end?"

I reached for my smokes and lit up while I let my temper wane. "Here's where I remind you this is the reason I argued against this case. Legally, Amery is powerless. Her grandfather can do whatever the hell he pleases with his money. It sucks that Prairie

27

Gardens just arbitrarily raised their rates and are displacing old people. Do I think the rate increase has bearing on this case? No. Granted, there is an issue with Gramps sneaking out and the lax security measures, but it doesn't seem Amery is asking us to focus on that issue. Was she?"

"No."

"In order to make any kind of accurate assessment of Prairie Gardens supposed security problems, we'd have to be there, or live there twenty-four/seven and God knows there isn't a retainer big enough to make me do that. Amery doesn't have that kind of cash or she would've hired a lawyer to deal with the power of attorney or legal guardianship bullshit."

His smile was half-feral. "Jerking a knot in my tail, partner?"

"I know you, Kev. You were all soft and sweet with her, which means you've developed a big-time crush."

"So?"

"So, are you thinking helping her out will make you more appealing on the 'Trust me I'm a big dick' front?"

"Did it for you and Martinez? He's constantly mooning around you."

I wasn't surprised he'd brought up that sticky situation. I'd worked for my lover, Tony Martinez, once officially before we hooked up, once as a favor after we'd established a relationship. True, our relationship came about only because Martinez had hired me, and as much as my inner tough girl sneered, I'd be utterly lost without that relationship.

Still. Kevin was comparing what I had with Tony to his crushlike feelings for Amery? Wrong.

"It's not the same."

"Why not?"

"Because Tony and I knew each other months before we became involved."

"You mean before you slept with him."

"I can't believe you'd be stupid enough to sleep with her right off the bat."

Kevin aimed his gaze at the brownish pile of snow outside his grimy window.

"Shit."

"Yeah."

"Jesus. When?"

"Yesterday." He squirmed. "She showed up around quitting time, right after you'd left. We went out for happy hour, one thing led to another and . . ."

"And she made your Mr. Happy *very* happy."

Silence.

"Thrilled as I am that you finally got laid—"

"Tread lightly here, Jules. I'm not going to provide a play-by-play of how she ended up in my bed."

Damn. "Am I your friend right now? Or your business partner?"

"Partner."

I sucked down the last of my cigarette, swishing the spent butt in my empty Diet Pepsi can. "I vote we go with my original suggestion and follow Luella and

Vernon. It's not like we have anything else to do."

"True." Kevin closed his eyes, nestling his neck in the headrest. "What time was Luella picking Vernon up?"

"One o'clock. About five minutes from now." I glanced at his profile and saw the smoking hot man he was. No wonder Amery jumped him last night. Sometimes I forgot my partner was such a delish dish. When Reva caught sight of my "hot partner" her baby blues would bug right out of her head.

"Christ, I'm tired."

"Marathon sex 'til the wee hours will do that to you."

"You would know."

Not recently. Not that I'd share that tidbit with him. "Shouldn't you park where we can watch both entrances?"

"Probably." He drove us to a better vantage point. "Do you know what Luella looks like?"

"Indian. But we shouldn't have a problem recognizing Vernon."

"Yeah? Describe him, smarty."

"Old man. Stooped over a cane. Fluffy white hair. Big nose. Wrinkled face. Dentures." I hunkered down in my seat, cold, despite Kevin leaving the Jeep heater running.

Kevin snorted. "You just described Einstein. You have no fucking clue what old Vern looks like, do you?"

"Nope. Does it matter? How many old guys will be getting picked up in private vehicles by an Indian woman in the next few minutes?"

"Fine. So what if Luella takes him to Albertsons?"

"We'll split up inside the store. See whether they're shopping for groceries or picking up prescriptions. Same goes for anywhere else they end up."

"Even if it's a doctor's office?"

"Yep."

"And if they go both places?"

"We will, too."

"You don't think they'll notice us following them?"

I glared at him. "How the fuck should I know? You're supposed to be the expert in this stealthy PI shit, Kev."

He grunted.

Which pissed me off. "You know what? Forget it. I'm sick of trying to work around you, and the truth is, we shouldn't have taken this goddamn case. I don't give a crap what you tell Amery. Let her take the two hours we owe her in your bed." I dug my cell phone out of my purse. Flipping it open, I scrolled through my short contacts list.

"What are you doing?"

"Leaving. Martinez will send someone to pick me up and take me back to the office."

Kevin grabbed my phone and snapped it shut.

"Hey, what the hell—"

"Look." He pointed to the carport at the front entrance. "I think Luella just pulled up."

CHAPTER 3

THE DRIVER'S SIDE DOOR ON A SILVER CADILLAC
opened. A chunky woman climbed out, wearing a pink
houndstooth checked coat, black slacks, her reddish-
brown face visible beneath a rabbit fur trimmed hat.

Our tour guide, Dee, walked an elderly man out
and met the woman on the sidewalk. He wasn't the
crippled old-timer I'd described. Maybe this was
someone else.

"That's him," Kevin said. "Vernon Sloane."

"You sure? He looks pretty spry for an eighty-
five-year-old guy."

"Alzheimer's is a mental defect, Julie, not physical.
He's exactly how Amery described him."

I skipped the smart-ass retort. Vernon was feisty;
he wouldn't let Luella help him into the car. She skirted the back end and they were off.

Kevin put the Jeep in gear.

Luella putzed along little-old-lady-style; her speed never surpassed the posted legal limit. People like her caused traffic problems and gave people like me road rage.

First stop: Boyd's Liquor Mart on Mt. Rushmore Road. Well, well. Wasn't that interesting?

Kevin parked by the Dumpster.

"Who's going in? You? Or me?"

"You." I rummaged in the backseat until I found his brown Dakine knit winter hat. "Put that on."

"Anything else, bossy?"

"Yeah, get me a pack of cigarettes and a pint of Jack Daniels." I tossed him a crumpled fifty.

"Martinez's drinking habits wearing off on you?"

"No. The Jack is for Reva."

His mouth dropped open. "In the short amount of time you spent together she told you her favorite whiskey? What? Are you two drinking buddies now?"

As I watched Luella and Vernon enter the package store, I said, "It'd be nice to have someone to drink with since Kim is pregnant."

"Don't you spend all your free time sucking down free booze in Martinez's bars?"

"No." I faced Kevin and fussed with his collar. "That's better. Go."

"Thanks, Mom." He slammed the door.

I lit up, considering how long I'd do my Eskimo imitation in the freezing cold. On a whim I dialed Martinez.

He answered on the second ring. "Everything okay, blondie?"

"Yeah. Why?"

"Because it's rare for you to call me during the day."

"You're always busy." *Shit shit shit.* This was exactly why I didn't call him; he made me feel guilty when I did. "Is it a bad time?"

"Hang on." A clunk followed a muffled thump. The line crackled. Background noises disappeared. "Where are you?"

"On a stakeout. Where are you?"

"My office at Bare Assets."

I flicked an ash out the window. "You alone?"

"I am now. Why?"

"I wondered if you wanna have phone sex."

"With you?"

"No, with Kevin, Martinez. Jesus, *yes* with me."

He paused. "Wells isn't in the car with you."

"Nope. Just little ol' me, feeling *horn*-ibly naughty."

"You're just bored."

"Pretty much."

"I should be insulted."

"You aren't. You're actually thinking about saying yes."

Martinez laughed softly.

"So I'll take a rain check on the phone sex if you promise me the real deal tonight." I inhaled, holding the smoke in my lungs a good long time before I exhaled.

He didn't respond, but I heard him sigh. I could

almost see the resignation on his face.

"Forget it. I'll talk to you later."

"Julie, wait—"

"Crap. Our guy is on the move. Gotta go." I punched the *Off* button and snapped the phone shut. It'd drive him crazy if he couldn't reach me. Might be a petty thing, but it guaranteed the outcome: Martinez in my bed tonight. We'd been hit-and-miss on the sex front lately, and I needed a grand-slam home run in a bad way. A doubleheader would even be better.

I finished my cigarette, staring in the side mirror. Luella and Vernon climbed in the Cadillac. Kevin appeared a beat later.

He tossed the brown paper sack on my lap, eyeing the passing vehicle before he started the Jeep.

"What did they buy?"

"A liter of Jim Beam Select, a bottle of Prairie Berry Wine, chokecherry blend. A jug of that pre-mixed Mudslide crap, and a box of Swisher Sweets."

"That's all?"

"Yes, unless you count the jumbo box of extra-large Trojans."

I whapped his arm. "Not funny."

"The clerk knew them both by name."

"That's really not funny."

"I know." Kevin changed lanes, keeping the Cadillac in sight as we cruised up 8th Street past Dairy Queen and Wilson Park. "It gets better. Luella filled out the check and Vernon just signed it."

"Shit."

"Yeah. Makes me wonder how many other times she's done it."

"Aren't you glad we followed them?"

He didn't answer. I felt smug anyway.

I stared out the window at the tourist shops, closed except for Coleman Gold Company and Coyote Claw Sam's. Someone had to sell Black Hills Gold jewelry and Sturgis Bike Rally T-shirts in the off-season. I glanced at the new Sonic Drive-In. For some reason Martinez had taken a liking to it so we'd eaten there frequently in the last few months.

We turned left on Cathedral Drive. Medical facilities had popped up like metal warts in this area in recent years. Luella's Caddy bypassed Wendy's and Taco Bell to chug up the hill to the Rapid City Medical Center. She snagged a handicapped spot up front.

Kevin backed into a parking space in the very last row. "Glad I took the liquor store."

"Huh uh. I'm not doing this alone."

"As you so accurately pointed out earlier, I am the expert in stealth matters. My gut is telling me to stay in the car." He flashed me his dimpled grin.

"Yeah? I hope your gut is happy when your balls freeze and fall off." I slammed the car door.

Once inside the enclosed entryway, I took my time removing my gloves, unwrapping my scarf, and unbuttoning my coat. I kept a close eye on the receptionist's desk. If I timed this right, I could sneak into the waiting area without one of the Trained Attack Receptionists, known as TARs, grilling me about appointment time.

Truthfully, what nut job would hang out in a place full of sick old people if they didn't have to?

Four people entered and I scooted in behind them to a split waiting area. I had a 50/50 shot of choosing correctly, so I swung around the wall on the right side.

Bingo. Luella and Vernon sat in the center section. I forced myself to move slowly, claiming a chair directly behind them.

I swiped a large-print edition of *Reader's Digest* and settled in, studying the layout of the room and the clientele.

Nearly two dozen people were spread out, sniffling or sneezing or snoring. One codger in the far back corner hadn't twitched. The top of his white head rested against the wall; his jowls were slack. He looked dead. Still, I preferred the look of eternal slumber on those folks' faces who were long in the tooth to some rotten kid's ear-piercing shrieks.

Vernon and Luella didn't exchange a single word.

I studied her. Lakota, probably, not a full-blood. Sixtyish. Black hair chopped short surrounded a pudgy brownish-red face. Broad nose. Brown eyes beneath trendy, square-framed tortoiseshell glasses. Apple-shaped Luella was definitely a sturdy, attractive woman. I still didn't see her and Vern doing the wild thing though.

Thirty minutes ticked by.

I was about to give up when a nurse called out, "Vernon Sloane?"

He followed the nurse to the doctors' offices. Luella stayed put.

Two minutes passed before I made my move. I gathered my stuff and tossed it on a chair kitty-corner to Luella's. Immediately I noisily scattered the offerings on the coffee table beside her. She sensed me staring and looked up from *People* magazine.

My smile was strained. Meryl Streep had nothing on my acting chops. "Pardon me, when you're done with that issue, can I have it? I've been here long enough to read all the rest of these."

"Sure. What are you here for?" she asked suspiciously, as if I carried the West Nile virus.

"I'm waiting for my aunt. She's been in there forever."

Luella's expression relaxed. "The wait seems longer every time we're here, too."

I flopped in the chair and sighed. "Aunt Rose never wants me to go in the doctor's room with her either; she's a little ornery that way."

"Believe me; I know how that goes."

"You here with your husband?"

Her guarded look returned. "Why would you ask that?"

"Oh. I saw you sitting with that handsome older man and I assumed . . ." I aimed my eyes at the purple floral carpet in mock embarrassment. "Never mind."

"It's a natural mistake."

I figured I'd blown it by overplaying my hand. It surprised me when she asked, "Is your aunt here because she's ill?"

"Aunt Rose has complained of a stomach/head-ache thing for a couple of days. Probably nothing serious, but it's better to be safe than sorry. Especially since she's taking so many prescriptions. I'm afraid to give her any over-the-counter medications."

"What is she on?"

Think. "Um, Aricept for early stage Alzheimer's, methotrexate for rheumatoid arthritis, and Zestril for high blood pressure." Who said suffering through those pharmaceutical ads on TV didn't pay off?

Luella confided, "The gentleman I'm with? He takes Aricept and I don't see how it's helped him one bit."

It boggled my mind how easily older people just chatted about various health ailments—theirs and others—with total strangers.

"Is he here getting his meds changed?"

"To a combination of Aricept and Namenda. I hope it works. He's gotten so confused and forgetful in the last few weeks anything would be an improvement at this point."

"Sounds like you're a big help to him."

She brightened. "It's not like he has anyone else to rely on or to help him with day-to-day issues. The poor, sweet dear is all alone."

Big chomp mark on my fat tongue kept me from

retorting, *Except for his worried granddaughter.*

"Your aunt is lucky she has you. I work with the elderly every day. It's heartbreaking to see how many of them end up alone."

She'd thrown the door of opportunity wide open; I barged right through. "Are you a nurse?"

"No. Just a volunteer."

Right. A volunteer who got paid.

"That's really generous to take care of people and not get anything in return."

"Part of my Lakota heritage is to honor our elders. But helping these folks who've sacrificed to make this country great is reward enough. Besides, they deserve better than to be shoved aside out of sight and forgotten like an old pair of worn-out shoes."

Cue Old Glory and Lee Greenwood's *God Bless the U.S.A.* "Do you work for a specific volunteer program?"

Luella paused, as if to hedge the question. "Prime Time Friends. Currently we're only associated with Prairie Gardens Assisted Living Facility."

My jaw dropped. "You're kidding. My brother and I were just there checking out the facility for Aunt Rose." When Luella's spine stiffened again, I confided, "Dee gave us the nickel tour. Frankly, we didn't get to see all that much, or talk to any residents, which is important to me. And Dee certainly didn't tell us there was a volunteer program like Prime Time Friends where Rose could get such personalized attention from generous souls as yourself."

A little praise and she relaxed. "Dee is a wonderful administrator. It's a pity she can't spend more time with prospective clients to show all the benefits offered by Prairie Gardens. There are probably a few other aspects she didn't have time to discuss with you, either."

I nodded, hoping I'd prodded her in the right direction. "Such a difficult decision, knowing which facility will be the right one, especially when we suspect it'll be the last place she'll live. We're all the family she has left, and neither my brother nor I live close by."

"Where do you live?"

"Gillette. He lives in Denver."

I could almost hear the gears spinning in Luella's head.

"Tell you what, why don't you let me give you a more complete tour?"

"You'd do that? Really?"

"I'd love to. I wouldn't want you to make such an important decision only knowing half of what makes the Prairie Gardens family a good choice."

I smiled even when I couldn't make it reach my eyes. "I-I don't know what to say."

"Simple. Just say yes. I'll have to check my schedule." Luella rummaged in her purse.

I expected she'd pull out a BlackBerry. Wrong. A day planner, the cover plastered with all shapes and sizes of teakettles.

Hard to believe the devil indulged in drinking tea.

"Let's see . . . I'm free at eight o'clock tomorrow

morning. Would that work for you?"

"That'd be perfect."

Kevin would shit bricks when I told him how far I'd taken this charade. Still, his mattress monkey needed to ante up more bananas before I'd keep the appointment. She'd run her retainer dry.

The back of my neck tingled. I noticed Luella staring at me strangely. Was my gloating premature? "Something wrong?"

"Yes. I just realized I don't know your name."

Whew. "Oh. It's Kate. Kate Sawyer."

"I'm Luella Spotted Tail, Kate. It's so nice to meet you."

"Same here."

Luella passed me a business card with the appointment time jotted on the back. "You can reach me at those numbers in case something comes up and you need to cancel. My home number is on there, too."

"Thanks. Speaking of, where should I meet you? At the receptionist's area?"

"Why don't you come to the east door instead? It leads to the common rooms. That way we won't have to worry about explaining this to Dee. Wouldn't want to step on her professional toes. She's touchy about this sort of thing."

Yeah, right. Her concern was for *Dee*. "No problem." I frowned at the clock. "Wow. I didn't know it was that late. I think I might head down to the lab. Last time we were here the doctor sent Aunt Rose downstairs for tests and no one told me. With as long as I've been waiting it's probably happened again."

"Good luck. I'll see you tomorrow, Kate."

My giddy sense of relief overtook my common sense; halfway across the parking lot I realized I hadn't put my coat on.

Kevin picked me up. Shivering, I wrestled with my outerwear as I clambered into his Jeep.

"What the hell happened? I've been calling you for an hour. Why didn't you answer your cell?"

Damn. I forgot I'd turned it off in a fit of pique with Martinez. "I was busy getting this." I waved the business card in his face.

"What? An appointment with a psychiatrist?"

"Ha fucking ha. No. I have an appointment with Luella tomorrow. She's giving me a more personal tour of Prairie Gardens than the one you got from Dee."

"How the hell did you manage that?"

I relished his look of awe. "Trade secret, my jealous friend."

"Seriously, Jules. How?"

Okay, I might've embellished the details in the retelling, but still, Kevin was suitably impressed.

"You think you can get into Vernon's apartment?"

"Sure as hell gonna try." I didn't bother tiptoeing around the elephant in the front seat. "Do you want me to talk to Amery about making another payment on her initial retainer?"

"Julie—"

"Don't even think about arguing this point. She's a client. We're professionals. If additional man-hours are justified and she wants us to continue with this case, she will have to pony up the cash, Kevin. Period."

His jaw tightened but he didn't dispute a word.

"And don't bring up Martinez. He paid us a pile to look into the Black Dog case *before* he and I became involved on a personal level, so it's not the same."

A Rapid City Western Meats truck passed us on the left. It caused hunger pangs even as the cold silence sat in my empty stomach like a block of ice.

I sighed. "Let me handle this for you, okay? It'll be easier for me to ask her for money after I've filled her in on what I learned. Besides, I'm not sleeping with her, so I won't get mesmerized by the sight of her bodacious ta-tas."

Kevin didn't smile . . . at first. Then he smirked. "They are pretty bodacious."

And he clammed up again.

So I whipped out my oyster knife to pry him open a bit. "Besides being partners, we're still friends, Kev. You don't talk about this kinda stuff with me anymore, but if you wanted to talk . . . well, I wouldn't be a total dick about it. I'd listen and try not to be a smart-ass."

"I know."

"Good. Just thought I'd put that out there."

"Thanks."

The tires threw gray slush on top of the piles of dirt-colored snow heaped along the street. The morning forecast called for more white stuff and arctic temperatures.

As we waited at the red stoplight on the corner of Mt. Rushmore Road and Saint Joseph Street, Kevin said, "Amery wasn't the first woman I've slept with since Lilly died. You don't need to worry if I'm feeling guilty about it, because I don't. I've moved on."

I didn't ask him when he'd made that decision. I knew. After I'd been shot and almost died late last fall. After he realized my thing with Tony Martinez wasn't just another sexual fling. So while it stung that he'd denied sharing those important changes in his life with me, I understood his reasoning because I no longer shared those intimate things with him.

He parked in his usual spot next to my truck. "Been a long morning and we didn't eat. You hungry?"

"Yeah. Pizza sounds good."

"Why don't you call it in and I'll call Amery and update her."

I buttoned my coat under my chin, preparing to brave the tundra. "Should I order enough pizza for Amery?"

Pause. "For her and Kim. Once Kim gets a whiff of meat and cheese, she'll be up for her midafternoon snack."

My bud Kim had bypassed the barfy stage of her pregnancy and settled into the eat-everything-in-sight stage. Since she'd sworn off alcohol, I did my level best to corrupt her with food.

I closed my office door and typed up everything

from my conversations with Reva and Luella to keep the details fresh. I'd crushed out my third cigarette when Kevin knocked. "Food's here."

"Be right there."

Amery had cocked a hip on the conference table like a *Fortune 500* CEO decked out in a form-fitting black and gray pin-striped business suit with a satiny white blouse unbuttoned to reveal her generous cleavage. The spiked heel black patent leather boots hitting below her knee were straight out of a dominatrix's closet. Her lustrous blond hair brushed her shoulders, the cut and color resembling Marsha Brady's: smooth, silky, and impossibly shiny.

I couldn't help but compare her to a business shark in such severe work clothes. Yet, the flustered smile she offered was sweetly appealing and I saw why Kevin was smitten.

Didn't mean I liked it. He was too goddamn old for her; she was too goddamn young to appreciate him.

I didn't voice my concerns; I merely smiled back at her. "Amery. Thanks for coming on such short notice. Even through the snow and cold."

"No problem. I don't mind the cold or the snow after living in Minnesota. It's been a slow day anyway."

Amery schlepped bus tours and airline tickets as a travel agent. Why weren't people clamoring to get the hell out of this cold snap and book a cruise to the Bahamas? Even Martinez and I had discussed a tropical getaway.

"Kevin said you'd had some success today?"

I filled her in while we polished off the pizza. I tried to concentrate on recounting my adventures and not on the hungry stare Kevin gave our client rather than the food.

After I finished speaking, I watched her process the information as she picked at a discarded crust with fingernails bitten to the quick.

"I knew something was going on, although part of me wishes I'd been wrong."

Kevin placed his hand over hers and squeezed.

"Do you want us to continue looking into this matter?"

She raised her gaze to mine at my overly formal tone.

I expected glimmery tears in her baby blues, not steely determination.

"Yes. How much more will it cost? Not that it matters, because Grandpa is all the family I have left."

"Another five hundred. If it takes us less time, we'll refund you the difference."

"Sounds fair." Amery slipped her hand from Kevin's to reach for her leather satchel.

I caught a glimpse of her checkbook cover before she flipped it open. For Christsake. The plastic was plastered with happy, fluffy, roly-poly puppies. Puppies! I dreaded seeing whatever cute critters decorated her actual checks.

She wrote the amount in the register, ripped the check out with painstaking precision, and handed it to me.

The face of her pastel pink checks were dotted with a variety of stilettos. "Would you like a receipt?"

Kevin said, "I'll give her one. I have to write her a new contract anyway."

Hey. Office drone shit was my responsibility, not his. Then again, the gaga eyes they were leveling at each other made me want to hurl.

"No need for you to stick around, Jules. It's a standard form. There's nothing else going on today, either."

An escape. "Cool. I'll just pop down and say hello to Kim before I leave."

Kevin hadn't taken his eyes off Amery. "You do that."

I gathered my coat and purse from my office and booked it downstairs.

The hair salon was as dead as every other business this time of year. Jenny—a ditz with a bra size bigger than her IQ—deigned to glance up from the fashion magazines spread across the check-in counter. The wad of purple gum she chomped matched the gloss on her collagen-enhanced lips.

"Is Kim around?"

"Nopers. She went home early."

"When?"

"About two hours ago."

"Was everything all right?"

"Yeppers."

Jesus. I hated her cutesy answers. "She still having

problems with heartburn?"

"Yeppers."

I left before she subjected me to more of her creative vernacular and I subjected her to what constitutes proper professional etiquette.

Dammit. I missed Kim. As much as I wanted to check on her, I knew she'd suffered with trouble sleeping and she deserved a quiet, uninterrupted afternoon nap.

So, what now?

Home. I bundled up and reached in my coat pocket for my gloves, only to come up empty-handed. Great. I'd set them on my desk and they were my spare pair. My favorite leather gloves were in Martinez's Escalade.

Back upstairs. I'd cleared the reception area when I noticed the door to the conference room was cracked open. "Oh, Kevin. Yes. Yes. Right there," wafted out on a seductive sigh.

I froze. I heard Kevin's low voice but couldn't make out his exact response. But Amery's next phrase rang out loud and clear:

"Harder. Oh. Just like that. God. That is so good."

No. It couldn't be. They were *not* doing it on the conference table. Maybe Kevin was giving her a neck rub or something.

Then a rhythmic thumping started.

So much for my back rub theory.

My feet shuffled forward even when my brain attempted to superglue them to the carpet.

Don't look. You don't want to see this.

But I did. Some perverse part of me for sure. I tiptoed across the room. My heart raced; my blood pounded a countertempo to the steady noises echoing back to me. One more step and I'd be at the door.

Don't do it. Walk away. Run *away.*

Ignoring the warning, I placed my cheek against the wooden door trim and peeked inside.

Holy shit.

Amery was splayed on the conference table, à la 1950s-pinup-girl-style; back and neck arched provocatively, her blouse undone, lacy bra cups dangling by her armpits, her skirt shoved up past her hips, her legs clad in sheer black thigh-highs were wrapped around Kevin's waist. I couldn't tear my eyes away from the sight of her shiny black boots contrasting with the white skin of Kevin's naked ass.

"Don't stop. Please, don't stop," she wailed.

Theatrics? Or was Kevin really that good?

Kevin's pants were around his ankles. Besides that he was fully clothed. He'd pinned Amery's arms above her head as his lower body thrust against hers, rocking the table.

My cheeks flamed. While I understood Kev taking a little afternoon delight when it was offered, he should've locked the goddamn door—any door. He'd left the office wide open. Anyone could've waltzed in and seen the up-close, personal service we offered while he was servicing our client.

Fucking idiot. When had he become so . . . reckless? Kevin was supposed to be the responsible one in this partnership.

It'd serve him right if I yelled, "Eww! I have to eat on that table!" or "Quit fucking around and get back to work." But I wouldn't.

Still, I didn't bother to slink away like some guilt-ridden Peeping Tom. I slammed the door before I locked it from the outside and reset the alarm.

When my cold fingers connected with the ice-covered handle on my truck, I realized I'd forgotten the reason I'd gone back to the office in the first place.

Screw that. I'd rather freeze my fingers off than have more images of Kevin and Amery going at it burned into my brain.

CHAPTER 4

MARTINEZ SHOWED UP EARLIER THAN I EXPECTED.

More pissed off than I'd expected.

His door slamming brought me into the living room PDQ and I jumped at his angry manner.

"Glad to see you're not half-dead in some goddamn river bottom, blondie."

I flinched.

Martinez didn't care; he wasn't done chewing my ass. He threw the gloves I'd left in his SUV on the coffee table. "I've been trying to call you for four hours. Where the hell's your cell phone?"

"In my purse."

He paused, trying to melt my surliness under the full weight of his tough guy glare. "So you turned it off."

"Yeah."

"Why?"

I shrugged.

"Christ. Because I wouldn't have phone sex with you?"

"No, I turned it off because I was working."

"Why didn't you turn it back on when you were done working?"

"What is your problem? I just forgot, okay?"

"No, it's not okay. Especially after what happened with Leticia. You know it drives me crazy when I can't get a hold of you for hours on end." He heaved his leather jacket on the recliner. "You weren't here and nobody answered the phone at your office."

"That's because Kevin was too busy fucking our client on the conference table to bother with anything trivial like locking the goddamn doors or answering the goddamn telephone."

Martinez lifted a brow. "Run that by me again?"

"You heard right." I rubbed the sharp pain between my eyes with my thumb, attempting to stave off a headache. "Look. I've had a shit day. Not only did I spend hours dealing with cranky old people, I had a front row seat to Kevin nailing our very young, and as I discovered, very vocal client. I'm not up to dealing with your pissy mood. So if you can't be nice to me, go away."

I pushed my body from the doorjamb and returned to the kitchen. I craved a warm drink, something sugary and soothing. Coffee was out. Ditto for the perfumy tea Brittney had passed off as my Christmas

53

gift. My fingers curled around the box of instant cocoa and my belly muscles tightened. It was impossible not to dwell on the last time I'd made hot chocolate in this kitchen—for my nephew, Jericho, who'd since disappeared from my life, probably forever. No, hot chocolate wouldn't be soothing at all.

The floor creaked. I looked up. Martinez shut the cupboard door, coiled his fingers in my hair, and pressed his mouth to mine.

It was a surprisingly sweet, but extensive kiss. He mollified me in a way nothing else—not even chocolate—ever had or ever would.

He tipped my face back to meet his dark eyes. "See? I can be nice."

"You can do better."

"Yeah? Maybe I'll give it a shot if you do something nice for me."

"Which would be?"

"Don't turn off your phone. Put it on vibrate, but I need to know I can get in touch with you at all times."

Not a casual request, and my warning bells jangled. "Tony, what's going on?"

He sighed. "Some Hombres shit."

I treated him to the narrow-eyed stare he usually leveled on me. "Not a good enough answer. Try again."

"Until I know more that's all I can tell you."

Or all he would tell me. "Is that why you barged in here? To put the fear of Verizon in me?"

"If that'll work."

"Fine. I'll sleep with the goddamn thing if you'll stop nagging me about it. Seems I could use a bad dream talisman anyway." I sidestepped him and opened the refrigerator. "Am I cooking dinner for two? Or did you just show up here to piss me off before you leave me to my own devices again?"

Martinez didn't move. I felt his searing gaze on my neck as I studied the humble contents inside the fridge.

"Why didn't you call me last night after it happened?"

"You'd've driven out here at two in the morning to hold my hand?"

"I'd've been here in a fucking heartbeat, Julie, and you damn well know it." He paused and asked, "Who?"

The unwanted images slammed into my head. I couldn't pretend the horror in my dreams was a freak-ish one-time-only nightmare. The faces might change, but the truth didn't: I'd killed someone. My subconscious decided I needed to pay for that. Repeatedly.

"Tell me," he demanded.

"It was you this time, okay? So you understand why I didn't rush to the phone to spill my guts that we were in a shoot-out and you killed me."

"Fuck."

I swung the door shut. "Yeah. Forget it."

"No."

"Tony—"

He spun me and clamped his hands around my biceps. "You don't have these goddamn nightmares when I'm in bed with you."

"No shit."

"When are you gonna admit . . ."

His shrewd gaze lingered on the dark circles under my eyes that makeup couldn't hide. I stayed mum and stared back defiantly.

"I will hammer away at you until you talk to me about this."

How well I knew that. "Fine. Everything was in bloody extreme slow-mo. A light flashed and we were blowing chunks out of each other. When I inhaled, my lungs hurt so fucking bad it was like I was breathing lead, which made it worse because everything smelled like you, then rot and death. And I was crying except when a bullet hit you, I'd laugh. *Laugh*, like she did after she shot me, and then I woke up alone." Screaming. I didn't tell him that part, but I suspected he knew anyway.

Martinez didn't haul me into his arms for a hug. His hands dropped like I'd become radioactive.

Great.

I fled to my bedroom to avoid the argument. Martinez's solution to my nightmares was simple: sleep with him every night, wherever that might be. It wouldn't be an issue if it meant crashing at his house regularly. But we spent less time at his hilltop fortress than any other place. I didn't mind spending the night in his private rooms at Fat Bob's, the biker bar he owned, or at Bare Assets, the strip club he owned . . . once in a while. Problem was, even he didn't know where he'd end up after last call, and I didn't enjoy playing musical beds.

Consequently, we weren't together every night—a situation he blamed on me. And it drove him insane he wasn't around to protect me from myself, which was sweet, if an unrealistic expectation on his part.

I pressed my hot forehead to the window, welcoming the cool sting of icy glass. Would he leave or stay?

After a time, footsteps stopped behind me and I was surrounded by the familiar scent of leather. Of him.

His heavy sigh stirred my hair. "I'm late for a meeting."

"So go."

"Jesus, Julie. Don't." Warm lips brushed the back of my head. "I know you want me to stay, and I wouldn't leave if I had a choice. I hate that I don't have a fucking choice tonight. There's some shit I can't . . ." His fingers swept my hair behind my ear and he leaned in to whisper, "Keep your cell phone on, blondie."

"Fine."

"Promise me."

"Okay, okay. I promise. Since I'll be sleeping alone again tonight, maybe I *will* keep it very close . . . and on vibrate."

Martinez's soft laughter sent a hot burst of longing through me. I missed him. I missed us. He kissed the spot below my ear and left without another word.

With half a dozen shots of Don Julio as a sleep aid,

not only didn't I hear the phone ring, I didn't dream at all.

The next morning it was snowing and blowing. I was half-tempted to call Luella and cancel our appointment. But I'd have to let Kevin know the change in plans and, frankly, I'd rather deal with a ground blizzard than with my randy partner.

I resembled a hockey player when I crawled in my truck; warmth won out over fashion for me every time. Visibility on I-90 East into Rapid City was better than I'd expected.

Luella paced by the side door at Prairie Gardens and flung it open at my approach. "Kate! I was afraid you weren't coming."

Kate. Right. I'd forgotten my cover. "It's not as bad out there as it looks." I stamped the snow from my boots on the rubber floor mat. "Cold though."

"Then I won't offer to take your coat."

We wound through the tables of a mostly empty common room and stopped at a metal counter that separated the kitchen from the rest of the space.

"Coffee?"

"Please. Black is fine." This was the part I hated, making small talk. I preferred to get down to business.

We sipped our coffee in silence broken by the distant buzz of a TV.

I smiled. "Is this the only food service area?"

"No. The main cafeteria is in the long-term care wing. This"—she gestured around us—"is used for snacks, parties, family gatherings, and such."

"It's very nice. Handy." My gaze swept the walls as I searched for polite chitchat topics. "What are those plaques for?"

"Oh. Memorial contributions."

"From . . . deceased residents? Like a wall of death?"

She studied the configuration from afar. "I never thought of it that way. Not very appetizing, is it?"

Before I responded, three loud beeps sounded from the black box clipped to her belt. Luella unclipped it and read the tiny screen. Her lips made an *O* before turning into a deep frown.

"Bad news?"

Her head whipped up. "Why would you ask that?"

Talk about suspicious. "You don't look happy."

"I'm not. Just something I have to take care of."

I watched her weigh the pros and cons of asking me to accompany her. "Anything I can do to help?"

"No. This'll just take a minute. Might be best if you—"

"I'll tag along. It'll give me a chance to look around."

"But—"

"No really, I don't mind at all."

She didn't argue.

As I trudged behind her into the hive I noticed several big green signs declaring, "I'm OK," hanging from the knob. Was that the check-in system Reva told me about?

My nose wrinkled. Man. It smelled rank. Why didn't anyone notice? Why didn't someone do something about it? There had to be industrial-sized air fresheners that could mask the scent.

A young male in uniform, about six feet four and severely underweight, shifted nervously at the end of the hallway. The second he caught sight of Luella, he pushed his mop of Day-Glo orange hair from his eyes and lumbered closer.

"I'm sorry. I didn't know what else to do. No one is at the front desk or answering the phone in the acute care wing and Ricky is late because his car won't start—"

"Damon. It's all right. Calm down."

He swallowed and nodded.

"Tell me what happened."

"I was doing rounds and I got to the end of the hall when I noticed there wasn't no sign up on this apartment and the door was partially open."

"What did you do?"

"I peeked inside and saw him lying there. Then I smelled him."

Luella squeezed past him and pushed open the door.

A sickly scent of rot, unwashed skin, urine, and shit wafted out from inside the room.

60

Someone was dead.

My fingers sought the handicapped railing behind me and I held on. Nice fucking start to my day. I looked at the room number.

"Damon? Could you come in here?"

His bulk had blocked most of the doorway and now I had a birds-eye view of the dead, if I chose to look.

Don't.

I didn't want to, but my gaze wandered that direction anyway.

An old, naked Indian man was sprawled on his side. I couldn't tell if he was fat or just bloated from death gases. His thick neck was cranked so his bald head faced the door; his eyes were open as if he'd been waiting for someone.

I figured even if I moved closer I wouldn't see a pool of blood anywhere, just the usual puddle of liquid from his bowels emptying. No foul play here. Only the final indignity of death.

Still made me want to throw up. I could've gone the rest of my life without seeing another dead body—even one from natural causes. I closed my eyes and listened to Luella calling 911 for a nonemergency situation.

When she said, "Kate?" I nearly jumped from my skin. "Sorry. I didn't mean to startle you. Why don't you head back to the common room? I'll meet you there when I'm done."

"How long will you be?"

"Half an hour or so."

"Okay." That'd give me enough time. I spun toward hallway two. And luck was with me when I noticed the green "I'm OK" sign on his door. I knocked.

Vernon Sloane answered by yelling, "What do you want?" through the closed door.

"Luella sent me to tell you she might be late."

Silence.

"Mr. Sloane?"

The door opened. He blinked at me with vacant eyes.

"Hi, I'm—"

"Susie? Is that you?"

"No. My name is Kate. Is it all right if I come in?"

He didn't answer. Instead he demanded, "Where's Susie?"

"I don't know."

"Is she coming?"

I turned sideways and slipped past him.

Luckily he didn't throw me out, but closed the door.

The apartment was unbearably hot, and I loosened my coat as I looked around. Typical bachelor pad; beige walls and carpeting. Navy blue couch. One battered tan recliner facing the window and the TV. No kitschy doodads anywhere. It was depressing as hell. Stacks of word search puzzle books were piled on one end of the coffee table. Two simple black frames hung above the sofa. A black-and-white wedding photo and a picture of a much younger Vernon sitting behind the wheel of a big old car. I stepped forward to take a closer look at the pictures.

"She's a beauty, isn't she?"

"Yes. When was it taken?"

"Oh, 1948. The same year I bought it."

He wasn't talking about his wife, but the car.

"I loved that Roadmaster. See, it's a convertible? 'Course, you can't tell the color, but it was the creamiest soft yellow, the shiniest paint Buick ever put on a car. Reflected like a mirror. Still looks pretty good for an antique. I'd offer to take you for a spin, but she's kind of touchy in the snow. Nothing like those four-wheel drives everyone has these days."

Hadn't Amery told us her grandfather had totaled his car, resulting in the loss of his driver's license? What was I supposed to do? Correct him? Play along?

Better change the subject.

I turned around and smiled.

His eyes clouded and he backed away, slowly, hands in the air in front of him like I'd jabbed a gun in his face. "Why are you here?"

"Luella sent me, remember?"

"You look like her, but you don't sound like her."

Maybe he was blind, too, because I hoped to hell I didn't resemble a sixty-year-old woman. "Who? Luella?"

"My Susie."

"I'm not Susie, Mr. Sloane." I sat and hoped he'd do the same. "But as long as we're on the subject, why don't you tell me about her?"

"I can't. They'll kill her."

Man. I was so out of my league. I'd never dealt

with this type of situation. "Okay. Why don't you tell me about your granddaughter, Amery, instead?"

"Who?"

"Amery. Susie's daughter."

"I don't know who you're talking about. Susie is just sixteen years old. She's a baby, not old enough to have a baby. Are you trying to trick me into telling you where she is?"

Over your head, Julie. "Ah. No."

"Who is this Amery person?"

"Never mind. I should—"

"Susie went away because I couldn't keep her safe. They wanted to hurt her. Sometimes she sneaks in here to see me. I have to hide her from them. But that means my sweet girl has to hide from her papa, too." His vacuous eyes flared panic. "You won't tell them she was here, will you?"

"No. Your secret is safe with me."

His gaze pierced my forehead as if he could see my brain to gauge whether or not I was lying. "I'm paying them to keep her safe now. She's in a place no one will ever find her."

"Paying who?"

"Wouldn't you like to know?" he snapped off.

Mr. Sloane was getting more riled up. I knew I'd made a mistake barging in here. Problem was, I didn't know how to fix it. He kept muttering and gesturing at me like he was warding off an evil spirit. It didn't help I felt like I'd slipped on the devil's skin.

My frantic gaze landed on the coffee table. "I used to love to do word search puzzles."

Vernon Sloane glared at me. "You're lying. Why are you really here?"

Shit.

"For more money?"

I stood. "Look. I didn't mean to upset you. I'll go."

"I know your type. You smile while you lie so it'll be easier to trick me."

My cheeks burned.

"How much are they paying you?"

Not nearly enough. And while I hurt for Amery, having to deal with a deranged grandfather, I figured she was money ahead if someone like Luella shared the emotional burden. Whatever Luella was making wasn't nearly enough. Sounded callous but I didn't care.

"Mr. Sloane. It was nice meeting you." If I hadn't been wearing clunky boots I would've sprinted for the door.

He called out, "Don't hurt her. Please. I'll do anything to keep my Susie safe. Take my car. Wait. I'll find the keys. They're here someplace."

Made my ears burn with shame to hear his pleading tone. "Susie is safe, remember? I don't need your car."

He didn't respond. I was afraid if I stuck around I'd hear him crying. Making an old man cry. What a fucking great thing to add to my day after seeing a dead guy.

I stepped into the hallway and pressed my back to

the wall to slow my guilty breathing.

Screw this. Since Kevin wanted to take this case so fucking bad he could finish it. I had no reason to stick around and talk to Luella. I'd gotten more than I came for: proof anyone could take advantage of Vernon Sloane. Proof he needed acute care.

One thing left to do. I peered around the corner.

Rubberneckers filled the hallway, mesmerized by the workings of the ambulance crew. Probably some kind of morbid entertainment for the residents. No one paid attention to me as I headed down hallway four and knocked on door 407.

CHAPTER 5

FIRST THING I NOTICED WHEN REVA OPENED HER apartment door were all the bookcases. The second thing I noticed was the way her eyes lit up when she saw me.

"Julie! Was your nose itching? I was just thinking about you."

"Am I in trouble?"

"Pooh. Don't stand there; come in. Would you like a cup of tea? I just made a fresh pot."

My mouth opened to refuse. But would it kill me to stick around for more than two minutes? No. I wasn't in a big hurry to go outside into the cold and snow anyway. "That'd be great."

"Sit."

"What can I do to help?"

"Be witty and entertaining because Lord knows

I've been bored out of my skull lately."

Everything in her kitchen was proportioned for her wheelchair. She took two dainty gold-rimmed teacups from a drawer and placed them on matching saucers. Then she lifted a crocheted tea cozy from the teapot and poured the steaming liquid into the cups.

"Carry those to the table and I'll rustle up some cookies."

While she fussed, I peeked in the sugar bowl. Yep. Sugar cubes. I snatched one with the fancy small silver tongs and thought of Martinez. He loved the damn things.

Reva rolled up to the side of the table without a chair and slid a plate of Walkers butter cookies in the center. "There. So tell me, Miss PI, what brings you here on such a nasty day?"

I sipped my tea, hoping the sugar would mask the flowery taste. "I had an appointment with Luella. But right after I got here she had to deal with . . ." Hell. I didn't know if Reva had heard about the dead guy yet.

"Walter Jumps High's bloated body."

"You knew about him?"

"I was making my morning rounds when that red-headed punk puked in the hallway." She blew on her tea. "I wasn't surprised. Walter was severely diabetic, severely overweight, and had heart attack written all over him. Not that he did anything to change his bad habits, so no one wanted anything to do with him. Like those of us who don't have family, he mostly kept to himself."

That was a little unsympathetic. Because he was Indian?

"Besides, this is an old folks' home. Someone is always found dead. It'll be old news by noon."

"Well, it was a shock to me first thing, especially when Luella was the first one called. Shouldn't that responsibility fall to a nurse or someone qualified?"

"Usually it does, so I think they're short-staffed today. Used to be one of the nurses from Acute Care would do rounds with Security. Now those minimum-wage idiots do the checks. If they feel like it. I told you what happened to my friend." Reva chomped on a cookie. "Why were you going in room 208?"

Talk about an eagle eye. "I thought I was discreet."

"Don't worry, no one else noticed. But I was sur-prised to see you going into Vernon Sloane's room."

"Do you know him?"

"Not really. Like Walter, he kept to himself until Luella took over. She acts like him playing chess with other residents will cure his decline into demen-tia. It's surprising he's still allowed to live by himself, especially since all he ever talks about is his stupid car when he does deign to leave his room."

"I kinda got that."

"Did his family hire you?"

"Why?"

"That's the thing. I didn't know he had family since I've never seen him with anyone."

A weird tingle danced up my spine. "Maybe they prefer to meet privately."

She shook her head. "Trust me, anyone who has family visit makes sure everyone in here *knows* they have family, because so many of us don't."

"You've never met his granddaughter?"

"Nope. What's she look like?"

"Young. Blond. Really pretty."

"I would've remembered her. Did you ask him about her?"

I nodded. "He didn't know her at all."

"Shame. If I had grandkids, you can bet I'd be parading them up and down the hallways in a dog-and-pony show."

"You don't have kids?"

"Nope. My husband and I weren't particularly upset by it at the time. Kinda lonely now."

I reached for a cookie and saw Reva squinting at my chest. "What?"

"That's quite the necklace. Lovely color. Matches your eyes. Did you get that from your sweetie pie?"

Calling Martinez my sweetie pie? Right. My fingers automatically twisted in the thick silver chain. "Yeah."

"What is that? A sapphire?"

"A star sapphire." I'd had to look it up online since I'd never seen a stone like it.

She leaned forward and whistled. "That is one big stone. What is it, about fifteen karats?"

"Twenty, I guess."

"He must really like you, sweets. Is there a story behind why he gave it to you?"

I squirmed because I didn't know.

A few weeks ago, a white box with a big blue satin bow had shown up on the coffee table in my living room. No card. I'd opened the package to find the gorgeous necklace nestled in midnight velvet. Later, Martinez called to ask if I liked my birthday present. That'd been the extent of it. I reacted as coolly as he had, because I'd never had a man give me jewelry. Afterward I suspected Martinez had as much experience giving it as I had receiving it so I'd been leery of asking questions.

"Julie?"

"It was a birthday gift from my boyfriend."

"My late husband was romantic to the core. You'd never know it by looking at him, a big, rough, dirty Wyoming oil rigger." Her blue eyes were soft, her smile wistful. "He's been gone ten years and I miss that sweet, gruff man every damn day."

I didn't do well with tears. "The librarian and the roughneck? Sounds like the makings of a fine romance novel, Reva."

A sly wink. "More like an erotic romance novel."

I lifted my teacup. "Here's to men who are a little rough around the edges and the edgy, rough sex."

"Amen." She chinked her cup against mine.

"Thanks for the tea party. Next time, maybe we should toast with something stronger. Like this." I set the bottle of Jack Daniels next to the cookies. "Thanks for your help. Don't drink it all before I come back, okay?"

Reva's mouth opened and closed. Tears shimmered in her eyes.

Ah, hell, I hadn't meant to fluster her. Dammit. Apparently I sucked at the gift-giving thing as much as my sweetie pie did. "Consider it a bribe. I'll be around to pick your brain some more."

"You're really planning to come back?"

I said, "Yes," and meant it.

She watched me closely as I wrapped up in my winter gear. "Be careful out there, Miss PI."

"I will. You be good. And if you can't, have fun being bad, spy girl."

Guilt made me search out Luella before I escaped.

As I neared the employee break room, I heard male laughter.

"You're a fuckin' pussy, Damon, blowing chunks in the hallway."

"Yeah? Well, it was fuckin' gross. Seeing that fat gut-eater in a pile of his own shit and piss. Smelled like bad Indian tacos in there."

"So? I wouldna puked."

"Bullshit. You think you're so fuckin' tough, Ricky."

"No, I'da been happy to find spooky fucker dead. He freaked me out."

"Why? Think he'd do some Indian voodoo shit to you? Make you wear feathers in your hair? Do the Sun Dance and pierce your man titties? Force you to call him chief and smoke the peace pipe?"

"Fuck you. I ain't afraid of no fuckin' red-skinned hoop. Weirdo never looked me in the eye. Just mumbled and shuffled his moccasins if I asked him something. Always stunk like booze and that stupid incense shit he burned in his room, too. I'm just fuckin' glad he's gone to the happy hunting grounds."

They both laughed. "Another one bites the dust."

A slap of hands in a high five. "Maybe we'll get someone in there now who isn't a fat fuckin' welfare case and they'll tip us for all the shit we do."

I made myself visible in the doorway. I hoped I looked as pissed off as I felt. "Good acoustics in the hallway. Which means I just heard every disrespect-ful, stupid, racist piece of garbage that fell out of your big, stupid mouths."

Surprise, followed by defiant looks.

"What in the hell is the matter with you two? It's not enough a man is dead? You have to rip him and his heritage to shreds? In public? Why? To make yourselves look like big men rather than whiny-assed babies?"

"Who the fuck are you?"

"Someone who will go out of her way to make sure your boss knows every inappropriate word you've spewed and how unprofessional you've acted."

Another round of laughter. "Right. Like anyone cares what we said about another dead fuckin' Indian."

"You think you're above him? You're a *janitor*, smart-ass. That man paid your goddamn salary and he deserved your respect, not your scorn."

"Ooh, Damon, looky here. We got a prairie nigger lover who's gonna rat us out. We're shakin' in our boots. You ain't got no power over us, so get the fuck out of here."

"She doesn't have power over you, but I do."

I turned and their gazes snapped to Luella.

Absolute silence.

The red-haired kid actually looked mortified. The other young man, a runt with long, greasy hair that didn't mask the zits covering his face, still appeared defiant.

"You ain't got no power over us"—he sneered—"and you know you can't fire us 'cause you'd be fucked. No one wants this shitty job anyway."

Another awkward moment.

"Besides, everyone knows you hoops stick together, no matter what, so ain't no one gonna believe what you say."

"Break is over. Get out of my sight or I'll scalp you, eh?"

Hiking boots hit the linoleum floor and Mr. Big

Mouth and his companion strode out.

Luella didn't look at me. "I'm sorry you had to hear that. Not exactly the family image we want to project to potential customers, is it?"

"Unfortunately, it's typical of just about everyone's attitudes around these parts, not just here." It'd probably rile me worse, but I had to ask. "Do you get that attitude a lot? Since you're Indian?"

"The mind-set that the only reason an Indian woman has attained a job at this level is because of racial profiling?"

"That, too. But I'm wondering about the attitudes of residents you're caring for?"

"*Shee.* Some residents doan want me in dere apartments because dey tink I'm gonna steal from dem, hey. Dey tink 'cause I'm Sioux dat I doan got no education and de only ting I know 'bout business is how to apply for subsidies, hey." Her sorrowful brown eyes finally met mine. "Yes. I hear that quite frequently. It never gets any easier hearing that garbage."

"People suck. And it really sucks you get that from co-workers."

"They don't care. Kids these days don't respect anybody. But thanks for calling them on their comments. Most folks would've walked away."

"I'm a rebel with a conscience, not an agenda." Well, except for the one involving Vernon Sloane.

Luella cocked her head. "I see that, and I'll admit I'm confused by it because you don't look Indian."

"I'm not. My half brother from White Plain was. I watched him struggle with stereotypes his whole life and I hated it." I slumped against the wall. "He's dead and I still hate it."

"I'm sorry."

"Thanks." I signed and buttoned up my coat. "Sorry if you've gone to trouble, Luella, but I'm not in the mood for a tour right now."

"That's fine. I understand completely, Kate. I just hope you haven't written Prairie Gardens off completely."

"I haven't. We'll be in touch."

"Be careful out there."

I fled into the snowstorm.

CHAPTER 6

My windshield wipers worked overtime as I crept through town. Because of the extreme cold, it wasn't a heavy, wet snow comprised of big, lacy snowflakes. The white stuff was a fine dust, the consistency between talcum powder and sugar crystals. When the 40-mph wind caught those icy crystals, it wasn't like being in a pretty snow globe; it was like being in the middle of a sandstorm.

The mucky gray sky gave no hint to the time of day and I'd lost track. I glanced at the clock. Noon. Damn day wasn't even half over. I just wanted to go home and hunker down until the storm passed.

The parking lot of Safeway on Mt. Rushmore Road was jam-packed as locals prepared for the worst. Maybe the forecasters were right for a change, and we were in for a big blizzard. I shivered and the urge to book it home tripled. But being a responsible partner, I dialed the office to make my report.

Kevin answered on the second ring.

I said, "I'm done at Prairie Gardens."

His sticky silence competed with the static from my cell phone.

"Kevin? You still there?"

"Yeah. Look. About what you saw yesterday—"

"Save it." I craved a goddamn cigarette. But I couldn't smoke, talk on the phone, and drive in a snowstorm all at the same time. "Is there any way you can get Amery to come in, in the next hour? As far as I'm concerned, this case is done."

"That won't be a problem. She's . . . ah, already here. We were having lunch."

I *so* did not need the mental picture of what Kevin meant by *having lunch*.

"Good. I'll be there in ten. Bye."

"Julie, wait."

"What?"

"Be nice when you get here."

"Why the fuck would I wanna do that?"

"Because I'm asking you to, all right?"

"Whatever." I hung up.

People parked like idiots downtown the second they saw white fluff. The leased lot was closed. There wasn't an open spot within two blocks of the office. By the time I'd hoofed it upstairs, nearly twenty minutes had passed. I unwrapped my scarf, peeled off my gloves, unbuttoned my coat, and jammed a lit cigarette between my lips before I'd made it into the haven of my office.

I slammed the door, needing a minute to find my "nice" persona. I'd probably left it in my bottom desk drawer next to my spare box of rainbows and butterflies.

Give me a fucking break.

By the time I'd finished Marlboro #2, I'd shed some of my abominable snowman attitude.

Kevin knocked. "Can we come in now?"

"Yeah."

He opened the door for Amery and pointed to the buffalo skin chair to the left of my desk. How sweet.

Amery looked to Kevin before she spoke to me. He gave her an encouraging smile. How nauseating.

"Kevin said you were just at the retirement center. Did you find out anything else?"

"Yes. But I'm not sure it's what you want to hear, Amery."

Another panicked doe-eyed look at Kevin. "I don't understand."

"How much time have you spent with your grandfather recently?"

"Not much. I told you—"

"That he has Alzheimer's, yeah, I know. I had no idea how bad it was until I talked to him this morning."

She blinked those big blue eyes. "You *talked* to him? What did he say?"

"Nothing but gibberish. He thought *I* was your

79

mother. Then he told me he'd hidden her away because 'they' were trying to kill her, and he begged me not to tell 'them'—whatever the hell that meant. He babbled about paying more money to keep her safe, trying to find his car, and by the time I left, he was ready for a straightjacket."

Amery gasped softly.

"Julie, that's enough," Kevin warned.

I ignored him. "So here's what I think. All this polite bullshit aside. You're damn lucky Luella is taking care of him. At least someone is. Whatever she's getting paid is not nearly enough. With what I saw today, and what you've told me, I think the best thing you could do for him is move him to the acute care wing."

"But that's not—"

"—what you wanted to hear?"

"No. That's not why I hired you. You're supposed to be finding out who is taking advantage of him."

I lit another cigarette. "No, Amery, you hired us because you were concerned about your grandfather's well-being. And I'm telling you that your original concerns were legitimate. But the only way to make sure he's not taken advantage of again—financially or emotionally—is to have him moved to a unit where qualified staff can keep an eye on him at all times." I filled my lungs with smoke. Exhaled. My cynical side counted on her outbreak of tears; my other cynical side hungered for her show of temper.

Amery took a deep breath. "All polite bullshit

aside, Ms. Collins, I thought you were a professional investigator. You suggesting that I lock him away, when we all know there are illegal activities going on in that facility, is a cop-out."

"No more of a cop-out than you ignoring him and getting all pissy when someone else starts paying attention to him."

"Julie—" Kevin tried to intervene.

"No. Let her finish, Kevin."

I didn't glance over at him because I didn't know if I could stomach the look on his face. "I talked to other residents, Amery. I know you don't visit him as often as you say you do."

Her chin drooped to her chest.

"I'm right, aren't I?"

She shook her head. "It's true I don't visit him in the common room. If you saw how confused he was today, then you can imagine what he's like when he sees me." She slowly lifted her face to meet my eyes. "Did you ask him about me?"

I nodded.

"He didn't know who I was, did he?"

"No."

"That's because he thinks I'm my mother. I look just like her. Sometimes he even thinks I'm my grandmother. I suspect part of him knows they're both dead, and that's why he gets so flustered when he sees me. Yes, he has reality issues, some idea that my mother was kidnapped. Sometimes he claims a man took her;

sometimes he claims he paid a man to take her to keep her 'safe.' So, no, when I visit him we don't hang out in the common room. Because, like you said, they'd put him in a straightjacket.

"He might be old and confused, but he does deserve some dignity. You want to know why we hide in his crappy apartment? Because I'm selfish. I want to spend time with him even when he doesn't know who I am.

"So you're right. It is a cop-out. But I'd rather those nosy residents felt sorry for him because he didn't get any visitors, than have them ridicule him because they think he's crazy."

This case had been fucked up nine ways 'til Sunday from the beginning, and my defense of myself wouldn't change that.

Amery stood abruptly.

"I-I have to finish up some things before I leave on my trip. I'll see you later tonight, Kevin."

"Wait. I'll walk you out."

I sparked another cigarette and swiveled my chair to face my blank computer monitor, bracing myself for yet another butt chewing.

A few minutes later, Kevin wandered to the window and kept his back to me. Hands jammed in the front pockets of his dark green suit pants; shoulders hunched nearly to his ears. "You happy now?"

"Happy about what, Kev? Happy that I saw a bloated dead body first thing this morning following up on a case I didn't want to take in the first place? Happy that I spent ten minutes trying to talk to the client's grandfather and then another ten trying like hell to get away from him? Happy that I've been the one dealing with ageism, racism, and sexism? And you haven't done a fucking thing on this case you insisted we take? Happy that your client questioned *my* investigative skill and *my* ethics, in *my* office, and you fucking sat there and *let* her do it?

"Or are you asking if I'm happy that I saw you screwing our client, in the middle of the goddamn day, in the middle of the goddamn conference table, when you didn't bother to check the goddamn locks on *any* of the office doors? Which one should I be the happiest about? 'Cause I'm dying of fucking curiosity to know which one *you'd* choose."

I swore I heard his molars crack from him clamping his jaw so tightly.

"It was stupid of me not to lock the doors yesterday."

Not exactly an apology. I waited for . . . something. A sheepish explanation. A lewd joke. Nothing. Looked like I'd be holding my breath for a long time for anything besides another confrontation.

Screw it. I'd had enough confrontations. I snuffed out my cigarette.

Kevin didn't turn around until I was bundled up and ready to leave. He seemed surprised. "Where are you going?"

"Home. And if it's like this tomorrow I won't be in."

If I thought my partner might stop me so we could have a serious dialogue about all the shit that'd gone down, I thought wrong.

I'd passed the Deadwood Avenue exit on I-90 West when my cell phone rang. I didn't bother to look at the caller ID. Not only because I couldn't take my eyes off the shitty road conditions, but I figured it was Martinez checking up on me, making sure my phone was attached to my hip.

"Hello?"

"Julie. Thank God I got a hold of you."

Nothing good ever comes from that conversational start. "Hey, Trish. What's up?"

"The kids and I are in Denver and I can't get in touch with your father. I've tried the house phone and Doug's cell. I even tried calling Melvin, the hired man. I'm starting to get really worried."

Oh, hell no. Don't even ask.

"I hate to ask you this, because I know how things are between you and Doug, but would you please go out to the ranch and check on him to make sure he's okay?"

"When was the last time you talked to him?"

"The night before last. I didn't talk to him at all yesterday, and I've been trying to call since six o'clock this morning. I know he didn't go anywhere—he wouldn't leave the cattle even for three days to come with us. And now I see on TV there's a blizzard warning for western South Dakota. Is the weather bad?"

"I-90 isn't too terrible." *Liar, liar, Julie.*

"If you're already out and about, can you swing by the ranch and make sure he's all right?"

Crap. I fell right into that snow trap. "I'm sure he's fine, Trish. He's probably just busy and forgot to charge his cell. You know how much he hates to talk on the phone anyway."

The ugly, thick silence my comment caused burned my ear like a case of frostbite.

"Trish? You still there?"

"Yes. You know I never ask you for anything, but I'm begging you this time, Julie. Please, I have a bad feeling. Doug is not as young as he used to be. It's calving season and if he's there alone... so many things can go wrong. You know how exhausting it is."

I did, which was precisely why I didn't want to go to the Collins ranch. "I'll try to call him from here. Maybe you're in a 'no service' area or something."

"Wrong. I'm not on my cell phone."

So much for that theory.

A tug-of-war over the receiver ensued, followed by fierce whispers. "Hi, sis."

"Hey, Britt."

"My mom is totally freaking out, and it's freaking me out. So would you please, please, please with sugar

85

on top go and check on Dad?"

No.

"For me?"

Hell, no. I hated the pseudosweet baby talk tone she used.

"What if he is hurt? Won't you feel really bad that you didn't at least *try* and check on him?"

No, no, no, no, no.

She sniffled. "Can you think about me for a change, instead of yourself? I don't want my daddy to die. Even when you pretend you're all tough and say you don't care, I don't think you really want him dead." She paused to let that tidbit sink in.

Fuck. *Send in the ringer, why don't you, Trish?*

"Fine, I'll check on him. But if I drive all the way out there and he's napping on the couch? You're on latrine duty. I'll expect you at my house every Saturday morning for a month to scrub toilets. With a toothbrush."

"As if I'd ever do that. So you'll call us and let us know what's going on?"

"Right away."

"See you later," Brittney said.

"Not if I see you first."

She giggled in a falsetto tone, which struck a wrong note with me, and my subconscious said, *sucker.*

CHAPTER 7

THE CONDITIONS OFF THE INTERSTATE IN BEAR Butte County were beyond horrible. The snow was a sea of white so blindingly bright I slipped my shades on. I inched along County Road 12, plowing over snowdrifts and sending up a little thanks to the car gods for my four-wheel drive Ford truck.

I didn't encounter a single vehicle in that five-mile stretch of road, which was good because I drove straight down the middle. Most people were smart enough not to venture out during a storm. Usually I was one of those smart people.

The wind whistled through the ventilation system and shook my three-quarter-ton truck like a Yugo. I kept an eye on the odometer since none of the natural landmarks were visible. I'd always bragged I could drive this gravel road with my eyes closed. Well, my eyes were wide open and I couldn't see shit.

I eased the truck to the left side and tried to make out the big elm trees lining the driveway, marking the turnoff to the ranch. I swiped fog from the windshield with my gloved hand. A momentary break in the wind and swirling snow showed the familiar skeletal trees. I braked, turned, and busted through two-foot-high drifts.

The shelterbelt surrounding the ranch buildings did what it was designed for, providing a modicum of protection. The amount of snow accumulation was the same as on the road and in the fields, but the trees blocked some of the wind gusts. I pulled up to the front of the house rather than my usual spot by the machine shed.

A grim feeling spread in me when I noticed my dad's pickup wasn't around. I left my truck running and ran up the snow-covered porch steps and into the foyer.

"Dad?"

I hadn't expected him to answer; the house had that empty feel. I checked every room upstairs, downstairs—even the cellar. Nothing. And I couldn't tell if he'd been here earlier in the morning. No coffee cup sat on the dining room table or dishes were left drying on the dish rack.

Next stop was the barn. The snowdrifts were knee-high in front of the big doors. I snagged the shovel out of the back of my truck and managed to get the side door open far enough to sneak inside.

The barn was hot, dark, and smelly in the summer,

and cold, dark, and smelly in the winter.

"Dad? You in here? It's Julie." I wandered past the darkened stalls and tack room to the largest section with the hayloft. Little hay, no sign of Dad, his hired man, cattle, or newborn calves. The horse stalls were empty, too.

I didn't know what to do next. A blizzard raged. Windchills were probably in the zero range. Skin could freeze in seconds. It'd be stupid to venture out and risk my safety. Not only didn't I have the basic winter wear; I had no idea what direction he'd gone. Highly doubtful I'd see his tire tracks. What could I do even if by some miracle I found him? Especially if he was injured? Or worse?

I don't think you really want him dead.

Did I? Could I walk away?

No. My subconscious called me a pussy when I entered the tack room looking for extra clothing. Dad never threw anything away, so I found an extra pair of old Carhartt overalls hanging on a peg in the back. In addition to being stained, faded, and ripped in spots, they were ginormous on me. I cinched them as tight as I could, put my outerwear back on, and grabbed two pairs of leather work gloves. I added three nylon ropes, and four heavy saddle blankets to my pile, hoping like hell the wind wouldn't rip them from my arms before I made it back to the truck.

Once I was safely inside the cab and my face unfroze so I could move my lips, I redialed Trish's number. No answer. I tried again. Nothing. Looked like the phone outages were on this end.

Since it was calving season it surprised me the cattle weren't close to the barn. Meant chances were good Dad was at the cattle shelter and not out on the frozen prairie. If I followed the fence line I'd practically run into it.

If I didn't get stuck in a snowdrift first.

I opened the gate and drove through.

The uneven terrain made for a bumpy ride even when I inched along. The driver's side window continually iced over, forcing me to roll it down to keep the fence line in view. Flakes swirled inside the cab. My nose was frozen. The sunglasses offered some protection from the wind, but I still had to squint to see through the snow squalls.

At the next hump, I lost sight of the fence line and I rolled to a stop when I realized way out here the mounds of snow covered the fence completely.

Being surrounded by the intense whiteness was like being trapped in a glass of milk. I cupped my hands around the digital clock on the dash to check the time. A half hour had passed. I still had a third of a mile to go, according to the odometer.

Or . . . I'd driven over the fence and was going the wrong direction. Only one way to find out. I uncoiled the rope and hopped out of the truck cab. The flakes stung, cutting exposed skin like tiny daggers. My body weight had as much impact as a feather against the thick crust of snow. I tied one end of the rope to the door handle in a quick release knot and the other through a belt loop on my coat.

Wind lashed and blew through the multiple layers of clothes.

Fuck, it was cold as a witch's tit, a well-digger's ass, a banker's smile, and all those creative colloquialisms we out here in the frozen lands tossed around regularly.

I started to walk in what I thought was a straight line. I kept my face pointed down, trying to look to the left for anything resembling a fence post. The scarf covering my mouth became soggy from my warm breath getting trapped in the icy wool. I couldn't feel my skin where my cheeks were exposed. I'd only counted fifty steps and I was already frozen to the bone.

And the wind kept howling.

Never-ending wind could drive a person crazy; I knew that from spending most my life in South Dakota. Wind wasn't a new phenomenon. Historical documents detailed the isolation of Dakota Territory pioneer settlers. Stuck for months on end in raging blizzards, alone on the vast prairie, where the biggest dangers weren't starvation and Indian attacks, but the persistent wind. Murder of entire families was commonplace, stories with the "wind told me to kill them all" theme. Some folks chose to follow the wind's shifting voices and were found frozen mere feet from their homestead during the spring thaw.

I stopped to catch my breath. Smoker's lungs, plus

a 50-mph headwind, and dragging ten extra pounds of snow-caked boots? Not good. Not a comfort that the most devoted gym rat would be sucking air just as hard as I was right about now.

By placing my hands on my knees and bending over, I hoped to force air into my lungs and block some of the goddamn Gulf Stream, if only for thirty seconds. Somehow I lost my balance. The wind provided an extra push and I rolled down the incline like a runaway log.

The damn rope didn't yank me back. No, I skidded to a stop on my face. A razor-sharp ridge of ice sliced my cheek and peeled the scarf from my mouth. My teeth dug into my lips, even as my lips dug into the crusted snow.

I laid there breathing hard. Freezing. I thought about burrowing into the drift like an Iditarod sled dog and napping until the storm blew over. I thought about my Viking ancestors hunkering down in warm furs inside snowbanks. Piece of cake. If I went to sleep, I'd probably just wake up refreshed. Alert. Ready to climb Everest. I closed my eyes. The wind crooned a special lullaby just for me.

Ssssssssssssssssssssssssssssssssssssss–sleep, sssssssssssssssssssssssssssss–sleep.

I was tired. My leg cramped up and I jumped at the sharp pain. My mouth smacked into the snow; I licked my lips and tasted blood. Yuck. Where else was I bleeding? Did blood turn purplish-black when it solidified in such extreme cold? Or did it stay bright red? Maybe it crystallized. Mmm. Like the red sugar sprinkles my mom used to decorate Christmas cookies. That'd be pretty. Blood on snow. Vivid red on such pristine white. I remembered candy canes and velvet ribbons draped on a flocked evergreen tree. Red ink swirls on crisp white paper cards. Mounds of canned whipped cream sprayed on Cherries Jubilee.

The white knuckle of my father's fist becoming bloodied after he'd hit me.

My body spasmed and I jerked awake.

Jesus, Julie, focus.

As I lay there, tired, cold, half-pissed-off/half-delirious and splayed in a grotesque distortion of a snow angel, my melancholy morphed into fear. I could die out here. Hell. Maybe I was halfway there.

My thoughts floated to a sad story about a kid a few years older than me in school. His parents had been trapped in a stalled car, after an accident out in the middle of nowhere, during an ice storm. Knowing they were going to freeze to death, the mother wrote a good-bye letter to her son. The morbid rumor circulating afterward claimed the letter was gibberish and that the final word trailed off at the end into one long line of nothing. Like she'd slowly dragged the pen across the center of the paper as she'd frozen to death and died.

Cheery thought. Maybe you should think about that Dr. Jekyll and Mr. Hyde made-for-TV movie you watched as a kid, where in the end the woman froze to death on the ship and her beautiful blue eyes were wide open and completely iced over.

The image still haunted me.

Wasn't delirium a fugue state right before death?

Last time I'd been in a dreamy pre-death state, my dead brother had shoved me back toward the land of the living before he disappeared into the great unknown.

Come on, Ben, I could use some wise Lakota words about now.

I heard nothing but the roar of the wind and a faint . . . *Mooooooooo.*

What the fuck?

I listened.

Moooooooooo.

I had to be hallucinating.

Moooooooooo.

I lifted my head and heard it again.

Not one moo, but a collection of moos. A chorus of moos. High and low notes ringing out dissonance across the prairie amphitheater.

Great. I was dying in a fucking cow pasture, being serenaded by a phantom bovine choir.

PETA would have a field day with this.

Field day? Jesus. I was in a field. That was goddamn funny.

I started to laugh. I laughed until the frigid air lined the inside of my lungs and my stomach hurt. I thought I might laugh until I cried. Or until I died.

But I wanted neither to die with tears on my cheeks, nor to live with the telltale tracks etched into my skin like a brand of shame.

In order to survive I had to move my ass.

Somehow I managed to lift my stiff body to my hands and knees. I sat up and rested on my heels. Flying daggers of ice slashed my face when I stood. I clenched my teeth and shook off the stinging pain. With my shoulders hunched against the wind, I shuffled through the powder, using the rope as a guide back to my truck and inside the blessed warmth of the cab.

Once I'd thawed some, I realized I'd lost my sunglasses. I also realized I was seeing better without them. Maybe since I wasn't so damn snow blind I could see the fence line. Too late to give up. I was already out here. It'd be stupid to go back.

I rubbed a foggy spot at the bottom of the windshield and saw a flash of red. I blinked, afraid it'd been another illusion.

Nope. A red streamer fluttered in the wind. I rammed the truck in gear and gunned it about twenty feet. Sure enough. My dad had fastened a long strip of red plasticlike lumberyards used to a twelve-foot two-by-four I knew it marked the turnoff to the cattle shelter.

I cranked the wheel a hard right, hit the gas, and plowed through a snowdrift. By the time the windshield wipers slapped away the snow, I saw the ass end of my dad's Dodge and narrowly avoided smacking into the open tailgate.

My adrenaline kicked in when I noticed the driver's door was open and a dark shape was half-buried in the snow by the front tire.

Stages leading to hypothermia:

Frostnip: characterized by skin pain and numbness, exposed body parts become blanched (white).

Frostbite: redness, swelling, formation of blisters or water blisters (blebs) followed by gangrene of tissue and underlying fat, resulting in black, leathery dead skin, requiring amputation.

Clinical stages of hypothermia:

Excitatory: rapid breathing, increased activity as victim shivers, attempting to warm up, as blood vessels constrict to conserve heat. Heart rate drops as the amount of blood ejected by the heart is reduced. Fatigue and confusion set in.

Adynamic: victim is without movement; breathing slows as the respiratory center reflects total metabolic slowdown. Confusion gives way to delirium. Reflexes disappear, including loss of muscular power and coordination. Skin becomes cold as blood is shunted into deeper tissues.

Paralytic: as the core temperature drops, the victim becomes comatose and neurological centers cease to function. Cold exposure produces excessive urination (diuresis), causing dehydration and cardiovascular complications. The heart quivers uselessly without pumping blood.

Death.

CHAPTER 8

I shut my truck off but made sure I left the keys in the ignition before I climbed out. The shape wasn't big enough to be Dad. I slammed his pickup door shut on my way past and stared down at the dead calf.

The tiny black animal was already frozen stiff.

My gaze zoomed to the rickety wooden structure in front of me. Not like a barn, not really even a building. The cattle shelter was a temporary break from the elements. It was twenty feet long and eight feet high. Three sides were enclosed, although an inch gap showed between the boards, like in a corn bin. In the far right corner, a couple of sheets of plywood had been tacked up, turning it into a makeshift stall.

Maybe it was wishful thinking, but it seemed the wind had died down. I crept along the back side of the structure. Too late for me to worry about not spooking the cows so I yelled through the slats, "Dad? You okay?"

No answer except the continual bellow of animals.

I repeated the process every five feet. Not even a blizzard could mask the rank odor of manure and animal flesh. I rounded the last corner, not knowing what I'd find.

Twenty or so head were jammed shoulder-to-shoulder, head-to-butt, butt-to-head. I pressed myself close to the wall, hoping I could make the entire length without a hoof connecting with some part of my body.

"Dad?"

Crack. A powerful kick connected with the siding and glanced off my knee. Oh, shit. *Oh, fuck. That hurt.* Stupid cows made a game of it and I was nailed a half-dozen more times before I made it to the stall.

One momma with afterbirth hanging out of her rear end bellowed mournfully, over and over, calling for her dead calf. Casualties were high in the cattle business during blizzards.

I peered over the edge and saw him. His head rested on the back wall. Eyes closed, mouth slack. He could be dead; he could be asleep. Loudly, I said, "Dad."

He jumped and rubbed his eyes like I was an apparition. "Julie?"

"Yeah, it's me."

"What the devil are you doin' out here?".

Saving your sorry ass.

"Trish sent me. She hadn't heard from you and she was worried."

"So she guilted you into comin' after me? In a blizzard?"

"No. Brittney did." I counted to ten. Why was I surprised he wasn't happy to see me? Did I really expect he'd throw his arms open in welcome? Right. And then the cows would sprout wings and fly us to the moon.

"How long have you been out here?"

He harrumphed. "Since first light. I knew we was in for a bunch of snow. I'd dropped off extra hay when I noticed a few of my two-year-old heifers were gone. Tracked them here to find them laboring. Stupid hired man dropped cake out here. What a worthless SOB."

The word *cake* threw me and I had to think for a second. Cake was pelletlike food ranchers sometimes used in the winter for feed in addition to hay. "Where is your hired man?"

Dad didn't answer; instead, he offhandedly said, "First-time mommas, you never know how it'll go. I stuck around. Ended up losin' the first calf."

"I saw it out by your truck." I slapped a flank, and the back end of the cow blocking me in moved, but the snap of the tail nearly caught me in the face. "By the way, your truck door was open. Hope you hadn't left it that way on purpose, because I shut it."

"Battery dead?"

"Didn't appear to be."

"The wind musta blown it open."

A laboring heifer lay on either side of him.

"How'd you find me? Use some of them PI skills?"

"No. I followed the fence line, saw the flag, and *voilà*, here I am."

"Surprised you remembered how to get here."

"Yeah? Can't say I'm surprised that you forgot I helped you with calving for two years before Trish entered the picture." Not that he'd given me a choice and I sure as shit had tried to block it out.

He didn't have a smart remark for that. We listened to the ceaseless sounds of the wind.

"Are these the last two in labor?"

"For now. I don't have a good feelin' about either of 'em. This one keeps wantin' to stand up. This one is flopped down like she's already given up on the birth. If I try to get 'em to move, they go into further distress. Ain't neither one of 'em particularly docile. If I leave 'em unattended, I'd likely lose two cow/calf pairs, rather than just two calves."

"How long you planning to stay out here?"

"Long as it takes. Got the calf puller ready to go for that one." He pointed to the heifer lying down, breathing hard. "I was jus' takin' a break."

God. I hated to help pull a calf. It was a last resort, hence the use of extraction tools, and potentially dangerous to the calf. Plus, it was just a gross, nasty process.

Even though we were somewhat sheltered, we were still outside and it was still damn cold. I stamped my feet and leaned inside the stall. "Wish I woulda thought to bring coffee."

He grunted and tipped his head back, closing his eyes.

I had nothing better to do so I studied him. I don't know what I expected to find. More gray hair threaded within the black strands? Deeper wrinkles by his disapproving eyes and frowning mouth? Or a softness in his sleeping hours, which was absent when he was awake?

There wasn't a soft thing about him.

I should leave while I still could.

"It ain't polite to stare. And I know for a fact your mama taught you better than that, girlie."

Before I could snap off a response, the heifer shifted and tried to stand.

"Whoa, whoa there, little gal," he said, shifting to his knees. "Let's take it slow."

The heifer began to thrash and make horrid noises.

"What the hell is wrong with her?"

"Her water bag broke more'n hour ago. She's panicked and in pain 'cause that calf ain't moved. Might be hung up on the pelvis. What do you recall about pullin' a calf?"

"Besides all the liquidy shit?"

"Guess you remember enough." He pointed to the bag in the corner. "Toss it over."

I dragged the big canvas bag behind him.

Dad ripped off his right leather work glove and ran his bare hand down the heifer's heaving side. Then he squirted antibacterial gel on his arm from his hand past his elbow. At least I wouldn't be sticking my hand up where no one's hand belonged.

I noticed he'd already attached the breech spanner of the calf puller below the heifer's puffed-out vulva, and secured it around the backbone to keep the tail in place.

He slid his hand inside the birth canal. Made a squishy sound as he gently moved it around. "Front hooves are pointin' the right way, but I can feel the calf's nose and the tongue started to swell."

I knelt along the cow's spine. She was too focused on expelling the calf to be skittish at my strange and tentative touch. Dad's and my hands were a foot apart on her belly and I could feel the hard clench of the external muscles as the internal muscles worked hard to disgorge the calf.

He and the cow both grunted as he rooted around, attaching the chain ends to the calf's legs. "Let's work the SOB out a little at time, alternating pullin' on these blasted chains."

"Do you need me down there to pull one while you pull the other?"

"No. Too risky, 'specially since you ain't done this for a while. Need you to open her up."

Eww. I didn't argue; I didn't ask questions. There were a million places I'd rather be than in the middle of a blizzard, in zero degree cold, with my father,

103

covered in cow shit, with my hand spreading open a cow's birth canal. I lifted the flaps of skin, pretending it was nothing more than her gums. "What now?"

He said, "Hold tight. Rest when she rests. Pull up when she strains. Here we go." His arm slipped out. Dad muttered under his breath. Once his hands were out of the warm, wet birth canal, and he touched the icy cold chain on the ground to start pulling, his hands froze to the metal and ripped the skin clean away. He didn't let it deter him. He was a tough old bastard, I'd give him that much.

My arms shook from the effort of holding open the vulva. Sweat poured down my temples but I was still cold.

"Don't let go."

"I'm not."

"Come on." He was pulling straight back, cranking the winch, taking up the slack. "You're about done, little gal. Work with it, not against it."

Dad wasn't talking to me, but the heifer.

"Almost there." He grunted. "There's the head." He switched angles to a downward arc when the shoulders and the rib cage emerged.

The calf slid out in a liquid ooze that stunk to high heaven. I held my breath and let go of the folds. Dad immediately tickled inside the sodden calf's nose with a piece of straw to help it get its first breath. It worked. I'd breathe, too, if someone was jamming something up my nostril.

The momma made no move to get up and lick her baby clean.

"This ain't good. Come on, girl, get up."

Finally after a few minutes, he picked up the calf and placed it on an old blanket to drag it up to the momma's head. The heifer let out a soft moo and the thick tongue lapped at the yuck coating the shivering baby. Then stopped.

We watched. Waiting for something. Anything.

The heifer strained and twitched hard and paid no attention whatsoever to her calf.

My breath was coming in short pants and a gust of frigid wind reminded me where I was. This was another danger to ranchers: exertion resulting in a false sense of warmth and constant exposure to cold made them complacent, resulting in frostbitten fingers, toes, ears, noses, and sometimes death. Spent, I crawled forward.

The move startled the heifer and she kicked me in the stomach, knocking me back. The blow nicked the bottom of my ribs, sending a white-hot stab of agony through me. "Fuck!"

"Watch your mouth," Dad warned.

The cow violently convulsed again. Her head smacked into the stall wall, her big tongue lolled to the side, and she went still.

We both watched the form for signs of life.

When nothing happened, Dad yelled, "Dammit!"

I turned to look at him. His face held that angry look of temper that'd warned me to run. Even if I'd wanted to run I had nowhere to go.

He scooped up the calf and took it to the dead cow's teat, while the calf-less heifer on the other side of the partition bawled.

Dad rummaged around in the bag, cursing, and disappeared outside.

With nothing else to do, I followed him.

More snow whapped me in the face and I hunkered deeper into my pilfered winter wear.

Dad dropped to his knees beside the dead calf and rolled it over so the belly faced up. He inserted a long, curved knife below the neck and sliced the skin straight down the center. He sawed the hide from the fat, cutting the skin away. Then he flipped the carcass over and tugged, peeling the hide from the body like the skin from a grape. Even part of the head ripped off, and he snapped the spine clean.

I clenched my teeth to keep the bile down. I knew Dad hunted and dressed the game. I knew he butchered his own cattle. But the harsh fact remained: he'd skinned the animal in under three minutes. At least he hadn't gutted it. No blood and entrails discolored the snow as he dragged the carcass to the back of his truck to dispose of it elsewhere to keep predators away from the herd.

When he turned around, covered in blood, mucus, and an oily substance that glistened like Crisco, holding a chunk of leather in its purest form, and a bloody knife, I retched.

Dad didn't care. He snapped, "Get yourself to-gether, girlie; we ain't done," as he passed by me.

And I was too damn cold and numb to do any-thing but obey.

Inside the shelter he draped the calfskin over the newborn live calf and took the bleating, shivering little thing to the calfless mother. She sniffed it. Repeat-edly. Her mournful sound changed, and the calf dove beneath her belly and began to suckle. But she wasn't convinced. She pushed it away and sniffed it again.

"Will she just accept that calf as her own?"

"Chances are still better'n fifty-fifty she'll reject it. Nothing we can do. Nature will win out every time."

Did that hold true for all animals? Even humans? True natures can never be masked?

I shivered. It'd be dark soon. I couldn't stop him from staying out here all night, but that didn't mean I had to bunk with him.

Almost the second I plotted my escape, the other heifer became restless and stood. She didn't care about the dead heifer beside her. Even to my fairly untrained eye, with a fluid bag dangling between her legs, she looked ready to pop.

Dad crouched down to check her. Then he glanced up at me. "Same drill as before. You ready?"

"I guess."

The process wasn't much smoother. The heifer wouldn't lie down. We put her head in a "catch" and I found myself on the business end of a hoof more than once before we hobbled her. The birth was stinkier and messier, too. The amnio sac was filled with liquid and calf shit and burst open when the hooves emerged. Dad was covered in way more gunk than I was and he didn't seem to notice. Might make me a wuss but I couldn't wait to crawl into a hot shower.

Chink clunk. Dad haphazardly tossed the birthing instruments in the bag. He must've sensed my intention to speak because he cut me off before I even opened my mouth.

"How much gas you got in that rig?"

"About a half tank. Why?"

"It's gonna be slow goin' getting back to the house."

"I'm following you?"

"Unless you wanna ride with me." At my look of horror he gave me a mean smile. "Didn't think so. Let's go 'fore it gets worse."

"You're just leaving them?"

"Ain't nuthin' more I can do here. They've got food and shelter."

The cold stole my breath the moment I was completely exposed to the elements. In the last two hours, while I'd been a heifer midwife, the snow began to accumulate on the ground. Where before it'd only been up to my ankles, now I trudged through shin-deep powdery fluff. The wind had died down, but that was a catch-22; rather than blowing the snow to Wyoming, it piled it up.

Dad yelled, "Keep your headlights on. Stay close. If

you need to stop or if you get stuck, lay on your horn."

The drive back was worse than the drive in. In some places the snow was two or three feet deep. Darkness fell. My world boiled down to the red taillights ahead of me and the constant slap of the wipers.

Every once in a while, big chunks of snow would fly from the hood and splat on the windshield, blinding me. I panicked every time, worried when the wipers cleared the snow I'd see nothing in front of me but inky blackness.

Dad cut a hard right and his bright headlights swept the side of the barn. Finally. It'd taken us an hour to travel a mile. But my relief was short-lived when I saw the size of the snowdrifts blocking access to the driveway and the county road beyond it.

There was no way I was going home tonight.

I'd convinced myself things couldn't get worse. As usual, famous last words. Once we'd trudged into the house, we discovered the electricity was off. Then neither the generator nor the backup would kick on. Vaguely I remembered hearing someone say my dad didn't keep his equipment in top-notch condition, but I didn't ask questions. At least we still had the wood-stove in the living room as a source of heat.

Dad tracked down a couple of flashlights and I lit the way as he shoveled a path to the woodpile. We hauled the split logs and stacked them on the porch. I tripped with an armload full of firewood, and a chunk of wood sliced me under the chin, slammed into my rib cage, and bounced off my shin.

My toes and face were cold, yet everywhere else I sweated like a pig. After I filled the wood box, I returned to my truck. Keeping the window cracked, I lit a cigarette and flipped open my cell phone to call Martinez. Completely dead. Not good. No one besides Trish and Brittney knew where I was.

I'd worry about dealing with Martinez later, since I had a more pressing problem to deal with right now: being stuck alone with my father.

CHAPTER 9

DAD STOKED THE FIRE. FOLLOWING HIS LEAD, I'D taken off the coveralls and the rest of my borrowed outerwear in the small entryway. Sweat plastered my clothes to my body and I wanted a shower something fierce. But no electricity meant no hot water. Yippee. A cold sponge bath.

My stomach rumbled. I hadn't eaten all damn day. I suspected Dad hadn't either. I was too tired to pull any of that feminist a-man's-capable-of-making-his-own-meal crap. He'd started the fire; I could rustle up dinner.

I rummaged in Trish's kitchen, finding roast beef, ham, cheese, lettuce, tomatoes, spicy German mustard, everything to make hearty sandwiches. I added a slice of homemade apple pie, and a side of canned peaches. By the time I brought Dad a plate, he'd fallen asleep by the fire. No reason to wake him. Wasn't like the food would get cold.

Plus, I'd rather listen to him snore than listen to him talk.

After I ate, I set my head on the table and closed my eyes.

I dreamed. Wind howled and snow gusted through the cracks in the settler's cabin, an abandoned shack where I'd seen horrific things. A location my mind returned to again and again whenever I was stressed out. Snowdrifts covered the windows. My gaze tracked the ghostly snow snakes slithering across the dirty plank floor. They dissipated upon reaching the discarded bodies.

I couldn't escape the vision of those bodies, even in my sleep.

Bodies once full of life, once smooth flesh plumped with blood, were deflated like forgotten balloons. Dried husks of skin and brittle bones, a human powder that would blow out through the cracks of the shack like earth's dust had blown in.

A baby cried. The wind shifted tones, masking the mournful wail. But I knew that sound. Was that my baby? I saw the manger in the corner and ran. Before I reached the brown box where a bloody chained hoof waved at me, the roof split open. Mountains of snow crashed through the gaping hole, sleet stung my face, flash-freezing my eyeballs. I tried to scream, but the snow funneled into my open mouth like a white tornado. Spinning, filling me with coldness, first my toes, then my legs, packing my womb with ice, distending my gut, coating my throat with frost until I couldn't breathe.

The *clank screech* of the woodstove's iron door jolted me awake.

Whoo-ee. Talk about a nightmare. Not the bloody carnage and Old West shoot-out variety I'd recently had, but bad enough.

Thud thud sounded as Dad tossed two split logs into the black-bellied stove and slammed the door. Both sandwiches I'd made him were gone. He'd shoved the empty dishes to the center of the table. I imagined he'd expect I'd clear them. I imagined I would do it despite not wanting to.

I wondered how long I'd been asleep and I scooted my chair closer to the fire. Molten red embers glowed through the ventilation holes at the base of the stove. Hot air streamed out as the dry wood crackled and popped. There was something soothing about staring at a contained fire. In recent months I'd spent many hours gazing into the big fireplace in Martinez's living room.

Dad didn't make small talk. He'd propped his feet on the brick ledge and leaned back in his chair, Wyoming Cowboys ball cap pulled low on his wrinkled forehead. Couldn't tell if his eyes were open.

I craved a cigarette. Standing in the subzero wind to sate my nic fit would cause him to make a snide

113

comment, and the silence between us was at least tolerable. I shifted in my chair. The aches and pains from the hellish afternoon were making themselves known, and I was uncomfortable in my own skin.

"See you're still as fidgety as you were when you was a kid."

When our life was somewhat normal—before my half brother Ben showed up and my mom was another drunk-driving statistic—he used to call me flibber-gibbet, in a teasing, affectionate tone I hadn't heard since.

"Brittney's just like you. Girl can't sit still to save her life."

I smiled, thinking of the freckle-faced waif. "I noticed."

"I'm surprised you're takin' an interest in her. 'Course I'm pretty sure I know why you ain't interested in DJ."

Don't ask, Julie. Keep your fucking mouth shut.

His feet hit the floor and I flinched. He stood to throw in another piece of firewood. Finished stirring the fire, he sat down with a sigh. "You ain't gonna answer that, are ya?"

Evidently he wasn't finished stirring me up. I feigned interest in the flames, ready to fight back with words, or with my fists if he took a shot at me.

"Ain't surprised. You're stubborn, just like her."

"Who? Brittney?"

"No. Your mother."

I looked over at his face hidden in the long shadows.

"I don't remember her being stubborn."

"That don't surprise me neither. She was one hardheaded Norsk. Once she'd made up her mind someone was in the wrong, she'd dig in her heels and then, look out."

"What would she do?"

"She wouldn't think of raisin' her voice. In fact, she wouldn't talk at all, which was worse." He adjusted his cap. "First year we were married she wanted some expensive cake pan she had to special order from Norway. I said no and told her to use a cake pan she already had. Got the cold shoulder all week. The followin' weekend I went lookin' for my ratchet set and found out she'd taken all my tools out of the garage, leavin' me with one screwdriver.

"When I demanded she tell me what she'd done with my tools, she suggested I use the screwdriver I already had. I lectured her about needin' the right tool for the job, and realized I'd proved her point."

"So she bought the cake pan?"

A pensive look crossed his face. "She bought the whole set."

I'd never heard this story. In fact, I knew nothing about my parents' marriage. As a child I'd been too self-absorbed to care. As an adult I'd been too full of hate.

"You're getting close to the same age she was when she was killed."

"That's a cheery thought."

"Just sayin'. . ." He shrugged. "You look like her.

Not a little; a lot. You could be her twin, 'cept for your eyes."

For the first time I wondered if that was the reason he'd become so violent. Looking at me was a constant reminder of what he'd lost. He couldn't take out his frustration at her for being dead, so he took it out on the closest thing to her: me.

Fucked-up logic. Probably made perfect sense to him.

I glanced over to see his ropy forearms resting on his thighs and his face aimed at the floor. My stomach pitched as my mind returned to another memory I'd blocked out.

The day after my mother's funeral I'd seen Dad in the same morose position on the end of their bed. My mother's favorite nightgown twisted in his big hands, pressed against his face while he cried.

He hadn't noticed me, would've beaten me for witnessing his grief. But peeking through the crack in the door, hearing him sobbing her name, a cruel sense of satisfaction surfaced in me that *he* was hurting for a change. Again, fucked-up logic, because I'd been hurting too. I hadn't understood why my triumph had been so bittersweet.

Bad time for those long buried emotions to surface. I didn't trust myself to deal with them fairly and nearly leapt to my feet to escape. "I'll fill the wood box. Then I'm going to bed. Thought I'd sleep on the couch. That way I can keep an eye on the fire."

No response.

I donned the stiff outerwear again and ventured out. The snow was still coming down hard, blowing sideways. I smoked a cigarette and studied the driveway leading away from the house. The plows would be by tomorrow. They had to be. I didn't know if I could survive another day with my father.

Wood stacked, fire stoked, I rolled out the sleeping bag I'd found in the hall closet and crawled in fully clothed. I didn't know where my dad had gone and didn't care.

I expected the day would dawn bright and sunny, with a clear blue sky, as it so often did after blizzards. Doomed to disappointment again. The continuing frigid air and monumental snowdrifts were Mother Nature's big *fuck you*—a reminder of who was in charge. A reminder I probably wasn't going anywhere today.

Yippee fucking skippy.

Gray light barely peeped through the window blinds. The fire burned steadily, though we were nearly out of wood again. I ignored the useless coffeepot as I poured my second bowl of Peanut Butter Cap'n Crunch. At least we had food.

I'd slipped on my boots when the front door opened. Dad shuffled in and slumped against the

117

door frame, his face pasty white as the sky. His glove-less right hand was pressed to his chest.

"What's wrong?"

He turned his palm and I saw blood. Everywhere. Running down his forearm and staining his overalls, dripping on the floor.

"Shit. What happened?"

"Cut myself trying to fix the generator."

I crossed the room to stand in front of him. "Let me see."

The deep gouge started at the knuckle of his index finger and ran crossways into his palm, stopping at the bone on the inside top of his wrist. Jesus. He'd almost cut his hand in half.

"I had hold of the wire, the engine fired and yanked it clean out of my hand. Started bleedin' like a son of a bitch right away."

He had to be damn near delirious from pain to curse. "Can you move your fingers?" With the way it was oozing I was worried he'd cut clear through the tendons, though I couldn't see bone with my naked eye.

Gritting his teeth, he curled his fingers to his palm and slowly straightened them.

"Good. Go into the kitchen so I can take a closer look at it."

"I'm fine."

"I'm not gonna pull out my sewing kit, but it needs to be cleaned."

I found a first aid kit under the sink in the bathroom.

When I returned to the kitchen, he was hunched over the sink letting water run into the cut. "Motherfucking son of a bitch—"

"Jesus. You're stubborn." I wrapped my left hand around his wrist, below the injury. "Let me do it. The last thing I need is you passing out, smacking your head into the stove so I have to deal with a goddamn concussion, too."

"Watch your—"

"Yeah, yeah, you lost the right to tell me to watch my mouth when I heard *motherfucking* coming from yours."

He hissed when I aimed the kitchen sprayer at the top of the cut and moved it across his palm. Blood poured out, mixing with the water spray, sending pinkish-red spots all over the white countertop. Watery red rivulets ran over my fingers, and down his forearm, disappearing into his shirtsleeve.

"Probably a good thing it's cold water. Might numb it a little." I studied the wound. "Better. Not perfect. Sit and I'll wrap it up."

He didn't protest. His face turned a shade of greenish-gray when I poured rubbing alcohol on a cotton ball and slicked it across the cut. Using two pieces of white tape, I fashioned a butterfly bandage to hold the split skin together and slapped on a large square adhesive bandage. I wound gauze from his knuckles to his wrist.

"I suggest you keep that flat and still for the rest of the day. I'll track down some Tylenol." I wiped off the scissors and repacked the kit.

"Where'd you learn so much about first aid?"

My fingers snapped the latch shut. "You really don't want to hear the answer to that."

"Yes, girlie, I do."

I locked my gaze to his. "From when you used to beat on me. I also got really good at applying makeup to cover bruises."

Not a lick of emotion crossed his face. Then again, had I expected an apology? No. The only thing I expected from this man was that he would piss me off, and in that regard, he'd never disappointed me.

"I've gotta haul in wood." I bundled up and escaped into the cold. Two cigarettes later, after I'd gauged all possible escape routes, I realized it'd be suicide to try to leave. But it might be murder if I stayed.

The day passed as slowly as the prehistoric Ice Age. I made lunch. I filled the wood box three times. I was too wired to nap. The last time I snuck out for a smoke I realized the snow had let up.

Dad hadn't said much, for which I was grateful. I wandered upstairs, briefly ducking into Brittney's room. She'd plastered the lilac-colored walls with posters of cowboys, the PRCA All-Around Cowboy,

Trevor Brazile, and bull riders Justin McBride, Travis Briscoe, Ross Coleman, and Guilerme Marchi. Pathetic I now knew them by name.

In the last few months, I'd learned Brittney was an avid fan of the Professional Bull Riders tour. She knew the rankings of the riders, back at least two years. Knew the points spread for the top fifteen riders. She'd even memorized the top ranked bull's stats. Urban kids were crazy for baseball statistics, so it made perfect sense pro rodeo garnered the same hero worship in the rural set.

For some reason her enthusiasm infected me, and I found myself watching VERSUS on those Saturday and Sunday nights Martinez wasn't around, rooting for the rider to outsmart the bull for eight seconds. I'd even gone so far as to check in to taking a road trip to Billings, Montana, in April—the closest the PBR Tour came to South Dakota.

On a whim I opened the door to my former bedroom. Frilly yellow curtains, a dressmaker's dummy, two sewing machines sat side by side. No sign of my Winger, Poison, or Def Leppard posters. Nothing of me remained anywhere in the house; it was as if I'd never lived here.

Back in the kitchen, while making yet another plate of sandwiches, I discovered a bottle of brandy. I knocked back four shots and nearly wept with gratitude for the immediate dulling of my senses.

It didn't last near long enough.

After supper, out of the blue, Dad said, "Whatever happened to Ben's kid?"

"Went back to Arizona. Abita got married and her husband adopted him."

"Huh. Did all that happen before or after you shot Ben's sister?"

What the hell? I knew he didn't care about Jericho or that I'd killed Leticia. He just wanted to piss with me. I had a mind to let him to see where it'd go. "After."

"You heard from her?"

"No." I doubted I would.

"Then that injun gal was smarter than she looked. Smarter than you. Ain't you afraid the Standing Elk family will be gunnin' for you for revenge for killin' their cash cow?"

"Why would you ask that?"

"No secret she was fundin' their place. The rest of 'em make poor ranchers. Now that she's dead, it's goin' up for auction next month."

"I hadn't heard."

"Didn't what you done to her go against what you was crusadin' for? Justice?"

"Justice was served. I killed her in self-defense."

"Maybe that injun family don't think so. Maybe they think you got off because you're white and no one cares about another dead injun. And you used to work for the sheriff. Maybe he was coverin' for you and let you get away with murder." He permitted a cruel twist of his mean lips. "See how this works?"

"How what works?"

"Breakin' the law. You, killin' like it ain't no big deal. First that guy you dusted with your bow. Then her. Who's next? Even if you get around the police, there ain't no escapin' the fact you're breakin' the Lord's law by killin' whenever the mood strikes you."

That killing mood was striking me pretty hard right now. I couldn't point out the kill shot with my bow wasn't done by my hand. I'd have to live with that lie forever. "Have you ever killed anybody, Dad?"

"Like I'd tell you, Miss *Pee Eye*."

"No seriously. Have you ever looked someone in the eye and watched the life bleed out of them?"

"If I said I had? What then? Would you mount an investigation?"

What the hell kind of paranoid answer was that? "Why? You have something to hide?"

He scowled. "You'd like nuthin' better than to see me in jail no matter what."

"Shut up. Nothing changes with you. You get bored and pick fights. Do you do this with Trish, DJ, and Brittney? Or am I just the lucky one?"

No answer was my answer. I skirted his chair and entered the kitchen to knock back another jelly glass full of brandy.

But he wasn't done goading me. "Not surprised you found the booze. Can't live without your vices."

"Nope." Just for shits and giggles, I poured another shot.

"Brittney told me about the tattooed freak who's at your place all the time. You embarrassed to introduce me to the spic who's warmin' your bed?"

"Yep. You've caused me enough embarrassment to last a lifetime." I drained the brandy in one long, delicious swallow.

"That ain't what I meant."

"I know. But I'm long past needing Daddy's approval for what or who I do."

"You think your mama would be proud of that smart mouth?"

I whirled around to face him. "Gee, this has been great. I'm guilted into coming here in the middle of a fucking blizzard, against my better judgment. Personally? I could care less if you froze to death with your beloved cows, but because Brittney gives a damn about you, by default, I had to, too. Never mind the fact I got the shit kicked out of me by your goddamn heifers. I feed you, I patch you up, I haul in wood in the middle of the fucking night to keep the fire going so we don't freeze to death, and this is what I get? Your fucking holier-than-thou attitude? You throwing my dead mother in my face when *you* are the one who should be ashamed of how you've acted toward me for the last twenty years? You think *she* would be proud of you?"

His jaw went rigid.

"I tried to make the best of this shitty situation, but know what? I'm done. My life would be so much easier if you were dead."

Childish? Yeah. I stomped outside. Smoked my last two cigarettes and only returned inside when I couldn't feel my feet. I dragged the sleeping bag up to Brittney's frigid room. I'd rather be a human Popsicle than spend another minute with him.

The next morning I woke to stillness. No wind. In the absolute stillness I heard the faint *beep beep* of the snowplow as it cleared off the gravel road. I didn't say anything at all as I fled the house. I put my truck in the lowest gear, busted through the snowdrifts blocking the driveway, and was on the road back to sanity.

CHAPTER 10

THE ROADS WERE STILL DICEY. BUT I WAS SO SICK OF being around Doug Collins I would've walked home. Uphill. Stark naked.

Bear Butte County snowplows cleared the main thoroughfare in my housing development, leaving a three-foot ridge blocking my driveway. I busted through it like an off-road pro. Eyeing the snowdrifts covering my porch and steps with distaste, I decided I'd deal with shoveling later. Like in the spring. All I could think about was a hot shower; dry, clean, warm pajamas; and my own soft bed.

I stripped off my filthy clothes before I stepped out of the foyer. The clock on the DVD player flashed 12:00, indicating the power had gone off here, too. Still wearing only my bra and panties, I plucked up the receiver and dialed.

Martinez's greeting was: "Jesus Christ, Julie, where the fuck have you been for the last two days?"

In hell. "Aw. I missed you, too, sweetie pie."

"Not funny."

"Yeah, well, the past two days haven't been a fucking yuk-fest for me either, pal. I got snowed in at the ranch with Daddy-O. So before you continue to bellow, let me say that the reason you didn't hear from me was because my cell phone died. Oh, and lucky for me, the electricity was off in the whole damn county so the phones at the house didn't work either. And I was fresh out of carrier pigeons to get a message to you."

"Still not laughing, blondie."

"Guess what? I've used up all my 'meanwhile, back at the ranch' jokes anyway."

I think I heard him snarl.

"I'm exhausted, and I can't stomach the thought of fighting with you, Martinez, so back off."

"You done?"

"Yes."

I waited, expecting he'd say something profane, but the pause lingered longer than usual.

"Look. I'm sorry you were worried."

His anger pulsed over the phone line; I swear the receiver throbbed in my hand even after I'd apologized, which was a rare occurrence for me.

"Fine. Be an ass. I just wanted to let you know I wasn't dead and lying in a goddamn river bottom someplace." I hung up and stumbled to the shower.

I lingered under the spray until not a drop of hot water remained. I couldn't get warm even snuggled in my super-duper thick terry-cloth robe. Wearing a towel wrapped turban-style around my head, I exited the bathroom and cranked the heater to the highest setting. When I rounded the corner to the kitchen, the front door opened.

Martinez stomped inside. He wore sunglasses and a heavy scowl. "Where's the shovel?"

"In the back of my truck." I started to tell him not to bother, but he'd do it anyway. The man had a weird obsession with shoveling, which made zero sense since he employed minions to do that sort of menial shit for him everywhere else he hung his leather coat. Why would he want do it here?

Who knew? He probably wouldn't be straight with me if I asked him, so I didn't bother.

I popped four Excedrin and returned to the bathroom to comb my wet hair. Still shivering in my robe, I was digging in the bottom dresser drawer for my fleece pajamas when I sensed him behind me. Mostly, I sensed him ogling my ass.

"I already told you, I don't want to fight with you."

"You think that's why I'm here?"

"Maybe."

"Why would you think I'd want that?"

I slowly straightened, glad he couldn't see how much the simple movement hurt me. "Because after we yell and scream, clothes start flying and we're rolling around naked. Then I forget what the hell we were fighting about."

"You dangle hot makeup sex in front of me and I might just pick a fight." He gently turned me around. His eyes searched my face and I winced when his palm pressed too hard into my hip.

"What's wrong?"

"Nothing. Just a sore spot."

"Sore from what?"

"Forget it, okay?"

"No. Let me see."

I sidestepped him and he stopped my retreat by latching onto my ribs. "Ow. Shit. Fuck. That hurts. Let go."

"Then stand still."

"Just—"

Martinez untied my robe, pushing it off my shoulders. His hands froze midair as he caught a glimpse of my various body traumas. Then his eyes narrowed and he assessed my injuries, starting with my swollen and chapped lips, and then the scratch trailing from my chin down my neck. His attention slowly drifted down my body to the bruises scattered around my rib cage like purple polka dots. He followed the pinkish scuff marks on my belly, which were parallel to the huge, angry red welt on my hip bone. And finally, his hard gaze gauged every cut and bruise on my thighs and shins.

He lowered his hands by his sides, clenching them

into tight fists. He didn't speak. He didn't look me in the eye. His breath came hard and fast—angry, like a bull fighting in the bucking chute.

"What did he do to you?"

Martinez's menacing tone still had the power to scare the crap out of me. Chills broke out across my exposed skin. "It's not as bad as it looks."

"Answer the fucking question. What did he do to you?"

"Nothing. It's not his fault—"

Lightning fast, Tony's thumb pressed against my lips as his hand snaked around my neck to keep my jaw from moving. His black eyes burned inches from mine. "Did you think you could hide this from me?"

"No. Let go. You're hurting my mouth."

Immediately, he dropped his hand but continued to stare at my distended lip. "That son of a bitch hit you in the face?"

"My dad didn't do this. You know I'd never let him smack me around. Ever. Things got hectic when we were at the cattle shelter during the blizzard and a couple of cows stomped the shit out of me. That's all, okay?"

"*Cows?* Are you fucking kidding me?"

"No." I sighed. "Will you let me explain?"

"Start. Now."

I shrugged back into my robe and perched on the end of the bed while Martinez paced. The details tumbled out in a jumbled mess, as if the past forty-eight hours happened to someone else.

"Now you know why I'm beat *and* beat up."

"I cannot believe the shit you get into."

"Literally. You should've seen me when I got home. No. Scratch that. I'm glad you didn't see me. I was covered in cow shit and birth gunk and wood-chips." And hate. I tugged the robe more tightly, grateful it at least covered the physical scars—old and new. Nothing I could do about the emotional scars, but they weren't readily visible. I glanced down at my chapped hands and ragged nails. Why was I always such a mess around him? Why didn't he care?

My stomach trembled when Martinez knelt on the floor in front of me. "You still mad?"

"No. I never was mad." He set the side of his face on my thigh and lightly stroked the backs of my calves with his rough fingertips. "I was worried something else had happened."

"What?"

"I'll tell you later." He sat up. "First I need to take a closer look at you to make sure you're all right."

"Tony, I'm fine."

"I'm not." He smoothed his palm down the side of my head and twined my wet hair in his fingers. I was surprised his hand shook. "Julie. Let me do this."

Why was he fussing over me? From guilt because we'd had a fight the last time we'd been together?

No. He's doing it because he cares about you.

"Do it quickly, because I'm cold."

Martinez stood. "Hang tight." He disappeared for a minute and returned with a bottle of peppermint schnapps. "This'll warm you up."

I swallowed two mouthfuls. The minty sweetness heated me from the inside out. Three more big gulps and I was completely relaxed, my limbs pliant, my head pleasantly muzzy.

His initial examination was very clinical. Testing my ribs for fractures, making sure the scratches weren't infected, checking bruises for abnormal swelling.

His second inspection was personal. Intensely personal. Every bruise, every cut, even the smallest mark received a tender caress and the healing touch of his warm mouth, until no part of my body had been left untended.

Those soft kisses and gentle strokes drugged me more thoroughly than the schnapps, soothing me with the lover's care and concern that no other man in my life ever bothered with. Tony's attention was so much sweeter because it was so unexpected.

I made a sleepy protest when he tucked me between my flannel sheets. Alone.

"That's it?"

"For now."

"You'll stay?"

"Yeah. I'll stay."

"All night?"

"If that's what you want, blondie."

"That's what I always want. Thank you for . . ."

Everything seemed too broad, too telling, and I was too wiped out to come up with something raunchy that'd make him crawl in bed with me and forego all thoughts of sleep. "Thank you for being nice."

"You're welcome."

The next morning I woke to the tempting smells of bacon and eggs and coffee. Martinez had prepared a feast and he watched me to make sure I ate every bite.

Finally, he said, "I called Wells yesterday afternoon to let him know where you'd been."

"Why?"

"He knew I'd been trying to track you down."

I reheated my coffee and his. "Wow. You must've been desperate to contact him."

"Smart-ass."

"Bet he didn't even know I was MIA, did he?"

"No. That first night of the blizzard some chick answered the phone. Thought I'd dialed the wrong number. So I called again. Evidently she'd gotten snowed in with him." He dumped five sugar cubes in his mug. "Is she the new client?"

"I imagine. What'd Kev say when you talked to him yesterday?"

"Not much. He was on his way back from the airport.

133

Said to tell you not to come in today if you don't feel up to it."

I smiled at Martinez over the rim of my cup. "I feel up to a lot of things this morning."

His I'd-like-to-have-you-for-breakfast bad-boy grin made my skin sizzle. "Oh, yeah? You admitting you missed me?"

"Mmm hmm. You wanna feel me up?"

"Like you wouldn't believe."

His cell phone rang. It never occurred to him not to answer it. He said about two words and then, "On my way." After draining his coffee, he stood to rinse his cup. He kissed the top of my head. "Hold that thought, blondie."

I didn't feel that great—then again, I lived on cigarettes, tequila, and coffee and was used to feeling lousy every damn day. Better to go to work than sit at home.

On the drive into Rapid City I was stunned by the variances in the amount of snowfall. In some spots the fields were barely covered. The frigid temperatures lingered, the only snowmelt was courtesy of salt on the roads, and it hadn't done much good. Piles of plowed snow lined the interstate, but it was nothing like the drifts at the ranch. Bear Butte County had been hit the worst, which wasn't unusual.

Kevin's Jeep was in the leased parking lot. I climbed the stairs. The aroma of freshly brewed coffee teased my senses when I opened the office door.

Before I could boldly announce myself in case Kevin

and Amery were polishing the conference table again, Kevin appeared holding an HS Precision mug.

"Hey, Jules. How you feeling?"

"Like I've been a kicking post for a herd of cattle, thanks for asking."

"Martinez didn't go into much detail the last time he called."

"The last time? How many times did he call you?"

"The first night? Four. Total? Seven."

Whoa. I unwrapped my scarf and let my eyes drift to the conference room.

"Amery's not here. She's in Vegas."

Thank God. "Doing what?"

"Travel agents' conference. She was supposed to leave the day of the storm, but the Rapid City airport closed and she wasn't able to get a flight out until yesterday morning."

"How bad was it here?"

"They advised no travel due to the whiteout conditions. Amery swung by my place and ended up snowed in with me."

"Lucky you."

"Were you really stuck at the ranch, alone, with Doug?"

"Yeah. It sucked in more ways than I can get into. And I'd like nothing better than to pretend it never happened." I detoured to the conference room and poured a cup of coffee. "What's on the agenda today?"

"Not much. I'm surprised you came in."

I headed to my office for a cigarette to make my morning ritual complete. When I spun my chair around after firing up my computer, I was surprised Kevin sat across from my desk, looking . . . uneasy. "What?"

"I want to apologize."

"For?"

"For letting Amery say what she said to you. She didn't know what the hell she was talking about. You're a damn good investigator. You found out more than I would have if I hadn't been so goddamn busy thinking with my dick."

"You're admitting the little head led the big head astray? What's next? You gonna take Kim up on her offer to teach you how to knit and start spewing Dr. Phil?"

"Fuck off." He pointed his finger at me. "This is why it's hard to be nice to you. Because you don't know how to act. Or how to graciously accept an apology."

My thoughts backtracked to Martinez's ministrations last night. Talk about nice. Maybe I was only gracious to those who deserved it. I smoked, waiting for Kevin to get to the point.

"Anyway, while we were snowed in, Amery and I spent a lot of time talking about her grandfather. She didn't want to hear it, but in the end she realized you were right."

I sucked back a *neener neener* smart retort with a lungful of smoke.

"She told me when she returns from Vegas her priority will be to get him moved into the acute care unit at Prairie Gardens."

"Any idea on how she plans to do that? Management wasn't too keen on helping Amery before, which was why she hired us."

"She mentioned hiring a lawyer. Or at least contacting AARP to see if they can recommend an elderly rights advocate."

"Smart move, allying with a qualified professional who's better suited to deal with Vernon's problems. She shouldn't try to buck the system on her own."

Kevin gave me a strange look.

"What?"

"Nothing. Just been a while since you agreed with me on anything."

"Where's the fun in that, partner?" I stared back at him with equal curiosity.

"What?"

"So this . . . thing between you and sweet young thang. What happens now?"

"What do you mean?"

"I assume we're done working for her."

He fidgeted, an unusual "tell" for him. "Yeah. So?"

"So why didn't you jet off to Sin City with her? It's not like we have pressing cases. I can't believe she didn't ask you."

"She did."

"Why didn't you go?"

Kevin's sharp green eyes cut through the crap and right to the truth. "Because you were missing.

Martinez isn't the only person who cares about you, Jules."

A heavy pause hung like a slab of rotten meat.

"As far as what happens when Amery returns? I don't know. I like her. She's . . . different from Lilly."

"Duh. Because she's about twenty years Lilly's junior."

"Ha ha. If I recall, your former boy toy Kell was the same age as Amery."

"True." I ground out my cigarette. "Don't know what it is, but Amery seems younger."

"You wouldn't say that if you knew her. In some ways, she's old beyond her years."

I *so* didn't want to know if he was alluding to her sexual experience or his perceived age of her soul.

Kevin's cell phone jangled. He frowned at the caller ID before he answered, "Hello," brusquely. The corners of his mouth turned up in a soft smile. "Hey. No, I'm sorry I didn't recognize the number. I forgot you didn't have your cell. How's Vegas?"

I didn't pretend I wasn't eavesdropping. If he wanted a private conversation he could skip out of my office.

"Slow down. I didn't catch that." His eyebrows drew together. "When? Why didn't they get in touch with you before you left? Oh. Right." Pause. "Amery, come on, doll, slow down. I can't understand you."

Doll? Eww. Then again, could be worse. At least he wasn't calling her sugar tits.

"They're sure?" His gaze snapped back to mine.

"No problem. Don't worry; we'll check it out. Yes, I promise. The minute I know anything. I can reach you at this number? Good." Pause. "I know. It'll be okay. Try not to think about it. I'll be in touch."

Kevin clicked his phone shut and stared at me—through me, really—but didn't offer a clue to the cryptic conversation.

"What's going on?"

"Amery's boss here in Rapid called the hotel in Las Vegas a couple of hours ago. She left an emergency message. Seems Prairie Gardens has been unable to reach Amery."

"Why not?"

He scratched his jaw with the edge of the antennae. "The day the blizzard hit she left her cell phone at the office. Then she spent the next day snowed in with me. She went straight from my house, to hers, to the airport, so they couldn't reach her at home and the travel agency has been closed until today."

"What's so urgent?"

"Vernon Sloane is missing."

"For how long?"

"That's the thing. No one knows. They're thinking since the day of the snowstorm. Since the day you saw him."

A queasy feeling sloshed the coffee around in my stomach. "Did they talk to Luella? She was scheduled for a home visit with him later that morning."

"No one has seen her either." Kevin quit twirling

his cell phone and dropped it inside his suit jacket pocket as he stood.

"So what is the staff at Prairie Gardens doing to find him?"

"According to Amery, nothing."

"Nothing? Then why the hell did they call her?"

"She doesn't know. Whenever she calls back to get more information, they just put her on hold. She's going crazy and asked if I'd—if we'd—go check it out." He looked at me. Pleadingly.

Say no.

"Hang on. I'll get my coat."

CHAPTER 11

When we arrived at Prairie Gardens, no one would talk to us. They shepherded us to a tiny reception room in the butt-fuck Egypt part of the building and told us to wait.

Kevin tired of waiting. He called 911.

Nothing gets attention like cop cars, fire trucks, and an ambulance. The first cop on scene knew Kevin. While he was pissed off about the tactic Kevin employed to get action, on some level he understood.

We waited for the manager to show up. And rather than waste time and manpower, the firefighters and the ambulance crew knocked door to door, asking if any residents had seen Vernon Sloane. By the surprised expressions, I doubted anyone had performed this task on the general populace. Why not? Why weren't the security teams and the caretakers doing their job? For

Christsake, a man was missing. Didn't anyone care? No wonder Amery freaked out.

Dee was practically in tears as she fluttered about, trying to calm residents, insisting everything was a simple misunderstanding.

Officer Smith stayed with us when we entered Vernon Sloane's empty apartment. Didn't look any different than it had a couple of days ago, which meant nothing. Searching for a missing coat, boots, or a suitcase was pointless, too.

The three of us were loitering outside the door when a man sashayed down the hallway. He was somewhere around fifty, with slicked-back reddish-brown hair, a face free of signs of aging, courtesy of Botox. He wore dark tan pants, a wool blazer, and a cream-colored turtleneck. It surprised me he wasn't stroking a yippy poodle or a groomed terrier.

I could give a crap about sexual orientation, but this gent was so gay he actually swished when he bypassed me.

"Officer. I'm Bradley Boner."

Oh, yeah, I totally felt the urge to snicker like a third grader. Not only because of the guy's name, but when he shook Dave's hand, I noticed he wore a diamond-studded ring on his pinkie.

"You the manager?"

"Yes. And frankly, I'm disturbed by why it's necessary to have all this"—he pointed to the EMTs standing at the head of the hive—"commotion. We've followed procedure—"

"Bull. If your security team had followed procedure, then these residents would've known Vernon
Sloane was missing," I said. "Instead, you hid the
information. Which makes us think you're hiding a
helluva lot more, which is exactly why we caused this
commotion."

Boner's poufy red lips made a girlish moue of dis-
pleasure. "And just who are you?"

"Julie Collins, of Wells/Collins Investigations.
Amery Grayson is out of town and she hired us in her
stead to find out what happened to her grandfather."
A little white lie. "Seems he's been missing since the
blizzard struck? When we discovered that your crack
security team *hadn't* followed procedure and contacted
the police"—I smiled sweetly—"we thought involving
law enforcement would speed things along."

"If you'll accompany me to my office, be assured I'll
get to the bottom of it." He spun on his spit-and-pol-
ished dress shoes without waiting to see if we'd follow.

Dee gave me the evil eye when we passed the desk.
I gave her one right back.

Bradley Boner's office sparkled as if it'd just come
off the office supply truck. Not a spare paper clip or
file folder or Post-it Note anywhere. No computer.
Not even a Cross pen set. If I had to guess, I'd say the
office hadn't been used before today.

After I leaned against the wall, Kevin and Officer
Smith snagged the two chairs in front of the enormous

cherrywood desk.

Officer Smith began. "How long have you been the manager here, Mr. Boner?"

"I took over seven months ago at the request of the new owners."

"Did you personally hire your staff?"

"Some. Others were holdovers from the previous administration."

"Including the volunteer staff?"

"Yes. Recently Prairie Gardens began a new active senior volunteer program, called Prime Time Friends."

"Don't you mean enforced a volunteer program on all residents, where the volunteers are financially compensated?" I asked.

Boner's face blanched, but he blithely continued, "Our head volunteer, Luella Spotted Tail, penciled in an outing for the day in question with Mr. Sloane. Logic says due to the poor road conditions, Ms. Spotted Tail took him to her private residence."

"Is that standard procedure? Ms. Spotted Tail hosting resident slumber parties on a whim?"

Officer Smith jotted notes. Kevin sat there like a toad.

Fuck this. "You've called Ms. Spotted Tail at her private residence and confirmed this?"

Boner didn't even look at me. "We're working on it."

"You either have or you haven't." I gestured to the shiny black phone on his desk. "It's not that hard.

Call her. Right now."

"You have no authority—"

"And you have no idea where Vernon Sloane is, do you, Mr. Boner? Do you even know how to use that phone? Or is it just another prop?"

"Miz Collins," Officer Smith said, "take a deep breath. We all want the same thing." He angled his head toward Boner. "Isn't that right, Mr. Boner?"

"Absolutely, Officer."

"Then you should have no reason not to answer Miz Collins's question."

Boner's self-righteous smirk faded.

"Have you, or any of your staff, been in touch with Miz Spotted Tail, either by phone or in person?"

"No."

"But you *have* phoned her?"

"Yes," he said tightly. "We learned some of the phone lines were down in that part of town, which might be a reason why she didn't answer."

"But the streets are cleared," I pointed out. "Why didn't one of your trusty staff members drive the company van over to check on her?"

No answer.

He cut me an icy stare. Might've been intimidating, if I hadn't been dating Tony Martinez—king of the piss-your-pants icy glare.

I crossed the room in three angry steps to slap my hands on his desk. "You slimy sack of shit. You didn't send anyone, did you? As a matter of fact, I'll bet you didn't even know a resident was missing. Who on your staff called you and warned you to get your prissy ass out of bed because the cops showed up?"

"Julie," Kevin warned.

"I will not sit here and listen to your insulting accusations," Boner said.

Officer Smith didn't jump in and chastise me. My ability to speak my mind was probably therapeutic for him—not that he could admit it. "Maybe you should take a breather, Miz Collins."

"Fine. I'm going. I need some fresh air since something sure stinks in here." To make my descent into good PI/bad PI complete, I slammed the door.

I didn't get far. Dee blocked my retreat before I hit the receptionist's area.

"Who are you?"

"Someone who is very, very pissed off right now, so get the hell out of my way."

"Not until you answer my question. Are you really a private investigator?"

"Yes."

"And you came here pretending to check out the facility so you could spy on us?"

"Pretty much."

Her face turned a mottled red. "You're despicable," she spit. "Lying, sneaking around, acting—"

"You know what I think is despicable, Dee?" I crowded her against the wall until her frizzy hair caught on the ridged wallpaper. "That an eighty-five-

year-old man has been missing for three fucking days
and *no one* cares. You're all too busy covering your
goddamn fat asses to get off them to find him. So the
day you can call *me* despicable is the day you stop worrying about your fucking paycheck and start worrying
about the people who are stuck with this facility's piss-
poor implementation of elderly care."

I stormed out the front door. The minute my boots
hit the pavement, I lit a cigarette and started stalking
the interconnected sidewalks. Fucking idiots. Wasn't
like Vernon Sloane was my grandfather. I don't know
why I'd gotten so worked up.

Yes, you do. Neglect is neglect; doesn't matter if the
person is five or eighty-five. Wrong is wrong. And this
is wrong.

Stupid ideology. My life would be so much easier
if my conscience would take a powder once in a while.

I smoked. And walked. And marveled that the
sidewalks were snow free. What was the point? Who
the hell was out here clattering around in a walker? I'd
bet not many octogenarians were clamoring to get out
in the fresh air and pop wheelies in their wheelchairs.

That thought stopped me. Vernon Sloane not
only wanted to get out of Prairie Gardens, but he'd
been successful at sneaking out. Several times. What
if he'd done it again?

What if he'd gone looking for his car?

Nah. Even if he had managed to escape, he
couldn't have gotten far with the arctic temperatures,

the blowing snow, and his advanced age.

A worse thought settled in, one too awful to contemplate, so naturally that's the one my brain stuck on.

I stopped and gauged where I was outside the complex in relation to the inside. Off to the right, way at the back of the acreage, were the separate buildings housing the acute care. Then the temporary care wings with separate entrances and parking lot. Around the corner to the left was the private condo wing.

If I followed the sidewalk straight back, I'd end up at the rear of the main building, by the hive. Each corridor had an exit. Where did the exits lead? To a common courtyard? Somewhere by the common rooms? No. I'd parked in the east lot and remembered the single unit apartments were to the west of the common rooms.

Since the emergency alarms on the exterior doors were disengaged, anyone could leave easily. What about the security cameras? Wouldn't there be a record? Why hadn't Boner brought it up?

Duh. Because there were no cameras. But at least that security oversight fell on his head. No matter what he claimed, that fact couldn't be hidden from the cops.

As I walked the perimeter, I began to pay very close attention to benches and bushes and trees. The machine used to clean off the sidewalks left the discarded snow in neat, uniform rows along the side. Snowdrifts behind the ridges were postcard pristine. No people or animal tracks marred the thick crust.

In my neighborhood, the snowy areas surrounding the houses were trampled from kids making snow angels or Eskimo forts or snowballs. Or from them carving a channel to the woodpile or a path to a friend's house. Even at the ranch, where the white space was vast, there were bumps and dirt everywhere; in the empty fields, in the shelterbelt, in the abandoned garden.

Here? Everything was neat and tidy. Here, I saw nothing.

Except that.

My stomach lurched at the snow-covered lump between the evergreen shrubs and the brick wall. It looked out of place. I stared at it for the longest time.

I scanned the area. No windows overlooked this section where two buildings intersected. The shrubs were an attempt to spruce up the hidden corner. But even those shrubs were straggly, neglected, and forgotten.

A shiver trickled down my spine as I took that first step. My boot broke through the unspoiled crust and buried my leg midcalf. To make progress through the thick layers, I had to raise my knees high, making me look like a demented majorette as I threw my arms out for balance. My blood pounded in time to the rat-a-tat-tat of a snare drum in the phantom marching band in my head.

Maybe I was mistaken. Maybe I'd reach that lump and find a sack of yard waste. Or some lazy person's discarded garbage. Or a bag of old, unwanted clothing.

Or an old, unwanted man.

My warm breath cut through the air. I crouched and gently brushed the snow away.

Please be wrong, please be wrong.

When my gloved fingers uncovered the frozen skin and hair, I shrieked and fell on my ass.

He appeared to be lying on his side, curled up in a fetal position. No hat. I couldn't tell if he wore gloves or a coat beneath the shell of snow covering him.

I didn't want to see anything else. This was not my job. I'd done my job in finding him. Period. Done done done.

Against my will, my fingertips reconnected to his face. I brushed away a little more snow just to be sure it was him. When his whole head was visible, I stopped. Vernon Sloane didn't look peaceful in death. He looked . . . pained. Cold. Terrified. Just like those frozen corpses at the end of the movie *Titanic*. But this wasn't a movie set where he'd get up, scrub off the makeup, and walk away. He was dead.

My vision became blurry. I stumbled back to the sidewalk and dialed Kevin's cell. He didn't answer until the third time I tried him.

"I found Vernon Sloane. Yes, I'm serious. No. I'm outside. Take the sidewalk heading east. In the corner." I glanced down at the old man. "No, I'll wait. Just don't bring a ton of people with you, okay? It's bad enough he died this way. He doesn't deserve to be gawked at like some kind of freaky human ice sculpture."

After I shut my phone, I peeled off my gloves, not caring about frostbite. I wouldn't wear them again. Ever. I rolled them into a ball and shoved them in the closest trash can.

God. I craved a cigarette, but I'd already fucked up the scene. I hunched deeper into myself, into my coat, and didn't budge until I heard Kevin shouting my name. Even then I didn't move very fast. I was too numb—in body and soul. I let him wrap me inside his big wool coat, soaking up his warmth and strength. I eased away from him when I could think again.

Kevin tipped my chin up to look in my eyes. "I'm sorry you found him."

"I know."

"You want to head back inside and I'll catch up with you when I'm done out here?"

"Hell, no."

He cocked an eyebrow at me. Since my near-death bout with hypothermia I tended to get cold faster than most people, hence my reluctance to stay in the cold, hence Kevin's concern over my willingness to do just that.

I'd survived calving in subzero temps with my father. I'd survive this, too. "Look, I don't want to be by myself, especially not in there. I'll wait for you."

"Then I'll make it fast."

Before I witnessed the Search and Rescue guys chipping away ice so they could load the body, Officer Smith escorted me back inside and took my statement. I don't know if my investigative skills impressed him or

scared him. But his solicitous act caused a headache.
I was damn glad when Kevin and I were formally ex-
cused from further questioning.

Kevin drove back to the office.

I gazed out the window. I'd had a lot of practice
in staring aimlessly into space, contemplating death in
recent months. "Did you call Amery?"

"Yeah. She's on her way home."

"I'm sorry, Kev. This'll be rough on her."

As I said it, the truth hit me. I could be in Amery's
situation right now. If I hadn't gone to the ranch, my
phone might be ringing with the news they'd found
my father frozen stiff. A niggling sense of unease surfaced for my petty parting shot of wishing him dead.
Was my guilty feeling because his behavior had turned
me into a recalcitrant child again? Or the fact I really
wouldn't be so broken up over his death?

Was Amery feeling guilty for flitting off to Vegas?
Probably. I shivered again.

Kevin flipped the heater to high. "She's taking it
hard. This situation raises more questions than answers."

With any luck he'd choose to counsel Amery in
a personal, rather than a professional capacity. And
I really hoped she didn't resent Kevin because they'd
indulged in a little slap and tickle during the blizzard
while Gramps became a permanent snow angel.

"Jules, you okay?"

"Yeah. But I think I'll go home. I'm not as fully
recovered from my ranch exploits as I thought." With

any luck Martinez would show up and we wouldn't leave my bed until morning. This time neither of us would be sleeping.

"Take care, babe. See you tomorrow."

I climbed in my Ford and smoked while the engine defrosted. My cell rang. The caller ID flashed—TM. Thank God. "You won't believe what—"

"Julie. Big Mike here. Hang on a sec, bossman wants to talk to you but he's on another line."

I rested my forehead on the cold steering wheel. I hated being put on hold.

Finally, Tony came on. "Something came up and I've gotta go to Denver."

"When?"

"Now."

Great. "Where are you?"

"Outside of Lusk and we're about to lose cell service so I thought I'd call you."

"Gee. Thanks."

Pause. "You okay?"

No. "Just tired. How long will you be gone?"

"A couple of days."

Immediately the pissy/whiny/clingy part of me pouted and demanded attention. What was I supposed to do when he was off at another Hombres secret meeting? Learn to knit? Get a fucking cat to talk to? Join a Bunko club?

Jesus. What was wrong with me? In the past I hadn't needed a man to entertain me or to make me happy. I oughta kick my own ass for being depressed. At least I wasn't IDing a loved one's body on a metal slab at the morgue tonight.

"Blondie?"

Buck up, tough up, suck it up, my inner bitch commanded, while my softer side lobbied to make kissy noises in the phone and coo for my man to be careful and come home to me safely.

Talk about unhinged.

"You still there?"

"Yeah. I'll see you when you get back." I closed the phone.

In the safety of my empty cab, I snapped, "I hate it that you're gone again, all right? And I'm pissed off that I need you, you stupid bastard. I'm even more pissed off that I can't seem to tell you I need you. Why in the hell don't you know how goddamn bad I miss you when you know every other thing about me?"

There. I felt better already.

I drove within three blocks of Kim's place, deciding to pop in and say howdy. See if she needed anything, or had a craving for Chinese food. Sounded heavenly to shovel in egg rolls and laugh at stupid baby names from her pregnancy books. Between my job, her job, her engagement to Murray, the baby's father, and my relationship with Martinez, we were woefully short on girls' time. I missed that. A little levity in my life after the last few days would perk me up, if only for an hour or two.

Kim's car was in the driveway. I rang the bell and studied the entwined wire heart festooned with ribbons she'd tacked on her door in honor of Valentine's Day a few weeks back. Hallmark had brainwashed the poor sap. She decorated for every holiday. Colored M&Ms were the height of holiday spirit in my house.

Damn. What was taking her so long? Even if I'd woken her up she should've waddled to the door by now. I rang the bell again and beat on the window for good measure.

Thump thump sounded from inside, followed by the locks disengaging. The door swung open and I smiled at Murray.

Whoa. Murray looked a little flushed. His glasses were on crooked, and dear God, was he wearing a . . . chiffon bathrobe?

Jesus. This was exactly why I didn't show up anywhere unannounced. I did not need another reminder that everyone in the free world was having sex but me.

"Julie. What a . . . surprise." He tried to discreetly tie the belt on his robe tighter.

"Nice to see you, Murray."

"You, too. Ah. Was there something you needed?"

A life, apparently. "No. Just thought I'd swing by

and remind Kim I'm . . . coming in for a haircut next week." Christ, that was a lame excuse for *coitus interruptus*.

Murray blinked. "Oh. Well. I'll be sure to tell her."

"You do that." I turned to leave, then turned back. "Next time, get dressed before you answer the door. Peach is so not your color."

I crawled in my truck and brooded. This was a perfect example of what happened when I ditched my lone wolf persona and started to rely on people; invariably they'd let me down. Usually when I needed them. Kevin. Martinez. Kim. Maybe I oughta call Jimmer and make it a four-bagger of disappointment.

The Circle S wouldn't let me down. I'd find plenty of chocolate solace in the candy aisle. I dumped my purse on the seat, searching for loose change. A white business card tumbled to the floor mat next to a crumpled cigarette package. Probably a dental appointment reminder. How could I look Murray in the eye again and not see him wearing ruffles?

I picked the card up, flipped it over, and read: Luella Spotted Tail. Ooh, looky, it even listed her home address. Which was only six blocks away. Maybe I should cruise by, make sure everything was A-OK with the A-Number-One senior volunteer—who got paid.

Or to confirm one of those fucking boneheads from Prairie Gardens actually deigned to check on her after the morning's fiasco.

Don't do it.

Enough shit had gone wrong today. I didn't need to add to it.

Did I?

Then again, what else could possibly go wrong?

I heard a chorus of mental groans from both Kevin and Martinez as I whipped a U-turn.

CHAPTER 12

I SHIVERED ON THE STOOP TO LUELLA'S HOUSE AND rang the doorbell. Twice. Be my luck if she answered the door in a full-out vinyl dominatrix outfit, complete with a ball gag in one hand and a leather flogger in the other.

The interior door opened. "Yes?"

Surely this stoop-shouldered woman wasn't Luella. "I'm looking for Luella Spotted Tail."

"I'm Luella."

Holy shit. And I thought I looked bad in the morning.

She squinted at me through the glass window of the storm door. "Who are you?"

"I don't know if you remember me. We met a couple of days ago?"

"Oh. Kate, right?"

"Ah. No. My name's not really Kate."

Luella frowned. "I don't have my glasses on, but you sure look like—"

"Maybe I could come in so I can explain who I am?"

"Why should I let you in when you just told me you're not who you said you were?"

Smart. "Do you want to see my ID?"

"No. But I'll warn you. If you come in it'll be at your own risk. I've been sick as a dog with the flu the last three days."

The glass and germ-killing cold separating us didn't seem like such a bad thing. "Thanks for the warning. I'll get right to the point. Did anyone from Prairie Gardens contact you today? Either by phone or in person?"

"I don't know. My phone's been out since the storm hit, and I've felt too lousy to care. You're the first person I've seen in days."

It finally dawned on her how weird it was that I was standing on her steps.

"If you're not Kate, who are you?"

"I'm Julie Collins with Wells/Collins Investigations. I was hired to check out a few concerns at Prairie Gardens for a client."

She considered me, and her back snapped straight. "I should've known."

"What?"

"Your eagerness to wiggle your way into checking

my routine and the facility. About needing care for your elderly aunt and praising Prime Time Friends. Everything you said was a lie, wasn't it?"

My face flushed.

"What about when you chewed out those workers? *Shee.* Was the story about your dead half-Indian brother just a way to get my sympathy so I'd talk to you because I'm Indian? We all stick together, right? Did you think I'd be so grateful that a white girl sees my worth I'd spill my guts about company secrets?"

"No. My brother was Sioux. What I said to those douche bags was how I really feel because they were wrong disrespecting you and you deserve better."

She snorted. "But you running into me at the medical center wasn't a coincidence?"

"No."

"It was a con? A way for you to sneak in, in plain sight? A way for you to get my trust?"

"I can explain—"

"Save it." Luella started to shut the door.

"Please. Listen. I know Vernon Sloane was your client—"

"*Was?*" She went motionless. "Dear God, what happened to him?"

"He's been missing for the last couple of days. We found him this morning."

"Where?"

I hated being the bearer of bad news.

"Tell me."

"Outside the complex on the east side."

Shock caused her to slump against the door frame. "Outside?"

"Yes. Evidently no one noticed he was missing. When someone did, a staff member from Prairie Gardens finally reached his granddaughter, who was out of town. We met with the manager and the police this morning on her behalf."

"Police? Was there a search party?"

"No."

"Then how did you find him?"

Karmic bad luck. "That's not important. What is important is that you help us determine how this happened."

"I have nothing else to say."

Luella slammed the door in my face. And locked it. I'll admit I was a bit stunned by her rude behavior.

Why? You tricked her. You expect her to confide in you now? To trust you?

As I returned to my truck, I questioned for about the millionth time what the hell I was doing. Scarcely six hours ago I'd been snuggled up in my bed, hopeful about a new day.

The lesson in this? Optimism doesn't pay. Ever.

Halfway home my cell phone rang. Annoying fucking

thing. Caller ID read: *Brittney*.

I exhaled another lungful of Marlboro goodness. "This better be about the gift you brought me back from Denver."

"Hey, sis! I did bring you a souvenir."

"It better not be a butt-ugly Broncos jersey."

She giggled. "It's not. Much cooler, because it's useful and you're gonna love it. So when can you come out here and pick it up?"

Never.

Brittney hadn't noticed my hesitation. She blithely continued on. Her constant exuberance grated on my nerves. And I didn't analyze why it did, which was unusual for me.

"—Mom said I could."

"Said you could what?"

"You weren't listening." She sighed dramatically. "Mom said I could surprise Dad and load up some hay from haystacks out by the road. By myself."

"With what?"

"With the tractor."

"Which tractor? The garden tractor?"

"No. The big one. The old one."

"You think you're old enough to run the tractor by yourself?"

"DJ did it when *he* was eleven."

"Then why isn't he doing it today?"

"He's at a rodeo club meeting."

"Why isn't Dad doing it?"

"His hand got infected because he was out doin' chores when he shouldna been."

Stubborn fool. "Don't you guys have a hired man to do shit jobs like that? Isn't he back by now?"

Brittney got quiet. Real quiet.

"Britt? What's wrong?"

"Nuthin'."

"Come on, kiddo, I know something's up when the chatterbox stops running."

"Are you changing the subject because you don't want to see me?"

Guilt, go away.

Stony silence.

The kid wasn't a teenager yet and she already had sullen silences down to an art. "What?"

"Why are you always like this?"

"Like what?" Half the time the kid was a serious brat, alternating blame and guilt. Part of me knew all kids had a thoughtless, selfish streak, but she attempted to disguise hers with saccharine words that burned like vinegar in the aftermath.

"Like, I thought *you* of all people would be happy I'm getting to do something only the guys get to do, driving the tractor."

The feminist in me cheered; the pragmatist remained skeptical. "I am. But why does it have to be today? Why can't you wreak havoc with the tractor when it's warm and the fields aren't full of snow?"

"Because I want to help out." Her voice turned

snotty and snappish. "Not that *you* would understand the hard work and what it's like to help out around here on the ranch. I heard Mom and Dad talking last night about the hay that needs to be hauled. With no hired man around, and Mom doin' everything else, they're shorthanded and I want to pitch in."

Brittney was nice, but not I-wanna-do-extra-chores nice. There was something else to it. *Bingo*. "You want to pitch in before DJ comes home, takes over, and gets all the credit."

"Exactly!"

Sneaky. I sort of admired her. I caught, "—but it's not as hard as DJ said."

I ground out my cigarette. "Speaking of butts, where's Dad?"

She snickered. "Mom took him in to the clinic in Sturgis to get his hand checked out. He had to pull another calf last night and now it's really swollen. He can barely use it."

I put the pieces together and found everyone missing except one. "Are you home alone?"

No reply.

"Tell me you weren't gonna get on that tractor when no one is home."

"It's not a big deal. I've driven the tractor with Dad lots of times and that haystack isn't very far away. It's not like you know anything about driving a tractor anyway."

"Jesus Christ, Brittney! You know better than

that. You'd better not be—"

Click.

The little shit hung up on me.

"Goddammit!" I threw the phone in the seat and sped up. I was gonna wring her scrawny neck if she didn't kill herself first.

The driveway to the house was cleared. I raced up the steps. Didn't bother to knock before I stormed inside. "Brittney? You'd better be in here."

No sound but the drone of the humidifier.

Back outside I heard machinery running out behind the barn.

I threw my truck in gear, then had to get out again to open the gate. Once I'd driven through and closed the gate, I heard the unsteady growl of machinery off in the distance. As I passed the far corner of the barn, I noticed a pile of hay strewn about. Had she been at it a while, way before she'd called me?

I fumed.

Even with my truck in four-wheel drive the path was treacherous. I caught sight of John Deere green against the backdrop of the pearly gray sky and white ground. In the corner of the field, close to the intersecting gravel roads, two fences made a "V" and a blue plastic tarp covered part of the misshapen haystack. Looked like a loaf of golden bread with a huge bite chomped out of the center.

I'd made a mistake driving out here, but with her head start and my smoker's lungs I'd never catch her if I hoofed it. I couldn't abandon my pickup in the middle of the pathway and chance Brittney nailing it with the tractor on the return trip. No place to turn around. No choice but to keep going.

I gunned it. Watching the tractor's back end skid out, not paying attention to my driving, I plowed into a thick ridge of snow. My seat belt jerked me back. The truck came to a complete stop. I dropped the drive shaft into the lowest gear. Hit the gas. The engine whined and mixed with the sound of rubber spinning on ice. High-centered.

"Fuck." No reason to sit and spin. I grabbed my phone, scrambled out, and slogged through the snow-drifts until I stood in front of my truck. Brittney had to have seen me. Avoiding me was making it worse for her.

She kept zipping along. In fact, she was going fast. Way too fast. Way, way too fast for the treacherous conditions. Out of control fast.

Her arms flailed inside the cab.

Oh shit. Oh no. Oh fuck no.

I ran.

The frigid air seemed to sear the airway to my lungs shut. I couldn't breathe. As my legs pumped, my heart threatened to explode from the sudden exertion. I slipped and slid on the ice but kept going. Somehow, some way, I had to stop that fucking machine.

The bucket on the front end bounced. Pieces of hay flew off the spiked tines like countrified confetti.

And Brittney was still headed straight for disaster.

Hitting that stack wouldn't be like jumping in a fluffy pile of fresh straw; it'd be like slamming into a brick wall.

I didn't want to watch; I couldn't look away. I felt useless and scared shitless that another tragedy was unfolding right before my eyes and I couldn't do a fucking thing to stop it.

Something must've gotten stuck or broke. I thought of Dad and his piss-poor equipment inspection. Had he neglected to tell his family of the problems with machinery? Did she even know where the emergency brake was? Why didn't she turn off the ignition? There were a million things she could've done. She did none of them.

How many times had she experienced pure life-or-death panic in her eleven years? None, probably, which was why she didn't know what to do but panic and freeze. Yet, she knew not to jump out of the cab and chance getting run over by those enormous back tires.

I'd never catch her, but if she'd just slow down her momentum . . .

I yelled, "Drop the bucket."

Come on, come on, come on, think, Britt.

I screamed, "Drop the bucket. Drop the bucket. Drop the bucket!" each time progressively louder, as if she could hear me.

Maybe she did. *Screech clank* echoed and the bucket slammed to the earth.

Instead of relief, I stared in horror as the wheels on the left side lifted from the uneven ground and the tractor listed to the right. This was an older model, not one of those new high-tech self-leveling types.

Immediately Brittney jerked the steering wheel to the left to correct the imbalance, except she overcorrected. Even as the tractor slowed, it clipped the corner of the haystack. Hay toppled over. The bucket's steel blade dug into the snow and dirt with a drawn-out *screech*. After demolishing the corner fence posts, the tractor came to a stop on an incline above the deep ditch.

The engine sputtered and died. I'd heard that bleak sound before and it hadn't ended well.

I half-slid/half-ran down the embankment. "Brittney!"

No answer.

"Hang on. I'm almost there."

The cab door was wide open. I looked around frantically, seeing nothing but mounds of snow. I'd taken a step back when a glimpse of dark blue entered my peripheral vision. I spun toward it.

My stomach plummeted.

Legs stuck up out of the snow twenty feet ahead of me.

No, no, please, no.

With each plodding footstep my vision blurred from intense concentration in such stark surroundings.

Upon reaching the half-hidden form I clenched my hands into fists, realizing my hands burned because I wasn't wearing gloves.

I would've frozen in shock at the sight in front of me, if I hadn't already been so goddamn cold.

I'd found a body.

But it wasn't Brittney's.

CHAPTER 13

If this wasn't Brittney, where was she?

I backtracked until I reached the open tractor door. "Brittney? You all right?"

No response.

Crap. I inched closer and stood on tiptoe to peer inside.

Brittney was buckled in the seat, motionless as a rag doll. She was unconscious; her chin nearly touched her chest and her arms dangled at her sides like sandbags.

The bucket blade wasn't firmly imbedded in the ground. I didn't know how smart it'd be to crawl into the cab to check her injuries. I doubted my weight would tip the heavy tractor forward, but I couldn't justify the risk. I'd leave her be. For now.

But we needed help. Fast. With temps only near ten degrees, before long hypothermia would be a real danger.

Already my hands weren't working well. I squeezed a tight fist and opened them wide like a starfish several times to get the blood flowing. When I felt tingles, I slid my hand into my pocket for my cell phone. I curled my fingers around it as I carefully pulled it out. If I dropped it in this deep snow, chances were good it'd be lost until the spring thaw.

I clutched the phone in my left palm and poked the buttons with my stiff right index finger. Using both hands, I held the cold metal to my ear.

"Bear Butte County Sheriff's Office."

"Missy? This is Julie Collins. I'm at my dad's ranch, and there's been an accident." I described the situation.

"Where exactly are you on the ranch?"

"Ah. I'm at the intersection where County Road 12 meets Dry Creek Road. That's the easiest access point."

"I've dispatched an ambulance and Search and Rescue. Sit tight, okay, hon?"

"Okay. There is one other thing. The tractor uncovered another body. A frozen one."

"Could you please repeat that?"

I did with as much detail as I knew, which wasn't a lot.

Missy said, "I'll let the sheriff know. Keep your phone handy. I'm sure he'll wanna see this."

Time passed in a blur of nothingness. I was cold, I was scared, and I could do nothing about either. I talked to Brittney until my voice became hoarse. Screaming hadn't done my vocal cords any favors.

I needed to move, to keep the blood flowing. My gaze locked on the body downhill. The second body I'd found today. And sad to say, but finding two bodies in one day wasn't even a record for me. I started toward the legs, out of more than morbid curiosity. It'd save the sheriff time if I identified the person beforehand. Although why I was still looking for ways to make the sheriff's job easier was beyond me.

When I reached the corpse I couldn't see the face, or the upper half of the body. I'd have to move it slightly.

Don't do it.

I placed my palm on the denim-covered shin and pushed hard. The cardboard rigid body toppled over, leaving the man prone.

"Shit, oh Jesus, that's fucking nasty." I jumped back from the gruesome sight. The man's head wobbled as if it was only attached to the body by the spinal cord. Dark splotches covered his face and I couldn't tell if it was blood or mud.

The tractor had ripped chunks out of flesh, in a couple of places, like a cleaver slicing away frozen meat. Were the holes in the cloth puncture wounds from the tractor tines? Or was the body too hard to pierce?

He wore the typical rancher wear: a flannel shirt and jeans. No coat. Yellow cotton liners layered under stained leather work gloves. The boots were a hybrid between hiking and old-fashioned rubber galoshes.

I had not a clue who this dead man was. But he was seriously fucked up.

The sound of approaching vehicles made me glance up and scramble back to the tractor. Not an ambulance, or patrol cars, or the volunteer fire department's extraction van, but two pickups. The men parked alongside the road climbed out. My dad's buddies, Don Anderson and Dale Pendergrast. Evidently they'd been listening to the police scanner again.

Dale rummaged in his truck bed while Don shouted, "Julie? You all right?"

"Yeah."

"Emergency folks oughta be here soon."

I didn't answer.

They started toward me, each holding a pair of heavy-duty bolt cutters. In no time flat they had the four remaining sections of the barbed-wire fence cut and rolled out of the way for easier access for the emergency crews.

Huffing and puffing uphill, they finally reached me.

The concern on their usually stoic faces made me jabber. "Brittney's still in the tractor. I don't know how bad she's hurt and I didn't want to chance moving her—"

"It's okay. You did fine. They'll get her out of there an' fixed up in no time."

Dale's gaze dropped to my bare hands. "Girl,

where are your gloves?"

"I-I'm not sure."

"Losin' your gloves is a damn good way to lose your fingers. Here." He tugged off his gloves and passed them to me, then grunted and lumbered back to his truck.

I almost wept when the warmth from the fleece-lined leather seeped into my hands.

"What else can we do?" Don asked.

"After they get her out of there . . ." I swallowed. My mouth was bone-dry from yelling and raw from the cold wind. "While I was chasing after her, I high-centered my truck. I'll probably need a winch to get unstuck."

"No worries. You got chains?"

"Yeah. I carry a little of everything in my truck bed."

"Smart."

Sirens wailed ever closer.

"Is your daddy on his way?"

I stared at him like an idiot. "They don't know. Brittney was home alone when she called me. When I found out she was climbing on that tractor by herself, I sped out here. Then this happened . . . and I didn't think."

"S'okay. We'll let 'em know. I got the number right here." Don dug his phone out of the front pocket of his bib overalls.

"Will you tell him it's not my fault? That I'd never

do anything to hurt her . . ." My throat closed and I couldn't finish.

Don's beady eyes narrowed on mine. "If it weren't for you, who knows what woulda happened to that little gal. If your daddy cain't see you saved her, then he's a bigger fool than I thought."

The ambulance screamed up, followed by patrol cars and the Search and Rescue van. I said nothing at all as I stumbled to meet them.

Didn't take long for the experienced crews to get Brittney out of the tractor. Knocked cold from the impact, she sported a goose egg smack-dab in the middle of her forehead.

Protocol demanded a trip to the hospital for routine tests. Since she was a minor and I wasn't her legal guardian, and she didn't require acute care at this point, the consensus was to wait until her parents arrived.

Brittney regained consciousness just as Trish and my dad pulled up. I hid off to the side, watching, scared, waiting, a part of it yet not.

The crowd surrounding the ambulance parted. Trish crawled into the back of the vehicle and my father stood there, lost. Displaced. Haggard.

Dad saw me. When he rushed up the embankment

I braced myself for his verbal onslaught. A punch in the stomach wouldn't have shocked me.

But his full body hug did.

He whispered, "Thank you." Then he released me quickly, spoke to Don, and climbed into his truck to follow the red and blue lights back into town.

I might've stood in the ditch forever in utter shock if Sheriff Richards hadn't pulled me aside.

"Collins?"

I blinked, expecting the surreal scene would vanish and I'd wake up. Nope. The sheriff loomed over me in his woolly coat like a big brown bear.

"You need medical attention?"

"No. Why?"

"You look a little dazed."

"I am. Cold, too. You wouldn't believe the day I've had and it's not even four o'clock."

He frowned. "Nothing surprises me when it comes to you, Collins. You wanna give me a rundown?"

I did. Starting with finding Vernon Sloane. His eyes stayed flat and emotionless until I came to the part about Brittney. My stupid voice hitched and he put his hand on my arm.

"She's lucky. Doan know what gets into people—not just kids. Third time in as many months something like this has happened. Two of those didn't turn out so good."

"I've sort of been out of it. What's gone on?"

"Remember Darvin Pearson? Ornery old rancher,

calls the office and complains 'bout Atberry's bulls getting out all the time? Well, he tipped over his tractor, fell into Old Woman Creek, and froze to death in his pasture walking back home."

"No."

"Yeah. Chris Greywolf used his ATV to pull his buddies on inner tubes. Lost control and ran himself and his friends into the side of a metal barn. Broken legs and arms weren't the worst of it. Cody Capshaw will be using a colostomy bag for the rest of his life. He's seventeen. So it coulda been worse."

"Sheriff?" Deputy Peach Fuzz yelled and motioned him over.

Richards sighed and ambled away.

I didn't know how long I'd have to stick around— at least until someone jerked my truck out of a snowbank. I needed a cigarette, but the thought of dragging ass up the embankment made me consider giving up smoking.

People wandered. More neighbors showed up, not strictly for the voyeuristic factor. This ranching community pulled together, for the most part.

Don and Dale slouched against the tailgate, chewing the fat, watching the activity, so I wandered in that direction.

"Feelin' better now?" Don asked.

"A little." I looked longingly at Dale's cigarette. "You have an extra one of those?" He took out a pack of generics, shook one out for me, and offered me the lighter. "Thanks." I inhaled deeply. God. Ambrosia.

"So, you worked for the sheriff, Julie. How long you think it'll take 'em to wrap this up today?"

"I was just wondering the same thing." Be impossible for Sheriff Richards to contain the crime scene. It'd been completely trampled, say nothing of how he'd gather evidence beneath three feet of snow.

"Well, his ma is damn near dead, from what I understand. This'll probably kill her, what with all the other stuff that's gone on."

My cigarette stopped short of my mouth. "They've already identified him?"

"Yeah." Dale squinted at me. "Din't no one tell you who got plowed up?"

I shook my head.

"Figures. Damn bureaucrats doan wanna tell nobody nuthin'."

Both Don and Dale made a harrumph of agreement.

"'Course, it doan look none too good, him bein' found on your daddy's place and all," Dale said.

"Yeah, 'specially not after him 'n' Doug got to arguin' at Chaska's Feed Store."

"Then again, some folks 'round here ain't gonna be sobbin' Melvin's dead."

"True enough." Don spit a wad of tobacco in the snow and reached for his can of Copenhagen for a fresh dip. "How long you figure he's been missin'? I sure ain't heard nuthin' about it."

"Me neither. Cain't recall the last time I seen him."

"With the way that blade hit him, and his head danglin' off his body like a worm on a hook, it's gonna be damn hard to tell how he died, doncha think?"

"Mebbe. Ain't all them people CSI specialists now? Looks to me like his head was nearly sliced clean off his body."

That made me think of how quickly my dad separated that calf's head from the spinal cord and I shivered. "What the hell are you guys talking about? Who is it? I'm lost."

Don and Dale exchanged a look.

"I forgot you an' Doug ain't on the best terms. You probably doan know. Guy's name is Melvin Canter."

Why did that name sound familiar?

Don angled his head at the body still visible in the snow. "That man was your daddy's hired hand."

Great.

Sheriff Richards returned for my statement. Darkness approached. Don and Dale and two other neighbors were able to get me unstuck without resorting to chains and winches. They waved off my thanks with good ol' boy smiles and encouraging pats on the driver's side door.

As I passed the house I called Trish's cell phone.

They were waiting on tests, but it appeared Brittney was fine, despite a mild concussion, whiplash, bruises on her collarbone, and a cracked rib. She'd spend a night in the hospital. I breathed a huge sigh of relief. Lucky little snot.

When Trish began to cry, thanking me profusely, I quickly ended the call. My emotions were too raw to deal with hers.

Not a single light burned inside my house. My haven looked dark and unwelcoming. If I had a choice, I'd go someplace else. But I didn't have a choice.

I fixed a can of Campbell's tomato soup. Couldn't muster up the energy to make a grilled cheese sandwich.

At loose ends, I did something I rarely do: I indulged in a long, hot bubble bath.

Cocooned in liquid heat, surrounded by the scent of a vanilla candle, the acoustic tunes of Godsmack, and the relaxing properties of tequila, I was able to put everything from the past couple of days out of my mind.

It was sheer bliss.

Naturally, it didn't last.

Right after I'd climbed out of the tub, Jimmer called.

"Jules. Lemme talk to Martinez."

"Hello, Jimmer. Why, I'm just peachy keen,

thanks for asking."

"Shit. Sorry." Pause. "Well? Is he there?"

"No. Why?"

"Do you know where he is?"

I wouldn't share Tony's private number with any-one, not even Jimmer, not to mention maybe Tony wanted his sudden trip to Colorado to stay hush-hush. "He's not answering his cell?"

"Nope. I can't track him down anywhere. Look. Next time he checks up on you, tell him to call me, pronto. It's important."

"Checks up on me? You mean when he checks *in* with me?"

"I meant what I said, little missy. You oughta know you ain't ever as alone as you think when it comes to someone like him. He takes care of what belongs to him, especially if he ain't around to do it in person."

Huh? "But—"

"Have him call me. Oh, and let's you and me go out drinkin' next week. Been a while since I've gotten into a knock-down, drag-out bar fight."

"I don't *always* fight when I'm in a bar."

Jimmer laughed. "Right. Pick a day and I'll clear it with Tony."

"I don't have to get his permission to spend time with my friends."

"Maybe not, but I have to ask him for permission to hang out with you."

"You're joking, right?"

"Wish I was. Later." He hung up.

Surely Jimmer was mistaken. Martinez wouldn't do that to me . . . would he?

I selected TM on my cell phone contact list. Immediately kicked me over to his voice mail. "Call Jimmer. He says it's urgent."

No reason to leave a personal message. What would I say? "Guess how many dead bodies I found today? Could you come home, crawl in bed with me, and chase away the nightmares?"

Right. I'd chase away my own damn nightmares, in the form of tequila chasers.

An hour later, I'd curled up on the couch, fuzzy pajamas on, a tumbler of Mexico's finest in one hand, a cigarette in the other. Things improved slightly at the twilight of the day from hell.

Four solid raps sounded on my door. *At 9:00 at night?* I flipped on the outside light and checked the peephole.

One of Martinez's backup bodyguards, a former Cornhuskers linebacker named—no kidding— Korny, stood on my porch. I undid the locks and opened the door. "What's going on, Korny?"

"Just a routine check Mr. Martinez asked me to do tonight."

"Why?"

Korny appeared confused. "Because he told me to."

Talk about a canned response. "Is there something going on that requires me to have drive-by protection?"

"No idea." He stared at me steadily. "Is everything all right? Anything you need?"

Yeah, to kick a certain man's proprietary ass.

Outwardly, I smiled with false sweetness; inwardly, hello uber-bitch. "Actually . . . I *have* been craving ice cream. Ben & Jerry's Chunky Monkey would be perfect. And I'm pretty sure the C-store up the road carries it. You don't mind picking me up a pint, do you? Oh, and a pack of Marlboro reds."

Korny's blocky face made a frowny-caveman-eyebrow squint.

I tried like hell not to smirk.

Finally he said, "Sure, Ms. Collins."

He headed down the steps to a Blazer with—surprise!—another Hombres spy huddled inside.

I yelled out, "Korny. I was kidding. I'm not sending you out for ice cream; I'm sending you back to the clubhouse."

His mouth twitched.

"But if I see another one of El Presidente's goons here checking up on me? You tell him I'm gonna use that Blazer or his Cadillac or any other car he sends for target practice."

Korny hesitated, assuming I'd repeat *just kidding*. This time I wasn't.

"Understood. I'll pass along the message. Good night."

I slammed the door. So much for a relaxing night

at home.

No big shocker when my cell phone rang within five minutes. He said, "You hate Chunky Monkey. And threatening to shoot up one of my cars? Not nice, blondie."

"Not a bluff. Remember what I did to Little Joe Carlucci's Corvette?"

"Vividly."

"That one will look like a door nick compared to what I'll do to the next spy car I see parked within twenty feet of my house. I am not a fucking pet poodle, and I won't be treated like I'm under house arrest in my own goddamn house when *you're* the one who's gone."

Silence.

"You don't get to check up on me, or dictate to me, or decide who I can or can't spend time with. No one needs *your* permission to be *my* friend, Martinez. Not Kevin. Not Jimmer. Not Kim. So take your body-guards and shove them up your ass."

A beat passed. "You done?"

"I don't know." I lit a cigarette and swigged tequila straight from the bottle.

"Can I say something?"

"This oughta be stunning."

"I miss you, too."

I choked on the booze, the smoke, and the imme-diate warm feeling in my chest. "That's *so* not fair."

"Life rarely is."

No kidding. Vernon Sloane's frozen face slid front

and center, followed by the board-stiff and heavily gouged body of my dad's hired hand. I squeezed my eyes shut to erase the images. No such luck.

"When were you going to tell me?"

"Tell you what?" *That I miss you like a limb?*

"About all the nasty shit that happened to you today."

My stomach clenched. "You know?"

"Some of it, not all. I figured I'd hear the rest from you tonight, and I haven't." He sighed. "Aren't we beyond this?"

"I'm trying."

"Try harder."

"I didn't tell you because you have enough shit of your own to deal with. I don't want to be the girlfriend who calls you up and unloads depressing stuff. Besides, you don't tell me anything about what's going on with the Hombres, so it's not like *you're* the only one who's suffering from nondisclosure."

"Fine. Now that you've gnawed my ass, start talking."

I didn't want to. I drank and remained quiet.

"Julie? Come on. I won't let it go."

I sighed. "Today turned into the never-ending-what-else-can-happen kind of day. When I came home I just wanted to forget for a while, but instead I get all these reminders that you're not here to talk to or to help me forget."

"Wish I was there, blondie."

"Me, too. Have you been gone a week?"

"Nope, not even a full day. I saw you this morning, remember? Been a week since we did more in bed than sleep."

"Maybe that's why we've been snarling at each other."

"Gee? Ya think?"

"You mocking me, smart-ass?"

"Yep. Tell me what went on today. Everything."

"How much time you got, bossman?"

"Much as you need. I'll make time for you. Always."

His sweetness was my undoing. I closed my eyes and let it pour out. Martinez was quiet after I finished the whole sordid mess I'd managed to get myself into again. "What?"

"And you're surprised I sent my guys to check on you tonight? Goddammit, Julie, they should move in with you."

"Not even funny."

I heard another male voice in the background. Our time was up. Strange to think this was the longest phone conversation we'd ever had.

"Sorry. I've gotta go." He mumbled something I didn't understand and hung up.

One of these days I really had to learn Spanish. I could always utilize new curse words.

I set the security system and shut off the lights. I peeked out the front window. No sign of a night watchman.

Instead of a warm body, the bottle of Don Julio accompanied me to bed. But it did the trick; it knocked me out cold and kept the nightmares away.

CHAPTER 14

EVIDENTLY MY BODY NEEDED TIME TO HEAL. I STAYED home from work the next day and managed an entire night of uninterrupted sleep.

Early in the morning the thermometer on my porch read a chilly nine degrees. I scraped my windshield and drove to the office.

Didn't look like Kevin made it in yesterday either. I checked the messages, shuffled through the mail, doing all the boring shit office drones do.

I flipped on the computer and scanned the headlines for the local online editions. Vernon Sloane's tragic death headlined the Rapid City paper. The article didn't shed new light on the situation. Didn't list me by name as the person who'd discovered the body. Good. I'd had enough press in recent months.

The article went on to say the matter remained

under investigation by the Rapid City Police Department. No family members could be reached for comment. The manager of Prairie Gardens also declined an interview for the story. Then it listed a link to Vernon Sloane's obituary. I followed it.

His funeral was tomorrow? Amery told us there weren't other relatives, but two days from aboveground to belowground seemed pretty damn fast.

No mention in any of the papers about the body discovered in Bear Butte County. I surfed the Net, checking my usual sites because I don't keep a computer at home. Most people found that odd and they'd bestow that pitying look upon me, as if I'm too proud to admit I'm computer illiterate. I'm not. I just don't see the appeal of e-mail. Ditto for cyber friends. Real friends were hard enough to keep up with.

I smoked. Drank a pot of coffee. Balanced my checkbook. By 2:00 I'd decided to call it a day. My cell phone rang in the stairwell. Trish. I couldn't stomach any more blubbering thanks for saving Brittney's life.

Ignore it.

She'd probably keep calling, so I reluctantly said, "Hello?"

"Julie? Thank God I got a hold of you. Doug is at the sheriff's office. I-I don't know what to do."

"Slow down. Take a deep breath and tell me what's happened. Why is he at the sheriff's office?"

Trish exhaled loudly. "Sheriff Richards called and asked Doug to come in for questioning about Melvin

189

Canter. And Doug just went! Is that even legal? Is he supposed to have a lawyer present? I don't know how any of this works."

I slumped against the cement wall. "Probably routine questioning. The dead guy did work for him and he was found on your land. Did they arrest him?"

"No!"

"Okay. Then he doesn't need a lawyer"—yet—"but he also does not have to answer all the questions the sheriff is gonna ask him."

"So if he says something they don't like, will they arrest him?"

"Not without evidence. Not without just cause. Not unless he confesses. Or says something stupid like he hated the son of a bitch and he deserved to die."

Trish clammed up.

"Shit. Please tell me I'm off base."

"I-I don't know. There's lots I don't know, Julie. Doug never told me he'd fired Melvin."

Maybe he didn't. Maybe he just killed him.

Not helping this situation.

"Melvin didn't show up for work last week. Doug shrugged it off. Then Don Anderson informed me Doug and Melvin were in a fistfight at the feed store. And everyone in the county knew about it except me? I don't know what to believe, and Doug won't talk to me. He always talks to me. It's like he's shut me out."

"When did Dad leave?"

"About ten minutes ago. I-I just . . ."

190

"Tell you what. I was on my way home. I'll swing by the sheriff's office first and see what's going on."

"Thank you. I didn't know if you would . . . I mean, I prayed for it, even when things have always been strained between you and Doug—"

"Trish, my other line is beeping. Sit tight." I shut the phone. Big fat lie; I didn't have another call coming in. I just couldn't listen to her doubts about my father when I had plenty of my own.

I'd returned to my alma mater, aka the Bear Butte County Sheriff's Department, a couple of times in the eleven months since I'd quit working as a secretary.

A new woman manned the front desk. Midforties, thick glasses, thick around the middle. No smile distorted the lines of her female mustache. "May I help you?"

Since she didn't call me by name, ergo, she didn't know me, I could lie my ass off about who I was. "Yes. I'm Doug Collins's counsel. Which room is he in?"

"I wasn't aware he'd asked for counsel to be present."

"*I'm* aware of it and that's all that matters. Which room?"

She debated and reached for the phone, but ultimately dropped her hand. "Room B. Before you get to stairs leading down to booking."

"Thanks." I hustled down the hallway, another savvy businesswoman keeping to a tight schedule.

I rapped twice and opened the door.

Three people sat at the conference table. Sheriff Richards, my father, and a buxom woman I didn't know. They all looked at me with surprise.

"Collins, how did you get back here?"

"Told the TAR I was Doug Collins's counsel, which I am. Excuse us a minute." I leaned down to speak in Dad's ear. "I don't know what you've said. If you haven't been arrested, you don't have to stay. Had enough?"

Doug Collins didn't snap or glare at me or tell me to mind my own beeswax. He nodded. His uneasiness with the situation was apparent, if only to me.

I straightened up. "Sheriff Richards, are you finished with your preliminary questions? If not, we'll need to confer with our attorney before you continue."

The sheriff excelled at the vapid stare. "I have enough for now. Thank you for your cooperation, Mr. Collins. You're free to go. I'll be in touch."

Dad stood off to the side of the door, black hat in hand, waiting for me. I lowered my voice, keeping my back to the conference table. "Go home. I'll see you later."

He clapped his hat on his head and left.

Richards told the young woman to leave and she bounced out. He gestured for me to sit.

"Before you start in on me, Sheriff, I'll remind you I know procedure."

"Well, so do I. Can't fault me for doing my job, Collins."

"No. But I doubt you told him he had no obligation to be here. Especially without a legal rep."

"He shouldn't be reluctant to talk to me if he has nothing to hide."

"That's crap and you know it."

Sheriff Richards set his elbows on the table. His meaty forearms nearly reached the other side. At six feet eight, his size intimidated and he used it to his advantage. "Why are you here?"

I don't know.

"Why do you care what happens to him? After everything he did to you?"

"Let's get one thing straight. He shouldn't have gotten away with beating on me for all those years. The system failed us both. But that has no bearing on this case."

"Oh. The case where *his* hired man was found dead on *his* land? That case? He had a physical confrontation with Melvin Canter in front of witnesses, where threats were made. A week later Melvin Canter winds up dead? On a section owned by Doug Collins?"

"You can't be one hundred percent sure Mr. Canter didn't get lost out in the snowstorm and tried to take shelter in the haystack and died from exposure. He wasn't even wearing a coat."

Richards said nothing.

"Where'd they take the body?"

"To the VA in Sturgis. They told me it might be a while before they get to it. DCI from Pierre is coming to assist. But I know what the facts are, Julie."

"What? No proof Canter was killed there, let alone dumped there. That mutilated body could've been outside the fence line when the blade hit it. Meaning in the ditch, which is public domain, which means anyone could've left it there, not necessarily my father."

"You think it's murder?"

Stumbled right into that one. "I don't know. But my understanding is that Doug Collins was *not* the only one in Bear Butte County who had run-ins with Mr. Canter."

"Who else did?"

I shrugged. I didn't know, but I sure as hell would find out. It was almost too pat, pointing the finger at my dad.

"You really don't believe your father had anything to do with this situation?"

"Beyond firing the victim? No."

"Yet you know he's capable of carrying out extreme violence?"

"Yes."

"Didn't you ever suspect that he might've killed Ben?"

The accusation provided a jolt. I'd considered the possibility although I'd never told anyone. "Moot point. He *didn't* kill Ben."

"Off record? Doug Collins is hiding something. If I have a suspect, he's it."

"Is that a warning?"

"A fact. If you think he didn't do it, prove it. Not like you ain't got the skills or the time. Or a plan to work on it anyway."

I snorted. I hated that he knew me so well.

His caterpillar eyebrows disappeared beneath the brim of his hat. "I've said all I'm gonna say, Collins. You know your way out."

He'd said more than he should and we both knew it.

The Collins ranch was the last place I wanted to go and the first place I headed.

Trish answered the door. The sour look on my face stopped her attempt to hug me. I didn't ask about Brittney. Still saw red when I remembered the stupid chance she'd taken and remembered the smart-aleck comments she'd made before she hung up on me.

"Where is he?"

"Kitchen." Trish shot a glance over her shoulder and whispered, "And he's been drinking."

"That's just fucking great."

"Yeah, well, good luck. I'll be doing chores." She

snagged her winter wear, slipped on her boots, and vanished.

I inhaled a deep breath and sauntered into the mouth of the beast.

Dad was hunched over a bottle of cheap whiskey and a half-empty tumbler.

Good plan. I doubted I'd get through this conversation without liquid courage myself. I snagged a Strawberry Shortcake juice glass from the dish rack and plopped across from him.

He didn't look up as I filled my glass and topped off his. I gulped a mouthful and shuddered. Stuff tasted like crap. My preference for top shelf booze hadn't come from him.

Holding his glass aloft, he said, "Why're you here?"

"Why do you think?"

Pause. "To gloat."

I let him rethink that asinine comment. "Wrong. But not surprising, since you always think the worst of me."

Another sip kept his denial in check.

"Did you do it?"

"What?"

"You know what. Did you kill your hired man and throw him in the pasture under a haystack?"

He grunted.

I drained the remaining bourbon and poured another glass. "You *are* gonna have to talk to me if you want my help."

His hand shook as he upended his tumbler. "Who says I want it?"

"Would it kill you to admit you might need it?"

Another grunt. Another long pause—where the *thwack thwack* of Trish stacking firewood reverberated against the side of the house and inside my head.

"If the coroner's report comes back with homicide as cause of death, Sheriff Richards will move you to the top of the suspect list on who killed Melvin Canter. He won't go out of his way to prove otherwise."

"And you will, girlie?"

"What's that supposed to mean?"

"I see the hatred in your eyes every time you look at me. I have for years. I'm s'posed to trust that you ain't gonna take—no, *enjoy*—the opportunity to put me behind bars? Even if I done nuthin' wrong? You're here outta spite. To get me to beg for your supposed expertise. Here's a hint. It ain't happenin'."

I stood up so fast I got an immediate head rush.

"You're right on one thing. I don't give a rat's ass if you spend the rest of your life in jail. Do whatever the hell you want to. You will anyway."

Trish paused in the entryway, horrified when I pushed past her.

Music blaring, head pounding, I sucked down three cigarettes on the way home. Cursing him. Cursing myself. Wondering why I'd bothered. Why I even fucking cared.

At home after I showered, I knew I couldn't spend another night alone in my house. I called Jimmer to see if he was game to move up our drinking date. No answer. Story of my life.

As I debated whether or not to call Kevin, my cell rang; he was on the line. "Divine karma, my friend. Wanna go to Dusty's and shoot pool? Hang out with me and Don Julio tonight? Been a while."

"That it has."

"Cool. Where are you?"

"Driving aimlessly."

Kevin never did anything without purpose. "Get your ass out here. On the way to Dusty's you can confess how much you've missed my oh-so-vindictive sense of humor."

He snorted. "I don't buy the Mary-fucking-sunshine act, babe. What's happened the last couple days when I've been a total selfish prick?"

I figured he'd pick up on my mood, but not that fast. "You wanna hear it in person?"

"No. Tell me now. It'll give me an indication on how much you're drinking tonight."

"Tons." By the time I finished relaying everything in clinical detail, he was parked in the driveway.

Without any prompt from me, Kevin climbed out of his Jeep and wrapped me in a hug. I missed his casual affection. Wasn't the same kind of affection Martinez gave me, but I realized I needed it just as badly.

"Thanks."

"You're welcome. You don't have to deal with this psycho family on your own, tough girl. Although, I don't know why you insist on . . ."

"What?"

"Letting them destroy you a piece at a time."

First time he'd commented on my relationship with the Collins family. "Next time Trish or Brittney calls me about helping Dad I'll hit call forward."

"Deal."

"Let's go."

In my truck Kevin said, "Uh oh. I know that look, Jules, and it's never good."

I pushed in the cigarette lighter, holding the unlit smoke between my gloved fingers as I steered with my left hand. "What look?"

"The I'm-looking-to-kick-the-shit-out-of-someone look."

"Wrong. I left my shit kickers at home. Despite what you and Jimmer think, I am not always looking for a fight."

"Doesn't matter. They seem to find you."

"Lucky thing I didn't bring my gun or my bow, huh?"

"Shit."

I smiled and stomped on the gas pedal.

CHAPTER 15

ALTHOUGH I'D SPENT PLENTY OF TIME IN BARS recently, I hadn't set foot in Dusty's in months. Nothing had changed. Same cavelike atmosphere. Same barflies holding court. Same smells of beer, tobacco, dirt, and sweat.

We wound through the happy hour crowd until we reached the line of booths in the back room by the pool tables. *Save a Horse (Ride a Cowboy)* blasted from the speakers.

Hadn't occurred to me to look for my psycho ex-boyfriend until we'd settled in. Kevin said, "Didn't see that asshole Ray hanging around anywhere, did you?"

"No. However, the night is still young."

"Jesus. You scare me sometimes, you know that?"

"That's what Martinez says right before he mumbles that I need a damn bodyguard."

"He would know all about that."

Not going there.

Carla, the uber-efficient cocktail waitress, breezed to our table. "Haven't seen you guys in here for ages."

"We'd better make up for lost time, huh? Bring us four shots of Don Julio and four Coors."

"You betcha. I'll start a tab."

Kevin leaned across the table. "Someone else joining us?"

"Nah. Just you and me, babycakes." I lit up.

His intent eyes locked to mine. Here was another chance to bare my soul about all the crap clogging up my life. I missed talking to Kevin about issues not involving the business, but tonight was about fun because we both needed it. "There's an open pool table. Wanna shoot a game?"

Kevin's gaze didn't waver; he knew my hedging techniques better than anyone. "Only if we're playing for money."

"I'm screwed."

He flashed his Tom Cruise pool shark smile. "And I didn't even bring my cue."

"Correction. I'm seriously screwed."

I racked. Kevin broke. He scratched on his fourth ball. I managed to knock in three balls before he ran the table. I also managed to knock back both shots of my tequila, one of his, and two of the Coors before league play started.

I slapped a twenty in his hand and dropped ten

bucks in the jukebox.

Carla lined up two more shots on my side of the booth. I licked the area between my thumb and first knuckle and poured salt on it. "Down the hatch." The liquid slid down my throat like candy.

Kevin lifted his brows.

I removed the lime wedge from my teeth. "What?"

"Been a while?"

"Yep. Carla was kind enough to bring them. Be a pity to let them go to waste."

"Altruistic of you."

"I thought so." Sara Evans sang *Suds in the Bucket* and my foot tapped. Catchy tune.

Kevin finished his second Coors and moved the empty can to the edge of the table. "Gotta see a man about a horse."

Sipping beer in my favorite bar with my best friend, good tunes on the jukebox, family shit forgotten. For the briefest moment, all was right with the world.

Naturally, my cell phone rang and destroyed my synchronicity with the universe.

I checked the caller ID. Martinez. I answered, "What?"

"Hello to you, too, blondie."

"Something you need?"

"Just a sec." He held his hand over the mouthpiece while he spoke to someone.

I hated not having his undivided attention even

on the phone.

He came back on the line. "Where are you?"

"Out."

Stunned silence.

Guess I had his full attention now.

I smoked, amused by the cowgirl in sparkly Western regalia cozying up to a cowboy with a monstrous belt buckle. Had he won it eating dirt? Or was the buckle a prop to pick up hotsy-totsy bunnies?

The pause continued.

My palms got itchy. "You need something?" I asked with forced sweetness.

A crash echoed in my ear. "Hang on."

I didn't. I hung up. Drank my last shot and signaled Carla for another round.

The booze hit me like a Wyoming coal train. *Woo-woo.* All aboard the 7:15 Julie express to Shit-faced-ville.

My phone rang. Martinez again. Big fucking surprise.

"What?"

"You gonna tell me where you are or not?"

Not. Surly girl pushed past the cobwebs in my head and demanded, "Why? Did we have plans or something?" I exhaled. "Oh, that's right, *no*, we don't, because you're in Colorado. Again."

Dead air. "You done?"

"Not even close, *bud*."

"You're drunk."

"Not yet."

Victorious shouts sounded from by the dart-boards.

"What the fuck happened today?"

"Nothing tequila can't fix. You'd know all about my shit day if you were here, but you're not. So I guess you'll have to read about it in the fucking newspaper like everybody else."

"Where are you?"

"I don't see why it matters where I am, Martinez."

His was an angry pause this time. I knew the difference even three sheets to the wind.

Screw it. "Later." I hung up and shut the damn thing off.

Kevin whistled and slipped back into the booth. "That was harsh. Even for you."

"Yeah, well, it's time he knew I can't always be—how did you phrase it? Mary-fucking-sunshine. And no, I don't want to talk about it."

He snagged a fresh beer and settled in.

I braced myself with a straight shot without the frills.

"Whoa, slow down there, partner," Kevin said. "How many of these did you have while I was gone?"

"Less than ten."

His gaze landed on the empty shot glasses.

"You okay?"

"Fine as frog's hair."

Kevin seemed to be watching me closely. Very closely. I tried to act normal. Sober. Serious.

Except things were getting fuzzy. And blurry.

"Ain't you Martinez's old lady?"

My head swiveled. Ooh, skank alert. Nyla, the meth-head crack whore from the Hombres clubhouse leered at me. Even my beer-goggles didn't improve her ragged appearance; runny nose, vacant red eyes, bruises down her right cheek, scratches on her neck.

"Yeah, I am. Why?"

"He around here?"

"No. Why do you care?"

Her chapped lips twisted. "Unfinished business."

"Wrong. You've got *no* business with him."

"You wish."

"Stay away from him and keep your filthy fucking paws off him."

"Or what?"

"Or I'll rearrange your ugly face."

She sneered. "Think you're so fuckin' tough. Lemme tell you somethin'."

"This oughta be stellar advice from a crank head."

A cheer rose from the dance floor when the band started playing; Nyla's mouth moved but the words were lost in the music and drunken revelry.

"—be getting in touch with you."

"What? I didn't hear you."

I squinted at Kevin because I was seeing two of Nyla, and that was two too many. I yelled, "What'd she say?"

"Hell if I know."

Closing one eye against my double vision, I looked up and Nyla was gone. "Hey, where'd skanky-ho go?"

"I have no idea. She seems out of place here. What did she want?"

"I think she wanted to fight me."

"You wish." He moved my half-empty beer next to the wall. "I think it's time you switched to coffee, babe."

"I think it's time we danced." I grabbed his hand and tugged, lost my balance, and slipped down in the booth, knocking a couple of empty beer cans to the floor. I laughed hysterically. "Come on, partner, I love this song."

"You don't even know what song it is."

"Sure, I do."

"Name it."

I stopped and listened. He was right. I didn't know. "Something about mattress dancing?"

"You're drunk," Kevin said.

"No shit," I slurred.

"Feel like you're gonna barf?"

"Hell, no. Barfing is for lightweights."

He laughed.

Whoa. Room spinning. Head rush. Maybe it would be easier to concentrate if I closed my eyes. And set my forehead on the table.

"Is she okay?" Carla asked somewhere above my head.

"Bring us a couple of Cokes—no ice—and a cup

of coffee."

Sleep beckoned like the perfect lover.

"Jules, you'd never live it down if you passed out in Dusty's."

"True." I lifted my head very slowly.

Kevin's familiar face swam into view. Made me happy and sad. "Sorry I'm such a sucky time."

"You are not a sucky time. For Christsake, don't say 'I love you, man' and get teary eyed."

"Fuck you. I'm not gonna cry."

"Then why are you sniffling?"

Because I love you, man. "'Cause I got a piece of lime up my nose." I fumbled with my cigarettes.

Kevin snatched my lighter. "Let me. Don't want you to start your hair on fire."

"I'm not *that* drunk."

"Right."

Carla dropped off the drinks. I sucked down both Cokes, popped three Excedrin, and suffered through the black sludge known as Dusty's coffee. Even asked for a refill. Twice.

After a bit, don't know how long—hours blur living on tequila time—I felt more in control, but nowhere near totally sober. I needed a distraction.

"Tell me what's going on with you and Amery."

It appeared he wanted to hedge, but he finally said, "I've been with her since she returned from Vegas. One minute she's fine; the next she's hysterical. Yeah, she's burying her grandfather tomorrow, so that's to

207

be expected, but honestly? I needed a break from her tonight." Kevin actually looked embarrassed. "Then there's her whole rant about suing the pants off Prairie Gardens because it's their fault he's dead."

"You know she probably has a good case."

"No argument from me. She could probably own that place if she gets the right lawyer."

"Much as we need the work, I certainly hope you aren't planning to help her with this case and her pursuit of justice in the form of cash."

A shadow fell across the table. We both glanced up expecting Carla.

But Big Mike towered over me. "Sorry to interrupt, but bossman would like to see you."

"He's back from Denver? Since when?"

"Just now."

"How the hell did he find me?"

Big Mike said nothing.

"Did those fucking sneaky goons of his follow me here?"

"I don't know. He wants to talk to you. Outside."

I snorted; it smelled like limes. "If he wants to talk to me, he can come in here."

"Not an option." He frowned at the pile of empty beer cans teetering on our table. "Come on, Julie. Five minutes. That's all he wants."

I shook my head.

He sighed. "What am I supposed to tell him?"

"Tell him he can kiss my ass."

Big Mike straightened to his full six-feet-six height; his eyes flattened to hard disks. He turned and stalked off.

"Was that smart?" Kevin asked.

"Probably not."

He mumbled something about a death wish.

I fidgeted in the seat. Thought about smoking another cigarette. Seriously considered ordering another shot. As my indecision wore on, the noise from the pool games and the dance floor escalated.

"Go," Kevin said.

"What message would that send him? That he can command my presence whenever the hell he wants? Fuck that." I crossed my arms over my chest, the picture of belligerent.

Kevin grinned in that devilish way that still charmed me. "Sounds like a perfect opportunity to tell him how you feel."

"You're just egging me on because I'm still half-drunk."

"Yep."

I crammed my crap back in my purse and buttoned up my coat. "Come looking for me if I'm not back here in five. Seriously." I bussed Kevin's forehead on my way past the booth. I'd missed hanging out with him.

In trying to dodge the flurry of twirling bodies and cowboy hats on the dance floor, someone bumped into me. Hard.

"Watch where the fuck you're goin', bitch."

I faced the snarling voice. Wow. The woman had the biggest nose and ears I'd seen outside a zoo. "You talking to me?"

"Yeah, I'm talkin' to you."

"*You* bumped into me."

"So?" Her big nostrils flared revulsion like a skunk crossed her path. "Maybe that means you oughta get the fuck out of my way." She pushed me.

Bad move.

I shoved her back with enough force she fell on her fat ass. "Now I'm out of your way. Stay out of mine." Her dance partner lifted her by her jiggly upper arms, holding her back while she screeched at me. My head pounded as I exited the bar.

The chill of the night air slapped my cheeks and quickened my pace. I tightened the belt on my coat and lowered my face into the lapels.

Screw this. Too damn cold to stay out here and fight with Martinez.

I spun around, a little unsteadily, to see Dumbo storming outside the exit, glaring. I figured she didn't really want to engage me. She'd act tough, keep a safe distance, and taunt me. I'd let her. But if she opened her trap and yapped insults, I *would* take a shot at her.

The reality was, few women went beyond nasty words to deliver a nasty uppercut.

Reality check: she barreled toward me like a Sherman tank.

CHAPTER 16

I braced myself as best as I could, considering my balance was slightly off. When she reached me, I stepped sideways and rammed my elbow in her chest.

She didn't see that one coming. *Wham*. She hit the ground like a brick.

I gloated above her. "Enough? Or do you want more?"

"Fuck you," she wheezed and grabbed my ankle, knocking me on my butt.

Even in my bleary-eyed state, I managed to make a safe fall. Hadn't injured anything but my pride.

Before I'd recovered my wits, she rose to her knees and took a swing at me.

I ducked, but not fast enough; her row of Black Hills Gold rings caught me in the right eyebrow like trailer park brass knuckles. Sharp, stinging pain galvanized me into action. I rolled and wobbled to my feet.

"Yeah, run," she jeered. "Just like she said. You ain't so tough. You know I'll kick your ass."

I ignored the weird "she" comment and repeated, "Run?"

"That was a lucky shot, and you know it."

"Bring it, Dumbo." I planted my feet in a right-side fighting stance. Resisted the urge to give her the "come on" signal Neo used in *The Matrix* before he fought Agent Smith. That'd be over the top, even for me.

The alcohol veil lifted. Why was I standing there like a cheesy movie hero giving her a second chance to rush me?

Fuck that.

I should've punched her in the nose since it was such an easy target. Instead, I pounced on her and gave her a dirt facial. Her head bounced. Her cutesy pink hair ribbon dropped to the ground. Grabbing her right arm, I jerked it straight up and put my foot on her lower back.

"Let go of me!"

"Still think I'm gonna run?"

"I said, let go!"

"Little hard for me to run with my boot on your ass, isn't it?"

She squirmed. Muttered insults. But I had her locked down and she knew it.

With my senses dulled by tequila, the noise behind me didn't register until it was too late.

A brawny arm wrapped around my throat and jerked me back. Unfortunately for Dumbo, I didn't release her arm, and the sickening sound of cartilage popping echoed before she screamed.

"Let go of her!" the baritone demanded. "Now!"

Aw. Her old man rode to her rescue. How sweet.

On pure instinct I swung around, using the foot I'd jammed in her back to catch her white knight in the knee with my boot heel.

He grunted and stumbled, loosening his grip on me. I went limp as a wet noodle and slithered out of his hold.

When he bent down to rub his kneecap, I clocked him in the jaw. Followed through with a snap-kick to his groin. But I missed and connected with his hip.

He staggered anyway.

My knuckles stung. Goddamn. No matter how many times I punched someone, I never seemed to remember how bad it hurt.

Feet scuffled in the gravel. I glanced up. We had an audience.

"Hit her again," some guy shouted.

"Rack him," a woman suggested.

The beaten pair looked at me.

"Are we done? Or should I take more suggestions?"

Dumbo scrambled to her feet and cradled her arm, cowering by the chubby man who was now rubbing his jaw *and* his knee.

Served them both right.

213

I stepped forward.

As one, they moved back.

Cool. This intimidation shit was heady stuff.

Between the adrenaline rush and the booze, I was ten feet tall and bulletproof. As I started to charge, two bands of steel pinned my arms to my sides and my feet dangled in the air.

"Three against one? That sucks!" Outraged, I thrashed. None of my dirty tricks worked on this moose. In fact, he'd completely immobilized me so I couldn't use a reverse head butt. I tried the limp noodle trick again.

He didn't fall for it.

I was tired. My head spun like a baton. I chanced a short breather while I figured out a way to take this guy down.

"Relax. I'm not gonna hurt you."

I recognized the voice and froze. "Big Mike?"

He chuckled. "Yep."

I was not amused.

"Leave. The show is over," he barked at the half-dozen people who were still gawking. Disappointed by the lack of real bloodshed, they trudged back into Dusty's.

"Let go of me."

"Not until they're gone."

"This doesn't concern you, so butt out."

He didn't say a word.

"And I was doing fine on my own before you

showed up. I sure as hell don't need your protection now."

"I'm holding you for *their* protection, not yours."

"Oh."

The couple didn't return to the bar. They sent me a fiery look of hatred, climbed into a turd brown Dodge minivan, and sped off. Probably to the hospital.

I told myself it was wrong to feel smug.

Big Mike released me.

I rolled my shoulders. The outer bar door flew open and Kevin stormed in my direction.

Crap.

I stood my ground, shakily, but stood it nonetheless.

He got right in my face. "I leave you alone for five fucking minutes and you're in a goddamn *bar* fight?"

"She started it."

"But you finished it, didn't you?"

"Uh. Yeah."

Kevin's gaze moved to my cheekbone. "For Christsake, Julie, you're bleeding."

"I am?" My fingers touched my eyebrow. Came away sticky. Eww. "Huh. Doesn't even hurt."

Big Mike snorted.

"You are not a superhero, despite your continual stupid actions to the contrary." Kevin lifted his arm and blotted the blood with his shirtsleeve. "Where else did she hit you?"

He thought the elephant woman bested me? Indignant, I said, "Nowhere. For your information, *I* won. And I'm fine."

"Shut up."

"Really, Kev, I'm f-*fuck*, that hurts!" I jerked from his poking fingers. "Quit it!"

"Quit being such a baby. You've had worse. Hold still."

Great. The adrenaline buzz started to wear off and now I was whining. So much for my superhero status. Definitely time to climb in the Batmobile and return to the cave.

"Come on, Kev. Take me home."

"No. *I'm* taking you home." Martinez materialized from the shadows.

A yelp escaped me. "Have you been here spying on me the whole time?"

Arms crossed over his chest, he stayed mute.

"See? That I-don't-have-to-tell-you-anything bullshit attitude is why you piss me off, Martinez. That's why I'm not going anywhere with you."

"Wrong. Give me your keys."

Wisely, Kevin and Big Mike retreated from the line of fire.

Another pause. Neither of us budged.

"Losing my patience with you, blondie."

I stomped toward him. "So fucking what? I don't even know why the fuck you're here. I told Big Mike I didn't want to talk to you."

"No, you told him I could kiss your ass."

"You're a bright guy; I figured you could read

between the lines."

He laughed softly. "You mean read between the cracks?"

"That wasn't supposed to be funny!" Yelling at him made my head throb. Made me feel like an ass, too. I said to Kevin, "Take me home."

Big Mike and Kevin exchanged a look.

Fine. Let Martinez dictate to them—he didn't dictate to me. I'd made it about ten steps when Martinez stopped me.

"Go away. I'm not talking to you."

His gaze flicked to the cut on my temple. "You're bleeding."

"Like you care."

Martinez stared at me. Through me. If I hoped he'd dispute my statement, lovingly assure me I was in error, that he cared about me deeply, then I was bound to be disappointed.

He leaned close enough to whisper, "Don't. Go. There."

Yikes. But he wasn't done.

"I'm so fucking mad at you right now that if you don't hand over your keys I will take them by force, tie you up with your purse straps, and dump your smart-ass in the back of your truck bed to see if a ride in the cold night air will cool off your goddamn hothead."

That was almost a soliloquy coming from Martinez. It was also scary as hell because he wasn't joking.

"Fine." I drew back, unzipped my purse, and

slapped my keys in his palm. "Happy now?"

"Ecstatic."

He sauntered over to Kevin and Big Mike. Said something to them I couldn't hear. They both nodded.

Kevin broke from their little he-man group and trotted back to me. "You okay with Martinez taking you home?"

"Like I have a choice."

"You do. Say the word and I'll call Jimmer. Or Kim. Or a cab."

I glanced at Tony studying me like a mountain lion eyes a lame fawn. "Maybe drunk and pissed off isn't the best way for me to deal with him."

Kevin pecked me on the forehead. "My money's on you."

Big Mike and Kevin climbed into a silver Cadillac Escalade and disappeared down the dusty road.

It was pitch-black in the far back corner of Dusty's parking lot. As I passed by empty vehicles, I wondered if Martinez's other bodyguards were out here watching us. Felt like someone was. I hated that feeling. Made me shiver.

I lost my footing on the running board on the passenger side of my truck.

Martinez caught me. "You okay?"

"No. My head hurts."

"I'll bet. Let me see." His gaze never made it past my mouth. He said, "Fuck it," pushing me against the truck to kiss the shit out of me.

I let him.

His lips broke from mine after about a year.

"I'm still mad at you," I said, fighting to catch my breath as he used his teeth on my throat.

"Same goes." He dove in for another openmouthed kiss that left my brain muddled, and the rest of my body hot and tingly.

In about two seconds my jeans would be around my knees and my bare ass would be pressing cold metal as he pressed inside me. I pushed him back.

"Stop. I'm not talking to you."

"We haven't been talking."

I mimed zipping my lip.

He sighed. "You drive me absolutely crazy."

"Me? What did *I* do?"

"Hung up on me for starters."

"So? Your phone manners suck every goddamn day."

"You refused to talk to me when I drove out here."

"I don't like being summoned, Martinez."

"I know. Why do you think I do it?" He used the back of his rough-skinned hand to trace my jawline.

A quiver rippled down the center of my body. Talk about easy. "Why am I letting you paw me when I'm mad at you?"

"Too much tequila. I'm a total bastard who has no problem taking advantage of the situation."

"Are we fighting again for the hot makeup sex?"

"Not entirely. I'm trying to distract you so you'll tell me what happened to you today."

Damn. The booze had worked for a little while and made me forget about my dad. I averted my gaze.

He tipped my chin up. "Fine. We'll deal with that later. Tell me how you ended up in another bar fight."

"I don't know. First she shoved me inside, then she was talking trash. I was content to let it go. She wasn't." I studied him. "How much did you see?"

Martinez grinned. "All of it."

"I won."

"I noticed."

Then I noticed his attentions had become obvious. I bumped my hips into his. "Jesus. Are you hard?"

"As a rock."

"Why?"

"Evidently seeing you drunk and kicking ass turns my crank."

"Eww. It's not a girl-on-girl thing, is it?"

"No." He swept my hair over my shoulder, letting it spill over his fingers like a waterfall. "Must just be a you thing, blondie."

Here was my chance to change this shit day into something meaningful. Something important. Something good. "Tony, do you love me?"

His eyes never moved from mine. "What do you think?"

"I think I'd like to hear you say the actual words."

"Same goes." His focus shifted to my cut. "I'll take you home and patch you up."

"I thought you were mad at me."

"I am."

"Then why are you going all Dr. Quinn?"

No answer.

"Is this where you tell me you'll kiss it and make it all better?"

"If you're lucky." His lips brushed mine.

My belly jumped. "That mean you're staying over?"

He opened the passenger door for me. "Do you want me to?"

"No," I lied.

"Good. Then I guess I am staying."

"Bastard."

Martinez laughed, placed his hands on my ass, and shoved me in the truck.

He'd barely slapped on the Big Bird Band-Aid when he had me naked, hot, and squirming under him in my bed. Then he had me naked, hot, and wet pinned against the wall in the shower. In the chair. On the floor. Then back in bed.

Exhausted and dazed, I murmured, "You *are* nice

when you're mad at me."

"Mmm." He'd situated us so half my body stretched across his; one hand clamped on my ass, the fingers of his other hand threaded through mine. His jaw rested on the top of my head.

This was the side of him no one knew. This was what I'd craved, the part of him that was mine alone. "I missed you."

"I know."

With his heat and scent and contentment surrounding me, my consciousness was floating away. "I feel it for you every day, Martinez, I'm just not so good at saying it."

"Try."

"I am."

"Try harder."

CHAPTER 17

THE NEXT MORNING KEVIN WAS ON FUNERAL DUTY with Amery so I had the office to myself. I brewed a pot of coffee; caffeine would dull the edges of my full body hangover, too much booze, too much sex—not that I was complaining about the latter.

The office manager for our newest corporate client, Tomahawk Ammo, e-mailed me a list of potential secondary suppliers she needed checked out right away. At least it gave me something to do.

I wrapped up the project and typed up the invoice. While I was dropping a copy on Kevin's desk, I noticed Post-it Notes stuck to his computer monitor, all relating to Prairie Gardens.

Last night he'd mentioned Amery ranting about suing the facility. Much as I hated to admit it, she had a good case. But a case I wanted no part of.

Our firm specialized in piddly-ass cases the larger investigative companies waved off as small potatoes. We refused to work with ambulance-chasing lawyers—where the big bucks were in the PI biz. We'd built up a list of repeat clients, secured contracts with enough places that small cases added up to a tidy sum. Neither Kevin nor I were looking to get rich. We liked what we did, we were damn good at it, and our client list was diverse enough we were rarely bored.

Kevin and I were equal partners with an equal amount of power when it came to making decisions. So far, we'd had few disagreements. But we'd have a big problem if he thought Wells/Collins Investigations would support Amery in her legal battle against Prairie Gardens.

I turned on Kevin's computer and backtracked his online surfing since we'd taken Amery's case. Routine stuff, tracing Vernon Sloane's social security number, DOB, previous addresses. But Kevin spent time tracking building permits. State regulations on nursing homes. Complaints from the Elderly Housing Authority, the arm of the state government that oversaw retirement homes and assisted living facilities. I couldn't tell from Kevin's scant information whether more than one entity dealt with violations.

This wasn't the type of info you tracked for fun. No, this was the preliminary documentation needed to justify a potential lawsuit.

Jesus. He really had been thinking with his dick.

Kevin mentioned the suing thing in passing, not even hinting he'd already begun the legwork. I scrolled to the last listing and watched it load as I lit a cigarette.

I hated flash sites for businesses, particularly when accompanied by crappy instrumental music (Iron Butterfly's *In-A-Gadda-Da-Vida*? Please shoot me now). The job of a Web site was to provide consumer information. Period. If I needed entertainment I'd visit YouTube.

The site, LPL, exploded with flashing graphics, but no information on what the hell LPL stood for. An intentional distraction? A brief moment of panic followed. What if Kev had been surfing for porn? What if LPL stood for lesbians—eww, I *so* didn't want to contemplate possibilities.

I found the site map. Three categories were listed: People—Places—Opportunities. I clicked on *People*. A standard Web site e-mail contact form addressed to webmaster@LPL.com. No help.

Next I dragged the cursor to *Opportunities*. A listing with a phone number and a P.O. box for an employment firm in Spearfish specializing in placing healthcare professionals—from janitors to administrators. Must be getting warmer.

The last tab was *Places*. Ooh, pay dirt. A list of LPL-owned businesses. Meade County Haven. Bennett County Rest Home. Deadwood Retirement Village. And Prairie Gardens. No links to those sites. At the very bottom of the page in teeny tiny letters:

For more information call LPL, followed by the number. With a South Dakota area code.

I dialed and took a quick drag from my smoke.

"Good afternoon. LPL. How may I help you?"

Should've thought of how to play it before I called.

"Hello?"

I coughed; not an act, because I choked as I exhaled. "Hi. Sorry. Something in my throat." I coughed again.

"You all right?"

"Yes. Thanks. This might sound weird, but I just stumbled across your Web site and I've gotta say, wow, it is really something."

"Thank you."

"I didn't see a Web site designer listed anywhere. I'm looking to update my own site and I wondered if you'd be able to tell me which company created LLP's."

"LPL," she corrected, as I expected.

"Right, LPL. What does LPL stand for anyway?"

"Linderman Property Limited."

I froze, but my brain started spinning, backtracking so fast my forehead heated up.

"If you'll hang on, I'll connect you with someone who can answer your question about the Web site designer."

I hung up, staring into space and finishing my cigarette.

Figure the odds. Bud Linderman. Entrepreneur. Asshole. I'd forgotten, or maybe a better phrase was *blocked out* my past association with him. Last time we'd crossed paths, Martinez threatened to chop Bud into pieces, after Bud made the mistake of manhandling me. In front of Tony. Without apology. Yikes. Not a smart move and Tony and I hadn't even been officially together back then.

It hadn't occurred to me when Kevin took Amery's case that Linderman might own Prairie Gardens.

Why hadn't Kevin mentioned the Linderman connection? He knew Linderman and I butted heads on the Chloe Black Dog case—didn't he? Damn. Maybe Kevin *didn't* remember. That fucked-up case happened right around the time his girlfriend died and he'd been MIA from the business. I'd dealt with the details and the fallout from the case alone.

Linderman's good ol' boy/pseudocowboy persona surfaced in my mind. He was the only person I'd met besides Martinez who employed full-time bodyguards. Linderman's hands were in a variety of pots: Deadwood gaming, car dealerships, athletic sponsorships, bars, real estate, and retirement homes. What I didn't know? If Linderman was as hands-on with his businesses as Martinez was with Fat Bob's and Bare Assets.

Normally this type of situation piqued my curiosity and I'd snoop around for information. Not this time. We weren't working for Amery. If I hadn't been adamant about that fact before, I would be now. Bud Linderman played dirty. And if he played dirty with me, Martinez would kill him. The easiest way to prevent the deadly outcome was avoidance, pure and simple.

I twirled the office chair around. I bumped the mouse and the previous "past history" screen filled the left corner of the monitor. My gaze landed on the Bad Doggie site.

As investigators, we had access to information sites private citizens didn't. Nothing like searching classified CIA files. Government sites were helpful, but usually as boring as government pamphlets. The local police department had to provide a voucher to the Web site owner/server, stating the primary function of our investigative business before they'd grant us access to the sites. And we paid a ton for the privilege of using the vast pool of information. Didn't matter we were the smallest fish in the pond.

Tip sites listed rewards, sightings, recent scams, and were primarily used by bigger investigative companies who also employed extraction and security specialists.

I clicked on the link. Bad Doggie was a snitch site modeled after anonymous tip lines in big cities. Each state had a page. Rewards were offered in some cases, but the site was not affiliated with any law enforcement agencies.

The site debunked two myths: A—that criminals were computer/Internet illiterate, B—that lawbreakers would turn on each other, but not turn to law enforcement.

South Dakota posts dealt with poachers, illegal fossil hunting, and child support issues. The posts were infrequent and out of the realm of our normal investigative business. It surprised me Kevin bookmarked the site last week.

Huh. What'd he been looking for? I imagined him checking my history files. Couples resorts in the Caribbean and the Pro Bull Riders Tour stats page. I shut down the computer and realized I'd lost two hours. Dammit. That was why I hated the Internet; it was a time suck.

My cell phone rang and I groaned. Nothing but bad news on that damn thing lately. Publisher's Clearing House Sweepstakes folks didn't have the number; this wasn't the million-dollar phone call. Honestly, I couldn't look at the caller ID; I just answered it.

"Hello?"

"Julie? It's Missy."

Missy? Not another Pampered Chef party invite. "Hey, Miss, how's it going?"

"All right. Look. I'm not supposed to do this, and if you tell Deputy John I called you, I'll deny it, but you'd better get to the sheriff's office right away."

"Why? What's happened?"

"Your dad is in jail."

"What? When—"

"Here he comes, gotta go."

Click.

Why the hell hadn't my pushy-ass family called me? Since they'd bugged me about every other minor fucking thing in the last week? Now Dad's in jail and my former co-worker had to break the news?

I bundled up and locked the office. The drive to the Bear Butte County Sheriff's Office was a complete blur, and, for once, not because of the weather.

I didn't go in the building through the administrative offices; I used the door around back in the half basement that led to booking.

In the tiny entryway, I shoved everything— my purse, my shoes, my coat, my belt, even the necklace Martinez gave me— in the plastic bin for personal belongings and pushed it through the Plexiglas partition.

After my stuff was checked and catalogued, the security guard buzzed me in and I passed through the metal detector. My blood pressure was near brain aneurysm range when I finally reached the booking desk.

Twee manned the area. She looked like someone's grandma. A stout, sweet-faced German descendant with salt-and-pepper hair, styled in a bouffant from the 1960s. An unassuming woman who wouldn't hurt a fly.

Wrong. I'd seen her fly over the counter and body

slam a two-hundred-pound biker who'd mistakenly made the same assumption. No one dared ask how she'd gotten her name, nor was anyone stupid enough to jokingly call her Tweedledee or Tweedledum. Twee was tough as shit, and luckily she'd always liked me.

She grunted. "Thought I might see you today."

"What's he in for?"

"Disturbing the peace."

"How long ago they bring him in?"

"Coupla hours." Twee cocked her head. "How'd you hear about it so fast?"

I hedged. "Who made the arrest?"

"Deputy John."

Could've been worse. He was a fair and decent officer. "Will John talk to me?"

"He ain't supposed to."

I waited.

"But I can call him and ask."

"Thanks, Twee. I really appreciate it."

After she replaced the phone, she said, "He'll be right up."

I nodded. My fingers rose to my throat to twist in the chain of my necklace, only to connect with bare skin. Strange how quickly the pendant became my worry stone.

Five long minutes passed before Deputy John appeared. No smile for me, which was odd. "Julie. Come on back."

We entered an interview room so small our knees

bumped in the chairs.

"You know I shouldn't be talkin' to you."

"I know. If me being here will cause problems for you, then I'll leave."

Deputy John sighed. "It won't. It would if it was anyone besides you."

I didn't know how to take that. "He was arrested for disturbing the peace, right?"

"Yeah."

"Where?"

"Bevel's Hardware."

"What happened?"

"What we've pieced together is Doug was buying a length of chain when he and BD Hoffman got into an argument. Pushing and shoving ensued. The manager broke it up. At the checkout BD said something else, at which time Doug Collins jumped the counter. Some say he punched BD in the face, breaking his nose. Some say it was an accident when he jumped the counter. One witness said Doug started to beat BD with the chain but we don't have corroboration."

I felt ill.

"Another customer pulled Doug off BD and held him back until we arrived."

"What now?" Dad could be arrested for assault. Should be, probably.

"Here's the thing: Doug Collins hasn't had so much as a speeding ticket in the last ten years. In fact, he's never been arrested for a damn thing."

How ironic that he'd finally been arrested for the very thing he used to do to me.

"Once BD shows up, I'm gonna suggest he not file charges."

Whoa. "Why?"

"No one is talking on the record. Which means no witnesses on the alleged assault. The Disturbing the Peace arrest will stand."

Better than a felony. "What did they argue about?"

"No one knows. Doug ain't talking. The witness said Doug warned BD if he ever repeated what he'd said to anyone else, he'd . . ."

"He'd what?"

Deputy John sighed again. "The witness didn't hear that part. Like I said, your dad's tight-lipped, and I suspect I'll get the same response from BD."

I opened my mouth. Closed it.

"What? Say what's on your mind. You're not exactly shy, Julie."

"Does Sheriff Richards know you're going to suggest that BD not file an assault charge?"

"He trusts me to do my job, so I haven't brought it up. I suspect he'd do the same, given Doug's clean record."

Be stupid to point out the sheriff probably wouldn't want the assault charge dropped, because it would strengthen the suspicions against my father in the unresolved Melvin Canter situation. Deputy John had to know Sheriff Richards brought Doug Collins in for questioning yesterday.

You don't work here. This oversight won't come down on you.

"So he's stuck in jail?"

"No. He's waiting to be bonded out." He frowned. "I thought that's why you were here?"

I hedged again. "Will Sheriff Richards be around when that happens?"

"Nah. He's at a conference in Sioux Falls the next two days and over the weekend."

Relieved, I slumped in the chair. "Has Trish been here yet?"

Deputy John frowned. "Who?"

"His wife. Did Doug call her?"

"No. I thought the only person he called was you."

He hadn't called me. Come on, poker face. Who had he called to bail him out?

"So you haven't told the family?"

"Not yet. Needed the facts straight first."

And big fucking surprise Dad expected me to do his shit work. Asshole deserved to spend the night in jail, even though he wouldn't. Maybe it'd wake his stubborn hide up.

"You always were logical. Things ain't the same with you gone. We all miss seeing you. I know Tom does, too."

Again, I didn't know how to take that. I stood.

"Thanks again."

"I'll walk you out."

I waved good-bye to Twee and collected my belongings. I warmed up my truck and stared at the jail portion of the building for the longest time. Must've smoked half a dozen cigarettes before I dialed my stepmother to tell her that her husband was a jailbird.

CHAPTER 18

MARTINEZ HAD MEETINGS ALL NIGHT SO I ENDED up at the Sturgis McDonald's for an early supper. I slipped into my usual spot, the back corner booth. My mind was a million miles away when the hair on the back of my neck prickled.

Someone was watching me.

I casually looked at the guy on the other side of the aisle. He paid more attention to the classified ads on the table in front of him than me. My gaze moved to the construction worker on the other side of the garbage container, shoveling French fries in his mouth at an alarming rate. The only other customer was a harried pregnant woman and her three young children.

Maybe I'd imagined the freakish sensation. Although, enough crappy things happened to me to justify my bouts of paranoia.

As I refilled my coffee, the man with the classified ads left and roared out of the parking lot in a green Chevy Blazer. Something about him felt wrong. I lingered inside, eyeing the screaming kids in the play area, wondering if I'd been born without a maternal longing. Or maybe it'd been beaten out of me. I liked children; I just didn't want any of my own.

I climbed in my truck. With no reason to rush home, I meandered through Sturgis. Billboards for Ratt, Poison, Rob Zombie, and Joan Jett were still up around town, although the concerts ended with the Sturgis Rally in August.

I'd motored past the formerly named F.O. Jolley Funeral Home, when I glanced in my rearview mirror and saw the same Blazer from the McDonalds. On a whim I stopped at Lyn's Dakotamart to buy two packs of cigarettes, a loaf of wheat bread, and a twelve-pack of Diet Pepsi. Didn't see the guy get out and lurk in the frozen food aisle and he didn't appear to be idling in the parking lot when I returned.

But as soon as I merged on I-90, he snuck in behind me again. At a discreet distance, sure, but this guy sucked at surveillance.

Yeah? Do you know how long he's been following you, smarty?

My paranoia gave way to annoyance.

If I stopped anywhere else he'd know I was onto him. I went straight home, scooted into the house, and locked all the doors. With the lights off, I peeked out the front window. That Blazer crept past my house every thirty minutes for the next four hours.

On one hand I was pissed. On the other hand I was . . . even more pissed. I'd told Martinez to call off his watchdogs. If he wanted me protected at all times, he oughta be here to do it himself. I rocked at pegging Hombres muscle; it infuriated me I'd missed this slimeball, even when he didn't look the part.

So what if it wasn't one of Martinez's guys looking out for me?

My dad's smart comment surfaced: *Ain't you afraid the Standing Elk family will be gunnin' for you for revenge for killin' their cash cow?"*

No. It was the Hombres. It had to be. I couldn't think beyond that.

I set the alarm, and brought my Sig Sauer to bed with me instead of tequila.

The next morning I craved sugary, chocolaty donuts and stumbled to my truck for the short jaunt to the Kum & Go. Within two blocks of leaving my house, a babysitter appeared. Not in the same vehicle. At least they were smart enough to change it up. My new shadow drove an older model Toyota 4Runner.

Enough. This ended today.

I opted not to call Dad to see what his bond ended up being and who he'd called to bail him out. The curious part of me wondered how Trish explained to the kids why he'd spent the afternoon wearing orange coveralls and paper shoes. Part of me wondered if Brittney would call me and chew me out for her daddy ending up in the place I used to work. She always found something to make me feel guilty, and I don't know why I let her.

At 9:00 I called Jimmer at his pawnshop.

"Julie! Wazzup wit yo' very bad self, sista?"

I rolled my eyes. He'd been watching 1970s blacksploitation DVDs again. Charming, if an odd choice for a former military man with an aversion to racial diversity. If at any point during the conversation he said, "Get out, shut yo' mouf," I'd break into the chorus of *Rubberband Man*.

"Nothing much. You busy this morning?"

"Depends. Whatcha got in mind?"

"You up for a little snipe hunting?" I explained what I'd planned, pacing and smoking while waiting for his reaction.

Ugly silence.

I exhaled, fighting the urge to blather. "Then again, I'm open to suggestions from the expert."

"You don't have nuthin' better to do, little missy, than to fuck around with this?"

"Nope. I need to know who it is, one way or the other."

"Better to beg for forgiveness than ask for permission?"

"Something like that." I played the card that always worked. "Come on, Jimmer. You love this kinda sneaky shit. Being armed to the teeth. Making guys piss their pants in fear. It'll be fun."

When he still wasn't acting gung ho, I added, "I'll even take you out for pie afterward. My treat."

"I'm in. You done any recon on this area?"

"What I remember is the entire stretch is fenced. Isolated. No residences, no secondary gravel roads. No place to turn around. No signage announcing any of the above."

"Cool. Looks like the weather's gonna cooperate, too. Snow and blow, baby."

"Be nice if something went right for me for a change. Will you be ready in half an hour?"

"Yep."

I explained where he needed to be.

"Gotcha back, kitty cat."

"For Christsake, Jimmer, you channeling *Shaft* now?"

"Nope. *Superfly.*" He laughed and hung up.

Bundled up and loaded for bear, I cranked the tunes

and burned rubber out of the driveway.

Bingo. Mr. 4Runner swung in place behind me on the service road.

I took my own sweet time driving up County Road 35, aka a dirt road to nowhere, keeping his vehicle within my rearview, even when the swirling snow tried to erase it.

Twenty minutes ticked by. We were on the far edge of Bear Butte County. Miles of snow-covered grazing fields spread out in an ocean of bluish white. The thick, jagged crusts of the snowdrifts were the foamy whitecaps; the rise and fall of gauzy snow mist was like the fine spray of saltwater. The occasional stark tree offered a visual break in the unwavering line of the horizon. Telephone poles listed to the left in an ongoing battle to stay upright against the never-ending South Dakota wind.

Easy to fall prey to the landscape's austere beauty and lose focus. My gaze zoomed to my rearview mirror.

Why hadn't my tail gotten suspicious? Driving deeper into the wilds didn't faze my follower. This setup screamed . . . *setup* to me. Had I been too quick to blame this on Martinez? Tony's guys weren't stupid.

My adrenaline pumped when I crested the last hill. I sucked a deep drag and smashed the cigarette butt into the ashtray. Placing both hands on the wheel, I floored it.

On the other side, I slammed the brakes; the back end fishtailed until I stopped sideways in the middle of the road. I threw it in reverse. The back tires bumped the gravel shoulder and slid into the ditch. I threw it in park, shut off the engine, and grabbed my gun from the seat as I scrambled out the passenger door.

I waited by the right front tire for my babysitter to run across my "accident." I only hoped he was a good enough driver not to run into me.

The rise and fall of the whistling wind surrounded me, and the soft *sssss* of hard snow crystals drifted over the road like icy, white, scaleless snakes.

A motor hummed on the other side of the hill, and the rolling thump of tires on snow-packed ground broke the monotony of the eerie stillness.

Come on, come on.

No screeching tires. No metallic clicking of an-tilock brakes. The vehicle simply slowed and stopped within my line of sight.

My heart beat so fast my eyes pulsed.

The engine quit. The door opened. Booted feet hit the road, kicking up a cloud of fine snow. A slight hesitation and then the feet stopped by the driver's side door of my truck.

I barreled around the front end, gun in hand. "You lookin' for me?"

A look of utter surprise.

"Hands above your head, asshole, and don't move."

He started to back away.

"I said, don't fucking move."

He didn't utter a peep; he just kept backing up.

Which pissed me off. I fired at the ground so close to his feet snow puffed over the toes of his boots like marshmallow topping.

Then he froze.

I inched closer and yelled, "On the ground."

He stared at me with his mouth hanging open so far I saw his fillings.

I fired again. "Now!"

He hit the snow.

"Stretch your arms above your head. Pretend you're Superman." I loomed over him. "You try anything while you're moving them up there and I'll shoot you in the ass."

Glove-covered hands zoomed up.

"You carrying?"

"Yeah."

"Where?"

"I-it's in the car."

"Where?"

"On the passenger's seat."

"Where's your cell?"

"In my pocket."

"Did you call this in to whoever is making you follow me?"

Pause. "Not yet."

"Lucky for you."

Crunching tires signaled Jimmer's arrival.

The guy lifted up, caught sight of the muzzle I'd

243

aimed at his head, and lowered back down.

The cold settled into my bones on a number of levels beyond the air temp.

Jimmer climbed out of his Hummer with a Remington 870 Wingmaster shotgun in hand. He sauntered over, held it aloft, and pumped it.

The man yelped at the distinctive sound.

Impressive.

Jimmer said, "You know who he is?"

"No. We skipped formal introductions."

"What's your name, boy?"

The guy turned his face to the left. "Dietz."

"What's he told you so far?"

"Just that he's got a gun on the front seat."

While Jimmer checked it out, I crouched five feet from my captive. "Who do you work for?"

No answer.

"Don't piss off a woman with a short temper and a big gun, Dietz. Who do you work for?"

"I-I can't tell you."

"You can, and you will if I have to shoot it out of you. Tell me who the fuck you work for."

"You don't understand. He'll kill me."

Jimmer said, "Start talking or *I'll* kill you."

"Do it. Because you don't scare me as much as he does."

"Wrong again. Talk."

I had a bad, bad feeling.

Dietz babbled, "Do you know what he'll do to

me when he finds out she picked up on the tail right away?"

"Actually, your buddy fucked it up last night, so I was on the lookout for another tail this morning."

Dietz looked me in the eye. "What?"

"Your buddy, in the Blazer last night at McDonald's."

"I don't know what you're talking about. Today's the first day we're supposed to—"

"Bullshit. I didn't imagine that snoopy fucker cruising by my house *eight* times last night. So try again."

Jimmer put the small gun he'd found in the Toyota at the base of the man's skull. "Answer the question. Who told you to follow her?"

No hesitation. "The Hombres."

Fuck.

"You a member? Or a hire?"

"I'm a pledge, man, I just do what I'm told."

"Who'd the order come down from? Did you verify it?"

I hadn't considered that. What if Martinez hadn't given the order?

"PT passed it along to me after the meeting last night."

There went that idea.

Jimmer dug the gun deeper into Dietz's neck. "Still don't answer the question, boy. Who gave the order?"

Dietz mumbled.

"What?"

"Mr. Martinez."

I slowly released the breath I'd been holding. Why did the mysterious *Hombres shit* he'd mentioned in passing somehow involve me to the point I needed constant surveillance?

"Why'd he pick a dumb fucker like you?"

"He was looking for a guy she wouldn't recognize. He thought I had experience."

"Why'd he think that?" I demanded.

"I lied and said I did, okay?"

"For that Martinez's security team will eat you for lunch."

"I know."

"Why'd you do it?"

"Because I wanted to prove I was worthy of the patch. I tried to do something that'd get me noticed."

"Got you noticed, all right. How do you think El Presidente is gonna react when he finds out you lied to him? And because of that lie, he trusted you with *her*. With her safety." He leaned in. "Do you *know* who she is?"

"Yes."

"And you're supposed to be protecting her? Did you even see me following you?"

"Ah. No."

"I'd be doin' you a favor if I killed you right fuckin' now," Jimmer snarled.

Dietz flopped on the ground. Probably wet himself.

Jimmer removed the gun from Dietz's neck. "Get up. Rush me, or try to take off, and I'll tell Martinez you were friendly with her. He'll slice off your shriveled cock before he feeds it to you."

Yikes.

Jimmer led me aside. "So now you know."

"But I don't know why."

"*Why?* Why are you fuckin' surprised, Julie? You know what he's like."

I turned away. Yeah, I knew what Tony was like, probably better than anyone, but something else was going on.

Martinez never pulled that I'm-the-big-bad-ass-biker-bossman-do-what-the-fuck-I-tell-you bullshit with me. He didn't treat me like property. Ever. Maybe he let the Hombres members believe he lorded over me, especially since I never voiced my opinion to him or any other Hombres member in public. I didn't give a shit what his brothers assumed about me or us; I knew the truth and that's what mattered.

Jimmer slung his arm over my shoulder and lowered his voice. "The arrogant bastard is so crazy fucking in love with you he'll do anything to keep you safe, little missy. Is that so bad?"

"No."

"So forget it."

"That's the thing. I can't." Would my reasoning sound fucked up and petty and . . . female?

"What? Why not?"

"I warned Martinez if he ever sicced his goons on me again without warning I'd retaliate." My glance at Jimmer was a silent plea for him to understand. "If I don't follow through, it'll look like I pussed out, not only to Tony, but to his security team. I don't wanna be seen as the type of whiny-assed woman who makes idle threats."

"Yeah? What'd you threaten to do?"

"Shoot up the next car he sent after me."

After about a ten-second pause, he handed me the shotgun. "Go for it."

"Seriously?"

"Gotta stand on principle. Or as Martinez is fond of saying: gotta have rules or chaos rules." He yelled at Dietz. "Whose rice burner is that?"

"Belongs to the club."

Jimmer grinned. "Perfect."

It was. I slapped the Sig in his palm, lifted the 870, and took aim.

Dietz scrambled back. "What the fuck are you doing?"

"Proving a point." I squinted. "I don't wanna blow it up. Where should I put the first one?"

"Gas tank is back half of the driver's side. How 'bout takin' out the side window?"

"Sweet." I braced the buttstock inside the ball of my right shoulder, locked my knees against the kick-back, and pulled the trigger.

Crack. Glass shattered. My ears rang. I wandered around to the right side and shot out the other back window to keep things symmetrical. Put a bullet in the front right quarter panel, reloaded three more shells, put another in the left front quarter panel, and two in the tailgate.

Jimmer didn't say a word when I swapped the shotgun for my 9mm and continued shooting.

I destroyed the headlights. And taillights. And fog lights. Eying the driver's side, I considered marking it with the letter *J*, but ultimately settled for *H* on both doors.

"Nice touch," Jimmer said.

"Thanks. Think he'll be pissed?"

"Oh, yeah. But I know that's how you like him best."

I grinned.

Jimmer motioned Dietz over. "I'm keepin' the gun. You tell *Mr.* Martinez I'll be in touch."

"That's it?"

"You want some more of me, boy?"

"No."

"Then get yo ass goin'. Ya got plenty o' other shit to worry about besides who I'm havin' pie with."

Dietz zoomed off. Jesus. He'd be damn lucky if he didn't get pulled over by the highway patrol before he made it back to Rapid.

Not my concern.

I returned to my truck. Jimmer gave me a push

to get the back end out of the ditch. He scowled at the snow-covered junk poking out of the truck bed. "Don't you ever clean this shit out?"

"Never know when you might need something like a—"

"—pink emergency makeup case?" he asked snidely.

"No, a crowbar, a log chain, and bullwhip for smart-ass men who get out of line with me."

"You ain't half as scary as you pretend to be."

"Wanna hear something really scary?" I belted out the chorus to *Cherry Pie* by Warrant.

Jimmer laughed until tears rolled down his face.

Then he followed me to the Road Kill Café for a slice of the real thing.

CHAPTER 19

THE LUNCH RUSH WAS OVER AND WE WERE THE ONLY ones in the joint.

Jimmer wolfed his pie. He'd started with cherry, eaten a slice of apple, and finished with blueberry. Red, American, and blue, baby; the man even ate patriotically.

I smoked, filling him in on all the not-so-fun stuff in my life. "So, Dad's not talking to me—nothing new—but I guess he's not talking to Trish either." I sipped my coffee. "What's your take?"

"Doug's a mean bastard. The hired guy pissed him off, he lost his temper and killed him." Jimmer shrugged. "Probably didn't mean to. Hid the body thinking it wouldn't be found for a coupla months. Then his ace detective daughter accidentally uncovers it and fucks all his plans nine ways 'til Sunday."

"Great."

Jimmer shoved the empty plate to the edge of the table. "So Kevin's found a new fuck buddy?"

"I wish. I suspect sweet thang is more than just a fling."

"Yeah? Why'd you say that?"

"Because Kev's being reckless, which is very un-Kevin-like, Jimmer. I'm pretty sure he's thinking of breaking some business rules to make her happy."

"No shit?"

"If that happens he and I are gonna have some big-ass problems."

"As far as the business is concerned? Or personally?"

I scowled at him. "What do you think?"

"You jealous of this baby chicklet, little missy?"

"No."

"What's she like?"

"Young. Pretty. Smart. Determined. A tall—"

"—blue-eyed blonde, strong-willed, yet with a hidden sweet side that makes the hardest men go all softhearted and protective?"

"Sounds like you already know her."

Jimmer leaned closer. "No, Jules, she sounds exactly like you."

That left me tongue-tied.

"Think on it. Give me a heads-up if it gets bad with Kev. I'll try to knock some sense into him, okay?"

"Okay."

He slid out and ruffled my hair. "Gotta run. You need anything, and I mean *anything*, you call me."

I smoked another cigarette, wondering when I'd hear from Martinez. My phone flashed and nearly vibrated off the table. Not him. Not yet, anyway. "Hello?"

Trish said, "I need to talk to you. Can I come over right now?"

"I'm not home. I'm at the Road Kill Café."

"Even better. Don't leave. I'll be right there."

Trish was true to her word. She scooted across from me five minutes later. Misty automatically brought her a cup of coffee. Weird to think Trish was a regular here, too.

"The county slapped Doug with a Disturbing the Peace."

"He's lucky."

"I don't know what he was thinking. It was so unlike him. I've never known him to beat on someone for no apparent reason."

My teeth sank into my tongue to keep from setting her straight. Then again, he *had* beat on me for no apparent reason, so her statement did have a bizarre ring of truth to it.

Trish sighed. "Everything is a mess. The kids are confused. I'm confused. Doug won't talk to me or to our minister. There's tons of work to be done and without a hired man, it's twice as hard on him."

"Is that your justification for thinking he didn't

have anything to do with Melvin's death? It would make extra work for him?"

Fire flashed in her eyes. "No. He wouldn't kill someone because it's against—"

"If you throw a Commandment at me as your reasoning for his innocence, I will walk out that door."

Her mouth shut.

Good. "Why was it so damn important for you to see me?"

"Because you have experience in this stuff."

"Meaning that I associate with jailbirds and murderers?"

Trish's back snapped straight. "Stop baiting me and quit being such a pain in the ass."

Whoa.

"And give me a damn cigarette." After she lit up, she sank back into the booth.

"I didn't know you smoked."

"I don't. I used to. I used to do a lot of things." She squinted at me through the smoke. "What I meant before you so rudely jumped to the wrong conclusion, was that you have experience in investigative work. I want to hire you."

Any time now Ashton Kutcher would jump out because I was being *Punk'd*, I just knew it.

Trish maintained a bland expression.

"No fucking way."

"Doug is too proud to ask you for help."

"He made it crystal clear he didn't trust me and he

didn't want my help."

"But I do. I need your help." She sucked in a mouthful of smoke and exhaled slowly. "Doug doesn't have to know."

"You want me to lie and sneak around?"

"Yep."

"Even if that lying and sneaking around reveals Dad killed Canter?"

"He didn't."

I stared at her giving her, a chance to recant.

She continued on, "I know you think the worst of him."

"Can you blame me?"

"No. That's why I've never pushed you to be part of his life. Which is why I'm confused you're willingly spending time with Brittney."

I shrugged.

"I'm not making excuses for his behavior, or offering explanations or apologies that aren't mine to give. But you have no idea how much he regrets what he did to you after your mother was killed."

I sparked a cigarette and realized one already smoldered in the ashtray.

"People lost in grief . . . everyone reacts differently. Some shut down. Some drink. Some become crusaders and some . . ." Trish's hazel eyes sought mine. "Some people lash out. With words or with—"

"—fists, or hangers, or whatever is handy?"

"Even that."

"Bullshit."

"Your mother's death devastated him."

"Please. He wasn't the only one, but you didn't see me whipping off my belt and using it on *him* to express my grief."

"He would've taken attention of any kind from you, Julie."

My mouth dropped open. "What the *fuck* are you babbling about?"

"Did you ever consider that he had *no one* to talk to? No clergyman. No extended family. You had Ben. And Kevin."

She was a fool. Dad could've talked to me, but instead he let his fists do the talking. And it didn't change the fact he'd started hitting me *before* Mom died, right around the time Ben showed up, so he had Trish completely fucking snowed. Jesus. How could she be so blind when it came to him?

"Every time he looked at you, he saw her, what he'd lost, and it was almost more than he could take."

Again, if Dad loved my mother so much, and I reminded him of her, it made even less sense that he beat me.

"In all the years we've been married, I've never heard Doug speak her name. Not once." She expelled a bitter snort. "The great love of his life and I didn't know her name until I ran across their marriage certificate in the safe."

I'd never considered that; I hadn't heard her name

either, not since the day I'd seen him crying as he'd repeated it over and over in absolute agony. She'd been just Mom to me. But Dad called her . . . not her real name, Annika, but a nickname . . .

Anka.

My breath stalled.

A memory floated in, an image of my father, looking up when my mother entered the room, absolute adoration in his eyes. Tugging her onto his lap as she laughed. Him peppering her face with kisses, repeating, "My Anka, my sweet, sweet Anka." Then more kissing and mommy/daddy stuff that made me flee the room with my crayons and coloring book.

How in the hell had I forgotten that?

Because you've blocked out the good and the bad memories.

A sanctimonious voice countered: *Yeah? Well, it's his fault because the mean bastard sullied them all.*

Hello, Bipolar Disorder.

Trish continued, "Your middle name is after her?"

"A shortened version." Childish, but I couldn't stand to hear Trish say her name. Ever. "Look, we're off track. What is it you want from me, Trish?"

"Help in figuring out what is going on."

"And if I don't want to help?"

"You will."

"Why would you think that?"

"You're not as coldhearted as you want me and everyone else to believe."

I squirmed. She was wrong. What would it take

to prove I really wasn't like everyone else? Or anyone she knew? That I always followed my own agenda, be it good or bad?

The bell above the front door jangled and for some reason I looked up and saw Tony amble in.

Speaking of bad . . . how had he found me so fast?

Jimmer. That rat bastard. Last time I'd buy him pie.

Screw Martinez if he thought I'd cower in the corner like a Chihuahua. I kept my eyes on his and a brittle smile on my lips.

He said, "Hey, baby doll, scoot over." Once he'd invaded my space, he kissed me. Not a sweet little peck; a real tonsil scratcher. Then he bestowed a dazzling grin upon Trish. "You must be Brittney's mother."

She was absolutely poleaxed. "Ah, yeah."

"I'm Tony."

"Ah. Hi. Tony."

Misty plodded over with a cup. "Mr. Martinez! Nice to see you again."

"Good to be here, Misty. Just coffee today, thanks."

All three hundred pounds of Misty floated off in the glow of Martinez's megawatt smile.

Jerk.

Trish was staring at him. Half-drooling, really, which pissed me off.

Finally, she managed a small measure of composure.

"So, you know Brittney?"

"Heckuva card player. She's kicked my butt in Crazy Eights a time or two when she's been at our place."

"Our place?" Trish repeated.

"Technically it's Julie's house, but I'm always there."

I bit back my retort, *not lately*, when Tony squeezed my thigh under the table as a warning.

"Oh. I didn't know you lived together."

"Really? We've been together for what? Almost nine months?"

"Eight."

"Time flies in a vacuum, doesn't it? Pass me the sweetener, would ya, sugar?"

Sugar?

Martinez doctored his coffee, chatting with Trish like it was old home week. "Julie's been reluctant to introduce the rest of her family. Which is unfair since my brothers know all about her and every crazy thing she does. She's a real pistol."

Oh, fuck.

Trish said, "Maybe you'd like to come over for dinner sometime?"

No no no.

"Pick the day and I guarantee we'll be there, won't we?"

He'd have to kill me first. And then drag my body behind his Harley.

Trish slipped out of the booth and zipped her parka. "Nice to meet you, Tony. I'll be in touch soon, Julie. Thanks."

Before Trish was out the door I hissed, "*Sugar?* Move your smarmy ass out of my way, Martinez, before I kick it."

"Not on your fucking life, blondie. You and I are gonna have a little chat."

"Yes, I will accept your apology along with a really expensive gift."

"Wrong. I had an interesting morning."

"Bully for you. Mine was the usual."

"Shooting the fuck out of stuff isn't *the usual* even for you."

"No, I meant the usual, I woke up alone again."

"Not touching the 'alone' comment, because technically, you weren't supposed to be alone."

"Technically if you aren't in *our* bed or *our* place I am alone, so try again, bucko."

He muttered something in Spanish.

"English."

"Fine. Let's start when Dietz calls PT and says he's blown the surveillance on you on the first fucking day. Then PT calls me, suggesting I haul ass to the clubhouse.

"So, Dietz rolls up in the bullet-riddled Toyota, and throws himself at my feet, begging for mercy, blubbering about my psycho old lady and your equally psycho sidekick. Meantime, my entire fucking security team is practically rolling on the ground laughing, *laughing* at what you've done to the goddamn car."

"Were you laughing?"

"No. Not then. Not now."

Damn.

"Your safety isn't something I joke about. Ever."

"Then you shouldn't have sent a dumb ass like Dietz to follow me. Besides, I warned you what I'd do if you sent spies after me again."

"And now, all the Hombres know you'll follow through on your threats. Not a bad way to get your point across. But that doesn't change the basic fact—"

"—that you sent someone to protect me and you still won't tell me why I need protection?"

Silent tough guy moment.

"Am I in danger?"

"You wouldn't be if you'd let me protect you."

"From what?"

Another no answer moment to add to the others.

"I don't need your protection. I can take care of myself."

We still hadn't made eye contact.

I'd done nothing wrong, and yet, I knew I'd crack first. My fingers twisted in the chain of my necklace. "It wasn't my intention to make problems for you in front of your brothers."

"Problems? Now the main problem is those brothers—mostly members of my security team—have started a Julie Collins fan club. They'd rather be protecting you than me, because apparently, you're more trouble."

"What?"

He faced me. "I know you can take care of yourself. That's why I'm pissed off. You take chances you shouldn't."

"You trying to protect me from myself?"

"Always." He threaded his fingers through my hair and brought my mouth closer to his.

My breath quickened in anticipation of a kiss he denied me.

"Paybacks are a bitch, blondie."

"Yeah? Bring it."

"Let's see if that 'fuck you' attitude holds after we have dinner with your dad." He teased his lips across mine. "Don't forget to clean your gun tonight."

Before I responded, he slid out of the booth, handed Misty a twenty, and stormed out into the storm.

Head to the office and fight with Kevin? Go to the ranch and fight with Dad? Choices, choices.

I finished my smoke and was about to leave when Don Anderson and Dale Pendergrast stomped in. They looked around, spied me, and—yippee! new companions joined me for the third time.

"Julie, girl, how you holdin' up?" Don asked as he sat across from me.

"All right, I guess."

"Shore was a shock that Doug ended up in a heap-in' pile of trouble yesterday."

Misty brought more coffee.

Don said, "I still can't believe he took a swing at BD."

Dale snorted. "BD had it comin'. Actin' all holier-than-thou, deacon of the church shit, after he'd been caught knockin' boots with the church secretary."

"What?"

"Big scandal, surprised you din't hear about it," Don said.

Recently I'd spent way more time in bars than behind stained-glass ones. "I'm a quart low on county gossip. What's going on?"

"You know your daddy and BD go to the same church? A month or so back, Doug stumbled on BD and Beth McClanahan doin' it in the vestibule."

"No."

"Yep." Don leaned forward. "Doug demanded BD get tossed offa the church council. BD pulled the whole Jimmy Swaggart 'I've sinned' line of bull; told everyone if God can forgive his trespasses everyone else oughta, too. And they did."

Stupid self-righteous religious bastards oughta swing from the rafters themselves.

"Which means, BD dropped extra cash in the collection plate and got off scot-free," Dale said slyly.

"What happened to the secretary?"

"Fired."

"How's that fair?" I demanded.

"It ain't, but it was Doug's idea she get canned. Take it up with him."

"So you think the fight between Dad and BD at Bevel's had something to do with that?"

"Prolly. 'Course, it don't help matters none that your stepmom and BD had some words a month back 'fore your daddy caught BD with his pants down."

These guys were gossipy as old hens. I considered how I could use it to my advantage. I sighed dramatically. "That doesn't clear up anything."

Don's ears perked up. "Anything we can do to help?"

Act reluctant.

I glanced around. "Promise this won't go any further than us?"

They both nodded vigorously.

"Didn't you guys tell me the day of Brittney's accident that few people would be upset because Melvin was dead? You have any idea who?"

Don and Dale exchanged a look.

"My dad's stubborn and figures if he's done nothing wrong he doesn't have nothing to worry about. We know the legal system doesn't work that way." Felt shitty to lie, but I did anyway. "Especially not in this county."

"She's got a point, Dale," Don said.

Dale refused to meet my eyes and clammed up.

I soldiered on, hoping to shake loose the pearls of wisdom from his tongue. "Anyone could've put that body on the Collins Ranch. What I'd like to know is who had a reason to."

"And if your daddy is guilty? What then?"

"Then I'll do the right thing."

"Even if the right thing's already been done, but it ain't the legal thing?" Dale asked cagily.

Did I look as confused as I felt?

Misty refilled coffee cups and coerced them each into ordering a piece of rhubarb crumble à la mode.

I gathered my stuff and handed them each a business card. "You think of anything, call me. Or stop by if I'm home. I'm not like my dad, guys. I don't know if you think that's a good thing or a bad thing, but it is a true thing."

I paid for their snack and tipped Misty big, hoping it would pay off in the long run.

CHAPTER 20

I SKIPPED A TRIP TO THE RANCH AND DROVE TO THE office.

No Kevin—just a note:

Jules—tried your cell earlier, no answer. I'm going to Pierre. Be back in a couple days. Need anything, call me on my cell—K

Pierre? What the fuck? I tossed his file folders for new contracts or deposit slips but found nothing.

As long as I was in Kevin's office, I used his computer. I opened the *Bear Butte County Gazette* online and scoured the obituaries for preliminary information on Melvin Canter. Survivors included his mother, Mary, and brother, Marvin. Huh. Pretty scant info. But I knew where to look for more.

Shoes off, coffee in hand, I typed the pertinent info and waited for the machine to do the work.

I don't know what I expected to turn up. Few people had endless enemies sworn to vengeance. Most fatal acts were impulsive, which didn't bode well for my father.

The program was taking forever to load. Damn cold weather affected everything. I stood to refill my coffee and the scent of Shalimar preceded Kim through the reception area.

"Hey, hot mama, long time, no see. You look good." No lie. Without makeup her creamy skin had an extra glow, and her auburn hair held a mirrorlike sheen, even clamped in a messy bun. Kim defined Earth Mother and dressed the part in hunter green corduroy pants and a tan woolen sweater, which covered her baby bump.

Kim grumbled, "Why is it that even the *smell* of coffee makes me have to pee? I'll be right back."

"I'm working in Kevin's office."

Kim sagged into the chair. I might kid her, but she wasn't to the waddling stage. Yet.

"How you feeling?"

"Tired. I hate being tired all the time. The Lamaze coaches tell me it's in preparation for after the baby arrives. Guess I won't get much sleep then, either."

"Bummer." Since I couldn't smoke around Kim my need increased exponentially. "How's business?"

"Slow. I'm beginning to think hair doesn't grow in South Dakota in February. Nails, either. The only person making any money is the masseuse and that's mostly because I'm her biggest customer. Damn back pain. I'll probably have hours of back labor."

"How's the heartburn?"

"Like an inferno. If I never eat another Tums it'll be too soon. But enough about me. What's new with you, sugar?"

Sugar. Reminded me of Martinez and I gritted my teeth. "The usual. Finding dead bodies, trying to shoot my problems, problems meaning situations with my dad, Kevin, Martinez, Brittney, and . . . am I forgetting something?" I paused. "Nope. That must be it."

Kim rolled her good eye; the glass one stayed in place. "You could've just said nothing, Jules."

How I wished to merrily smile and say nothing. Instead, I zoomed off on a tangent about what'd gone down on the ranch with Doug, and then Trish demanding my help.

"You aren't considering helping him, are you?"

I shrugged. Didn't count if Trish asked for my help, right?

"He deserves jail time."

"Given the chance, would you put your dad in jail, Kim?"

"In a New York minute."

"This isn't the same. He shouldn't go to jail now for what he did to me then. I'm not so sure he's guilty.

"They're always guilty."

A strange silence descended.

"So you came here to fight with me?" I asked with

saccharine sweetness.

"No. Murray said when you dropped by my place you mentioned you were due for a haircut."

"A lie I made under duress. I'm surprised he even remembered." I sipped coffee. "Maybe you should've bought him a robe for Valentine's Day instead of golf clubs."

She flapped her left hand. In dim light the gigantic diamond on her ring finger flashed like a beacon. "He's confident in his masculinity." She granted me a catlike grin. "As he should be."

"You set the big date yet?"

"That's one of the reasons I'm here. We're flying to Vegas the end of this month. His best man will meet us there, and we'll hold the ceremony on the twenty-ninth."

"Please tell me you haven't chosen an Elvis impersonator to marry you?"

"Lawd, Julie. We do have *some* class. We're getting hitched at the Star Trek Experience."

I choked on my Folgers.

Kim laughed. "Gotcha. We've narrowed it down to the Venetian. Better book your plane tickets and hotel room soon."

"Good idea. Hey, I'll talk to Kevin's new fuck buddy. She's a travel agent. Maybe she can get me an I'm-shagging-your-partner discount."

"Fuck buddy? That's crude, even for you."

So, I blasted her eardrums on what constituted

crude office behavior. When I finished, she wasn't leaping on the Julie's-always-right bandwagon like she normally did.

"Is this Amery person in Pierre with him?"

"I don't know." Why didn't I? As his business partner, wasn't I supposed to know?

Kim's palm made continual circles on her belly. "Is there a chance Martinez will come with you to the wedding?"

"I dunno. I'll ask."

"How are things going with him?"

"Shitty. He's mad at me. Again."

"Why?"

"Between his obligations and mine, we just can't seem to come to terms on where we're supposed to be together. Lately it's been hit-and-miss on us spending any time together at all. I get angry; he gets angry. Seems all we ever do is fight."

Kim didn't say anything; she just rubbed the magic ball that was her belly. Why was that so annoying? Almost like she constantly drew attention to the fact she was pregnant.

Christ. I needed a Marlboro in a bad way.

"What else is new with you?"

"I finally decided on a dress."

"Which one?"

"The ivory with the sweetheart neckline, the empire waist, and the layer of tulle down the back."

"I don't remember that one."

"It was next to the tangerine-colored strapless I liked for your dress."

My eyes narrowed. "Tangerine? As in orange? Eww. You aren't going to make me wear some butt-ugly bridesmaid's dress, are you?"

"No." She pushed out of the chair. "I'll tell you what. Why don't you forget the whole thing? You know, sharing the happiest day of my life? I'll find someone else to stand up for me in Vegas."

"What? I was kidding, Kim."

"No, you weren't."

She sighed. And rubbed her belly some more. She'd improved at the "pat your head and rub your tummy" exercise since she polished that bulge all the goddamn time—not that I'd comment since her sense of humor had vanished with her waistline.

"Lighten up. You can joke about Elvis but not a dress?"

"It's more than just a dress."

"Meaning what?"

"Meaning . . . do you miss hanging out with me, Julie?"

This was not headed in a good conversational direction. "Every damn day. Why?"

"You have any idea why we haven't spent much time together recently?"

Because everything changed when you knew I killed someone.

Kim didn't wait for my response; she answered,

271

"Because you are negative, cynical, and crude."

"You used to like that about me."

"You weren't like that all the time, Jules. You are now. You find something wrong with everyone and everything around you, no matter what it is."

I crossed my arms over my chest. Defensive? Yeah. So?

"Kevin's girlfriend died and instead of being happy he has the balls to start a new relationship, you're jealous as hell. And we both know you will go out of your way to sabotage it."

Wrong. But she was on a roll so I let her go.

"Why have you been hanging out at the ranch so much? You're kidding yourself if you think it has a damn thing to do with Brittney. She's using you, Julie, to test the boundaries with her parents. You're trying to prove you're worthy to both her and your father."

"I don't have the same daddy issues you do, Kim."

"Yes, you do. You just pretend you can handle it. I cut my dad out of my life like the cancer he is. You haven't. Do you really believe that if you help your father it'll erase all the horrible things he did to you? It won't. Nothing will.

"But rather than telling him to fuck off, like you'd do to anyone else who beat you like a dog, you run to the rescue, drowning in guilt and self-hatred for it. And then you turn your bitterness on the people who really do love and care about you. Kevin. Me. Martinez."

"That's not fair."

"It's the truth. Tony would do anything for you. What have you done for him? Besides keep him at arms' length? Why don't you believe he—or anyone else—could possibly love you? You sit up here, wallowing in worthless shit, dealing with dark aspects of human nature that don't allow you to believe in basic human happiness."

Wow. Those were some megadoses of self-righteousness in her prenatal vitamins. I waited; I knew she wasn't done. She'd probably saved the best for last.

"Are you ever gonna allow yourself to be happy?" Kim asked in her lilting Southern accent.

Count to ten, Julie. Think before you speak.

Fuck that.

"Yes. I'll be extremely fucking happy when I don't have to hear Zen happiness lectures from you, Kim. Jesus."

She flinched.

"And since you don't want me, the little black cloud of doom, sullying your perfect wedding day, maybe you oughta see if Kathie Lee Gifford will beam sunshine by your side as you float down the aisle. She's performing in Vegas. Bet she'd even sing some sappy tune."

"Julie, I didn't mean—"

"Yes, you did. Accept me for who I am, Kim. Accept that I'm not the one who's changed; you are."

I lit up. That'd get rid of her fast.

Kevin's computer beeped, signaling my records search ended. "If you'll excuse me, I have some worthless shit to

273

wallow in."

I spun in the office chair, hoping this insipid conversation was at an end, too.

I didn't hear her leave but I knew she was gone.

I suspected I'd have lousy concentration but the information on the screen was disturbing enough to make me forget yet another argument in my life.

Pertinent info on the dead guy. Melvin Canter, forty-four, born in Sturgis. Graduated from Sturgis Brown High School. Joined the U.S. Army at age twenty. Honorably discharged four years later. No marriage certificates. Spotty employment records, mostly janitorial work. The long stretches between employments usually meant incarceration.

I kept reading. Yikes. Melvin Canter wasn't just a registered sex offender; he was a convicted sex offender. Three counts of sexual assault over a twenty-year period, filed in three states. None in South Dakota. Melvin did five years in Nevada for the last conviction. He'd moved back here in November. As far as I could tell, he'd registered in Meade County, not Bear Butte County.

That was a no-no. But why hadn't Sheriff Richards said anything to me or Dad about Melvin's sex offender status?

It appeared Melvin used his brother's address to register, when in fact, Don and Dale told me Melvin lived with his mother in our small county.

Could it be that Dad hadn't known about the convictions when he'd hired Melvin? And later he'd found out? Was that why they'd fought in Chaska's Feed Store?

How was I supposed to get answers to what'd gone down, if I couldn't ask Dad about it? I picked up the phone anyway and dialed the ranch.

Brittney answered. "Hello?"

I hadn't spoken to her since her accident. "Hey, girl."

Pause. "You're really mad at me, aren't you?"

Yes. "That was a stupid stunt you pulled."

"I knew you'd say that. I knew you'd chew me out first thing instead of being nice and understanding."

Another count-to-ten moment in my life. The fact she wasn't the least bit sorry for all the trouble and worry she'd caused not just me, but everyone else, bothered me. "Is Dad around?"

"No, he and DJ went someplace. Did you wanna talk to my mom?"

"No, actually, I'd like to talk to you."

"I should've known the only reason you called was to lecture me."

Talk about surly. "This isn't about lecturing you. This is about the hired hand, Melvin Canter."

Her immediate silence was disturbing. Now that I

275

thought about it, she'd been unnaturally quiet the last time I'd brought up his name.

"Britt?"

"I know you found him after I wrecked the tractor . . . and I . . ."

"What?"

"I'm glad he's dead."

A shiver ran up my spine. "What? Why?"

After a ten-second hesitation, she blurted, "I might go to hell for saying that, but I was so happy when he didn't show up for work. I didn't like him. At all. He was creepy and icky and had these weird googly eyes that would follow you around all the time. Me and DJ hated doin' chores with him. Hated it."

My nonresponse made her backtrack.

"I'm sorry; I shouldna said that. You're probably thinking—"

"I'm thinking there's no rule that says you have to like everyone."

"There is in our family."

Everyone but me apparently. I said, "What do you mean?"

A suspicious, "You won't blab to my mom what I said?"

"No. Why?"

"'Cause she gets sorta mad about that kinda stuff and starts lecturing me about Christian charity."

"Really?"

"If I complained about working with him, she blew

a fuse. Then she demanded I find something nice and positive to say about him. It was really hard to do, because he wasn't a nice man at all." She sighed. "The only good thing was Dad didn't have a lot of work for him, so he wasn't around all that much."

"This is going to sound creepy and snoopy, but did Melvin ever make sexual comments to you?"

No response.

In for a penny; in for a pound. "Did he ever touch you inappropriately? Or try to touch you, especially when it seemed like he was helping you do chores?"

More silence.

"Did he try to get you alone?"

Breezily, Brittney said, "I don't gotta clue to what you're talkin' 'bout. And it kinda makes me mad you'd call me up just to ask gross stuff like that. Are you trying to make me feel worse? Because it's working." She sniffed. Loudly.

What a manipulative kid. She didn't stand a chance of lying to me face to face, or dodging my questions with emotional blackmail. I'd give her a couple of days before I forced the issue. "I'll drop it for now, but if you need to talk, call me. So, you all healed?"

"Pretty much. I still get headaches. I thought since I'd gotten hurt you'd show up here to take me out for ice cream or something. But I guess you're too busy."

I ground my teeth. It seemed the more I did for her, the more she expected.

"You want me to have Dad call you back?"

277

"No. In fact, don't even tell him I called."

"Okay. See you."

"Not if I see you first."

She giggled, but it didn't make me smile like usual.

I closed the office and implemented the "catch people off guard" line of thinking by heading to Fat Bob's. My rearview didn't pick up a tail. Didn't mean one wasn't there, just meant he was sneakier than Dietz.

My lifetime ban on hanging in the biker bar ended when the reign of Harvey, the Hombres former enforcer, ended. The bouncers waved me through. By the time I'd reached the door to the back room, Big Mike leaned against the wall.

His gigantic grin was a thing of beauty. "Nice shootin' earlier." His voice dropped to a whisper. "And if you tell bossman I said that, I'll deny it."

I mimed zipping my lip.

"He didn't tell me you were coming."

"He doesn't know." I skirted a bartender rolling an empty keg out of the walk-in cooler. "It's a surprise."

"Ah, he ain't one for surprises, but I'm sure he'll be appreciative after he's done with his meeting." Big Mike paused outside the steel door to the private suite.

"Then again, maybe it'd be best if you chilled at the bar with a beer until he's finished. Shouldn't be long."

"Who's he meeting with?"

He shrugged and looked away.

And then I knew. Tony was meeting with a woman.

Curiosity made the cat . . . catty. I pounded on the door.

The profusion of locks snapped. No-neck poked his head out and glared at Big Mike. "Didn't he tell you—"

"You didn't tell me," I said sweetly. "I'm the one huffing and puffing on his door."

"Julie. He's in a . . . a meeting. Maybe you should—"

"—do the same thing to this door that I did to the 4Runner today? I'd let me in if I were you. Right. Fucking. Now."

Big Mike muttered *shit* behind me as I strolled inside.

A leggy brunette almost dressed in a slinky scarlet cocktail dress was perched provocatively across from my man. They pored over stacks of papers on the coffee table, an open bottle of red wine and two half-empty glasses between them.

Martinez looked up, annoyed. "I said no—"

"You never say no to me, sugar." I bent down, kissing him exactly like he'd kissed me in front of Trish. "Thought I'd pop by and say hello. See if you had any more car problems."

His gaze threatened to char my retinas.

When I straightened, I feigned surprise at seeing the sexpot. "Oops, sorry, I didn't notice you. I'm Julie."

"Maddie."

I skipped the "nice to meet you" bullshit as I'd focused all my attention on Tony, gifting him with a sultry smile. "I won't bug you. What time will you be home tonight? Should I plan dinner?"

"No. It'll be late."

"Mmm. Too bad." I gave him another long kiss. "But I'll wait up. See you." I sauntered out and didn't look back.

Kim was wrong. Lots of things made me happy. In fact, I was feeling much happier already.

CHAPTER 21

My cell phone jolted me from deep sleep. I mumbled, "Hello?"

"Julie. It's Big Mike."

Big Mike? What the hell? Big Mike never called me unless Martinez was unexpectedly called out of town.

Not again. "What's up?"

"Bossman wants you to come to Bare Assets."

I yawned. "When?"

"Ah. Now."

"What's he doing there instead of Fat Bob's?"

"Business. He wants to see you."

I waited a beat. "Why?"

Silence.

"Christ. Is he pissed about me showing up at Fat Bob's earlier? It was supposed to be a funny payback after what he did to me! Why should I—"

"Don't bite my head off. I'm just doing what I was told."

"Why isn't he calling me himself if he's so hot to see me?"

"Because he's occupied with another matter." Big Mike paused, staying calm in light of his boss's girl-friend's bitchy attitude.

The clock on the DVD player read 11:10. My gaze swept my darkened living room but I couldn't remember why I'd fallen asleep on the couch rather than my bed. Waiting for Martinez, probably. At least I was still dressed and sober. I swung my feet to the floor. Cold air bit into my ankles, clearing the fuzziness from my brain.

"So, can I tell him you're coming or what?"

"Yeah. I'll be right there."

Big Mike expelled a sigh. "Good. Park in the private lot and come to the back door. About half an hour, then?"

"Roughly."

He hung up without another word, mimicking Martinez's phone manners to the letter.

I grabbed an extra pack of cigarettes and a Diet Pepsi before I bundled up in my subzero coat and winter wear. Damn arctic weather. I'd gladly welcome global warming when the thermometer on the porch displayed a glacial four degrees.

No moon made the sky an inky black. The absolute stillness in the air defied logic; the wind always blew in South Dakota, but I was grateful the windchill factor wasn't in the forty-below range. My boot steps made a *squeak* rather than a solid *crunch* as the thick tread of my sole broke through the snowy crust.

Took forever for my truck to heat up. I was so damn cold I didn't even fire up a smoke on the trek into Rapid City.

Bare Assets was hopping on a frigid February weeknight. The second I stepped over the chain separating the private lot from the alley behind the bar, Bucket materialized from the shadows.

I gasped like a horror movie queen. "You scared the crap out of me!"

Bucket looked like the Grim Reaper, acted like him, too: silent, watchful, and deadly. Black skullcap. Black trench coat. Big black boots. He carried at least one gun under the duster and probably a couple of knives. A Taser. The shudder rolling through me wasn't entirely from the cold.

Bucket didn't utter a peep—nothing new for him. He merely beat on the door four times with his gloved fist.

The door swung open and Big Mike popped his head out. His warm breath cut the night air in a cloud of white steam. He and Bucket exchanged a nod before he thoroughly scanned the parking lot. "Come on upstairs."

Bucket followed me inside, securing the service entrance behind us.

Big Mike unlocked the steel door to the staircase.

Being a big man, his heavy footfalls should've echoed down the short hallway as loudly as a buffalo stampede. But his boots made a soft *shush shush* on the Berber carpet. Why did the sounds seem magnified times ten?

He stopped in front of the door to Martinez's private suite and knocked, four solid raps, just like Bucket had done downstairs.

Weird. I'd never seen anyone on this level of the club, let alone anyone near Martinez's residence. Why didn't Big Mike—or anyone else—have keys to these rooms? Especially with all the damn locks and the rigid security measures?

Anxiety rippled up my spine.

The door opened. Big Mike let me pass through first. I was starting to get creeped out, not from the safety precautions—those, I was used to—but from the unspoken tension.

After Big Mike secured the room by snapping the half-dozen locks on another reinforced steel door, he spun around.

The wariness in his eyes scared the shit out of me. "What?"

"Julie, I have to tell you something. But I need your promise you won't freak out."

Then I knew why Tony hadn't called me: something had kept him from calling me.

"What happened?"

"Can you stay calm?"

"Tell me right fucking now what the fuck is going on. Where's Martinez?"

Big Mike and No-neck exchanged a look. Then Big Mike said, "Keep your voice down. You should sit." He gestured to the rumpled cushions of the sectional in front of the TV.

"The fuck I will." I marched up to Big Mike and got right in his face. "Tell me what happened."

"Tony was shot tonight."

Everything went blurry. My knees buckled. Big Mike caught me. I couldn't hear beyond my mental shrieks of NO NO NO and the instant vertigo. Someone dragged me to the loveseat and forced me to sit.

My innards ripped like I'd swallowed a studded snow tire stuck on spin. Black spots wavered behind my eyelids. I couldn't suck enough air into my lungs. I tried to put my head between my knees but the jack-knife position gouged my stomach.

A voice next to my ear said, "Breathe. Slow and easy. Don't pass out on me, Julie. Come on. Tough it up."

"Is he . . ." I couldn't make myself think it, let alone say it out loud.

"No."

My head snapped up and I blinked through the head rush. "Then where is he?"

"In the bedroom."

I tried to stand.

Big Mike's enormous palms clamped over my

shoulders and held me down. "First you need to listen to me."

I stared at him, unable to speak.

"Here's a brief rundown of his injuries. He was shot in the right thigh, above his kneecap. Another bullet grazed his ribs. The doctor's been with him the last couple of hours, monitoring him since he removed the bullet from his leg."

"So it's not serious enough to send him to the hospital?"

"It is serious. But we can't take him to the hospital—"

"Why the hell not?"

"Because cops ask questions about gunshot wounds."

Shit. "The Hombres doctor is a real doctor?"

"Yes, he's fully licensed, a full-fledged Hombres member, and he makes house calls. He's patched Tony up before."

Not the last time you'll deal with this, Julie.

"He's done everything he can. Tony was just making him wait for—"

"For what?"

Big Mike studied me for several long seconds. "For you."

"What? Me? Why me?"

"He refused to take any painkillers until he saw you first."

"Oh, Jesus." I remembered the agony from the

bullet wounds I'd received last fall and my thigh throbbed in response.

"I'll take you in to see him, but I need your promise you can hold it together until he takes the meds."

"But—"

"No buts." His blue eyes glinted a warning. "I'm not kidding. He has enough to worry about without worrying about you."

I nodded and swayed to my feet. I shook off Big Mike's oh-so-helpful death grip on my bicep when we reached the doorway. No-neck shuffled aside. I swallowed my fear, pushed open the door, and froze just inside the jamb.

Martinez lay flat on his back on the left side of the gigantic bed. Someone had stripped the puffy covers from the mattress and flung them in the corner. A metal IV rack loomed next to the headboard like a silver skeleton. Martinez's face was ghostly pale against the white sheet; he looked dead.

The instant I cleared the threshold, his eyes opened and his gaze caught mine. "Blondie."

Don't cry. Jesus. Be strong.

"It's not as bad as it looks."

A small hiccupping gasp escaped my throat before I could stop it.

The doctor snorted. "Right. Luckily the bullet missed the femoral artery. If it would've gone half an inch to the left . . ."

Martinez would be in the morgue.

I reached his side of the bed and fell to my knees.

He was trying so goddamn hard to hide the pain from me I wanted scream at him for his macho stupidity. Instead, I took his hand and curled it around my face, like he always did.

I managed to keep my voice steady. "I'd be pissed off if the bullet would've hit just a little higher up and nicked something *really* important."

Martinez didn't respond with a cocky comment or a make-my-heart-race grin.

"Matching tattoos are passé, so you decided we needed matching bullet holes?"

His sole focus remained on me. His thumb absentmindedly stroked my cheek. His eyes held pain and pride and something else I couldn't place—either fear or relief.

I turned my head and softly kissed the inside of his forearm, fully aware we had an audience, fully aware neither of us were into public displays of affection. "So you're beyond a Big Bird bandage or me kissing it and making it better, huh?"

No response.

"If I promise to stay and plump your pillows and be your private wet nurse, will you promise to take the painkillers right now?"

"Julie—"

"Nonnegotiable point, Martinez."

He closed his eyes and nodded. Then he patted the open side of the bed with his free hand.

I looked at the doctor, a sixty-something hippie with long graying hair and washed-out eyes, for approval or denial.

He frowned at me. "I don't really think—"

"She stays. Right here. With me. Nonnegotiable," Martinez said with concentrated effort.

The doctor heaved a weary sigh and shrugged.

"Hang on a sec." I stripped off my coat and snow boots. I tugged the soft wool blanket from the pile of discarded bedclothes and carefully crawled beside him.

Martinez immediately reached for my hand and squeezed it.

I ached inside like he'd clamped his fist around my heart.

The doctor injected a needle into the Y tubing of his IV. The doc and Big Mike conversed in low tones. I propped myself on my side and smoothed the damp hair from Tony's forehead. His skin was always warm, hot almost, never this cold, clammy flesh. My stomach roiled; I fought back an upsurge of nausea.

The doctor leaned over Martinez. "You feel worse at any point, you call me. Don't be a tough guy, *hombre*."

Martinez whispered something in Spanish. The only word I understood was *gracias*.

The doctor left. Big Mike trailed behind him and stopped in the doorway. "I'll be right out here if you need anything. Anything at all."

"I'm fine," Martinez said.

Little did Martinez know Big Mike's comments

were addressed to me, not him. I nodded.

Martinez sagged deeper into the mattress when the door clicked shut.

"They're gone."

"Good."

I kept touching him, knowing it would appease his mind and his body and mine. "Tell me how you really feel, Martinez."

"Fuckin' hurts like a goddamn bitch."

"You should've taken the painkillers sooner."

"I couldn't."

I counted to ten. Then twenty. "Why not? Too much of a tough guy?"

"You should talk about being tough, blondie. But no, that wasn't it."

"What, then?"

Martinez brought my hand to his mouth and dragged soft kisses across my knuckles. "I hated hanging around, seeing you drugged up, waiting for you to regain consciousness. I didn't want to put you through that because it sucks."

Don't cry, Jesus, suck it up, Julie.

"While I appreciate that you were thinking of me, next time take the damn drugs, okay?"

"Okay."

I noticed he didn't dispute there wouldn't be a next time.

He sighed. "I was about to give in when I caught a whiff of you in the main room, so it didn't matter."

My hand stopped moving on his forehead. "A whiff? You saying I smell bad, Martinez?"

"No. I'm saying I'd recognize you blindfolded in a room of perfume salespeople."

"Are the drugs kicking in already? Because that was almost romantic, in a twisted way."

He muttered something in Spanish.

"English."

"Maybe it was meant to be romantic."

My mouth opened but I couldn't think of a single retort.

"Guilty as I felt about being apart from you for another night, I'm damn glad you weren't around when that motherfucker opened fire."

"Me, too. I might've done something stupid like step in front of a hail of bullets to save your sorry ass."

"Careful. I might consider that romantic."

I pressed a kiss to his chin. "Maybe it was meant to be."

No answer.

His breathing slowed. I forced myself to break his handhold and brushed my fingers down his jawline. "Rest. I'll be here when you wake up."

"Good." He shivered violently.

"Are you okay? You want me to call the doctor back—"

"No. Just cold. Come closer and warm me up."

"I don't want to hurt you."

"Right now, you couldn't make me feel any worse,

unless you left me."

Not fair.

After covering him completely with the blanket, I scooted under his arm and carefully laid my head on his chest. The tremors stopped almost immediately.

I was content to listen to him breathe—just because he still could.

About an hour later Big Mike poked his head in. I untangled from Martinez's arms, reluctant for anyone to see us curled up like kittens.

I snagged my cigarettes out of my purse and flopped back on the love seat. After the initial drag, I said, "What happened? Every goddamn detail."

Big Mike set a bottle of Don Julio and shot glasses on the coffee table next to my ashtray.

"Bossman was conducting some last-minute business in the bar. Something pissed him off so he headed in the back room to chill out and regroup. He opened the service door to go out to his Escalade for some damn thing . . . Cal and I were right on his heels when we heard the shots."

Definitely needed that drink. I poured a slug, knocked it back, welcoming the trail of fire down my throat.

"I dragged Martinez inside; Cal took off after the shooter. I got him upstairs, got temporary control of the bleeding, and called the doc." Big Mike poured a generous helping of tequila in a lowball glass. "One minute. That's all he was out of our sight. One. Fucking. Minute."

"Not a random act?"

He shook his head and stayed quiet, studying the silver liquid in the glass.

"This isn't gonna fly with me, Big Mike. I don't give a shit if it violates some stupid Hombres' rules, not when he's lying in the next goddamn room bleeding . . ." Cold reality hit. I gritted my teeth and forced myself to focus on facts, not emotions. "I have a right to know it all."

He said, "Shit," and slammed another glassful of tequila.

"You know who's responsible, don't you?"

"Yeah."

"Who?"

Big Mike's hard eyes met mine. "Jackal."

Jackal was the former Hombres enforcer. "I thought he was under lock and key while he's on probation?"

"He was."

"*Was?*"

"Last week he killed the guy working on his 'rehabilitation' and Jackal used him to send a warning to Martinez before Jackal disappeared."

293

"How? If the guy was dead?"

"Jackal wrote the message on a piece of paper and attached it to the guard, via a knife to the eyeball."

"Holy fuck." That was just plain sick. "Last week? Why didn't Martinez tell me instead of making some big goddamn deal about me keeping my cell phone on at all times?"

"Bossman didn't want you to worry, especially after . . ."

Especially after the trauma I'd gone through a few months back when I'd killed someone. Martinez stuck around to pick up the pieces and I still didn't feel whole.

"We immediately put extra security on him. Which was why he was so pissed off when you went missing during the blizzard. Why he sent Korny to your house when we left for Denver. Why he picked Dietz to keep an eye on you. Why he's been watching everyone who approaches you, especially if they're tied to the club in any way. Any man or woman."

Any man or woman tied to the club. "Oh, shit."

"What?"

"Remember the night I was in the bar fight at Dusty's? I was pretty drunk for a while there. Totally forgot I saw Nyla from the Hombres clubhouse. She sauntered up to our table, high as a kite, beat to shit, and babbled something."

"What?"

"Don't remember what exactly. Chalk it up to me being wasted."

"Did you see her again that night?"

"Nope."

"Who was she with?"

"Not a clue."

"Fucking awesome news, Julie." Big Mike rubbed his temple so vigorously I thought a genie might pop out. "And you didn't think you shoulda shared that with Martinez?"

"A: I was drunk. B: without being crude, Tony and I didn't do a whole lotta talking that night." Despite his bevy of bodyguards, Martinez made sure our sex life was a hundred percent private. "Oh, and C: Tony and I haven't spent time together at all recently so it hasn't come up. Why does it matter?"

Big Mike sighed. "Now that I know she was at your local bar, I wonder who else was there. I thought that fight seemed a little . . . staged."

"Staged? Umm. Hello? That woman actually punched me in the face."

"No, staged as in someone putting that woman up to starting the fight, someone watching to see how well you fought, and to see how quickly Martinez showed up. Or if at all."

"Oh." Come to think of it, even under the alcohol veil that feeling of being watched had bugged me the entire night. I'd attributed it to Martinez and his bodyguards. "Does Martinez know Jackal was involved tonight?"

He nodded.

"Who else knows?"

"On our end? Cal, Bucket, Buzz, me, the doc, and you. And the shooter."

"Jackal wasn't the shooter?"

"No."

"Then you know who the shooter was?"

"Yeah."

"Who?"

He threw back a shot of Mexico's finest and didn't answer.

"What's this about? Jackal's vengeance for the humiliating incident at the clubhouse?" A few months back Martinez had made a very public mess of Jackal's face when he'd stripped him of his Hombres position.

"Partially."

I waited for him to elaborate.

Tequila swilling silence ensued.

"You're not gonna tell me what's going on, are you?"

"Not all of it. But we do need your help."

I studied him through the thin line of smoke rising from my cigarette. "Exactly what kind of help would that be? Since I can't know the pertinent details and all that shit."

Big Mike paused, nervous, which made no sense, unless he planned on asking me to find the shooter.

Or hunt down Jackal so they could kill him.

I'd do either without hesitation. I'd stepped over the line of ethical behavior so many times in recent months it was faded and damn near invisible in spots. That made some decisions easier than others. "Do you want me to track Jackal?"

"Martinez would have my head on a spike for suggesting it, never mind actually putting you within a thousand feet of that sadistic bastard."

But Big Mike hadn't automatically said *no*. "Then why do you need my help?"

"Right now? We need you to lie low with him for a couple of days until he recovers. We'll tell everyone the two of you are out of town for the weekend."

On the practical side, Martinez couldn't show weakness in front of his Hombres brothers or his business competition. On the personal side, I wouldn't leave his side even if his bodyguards attempted to throw me out the third floor window.

"Won't employees get suspicious if they see the doctor going upstairs with medical supplies?"

"Doc brought the stuff I can't buy. He made me a list of what we need. I'll get it at Wal-Mart after the bar closes. He won't be checking on him every day."

"Why not? I don't know how to clean wounds or replace his IV—"

"I do," Big Mike said.

"You? How?"

"Army medic during Desert Storm. Trust me. If something happens I can't handle, I'll be the first one on the phone to the doc."

"Good." That made me feel better. I crushed out

297

my cigarette. "I'll make a grocery list. How many of you guys will be on guard?"

"Two. Me round the clock in here. Cal and Bucket will take turns outside." Big Mike slowly pushed to his feet. "Thanks for doing this for us."

I looked up at him. "It's for me as much as it is for him. I can't believe . . ." My gaze wandered to the bedroom door. Knowing what lay behind it, I closed my eyes against a tidal wave of tears. I drew my knees up to my chest and sank my teeth into my kneecaps to keep from sobbing hysterically.

Be strong. No crybabies allowed. You can do this. You have to do this. For him. For you.

When I lifted my head, Big Mike recognized my hard-won emotional battle and awkwardly patted my shoulder. "He's gonna be okay, Julie."

"Yeah?"

"Yeah, especially now that you're here."

"Did he doubt I'd show?"

"Not for a single second."

That made me want to start crying all over again.

CHAPTER 22

WE WERE ON DAY THREE OF FUSSING OVER MARTINEZ and everyone's patience was wearing thin.

I made myself scarce while Big Mike and No-neck herded Martinez into the shower. It was pointless to get upset over Tony not wanting my help. I understood his pride even when it stung mine.

Being stuck in these windowless rooms was taking a toll on me. I'd watched the third season of *Deadwood*. I napped. I cooked but couldn't eat much. I smoked. I obsessively checked on Martinez. Probably good he slept a lot. My fretting would set him on edge.

One thing I hadn't done was cry.

The bathroom door opened and I heard the clatter of metal crutches. Low male voices. Tony's snappish response. I hadn't asked how they'd explain

Martinez's injury after our supposed return from the long weekend. He wasn't healed. But if anyone could will himself to heal faster, it'd be him.

After the bedroom door closed, I trudged to the shower. The scent of Tony's woodsy shampoo and lime shaving cream lingered in the humid air. An odd sense of longing swamped me as I stripped. Although I'd scarcely left his side, it seemed I hadn't seen him for a week.

Had Tony felt that way during my stay in the hospital after the showdown with Leticia? It'd taken me weeks to find my balance.

Unfortunately, hot water didn't turn my restlessness into lethargy. I exited the bathroom in Martinez's oversized silk robe, expecting to hear the TV blaring as Hombres security killed time in the living room. But the suite was unexpectedly empty. The doors were locked with a note from Big Mike asking me to engage the dead bolts.

Huh.

I crept inside the darkened bedroom. A barechested Martinez sprawled in the middle of the mattress, a plain white sheet covering the lower half of his body. He'd shoved the pile of pillows over to my side of the bed. Typical. He hated pillows; he preferred to use me.

I watched him sleeping. Part of me didn't want to disturb him; part of me couldn't stomach twiddling my thumbs in the living room, especially if we were alone for the first time in days. Truth was, I needed to be near him. I tried not to jiggle the bed as I crawled on and tossed the pillows to the floor.

Martinez automatically tucked my body against his, twining his fingers in my hair so we were touching from head to toe.

I finally relaxed.

"So damn tired," he mumbled.

"I know."

"Stay."

"I am." I kissed a tattoo-free section of bronze skin above his nipple and closed my eyes.

A series of gunshots woke me.

Terror beat from every pore; my heart thumped like a subwoofer. Where was I?

I caught a whiff of antiseptic. Then I remembered. I was in the suite above Bare Assets, not in a dirty alley in Sturgis surrounded by the putrid scents of restaurant grease and vomit.

But where was Martinez? I shifted and my hand smoothed down a muscled torso I knew as well as my own.

The skin was slick with sweat, not blood. No holes in his gut. I squinted at him. His brown eyes weren't open and vacant with death. His lips weren't bloodless and parted in a final parody of surprise.

Squeezing my eyes shut didn't block the nightmare image: Jackal brandishing an old-fashioned pistol, laughing at my anguished shrieks as he emptied the cylinder into Martinez's chest. Laughing at my hair, my clothes, my skin, my soul, all awash in blood. Tony's blood.

The unshed tears poured out, grief so raw, so real, I was living that alternate universe. Even when Martinez's heart beat strong and steady beneath my ear, and his chest rose and fell beneath my palm, I couldn't make the dream fade.

Get control of yourself, Julie.

My tenuous hold on my emotions snapped like a cheap rubber band. I cried in silent misery, half-crazy with fear, half-dizzy with relief.

I couldn't fathom going through gut-wrenching pain again. How would I survive another loss in my life? Especially him? I couldn't. I'd break. I was damn close now.

Martinez's fingers tightened in my hair a second before he said, "Don't."

Instead of laughing off his stern warning, air left my lungs in a frightened stutter and I sobbed harder. His chest was slippery, as wet as my face. My fingernails left crescent-shaped marks on his pectorals as I clutched him.

"Julie."

"I-I'm—"

"Ssh."

"I-I c-can't—"

"Stop."

Tears blurred my vision. "I can't—"

"Try."

"Oh, God, I'm suffocating."

"Ssh, baby, just breathe."

"I can't stop thinking"—I swallowed hard and my voice came out a hoarse whisper—"that you could've died."

An oppressive pause settled between us.

"But I didn't."

His gruff denial didn't shame my tears into submission. In fact, it had the opposite effect. The harder I fought for control, the more elusive it became.

My whole body shook.

"Julie."

Breathe. In. Out.

"Calm down."

A hiccupping cry escaped. "I can't be calm because you can't promise me you won't die. You can't promise this isn't the last time someone will try to kill you."

Tony's soothing circular caresses in the center of my spine stopped.

I gulped air. My salty tears and inability to suck enough oxygen into my lungs reinforced the sensation I was drowning.

"Blondie."

I burrowed into the spot where his arm and torso connected, searching for his warmth, using his flesh as a sound barrier, finding his scent as a balm to prove he was real.

"Look at me."

No.

He tugged my hair, gently at first. When I wouldn't budge, he pulled harder, trying to force my head back.

"I said: *Look. At. Me.*"

Slowly, I raised my chin and met his eyes.

Martinez placed his palm on my cheek, using his thumb to wick away the moisture from my face. He curled his hand around the back of my neck to urge me closer. "No more. Hit me. Jesus. It'd hurt less than wearing your tears."

"I can't—"

Then his mouth was on mine. Not the gentle communing of souls kiss I expected. But hunger. The need he showed only to me. He hauled my torso higher, alongside his.

The sensations of his taste, his scent, his warmth flowed over me as I let him lead us where we both wanted to go, understanding the importance of him proving to me he could still take us there.

In the silence of the room, his rough-skinned hands made a loud scratching sound on the delicate silk as he slid it down my body on the outside of the robe.

His lips moved to my ear. "Take it off."

"Tony, you're—"

"Fine." He tugged on the sash until the knot gave way.

"But I'll hurt you."

"Only if you say no." Hot, sweet, wet, hungry kisses tracked my throat, making me tremble and arch against him. "God. Please don't say no. I need this."

Not, I need *you*.

I went rigid, even when certain parts of my body had already gone pliant and damp with anticipation.

"*You* need this."

The damn tears started again. He knew me so well.

Martinez kissed me as he peeled the robe away, baring me completely to his expert touch. He flattened his palm on my left hip and leisurely followed the bend in my waist up to my rib cage. His fingertips idly caressed the underswell of my breast. Rubbing his lips over mine in a seductive, wet glide, he murmured, "I'm not dead, blondie."

"But—"

"But if you don't stop crying and put your hands on me right now, I might actually kill you."

I managed a laugh and he kissed the corners of my mouth. Only he had the ability to change my mood from fear to fire so quickly.

After drugging me with more soul-stealing kisses, he pressed his forehead to mine. "Not so easy being on the other side of the sickbed, is it?"

"No." I slid my mouth over his freshly shaven cheek, letting my hot breath flow into his ear, eliciting his deep shiver. Then I nipped his lobe with my teeth. "I prefer to be on top anyway."

"How well I know that."

I teased him with little whips of my tongue on the muscles straining in his throat while I eased the light-weight fabric sheet from his injured thigh. My lips mimicked the path my fingers created, trailing from his neck down his torso, leaving a sweet, breathy kiss on the wound on his rib cage, gradually making my way across the muscles quivering in his belly to his right hip, down to where the gauze covered his wound. I circled a string of kisses around the bandage.

He hissed.

"You sure this won't hurt you?"

"No."

Not the answer I wanted. My gaze connected to his across his battered body.

"But I'd rather take the chance it'll hurt than play it safe and feel nothing."

I had to look away.

He relaxed into the mattress, giving me control. It humbled me, having this man's unwavering trust. I used my hands, my mouth, my constant caresses to create his mindless pleasure. I took him over the edge and greedily returned for more, gorging on the dark, raw taste of him. Fueling my need with his.

"Julie."

"Ssh. Let me."

By the time he was hard and ready for round two, a desperate-edged hunger crackled between us like lightning.

And still I would not be rushed. Or denied my prize.

I straddled his pelvis, careful to keep my knee from nicking either his injured rib or his leg and putting an end to this before it began.

Aligning his sex with mine, I played a game of tease and retreat. Recently our trysts were fast, intense, and frequent—not that I had any complaints—but I craved the unhurried, sweet intimacy we'd denied ourselves in our usual blaze of lust-fueled passion.

"Julie. Please."

Was I hurting him? I quit moving. "Want me to stop?"

"No."

"What?"

"You don't need to go slow for me."

I paused. "Maybe I need to go slow for *me*."

He said nothing.

I studied him, bared before me. The tiny beads of sweat formed on his brow. The arc of his long, dark eyelashes. The warm breath expelled from his nose in shallow bursts. The slash of color across his high cheekbones. The set of his jaw and mouth, especially the ripeness of his lips. His face was a perfect mix of male ferocity and masculine beauty—an iron-willed man. A man strong enough for me.

Was I strong enough to bare everything to him?

I planted my hands flat on the mattress beside his head, angling my body so we were face to face as well as skin to skin.

"Tony. Look at me."

His lashes fluttered and he locked his gaze to mine. Everything I'd ever wanted was right there in his eyes.

"I'm done playing it safe with you."

He cradled my face in his shaking hands. "Meaning what, blondie?"

"Meaning, I love you." One push and he was buried deep inside me. I kissed him with the zeal I always did, but it seemed different. Truer somehow.

Martinez groaned. His hands slid over my skin and clamped on my ass as I rocked into him. The world fell away.

And oddly enough, my world finally felt right.

After Martinez dozed off, I ventured into the living area for a cigarette. Big Mike knocked four times and I let him back in the suite. Once the locks were secured, I realized he'd come alone.

He pointed to the bedroom. "Asleep?"

"Yeah. What's up?"

"I need to talk to you." He closed the bedroom door, unnecessarily, because I figured the soundproofing in the apartment would keep our conversation private. "Remember the night Martinez was shot and you asked if we needed you to track down Jackal? Turns out we do." Big Mike shot a quick look over his shoulder at the door. "But bossman can't know about it."

With the brutal honesty I'd just given Martinez, now I was supposed to lie to him? Christ. What bad things had I done in a past life? Because the universe fucking hated me. "Why not?"

"He'll see anything as a danger to you."

"Is it?"

"Maybe. Jackal expects Tony to handle vengeance personally. Which is what Jackal wants and I'm sure it's what Tony's planning. You helping us track Jackal down is letting us take care of the problem and protects bossman, which is our job."

"Wouldn't that be going against Martinez's direct orders?"

"We protect him even against himself." Big Mike squinted at me. "So, you in?

Jackal wearing a toe tag was beneficial to everyone, no matter who pulled the trigger. "Yeah. But fair warning. If Martinez catches us, I'm rolling on you. I won't fuck up my relationship with him for anyone or anything."

"Deal."

"I take it you have an idea where Jackal might be?"

"No. But Nyla does."

"Why?" I exhaled. "She Jackal's weakness?"

"No. Meth is Nyla's weakness. She'll surface when her supply runs out. Our sources swear she hasn't made a buy since the night you saw her at Dusty's."

"So? Why couldn't someone else be buying it for her?"

"See, that's a logical assumption. But crank heads ain't logical. That's why they're addicts. We're thinking she'll make contact with the supplier tonight or tomorrow night. The other thing; Nyla trades sex for extra hits. The main supplier she uses is into kinky shit and Nyla gets off on being the only chick around who'll do the nasty stuff. It's another drug for her."

I bit my curious tongue. Nyla's need for kink wasn't my business. "How's this work? You get the call, I'll go to where's she's being held and grab her?"

"No. The suppliers agreed to help us only if the shit don't go down at their place. She'll take her first hit at the suppliers, then take her stash back to wherever she's been hiding. If she's high she might not pick up on the tail. But we can't take a chance on multiple vehicles in pursuit, especially ones she recognizes, because she'll definitely notice that."

"Might not?"

"Don't ever underestimate her. Drug addicts are paranoid, so again, this is why she's been so slippery."

"Or you have someone on the inside feeding Jackal information on your plans."

Big Mike's jaw flexed. "*Had* being the operative word. I ain't gonna tell you who. But at least we know why it was so easy for the shooter to get at Tony."

Had to be someone working at Bare Assets. An

Hombres pledge? A bartender? A bouncer? A cocktail waitress? A couple of months passed since I'd slung drinks at the strip club as a favor to Martinez. I'd made more enemies than friends with the staff. Throwing in with Jackal was stupid and the snitch deserved whatever punishment had been—or would be—meted out.

"You still haven't told me what I'll do with Nyla once I track her."

"Keep her under surveillance. We'll see if Jackal shows. If he doesn't, then you'll go in and grab her."

"Right. A paranoid, hopped-up meth-head is gonna just open the fucking door to me? You trying to get me killed? Or just arrested for kidnapping?"

"You're tough as shit, Julie. Knock her ass out if she fights you."

"Why me? Why not use a Hombres member who's trained in this stealthy crap?"

"Because you volunteered, remember?"

Me and my big mouth. I had said I'd do anything to catch Jackal.

"Besides, we're not sure Jackal doesn't have someone else inside the Hombres working with him to tip him off. That's why we're keeping this between you and me."

"Let's say I'm successful and I grab her. What next?"

"Then you'll bring her to me. We'll detain her until the drugs in her system wear off. She'll be so desperate for her fix she'll tell us what we want to know."

After sucking down the last bit of my own fix, I crushed out my Marlboro. "There's a flaw in that line of thinking."

"What makes you say that?"

"Because Jackal wouldn't blab his secrets to a crack whore and he wouldn't give a shit what you did to her."

"He would if the crackhead was his sister."

"Get out. Jackal and Nyla are related? How come I didn't know that?"

"It's not common knowledge. In fact, Jackal don't know *we* know. Sick deal because they use a sexual relationship to throw everyone off, but they're both so fucking perverted they get off on it. So see, he's counting on the fact we'll discount her as nothing to him but a stupid meth-head chick he fucks and beats up from time to time."

"Jesus. That's disgusting. Who knows this?"

"Me. Martinez. Now you."

"How'd you figure it out?"

He smirked. "Interested in my investigative technique, PI?"

I rolled my eyes.

"Nyla showed up two weeks after Jackal was installed in the enforcer's position. Bugged me she's always had inside info she shouldn't and she seemed to be around even more after we put Jackal in lockdown. One night, I . . . ah, took one for the team, so to speak."

"Eww."

"Yeah. Made sure she wouldn't remember me asking the questions, just the false info I planted to see if she'd pass it to Jackal. She did."

"Okay. But won't Jackal notice if she's missing?"

"I hope so."

"So if Jackal or one of his guys is following her to see if anyone is tailing her, and he sees me, chances are good he'll take after me."

"Then he's out in the open, which is easier, and we nail the cocksucker either way."

Made sense. But I could see why we were keeping this from Tony; he'd be livid. "You aren't gonna kill Nyla, are you?"

"No. But we need to get the ball rolling on this. Martinez needs to get out of here and be seen tonight."

"What's the plan for explaining his injury?"

"Skiing—"

The bedroom door banged open. Tony hobbled out. "Don't let me interrupt whatever required you to shut the fucking door."

Busted. I pointed at Big Mike. "Blame him."

Big Mike glared at me. "If you weren't so goddamn loud and freaking out about—"

"Freaking out about what?" Martinez demanded.

"The stupid excuses he's come up with to explain

why you're on crutches." From the corner of my eye I saw Big Mike relax slightly.

"What'd he come up with?"

"Skiing!" I threw my hands up. "Nobody in their right mind would believe you injured yourself snow skiing."

"Why not?"

"Because you don't ski, Martinez."

He lifted a brow. "Yes, I do."

My jaw hitting my knees wasn't a dramatic touch.

Big Mike said, "Told ya."

"But . . . you ski?"

"Of course I ski. I grew up in Colorado."

"Why didn't you tell me? I never hear you talk about hitting the slopes or any of that 'gnarly powder, dude' kind of shit."

"I don't ski around here. Why do you think I've gone to Colorado more often this winter?"

I gaped at him. Why hadn't he told me if it wasn't a secret?

"What?"

"I can't believe I didn't know that about you." What else was he hiding, the man I'd told I loved not an hour ago?

"So now you do. What was your explanation for my injury?"

Should've known he wouldn't let it drop.

"When Julie argued about the skiing idea, I suggested we tell everyone she accidentally shot you with her bow when you guys were out target shooting," Big Mike said.

"That's fucking lame. I am a goddamn good shot and it pisses me off you even suggested it."

"Enough." Martinez settled in the corner of the couch and propped his leg on the coffee table. "Now I see why you shut the goddamn door." He looked at me, gifted me with his lethal grin, and patted the open spot on his left side.

I bounded over; if I had a tail, it'd be waggin'. Even if Martinez's secrets drove me bat shit, color me deliriously happy my man was on the road to recovery.

Big Mike sighed. "Don't get too cozy. I came up here to take Julie downstairs."

"Why?"

"You need to put in an appearance at Fat Bob's tonight."

Without *her* was implied.

"It's okay. I haven't been home in three days. Probably all sorts of shit waiting for me to deal with."

"Give us a couple of minutes," Martinez said, and Big Mike headed for the bathroom.

I murmured, "Are you really feeling up to doing this? Because there's no shame in taking another day to heal."

"Would you stick around and be my wet nurse?"

"Sounds perverted, but yes." Then I remembered why Big Mike needed to separate us. I couldn't tail Nyla if Martinez and I were playing grab ass. "But

Big Mike wouldn't be pushing for you to go out and be seen if it wasn't necessary."

"True." He angled my head where he wanted it and kissed me thoroughly. "Promise you'll charge up that cell the second you get home, blondie."

"Promise."

Martinez twined my hair around his finger and muttered against my throat. "*Te quiero mucho.*"

"What's that mean?"

"*Debes aprender a hablar español.*"

"Funny. You aren't going to tell me, are you?"

"Nope."

"Swearing at me? You must be feeling better." I gave him a big, wet, smacking kiss right on his smirking mouth. "Later?"

"Most definitely."

I followed Big Mike downstairs. Felt good to be out in the fresh air even if it was frigid.

He handed me one of those disposable cell phones while we were sitting in my truck waiting for it to warm up. "I won't call you on this unless something's going down. The number programmed in the call list is mine. Remember, only contact me on this phone, okay?"

And for the first time since I'd met Big Mike, I wasn't entirely sure I trusted him. This seemed too elaborate a scheme. Why not just have an Hombres member snatch Nyla at the dealer's place? Especially since she was everybody's crack whore? I'd bet a kilo of coke the Hombres were the dealer's distributors. If the dealers wanted continued business, they couldn't deny the Hombres' demand to detain Nyla until security arrived.

But . . . chances were good Jackal knew where Nyla scored her drugs. If he put the place under surveillance and if Hombres members showed up, it'd tip him off they knew about his relationship to Nyla. Then we might lose the best chance of flushing Jackal out.

On the other hand, if Big Mike suspected Jackal was living with Nyla, following her would kill two birds with one stoned chick.

God. Too many variables and I didn't have the energy to work them all out. I really wanted to go home.

"You're quiet. What's wrong?"

"Nothing. Just thinking. If I'm gonna help you do this, I want you to call off all surveillance on me."

Big Mike vehemently shook his head. "No fucking way."

"Listen. There's no reason for *me* to tail *her* if she sees people tailing me. You guys might as well do it and leave me out of the middle of it."

He was quiet for a beat. "Shit. I hadn't thought of that. But I can't call off your security detail. Not only will Tony know, the guy assigned to you will wonder why, especially in light of the fact Jackal is still out there on the loose."

"There's no other way to do this."

"Fuck. Do you know what he'll do to me if he

finds out not only are we going behind his back, but I'm purposely putting you in danger?"

"So you'd better figure something out fast. I'm risking my ass to save Tony's. I'd do anything to keep Jackal away from him, and so would you. That's what's at stake, Big Mike. You think I like being fucking bait? You think I like lying and sneaking around on Martinez?"

"No." He scrubbed the stubble on his face. "Fine. Let's just hope this goes down soon."

After he hopped out, I rolled down the window and yelled, "Hey."

"Yeah?"

"Take good care of him."

"I will. I'll be in touch. Soon."

CHAPTER 23

TOO SOON.

The blasted cell phone Big Mike snuck me rang at 3:00 in the morning.

"Julie. Haul ass. She just got there."

"Where'm I going?" Man, I was groggy.

Big Mike rattled off the address. "There's an alley on the left side. It's hidden, but it'll give you an un-obstructed view of the rear entrance. Yellow house, white trim, concrete stoop in the back. She'll take the rear entrance out. Once you get to where she's hiding, keep awake."

The late hour proved Nyla was smart enough to pick a time when there'd be little traffic.

"And for Christsake don't freeze to death."

Vernon Sloane's frozen body amidst the bright white snow flashed behind my dark lids and I was instantly wide awake.

"Call me and let me know where you are, but you're on your own. At least until dawn. Bossman is already suspicious about the changes in security."

"Great." I didn't want to know how Big Mike had pulled one over on Martinez. After minimal hygiene I dressed in layers. Long johns. Flannel jeans. Two pairs of cotton socks. A long-sleeved T-shirt. A lightweight wool sweater. A fleece pullover. Then the usual hat, glove liners, gloves, scarf, and subzero Thinsulate ski jacket.

I popped four Jet-Alert caffeine tablets. They worked way better for staying alert than energy drinks and I didn't have to pee all the time.

Cell phones, gun, restraints, big-ass bolt cutters, a blanket, a shovel, cigarettes, bottled water; I was good to go.

The area the dealers set up shop was familiar. A mere three blocks from the house I'd grown up in. The neighborhood hadn't gone to the dogs in the last twenty-odd years; it'd always been a mix of working class and low-income folks.

At the mouth of the alley I cut my headlights and hoped like hell the cops weren't patrolling. Nothing says criminal activity like cruising down an alley at 3:30 in the morning with your lights off. I parked by a chain-link fence and stared straight ahead at the back of the yellow house.

I shut off the truck. Nyla probably wouldn't

hear the engine idling, but I wasn't willing to take the chance. I studied the junky cars scattered on the street. A beige Ford Escort. A jacked-up Chevy Blazer. A rusted-out Honda Civic. A brand-spanking new Dodge Ram pickup. A beat-up Ford conversion van. A Buick.

By the time I'd pegged the crappy Honda as hers, Nyla burst out the back door, head down, and went right for . . . the conversion van. She backed out and headed south.

I started my truck, kept the lights off, and watched her taillights, staying as far back as I dared. A light snow fell, which was good for masking my vehicle but bad for visibility with no headlights.

Nyla drove aimlessly for fifteen minutes. I'd begun to think she'd made me when she changed directions again and parked in the far corner of the Kmart parking lot. I killed the engine and wished the sodium lights weren't a neon arrow pointing to my location.

After five minutes, she climbed out the driver's side door with a messenger bag slung across her shoulder. She took a quick look around, but never once my direction. Satisfied, she briskly walked to a seedy motel, disappearing at the edge of the building.

No choice but to follow her on foot. I jammed my gun in the outside pocket of my jacket and slipped out of the truck. Luckily, the snow wasn't blowing her tracks away, but I had to run to keep up.

I snuck along the back of the brick building. When

I reached the corner, I poked my head around. Nyla was at the front desk of the motel office. The night clerk handed her cash, a receipt, and an old-fashioned key fob. She didn't bother with another paranoid perusal when she exited the office. She headed straight for room 112, unlocked the door, and scooted inside.

I didn't budge from my spot in the shadows for at least ten minutes. Too damn cold to stay outside. I raced back to my truck and parallel parked on the street behind the motel, which offered me a clear view of Nyla's room.

Surveillance is boring as shit and the only time I allow my mind to blank completely. I think about nothing except what is in front of me. Or, in this case, how I'd restrain Nyla once Big Mike gave the all clear to bring her in. I'd brought a couple of Tuff-Tie restraints, in addition to my Sig. Times like these I really missed my stun gun. I made a mental note to have Jimmer order a new one. A whack to the head with a shovel didn't seem as glamorous as the high-tech device for knocking someone unconscious.

Hours passed. The sun rose and traffic around me picked up. I stretched and called Big Mike.

"It's almost eight. No one has come or gone. You ready for me to grab her? The maids started cleaning rooms on the upper level. Be a good excuse to get her to open the door."

"Gut feeling. Think Jackal's in there with her?"

"No. This place seems a random choice. If she'd

already been registered, she would've gone directly to her room rather than going to the motel office first."

"You armed?"

"Do ya think?"

"Be careful. Call me the second you have her."

I clicked the phone off and moved my truck to the open parking spot in front of her room. With the ties on my wrist, the bolt cutters in my right hand, and firepower in my pocket, I felt as bad-ass as "Dog" the Bounty Hunter. But with better hair.

Quick survey of the surrounding area revealed no one paying attention to me. I held my thumb over the peephole and knocked.

No answer.

I banged harder. Longer. "Housekeeping."

Finally, I heard, "Go 'way."

Heh heh. Another minute passed. I began the knocking process all over. "Housekeeping."

The second I heard the locks disengage I was ready. My adrenaline kicked in. The door opened as far as the safety chain allowed.

"Do you fuckin' *mind*? Some people are—"

I slid the bolt cutters around the chain, applied pressure, and snapped it in half. I had my gun in hand before the cutters hit the ground. I shoved the door open.

Nyla wasn't armed. She wasn't smart either; she turned and ran. Where the hell did she think she was gonna go?

I stopped her with a full flying body tackle that

would've made Howie Long proud. Some body part of hers cracked loudly when we hit.

She screamed and I smashed her face into the bright blue carpet to quiet her.

I rammed the barrel into the base of her skull. "Pipe down. Put your hands behind your back and I'll let you walk out. If you fight me, I will knock you unconscious and drag your skinny ass outside. Understood?"

"Uh huh."

"Good. Move 'em. Slowly. Palms up." I switched the gun to my left hand and slid the Tuff-Tie off my wrist.

Nyla was compliant. Once I had her bound, I dropped the gun in my pocket and yanked her to her feet. Her bare feet. Damn. I'd have to put her shoes on . . . unless tiptoeing through the snow would be an incentive for her not to run. At least she was dressed.

"Is anyone else here?"

"No."

I propelled her forward. The messenger bag, her coat, and snow boots were the only items in the room. "Put them on."

She slipped her feet in the boots. I marched her to the wall. "On your knees. I wanna see you kissing that ugly fucking wallpaper." She whimpered, but she did it.

I rifled through the messenger bag. First I found little packages of glossy magazine pages folded in squares and put in individual plastic baggies. I didn't have to open one to know it was a gram of crank, meth, tweakers, whatever the hell they called it; she had a thousand bucks worth of the illegal stuff, easy.

Cell phone. Empty prescription bottles. Pipe cleaners. Condoms. Wallet with four hundred bucks and a South Dakota driver's license. Mace. Car keys. Another ring of keys. And a little flowered notebook that looked like a diary/address book. I slipped it in my pocket.

Rule #2 in the PI biz. Never let them have it all. Give the client enough to keep them on the hook. Especially true now that I had trust issues with Big Mike. If I found information related to Martinez's shooting in the book, I'd turn it over to Big Mike. If I found other information? I'd turn it over to Martinez.

I draped the strap across my chest so the bag rested on my ass. After bringing Nyla back to her feet, I set the coat on her shoulders and zipped it up so it worked like a straightjacket.

"Do I need to gag you?"

"No."

I popped my head outside the room. Coast was clear. I picked up the bolt cutters and dropped them in the passenger's side of the truck bed in the snow next to the shovel before I helped her in and buckled her up. Glad I didn't have to use the shovel on her. Once we were out of the motel parking lot she spoke.

"Don't matter you're Martinez's old lady. You're gonna fuckin' fry for this. Kidnapping is illegal."

"Yeah? Last time I checked so was a bagful of meth. How do you know I'm not making a citizen's arrest and taking you to the cop shop?"

Nyla's head whipped around and I got my first good look at her. What a fucking mess. Greasy, matted hair. Glazed, bloodshot eyes. Snot dripped from her reddened nose. Her thin lips were chapped, cracked, and bleeding in places.

"Don't take me to the cops. I'd rather be dead than in jail. They don't understand how much I need—"

"Drugs? How long you been doing meth? Because the way I see it? You're gonna be dead in two years." I dug out the cell phone. "Your teeth falling out yet?"

Her tongue snuck under her lip, as if to check, giving me my answer.

"Well, you're lucky. I'm not taking you to jail. I'm taking you someplace where you can answer some questions."

Panic flared in her eyes. "I don't know nuthin' about it."

"About what? Gonna have to be more specific, Nyla, because there's questions about a whole buncha things."

"Where you takin' me?" Nyla licked her lips and didn't seem to notice the snot and blood on her tongue. "Look. Can't we cut a deal? I'll do anything you want. Sex, drugs, name it."

Yeah, sex with her was some incentive all right. I

hit *dial*. The phone rang once before he picked up. I kept my gaze on Nyla's as I said, "Big Mike? Where's the drop point? Good. Ten minutes."

My cold heart didn't melt at all when she began to sob.

Using a fireman's hold, Bucket carried a kicking and screaming Nyla into the back door of the Hombres clubhouse. Evidently Big Mike had found help with our nefarious little scheme.

A tiny bit of guilt surfaced. "You're not going to kill her, right?"

"Not on purpose."

I sucked down the last drag and crushed my cigarette beneath my boot heel. "I fucking hate this shit. I want that fucker Jackal dead, but I don't want to know how you get the information, all right?"

"You still can't tell Martinez about this, Julie. Might be a couple of days until we get her to talk. Maybe it'd be best if you didn't see him during that time."

I studied Big Mike. He'd said that too quickly, too eagerly. "I guarantee if you suggest he and I take a break, Martinez will know something's up."

"You're probably right." He sighed. "You're sure you didn't see anything else in her room?"

"Positive. Why?"

"Just makin' sure she didn't leave behind nuthin' that can be traced. Was the van still where she'd parked it?"

"I don't know. I didn't drive past it."

"We'll check it out."

"So my part in this is done?"

Big Mike nodded.

"I'm keeping the cell. You keep in touch with me and let me know what's going on or I blow the fucking whistle, got it?"

"Jesus. You're a hard-ass."

"Like that's a big surprise."

Been a long time since I'd pulled an all-nighter.

I needed a shower but had no desire to go home, so I headed for the office.

The message from Kevin said he'd be in Pierre through the weekend. Because Martinez's shooting happened on a Thursday night, Kevin hadn't missed me or my invaluable contribution to Wells/Collins Investigations. Even if he was here I couldn't tell him I'd spent the weekend holed up at Bare Assets caring for my injured lover.

At 10:00 I opened for business and took my big

mug of steaming coffee into my office. No clue what I'd do since we didn't have any pressing cases.

Twenty minutes later the outer door opened.

Bud Linderman loped into my office. Alone. No cowboy posse. I couldn't believe I was actually disappointed. I couldn't believe I was actually nervous.

"Mr. Linderman."

He removed his coat and hat and made his way to the chairs across from my desk. "Miz Collins. You look as good as I remembered."

Couldn't say the same for him. Bud had aged ten years since I'd last seen him. He'd dropped a good fifty pounds. His silver hair turned to cotton-white fluff and it needed a trim, as did his droopy mustache. His Western duds weren't pressed to perfection. He looked like a sad, lost man.

Don't feel sorry for him. Piece of shit threatened you. He threatened an innocent little girl. If he's fallen on hard times, it's no more than he deserves.

"Is there something I can do for you?"

Linderman nodded. "I know you don't think too much of me; cain't say as I blame you. In retrospect my behavior toward you was appallin'. I'd like to apologize for that."

I shrugged.

"You prolly don't care, but since we last crossed paths, I ain't the same person. My life changed."

If he confessed he'd accepted Jesus Christ as his personal Lord and Savior, I'd kick him to the fucking curb, old man or not.

"My wife, Mary, died suddenly. We'd been married forty-seven years. High school sweethearts."

"Look, Linderman, I'm sorry for your loss. But if I'm on your list of rights you have to wrong to ease your conscience, you're barking up the wrong tree. The person you need to make amends to is Chloe Black Dog, not me."

"I have. I started a scholarship fund for that little gal in her mother's name. I ain't gonna brag and tell you how much money I put in there, but it's a pile. She won't hafta worry 'bout how's she's gonna pay for her college education."

That floored me. "Donovan knows?"

"Yep. And I apologized to him, too." Linderman glanced up from twisting his gnarled hands in his lap. "So, will you at least listen to me?"

Say no. "I guess." I lit up, leaned back, and put my feet on the desk to keep my Skechers from getting dirty wading through Linderman's piles of bullshit.

"I know you found Vernon Sloane's body."

My stomach clenched, which allowed me to blow a really nice smoke ring.

"And I'm pretty sure after that you figured out I own Prairie Gardens. Made me sick to think of that old guy dyin' alone out in the snow. Made me even sicker to think the people workin' for me could've prevented it."

"How?"

"By doin' their jobs. I bought that place about a year ago. We'd started makin' the changes when . . ." He cleared his throat. "Anyway, I'd planned on runnin' it myself, but after Mary passed on, I couldn't."

"So you hired a worthless piece of shit like Bradley Boner to run it?"

"Not me. But you're right on about his character. See, Bradley is Mary's nephew. He showed up at her funeral, got to talkin' with my boys, and the next thing I knew, they'd named him executive director and put him in charge.

"I don't trust that fruity SOB; never have, even if he is Mary's kin. But it don't matter because the retirement places I own are at the bottom of my kids' priorities."

"Really? Why?"

He snorted and I caught a glimpse of the feisty Bud Linderman I'd remembered. "Carin' for old people ain't as glamorous as sellin' cars or managin' real estate or cowboy nightclubs. But it's profitable. My boy Rory would rather work where there's hot young chicks not, in his words, 'a bunch of old bitties.'"

"This does have a point, right?"

Linderman blushed. Jesus. Made me feel like I'd reprimanded a garden gnome.

"The point is, I wanna hire you to figure out what's going on at Prairie Gardens."

"You're joking."

"No, I ain't. You're a good investigator, prolly too

331

good. If anyone can make sense of it, you can."

His flattery meant nothing.

"That little gal whose grandpa died is gonna file a lawsuit against us. And if his death was due to neglect on our end, I won't fight her; I'll try to settle with her as soon as possible."

Lawsuit, the magic word that perked up my ears.

He leaned forward, his face earnest. "I'm done tryin' to cover up my mistakes. But by the same token, I ain't gonna let some high-priced lawyer run roughshod over us if we ain't at fault. I need someone unbiased to look into it."

Ethical dilemma. Did I tell Linderman that Amery originally hired us to find out if Prairie Gardens had been neglectful and deceitful? That broke client confidentiality.

But if we weren't working for Amery, the possibilities were wide open.

Why would I want to do it? I didn't like Linderman, didn't trust him either. Kevin would freak. Martinez would freak. While I weighed the factors, Linderman spoke up again.

"But here's the thing. I have to hire you on the sly—cash on the barrelhead. My kids don't want me involved. They think we should let Bradley handle it. I think we wouldn't be in this pickle if they'd kept a keener eye on what he was doin'."

"Without breaching client privacy laws, there's a good chance my partner made a verbal agreement with

Ms. Grayson on doing the legal legwork for her case *against* Prairie Gardens."

"Then that's perfect."

"How so?"

"If what you find helps her case, then you can turn the information over to her. If what you find out shows something other than our neglect caused Mr. Sloane's death, then justice will be served."

I blew a stream of smoke upward.

"You don't trust me."

"Why should I? Given what I've discovered about your facility, I'd say you aren't going to be so 'do the right thing' once I pass you a list of all the problems I've already uncovered."

"True enough."

"On the other hand, I have no way of knowing you aren't trying to save your own ass by manipulating me into working for you, so you can find out what angle my partner is working on for Ms. Grayson."

"That's also true. But let me ask you something. Who stands to benefit from Vernon Sloane's death?"

"Financially? From the lawsuit?"

"No. From his will. It's not Prairie Gardens. His granddaughter inherits all that money."

"What money? Vernon Sloane didn't have any money."

"Someone fed you wrong information. Vernon Sloane was worth more than five million dollars."

My eyes went *sproing*. "How in the hell do you

know that?"

"Company policy to have a will on hand for each resident."

"Are you shitting me?"

"Nope. It's not unusual when you consider the vast majority of the residents die at our facility. Saves time when we don't have disputes over personal property."

"Is that even legal?"

"Couldn't do it if it wasn't."

"But isn't that information supposed to be confidential?"

"Highly."

"Then how'd you know about it?"

Linderman became quiet for a minute. "I shouldn't know she's the sole surviving heir. So I gotta ask, who else knows? Who else is sharing that information?"

"Has this been going on since LPL took over?"

"I reckon. Here's what bothers me. The Prime Time Friends program was supposed to be strictly voluntary for residents in the hive. Not a requirement with a room rate increase straight across the board."

"The extra ten grand per month is a nice windfall. Where does the money go?"

"Straight into the Friends account. Bradley unearthed some donors from the get-go and set it up as a nonprofit organization, then titled himself the COO."

Nice. "How do they split the monthly income between the actual Friends employees?"

"Near as I can figure a grand each for the four volunteers, and three grand each for Luella and Bradley."

"Seems an unfair split. They do the shit work and the COO reaps the benefits."

"Something you gotta remember. These women are retired. They work two twenty-hour weeks out of the month. Their wages aren't reported because they're part of a volunteer organization and no one's expectin' them to get paid."

"Okay. Still not seeing how those workers wouldn't be pissed about the inequity. Especially since the rumor is, Bradley is never there. I mean never."

"And that's where Bradley sweetens the pot. If any of the volunteers get a resident to bequeath their estate to Prime Time Friends, she receives five percent off the top."

"You're kidding."

He studied me. "I thought maybe your client suspected the administration was siccing the Friends on residents who have a substantial estate, which was why she'd hired you to investigate."

Should I hedge? Nah. Linderman shared more information than was wise. Who knew what else he'd tell me if I appeared to divulge secrets of my own. "No. She was more worried about the large amounts of money her grandfather was withdrawing from his bank account on a regular basis that couldn't be accounted for." But Amery had pointed out influence being leveled on him from someone.

"How did this come to *your* attention, Bud? If you just became interested in the business again, I would think the information would be hard to find."

"That's the thing. It should be." A sad, bitter look crossed his face. "Dee lets me have access to everything. See, she thinks she's humoring me, that I'm just another worthless old man trying to relive his glory years. My kids are tryin' to muscle me out of all of the businesses I've spent my life building. After the office staff goes home for the day, I come in and poke around through the files and the computers and whatnot."

I had no idea on whether Linderman's kids were justified in taking over his business interests, and it'd be easy for me to get sucked into his well of pity. I focused on the facts. "Does Dee know how Prime Time Friends operates?"

"Yep. She gets a quarterly bonus for 'joint administrative duties' to the tune of a coupla thousand bucks. So, I was snoopin' and I found that two residents who had recently died bequeathed the bulk of their estate to the Friends program."

"Big amounts?"

"Eh. Just a coupla hundred thousand."

Linderman made it sound like small potatoes, but that was a lot of money to a lot of people, me included. "Which Friend received the kickback for bringing in the loot?"

"The program director, Luella Spotted Tail."

"What do you know about her?"

"Not much. She was a holdover from the previous owners. We initially kept her on in a transition position."

"Long transition. It's been what, a year?"

"Not quite. According to Bradley, because she's Indian, he ain't never been too sure she wouldn't sue if she was fired outright. When she officially left the payroll, we were no longer subject to the EEO standards. Some of the residents don't like her much. Bradley doesn't like her. Doesn't trust her either."

Not surprising. That attitude mirrored most local attitudes about Indians and it pissed me off, but I managed to bite back a smart retort. "Why keep her on?"

"'Cause I guess she could sweet talk a honeybee from a flower. She's added nearly half a million dollars to the Prime Time Friends coffers since they started it."

A kick in the gut couldn't have sucked the air from my lungs any faster. Money was one helluva motive. In addition to Luella's awareness of how the COO felt, she might be looking at a big score before she bailed out of the program entirely.

Honestly, I was as confused and conflicted about the case as I'd been at the beginning. I sighed.

"I hear that sigh a lot from my kids, Miz Collins."

"Sorry. Much as I appreciate it, you overloaded me with information, Bud."

"Does that mean you're saying no?"

"No. It means I need to think about it before I make a decision."

"Well, at least you didn't throw me out on my ear."

"Did you expect me to?"

Bud pushed to his feet and reached for his coat. "To be honest, I wasn't sure. You have quite the tough-as-nails reputation. You didn't get that by bein' an easy mark fallin' for every sob story comin' down the pike." He buttoned his duster and slipped on his gloves before he looked at me again. "But I've no doubt you'll do the best thing for everyone."

The man didn't know me. Our past association had been confrontational at best. Now he acted like he had my number cold. "Why?"

"Because puttin' the screws to me would be sweet revenge. And I'd do the same damn thing if I were in your position."

"I'm nothing like you, Linderman."

"I know. That's why I'm convinced you'll do the right thing, Miz Collins. Good day."

The open and shut case didn't seem so open and shut anymore.

CHAPTER 24

I MULLED OVER LINDERMAN'S VISIT.

It'd be reasonable to protect his business interests and blame Vernon Sloane's death on murder rather than negligence. But when the pieces were laid out, I realized I'd been just as quick to jump on the "accident" bandwagon as everyone else.

Why? Because no one wanted to believe someone could be so cold as to let an old man freeze to death? For money?

No one working at Prairie Gardens would blink about Luella taking Vernon for an "outing"—even out to die. At five percent, her personal cut of five million was substantial.

Just not as substantial as Amery's one hundred percent.

If I took the case, would it prove Kim's accusation

right? I'd do anything to make problems for Kevin and his relationship with Amery?

Wrong. It had nothing to do with Kevin. We weren't working for Amery. In fact, when I went through the file folders, I noticed he'd voided her last check and the contract. So if I decided to help Linderman, Kevin couldn't claim we were contractually obligated to Miz Grayson. The only conflict of interest was his personal relationship with the dead man's granddaughter.

What about the conflict Martinez has with Linderman?

Yeah, it might piss Tony off, but it was my business. I seriously doubted he wanted me sticking my nose into his affairs. I hadn't questioned him on the identity of the redheaded bombshell he'd been doing business with. Since Linderman was a shell of his former self I hardly saw him as a physical threat. Was it naïve to think Linderman had changed?

Are you hoping that helping Linderman will prove any man—including your father—is capable of change?

Again. Not the same thing. Sheriff Richards practically dared me to snoop around. It was as much about my ego to uncover information, or browbeat it out of people, to prove my worthiness as an investigator, as it was guilt out of helping Doug Collins.

Regardless. It was another fucked-up situation. It bugged the shit out of me I didn't know what my dad and BD Hoffman had fought about. Chances were slim BD would spill his guts to me either, but he was the only lead I had.

I closed down the office and made the trek to Bear Butte County. My damn truck was almost out of gas again. With the increased fuel prices, I'd begun to question why I lived so far away from work. As a county employee, I'd had to live in Bear Butte County. But it'd been damn near a year since I'd quit. Why was I still living there? Wasn't like I had a great house. Or fantastic neighbors. True, my place was only twenty-five minutes out of Rapid. Tony never complained about the drive, but I wondered if that was part of the reason we'd been spending fewer nights together and he'd been afraid to bring it up.

Right. Martinez had such a difficult time speaking his mind.

BD Hoffman owned a trucking business on the outskirts of the county seat. The building was a standard metal prefab set in the middle of an immense gravel parking lot. I parked between empty livestock trailers and ventured inside.

No receptionist. I guessed ninety-nine percent of the work was handled over the phone. I loitered politely, my midwestern manners intact, at least until the point I tired of listening to *plop plop* as the snow melted and dripped off my boots.

Although Bear Butte County is small, I'd never met BD, as he hadn't cooled his boot heels in the sheriff's office during my tenure. I'd caused enough problems locally that he might recognize me, so I disguised myself with a floppy knit cap, which hid my hair, and donned smart girl glasses with clear lenses.

I called out, "Hello?"

"Hang on," boomed from the belly of the cavernous building.

The guy growled like an angry grizzly. Probably looked like a lumbering bear, too. So I was surprised when a skinny runt rounded the corner.

I gave him a quick perusal. He was midforties, bowlegged, probably bald beneath his Peterbilt ball cap, short, wiry, with the typical cowboy goatee and mustache. He wore zip-up denim striped coveralls and stained suede hiking boots. His nose and mouth were swollen like he'd been punched in the face. I couldn't be sure if this was BD; cowboys liked to fight. Someone other than my father could've punched the guy.

He wiped his greasy hands on an even greasier rag. "Help ya?"

"I'm looking for BD."

"You found him."

Whoa. This guy had seduced the church secretary?

I didn't offer my hand. "Hi, BD. I'm working in conjunction with the Bear Butte County Sheriff's Office regarding the Melvin Canter case. I'd like to ask you a few questions."

Immediately he became suspicious. "Why din't Deputy John ask 'em when I was there a few days ago?"

"Because he's busy with county business while Sheriff Richards is out of town and he outsourced the investigation."

More squinty-eyed distrust.

Maybe I'd laid it on too thick.

"Don't know how much I can help ya, but come on back. I jus' made a fresh potta coffee."

"That'd be great." I followed him into a big open room, which was the garage/maintenance area. Concrete floors, gigantic garage doors, tires stacked in the corner, and belts hanging on the wall.

Six gleaming semitrucks with jewel-toned metallic cabs were parked in a straight line. Worth at least a million bucks each. Bright red rolling chests ringed the room, holding hundreds of thousands of dollars of ratchets, wrenches, and other tools. One truck was on a hydraulic lift. Heavy chains draped the steel rafters like industrial tinsel. The place smelled like oil and gas and for a second the distinctive scent brought me back to my childhood when my dad'd been a short-term truck driver. My visits to his place of employment had been rare, therefore memorable.

BD ducked through a doorway. I followed and entered a room filled with computer equipment and the aroma of freshly brewed coffee. Built-in cabinets and shelves took up one wall. A big glass window looked out into the shop; underneath it were two padded folding chairs. The office area was spotless and NO SMOKING signs were slapped up everywhere.

There went that idea.

He wiggled a Styrofoam cup from a stack and poured. "Cream an' sugar over here if you need it."

"Black is fine." I took the proffered cup.

BD gestured to one of the chairs. "Pull that up to the desk if ya want."

"Thanks."

"Now what can I do for ya?"

"I know you're a busy man, so I'll jump right in with my questions if you don't mind."

"Not a problem."

"What can you tell me about Melvin Canter? I understand you attended the same church. He moved back here recently and was looking for work. Did he approach you for a job?"

"Yep. Turned him down flat. Made some folks in the church unhappy. But I gotta look out for the interests of my employees rather than just blindly follow the idea of Christian charity."

Not the response I'd expected. "So you knew Melvin had done time?"

"Yeah."

"Did everyone in the church know about the years he'd spent in jail?"

BD shook his head.

"Why didn't you hire him?"

"He din't have no mechanic experience. Plus, my best mechanic is a woman. Knowing what he'd done . . . well, I ain't about to let him be around her at all, say nuthin' of bein' around her unsupervised."

I breathed deeply and evenly. If BD knew Melvin was a sexual predator, why hadn't he shared that information with my father? "How did you know Melvin was a convicted and registered sex offender?"

His soft brown eyes met mine and something defiant flickered. "I din't. But I've lived in this county my whole life. I knew Melvin growin' up, and I was here when my dad and a buncha other guys run Melvin out of town the first time he got caught years ago."

"What?"

He shifted in his chair. "I ain't real comfortable talkin' about this."

Too fucking bad. "The sheriff isn't gonna care about something that happened twenty years ago. He's looking for answers about this case."

"I suspect the past cain't be separated from the now. So that ain't exactly true."

"Maybe you should tell me what happened."

BD stood and returned to the coffeepot. As he spoke, his loud voice reverberated off the wall, but he kept his back to me. "Twenty-odd years ago Melvin Canter supposedly raped a twelve-year-old girl. No one did nuthin' because she was the daughter of a single mother who bartended at Dusty's. People thought she had it comin' or some dumb thing. A month later, another rumor floated around about Melvin and a young kid. Again, unconfirmed. No one paid attention until Melvin raped the preacher's eleven-year-old daughter."

My heart started to pound.

"My ma was the head of the Sunday school program, and she found her. The girl told her what happened. Just after my ma called the police, the gal's daddy showed up."

My heart switched from a steady bass beat to the rapid fire of a snare drum solo.

"The preacher din't want his daughter to hafta go to court, so she retracted the story as a lie. He said God would be the man's final judge. No charges were ever filed and the preacher and his family moved out of town.

"But my dad and a bunch of the elders from the church knew the truth. They rode out to the Canters' place and told Melvin to get outta town and not to come back. Even his brother left the immediate area 'cause he din't wanna be associated with a child rapist."

"Do you think the brother knows about Melvin using his address in Meade County to register his sex offender status?"

"No. Marvin's a stand-up guy. Melvin stayed away for years 'til his mother started ailin'. When he came back a 'changed man and born-again Christian' . . . well, it's been a trial for me, 'cause I know the SOB ain't changed. I din't know howta tell folks what kinda sick monster he was. The one person I trusted and took inta my confidence told me I oughta practice

Christian forgiveness."

"None of the church members remembered him or what he'd done?"

"We couldn't get no minister to take the call to our church after what happened. The church closed down. Coupla years later some teens were drinkin' in there, set it on fire, and it burned to the ground. A lotta the members back then were old and they've since died. Lost track of the rest."

So maybe my dad hadn't known. At the time he'd been a hit-and-miss Catholic—hitting me and missing church services, mostly.

"But Melvin worked for Doug Collins. Doug attends your church and is your fellow elder. Did you try to talk to him about not hiring Melvin, especially since Doug has a young daughter?"

BD still hadn't turned around.

I gave him a minute before I said, "Mr. Hoffman?"

He spun and glared at me. "Who do you think told me I oughta practice Christian forgiveness?"

My stomach plummeted like I'd swallowed a length of log chain. "Doug did?"

"No. His wife, Trish, did. She told me spreadin' rumors was the devil's work. That everyone deserved a second chance no matter what they'd done in the past."

Jesus. Trish couldn't be that fucking stupid, could she?

"Did Doug Collins know? I mean, as far as you know, did Trish ever tell him that you'd warned her

347

about Melvin?"

BD returned to his chair and picked at his grease-stained fingernails. "I don't know if I should . . ."

"Should what?"

"Is all this gonna go in your report?"

I shrugged. He'd tell me or he wouldn't. Cajoling him would only make me look suspect.

"Around that time, something else happened at our church with me and someone else. I tried to explain it wadn't what it looked like. Doug wouldn't listen. He lashed out and made a stupid decision. I guess I wanted to prove to him how damn dumb that decision was, so I tried to tell him what I'd told Trish about Canter. Then he accused me of tryin' to retaliate by comin' between him and his wife. Big mess din't need to be made bigger. I let it go."

"I'm strictly looking for facts, but I did talk to someone and they'd made mention of a rumor about you and the church secretary? What was her name again?"

BD's face flushed red as his toolboxes. "Beth McClanahan. We wadn't doin' what folks said we was. She was cryin' and on her knees prayin'. I was helpin' her."

Right. The old *on-the-knees* excuse.

"Beth lost her job in the most humiliatin' way. I tried to quit the elders' council and leave the church, after they fired her. 'Course they wadn't gonna let me do that since I give 'em so much money every year.

Sweet Lord Jesus, if anyone knew why she'd been cryin' . . ."

"Why?"

He cut me a dark look. "Keep her out of this. She's a good woman. Been through a lotta bad stuff in her life and she don't need no more."

Perfect example of how fourth- and fifth-hand information turned into personal speculation. Dale told me BD begged for forgiveness, but I'd bet Sunday's collection plate it wasn't for himself but for Beth McClanahan.

I figured she wouldn't talk to me since my father canned her biscuits, but maybe if BD was a buffer she'd consider it. "Would Beth talk to me?"

"Why?"

"To see if she had any dealings with Melvin Canter."

BD's gaze fell back to his coffee cup.

"She does have a job someplace around here?"

A moment of quiet, then he asked, "How'd you know Beth's been workin' here for me?"

I blinked. I hadn't known.

"She's a good secretary and I needed office help."

Getting off track, Julie.

"What did you and Doug Collins fight about at Bevel's Hardware?"

His mouth went hard and flat.

"Deputy John said you didn't file charges. Why?"

"To prove to Doug I can turn the other cheek."

349

Great. One-upmanship Jesus-style. "Did you overhear the fights Doug and Melvin were purported to have at Chaska's?"

BD shook his head.

"So you don't know what they were fighting about?"

Another head shake.

"BD, do you have any idea why Melvin Canter is dead?"

"No." His head hung so low I strained to hear him and he was a mere three feet from me. "And may Christ our Lord and Savior have mercy on my sinner's soul, because I can't find sorrow in my heart that he is."

A chill rolled through me. I stood and offered my hand. "Thank you for the coffee. If I think of anything else I'll be in touch."

As I drove home I wondered if he realized I'd never given him my name.

Something weird was going on with Beth McClanahan. Probably be worth it to run a background check on her.

I called Trish. I hadn't talked to her since Martinez's shooting.

If my luck held we could have the whole damn

conversation on the phone. My energy started to lag and I knew I'd crash on the couch soon as the last cup of coffee wore off.

Trish insisted on coming to my place. I didn't bother to pick up because I could give a crap about what she thought of my housekeeping skills; she wasn't my mother.

I was smoking and cleaning my gun when she barged in.

"I can't stay."

I bit back my response of *good*.

"I tried to call you for a couple of days. Where've you been?"

None of your business. I was punchy and I just needed to crawl in bed. "Out of town. Why? Did something happen?"

"No. Thank goodness. Did you find out anything?"

"Yeah, but I'm not sure you wanna hear it."

"What?"

"The background check on Melvin Canter."

She frowned but didn't argue why I'd taken that tack.

"Why in the hell would you insist on hiring him?"

The question threw her. "He needed money to help care for his mother. Doug needed a hired hand. And it was the Christian thing to do."

"Doesn't my father know when he needs help? Wasn't he livid when you announced you'd just hired Canter on his behalf out of the blue?"

"I resent—"

"—someone trying to tell you the truth?"

"What truth? Showing human kindness and compassion? The man needed a break."

"Jesus, Trish, the man is a fucking *pedophile*. How in the world could you ever justify having him around your children?"

Trish's face turned ashen. "What did you say?"

"You heard me. Melvin Canter is a convicted felon. Sexual assault. Three cases in three different states. He's done thirteen of the last twenty years in various jails. He is a convicted sex offender."

She leapt to her feet and stumbled to the bathroom. She didn't manage to shut the door, so I heard her retching. I didn't check on her simply because I couldn't stand to be in the room when she looked at herself in the mirror.

After a while Trish shuffled into the living room. I handed her a glass of water.

"Thanks."

I waited. Smoked. Watched her.

Finally she said, "How did you find out?"

"Like I said. Background check. But you could've known what kind of man he was if you'd only listened to the warnings."

"What warnings?"

"BD Hoffman for one."

Guilt put color back in her freckled cheeks. "I thought I was doing the right thing."

"No, you thought what you were doing would elicit the 'Trish Collins is a model Christian woman' comments from the church congregation."

She winced.

I didn't care about her discomfort, and I didn't stop hammering her. "Who would Brittney talk to if Melvin Canter touched her inappropriately?"

That sick realization distorted her face. "I thought she'd talk to me."

"Not if you'd been reminding her again and again to be extra nice and extra helpful to Daddy's new hired hand."

She winced again.

"She'd avoid talking to you if you were piling on the guilt about maintaining a Christian attitude toward Melvin, no matter what. So who else would she talk to? DJ?"

"Maybe."

"She wouldn't talk to Dad, would she?"

Trish shook her head.

"A teacher? Her best pal, Shelby?"

"No." She squinted at me. "What did she mention to you? Because if you're trying to protect her—"

"At least someone would be."

She covered her hands with her face and sobbed.

I let her cry. Out of spite? Probably. But I'd been Brittney's age when Dad began hitting me on the sly. I hid it from my mother because I'd been ashamed.

What if Collins history repeated itself? I imagined

Brittney's situation would be different because she had a protector in Trish. But Trish was as clueless as my mom had been.

And why didn't I resent Annika Collins for that? Because the childish part of me believed if she'd lived she would have stopped it? Yes. We all had our delusions about our past and that one was mine.

"What did Brittney say to you?"

"She said Dad's hired man creeped her out. It felt like he was watching her all the time. Then she said neither she nor DJ felt comfortable doing chores with him around. But they couldn't say anything to you."

Trish dropped her chin to her chest. "Stop."

She wasn't getting off the hook that easily. "If either of them made a negative comment, you'd reprimand them, and make them both say a positive thing about Melvin." I inhaled and exhaled. "Is that really how you want it to be? Your kids telling you what they *think* you want to hear? Instead of them thinking for themselves?"

"No wonder Doug was so livid. I totally screwed this up."

Zero disagreement from me. "Let me ask you this: what would Doug do if he found out Melvin was a molester?"

"Kill him." When she realized what she'd said, she amended, "I meant—"

"You can't take that back, Trish. But I will remind you that you swore to me Doug didn't do this." She opened her mouth to protest and I held up my hand. "No qualifications."

I wasn't asking her to submit to a philosophy I, myself, hadn't embraced. Tony was a man who did bad things. I accepted that was as much a part of his nature as the part of him I saw that no one else did. There was no qualification for me either when it came to how I felt about him.

Heavy silence.

"What do I do now?"

"Dad needs to tell you how he found out about Melvin. You need to demand to know why he didn't share the information with you."

She thrust a hand through her unruly hair. "Does it matter? Will you share your findings about Melvin Canter with the sheriff? It's apparent he doesn't know."

I doubted it. Sheriff Richards was probably biding his time waiting for me or someone else to make the connection.

"What if *your* suspicions land Doug in jail?"

"Whoa whoa whoa. How would *I* be responsible for Dad being in jail if *he* killed a man?"

Trish ignored my logic. "Because you're supposed to be finding information to exonerate Doug, not incriminate him!"

I was tired. Tired of the drama. Tired of the games. Tired of the shitty things family members did to each other, especially in my family. I could feel myself sliding toward the babbling phase from sleep deprivation. I managed, "Go home."

After she left, I gazed out the screen door in the kitchen, swigging Don Julio and eating Ritz crackers, staring across that mantle of endless snow, my warm breath fogging up the cold glass, letting the alcohol lull me into thinking everything might turn out all right.

CHAPTER 25

THE NEXT MORNING THE REMNANTS OF MY SELF-AP-
pointed sacramental communion lingered; I was hung
over as hell.

"Really. Would anyone miss me if I didn't go into
the office today?"

Surprisingly enough, the coffeepot didn't answer.

I sighed. At least if I had a dog it'd bark a response.
Right. Human companionship on a regular basis was
a must if I actually considered a canine an alternative.

Cold Hard Bitch by Jet serenaded me from the home
theater speakers as I readied for another workday. The
music wasn't too loud; I still heard the thumps on the
screen door. I turned the stereo off and checked the
peephole. Don Anderson.

I ushered him inside. "Surprised to see you,
Don."

He saw my coat and gloves on the back of the couch. "This a bad time?"

"I'm headed into work, but I can talk to you first. What's up?"

"I'll make it quick. You went to see BD yesterday afternoon?"

"How'd you know?"

"BD called me last night. Said some woman barged in and was askin' questions 'bout Melvin Canter and he spilled his guts to her on that nasty business from years ago. Said he never caught the woman's name. So it was you?"

"Yeah."

Don's shoulders slumped. "Good."

"Why the relief?"

"Look, I doan want you to think we was lyin' to you when we said we'd help with your investigation, but we, me an' Dale, but me mostly, got what you might call a vested innerest."

I pointed to the easy chair. "Park it and start explaining."

He wiped his boots before he sat down. "Lemme say that I wasn't involved in runnin' Canter outta town them years ago, but I knew the guys who'd done it. BD's dad, JR, Maurice Ashcroft, Buck Bevel, Red Granger, Clint Jenson, and"—Don looked at me—"Dale Pendergrast."

Don had come to me months ago during a case because he was worried his best buddy, Dale, had killed a man. Ultimately Don had been wrong, but it didn't change the fact he thought Dale capable of murder.

"JR, Red, and Maurice are all dead. Buck turned the business over to his son and moved to Arizona. Clint's still around, up at the VA. So's Dale. After that business with the preacher's daughter was shunted aside, Dale quit goin' to church."

"Can't say as I blame him."

"Well, you know how Dale is. He was more of the 'eye for an eye,' and he wanted to make Canter disappear permanently." Don's Adam's apple bobbed when he swallowed nervously. "Which is why I wanna assure you that Dale din't have nuthin' to do with Canter endin' up dead."

"You thought Dale might've been a murderer just last summer. Now you're telling me he's changed?"

"No. I'm tellin' you in confidence that he ain't strong enough to've killed nobody unless it was with a gun."

"I can't say as I disagree. So, back to BD. One thing I didn't ask him, because I didn't want to increase his suspicions of me, was the preacher's name."

"Why's that important?"

"I don't know if it is, but I want to be thorough."

"Shoot. His name . . ." Don tapped his chin. "Newman. Patrick Newman. Daughter . . . Lizzie? Something like that. Anyway, Dale and his missus spent November, December, and January travelin', and he din't know Doug'd hired Canter until two weeks ago. Dale paid Doug a visit right away and told him the whole story. Doug was ticked, rightly so, and that's when he confronted Melvin outside Chaska's. Apparently, that's why they had the fistfight."

"Does Trish know any of this?"

Don shook his head. "Doug said to keep her out of it and that he'd handle it."

"Seems to be a theme because BD tried to tell Trish what he knew of Melvin's past and Trish wouldn't listen to him. But BD said he tried to tell my dad, too, and Dad accused BD of making problems."

"Doug's a stubborn cuss, but I doan gotta tell you that."

"No. But you mentioned a vested interest. I'm not seeing one."

He twisted his gloves in his hands. "Dale doan know I came to you last summer with my worries about him and Red Granger. He doan know I'm here now. This thing with Canter needs to be made right, and I figure you're the only one who can do it."

"Dale disagrees?"

"He thinks you got it in for your daddy so bad you'll do anything to see him behind bars."

I kept quiet. Arguing wouldn't change a damn thing. "What else?"

"Well, BD is afraid you're gonna track Beth down and ask her a buncha questions. He said he'd try to keep Beth away from you for her own protection."

"Did you tell BD my name?"

He snorted. "No. I do have some evasive skills. But I will say one thing, and you can take this however you want. Why's that little gal need BD's protection? What's she have to hide?"

I clapped him on the shoulder in a show of solidarity, because I'd been thinking exactly the same thing. "Great minds, Don. I was wondering that, too. You'd make a fine investigator."

"Really?"

"Yep. I just hope you don't use your evasive skills on me."

"If I was really good, you'd never know, would ya?"

I smiled at his sly grin. "Got me there. Lemme ask you something. How old do you think Beth is?"

"Somewhere around thirty to thirty-five, which was why I couldn't understand why BD was protectin' her."

"She's not married?"

"Nope. She's divorced. Doug made a big deal out of her marital status I guess, durin' that hullabaloo at the church."

"Thanks for the info. Let me know if anything else pops up, okay?"

"Will do."

If nothing else shook loose at the office, at least I had three names—Patrick Newman, Lizzie Newman, and Beth McClanahan—to run through the database.

361

Kevin showed up an hour after I did.

Much had happened in the last five days and I couldn't tell him squat. I expected him to be standoffish; I wasn't expecting him to envelop me in a big hug.

"What was that for?"

"Because I missed you, dork."

"Missed you, too, doofus."

He sidestepped me and plopped in the buffalo skin chair. "I tried to call a couple of times. Something wrong with your cell?"

"No. Martinez and I were out of town and I forgot my charger," I freely fibbed. "I wanna hear every juicy detail about what crazy fun things you did in Capital City."

"Nothing besides ice fishing."

"What?"

"I went ice fishing."

"You don't ice fish."

Kevin leveled his gaze at me. "Yes, I do."

"Since when?"

"Since always. You don't know everything about me, Jules."

What the fuck was going on with the men in my life and their undisclosed love of winter sports? Martinez—skiing? Kevin—ice fishing? Would

Jimmer confess he was a closet pairs figure skater? I could scarcely wrap my head around the hidden sides of these men I thought I knew so well.

"Anyway. I needed time to clear my head."

"About?"

"The business."

"What about it?"

"It's been too slow. We need to expand. With two of us . . . I'm thinking of trying our hand at bond enforcement."

I blinked. "Like chasing bail jumpers and beating them up and shit?"

"Yeah."

"I am so totally all over that."

He sighed. "I thought you would be, so that's why *you're* not going to do it. I am. Besides, half the guys we'd be after probably are associated with your criminal boyfriend."

"You're fucking hilarious." But it explained why Kevin had started bookmarking sites dealing with that skip trace stuff.

"I also had time to think about Amery."

"I take it she wasn't with you?"

"No. I went alone."

Kevin didn't sound particularly happy about that. "Tell me something. Are you two officially broken up?"

"Wasn't like I asked her to go steady and demanded back my class ring when she stopped calling me."

Probably unproductive to point out Amery was young enough for the scenario to be true. "You know what I mean. Are you?"

"Why?"

"Are we still working for her?"

"No."

"Maybe I should rephrase that: are *you* working for her?"

He slouched in the chair and scowled at me. "Why the clarification?"

I smiled sweetly. "Why the evasion?"

"Touché. No, I'm not working for her. I'm not doing anything with her."

"Good. I didn't know how to bring this up, but guess who wants to hire me?" He lifted his eyebrow. Damn. Martinez had that little quirk, too. I found it sexy as hell on both of them. "Bud Linderman."

"You're joking."

"No." I detailed the visit from Linderman, my suspicions, and recapped my run-ins with him last summer in case Kevin didn't remember. Kevin didn't say much after I finished. In fact I sucked down the rest of my Marlboro in the silence.

"You would've taken the case without discussing it with me." A statement, not question.

"Yes, but not to be contrary. Linderman is not the same ruthless man, Kev. Loss changed him. We both know what that's like. He wasn't bullshitting me when he said if his facility was negligent he'd have no problem paying Amery compensation."

"And you bought into that?"

"Not until he told me Vernon Sloane wasn't some destitute old man, like Amery led us to believe, but worth five million dollars."

Stunned silence. Then, "What the fuck did you just say?"

"Vernon Sloane was rich. Linderman said Prairie Gardens has a copy of Sloane's will on file. Amery might not have power of attorney, but she is his sole heir." I lit up. And I'll be damned if Kevin didn't grab my smokes and do the same.

We smoked in hellish stillness. Affected pauses weren't the norm with him, which was what made them so dramatic.

Kevin extinguished his cigarette and stared at his shoes for the longest time. "Ever been walking along, minding your own business, not paying attention to anything, and you trip on something? After falling flat on your face, you take a quick look around to see if anyone saw you?"

I didn't answer; I didn't move. I barely breathed.

"That's what I feel like, Jules. I'm looking around to see if anyone saw me fall and make a fool of myself."

When he raised his gaze to mine, his eyes were that unusual shade of stormy green, a mix of fury, humiliation, and self-reproach. "Amery played me, didn't she? Big-time."

I still had no response, no "there, there, sweetie"

comforting words. I wished I did. God did I ever wish I had something profound or sweet or encouraging to erase that brooding look.

"How many clients have I slept with in the five years I've owned this agency? None. What was it about *her*? Why did *she* end up in my bed hours after we met?"

Rhetorical question, Julie.

"Her youth? Her vulnerability? Her looks? Her bodacious ta-tas? After we left the bar that first night, she couldn't keep her hands off me. Why? I'm not some muscle-bound twentysomething gym rat. I'm not that goddamn smooth. Not particularly funny. But damn if she didn't make me feel like all that and a bag of chips.

"I liked that she let me coddle her. Yet, I liked that she had a strong sense of self. I really liked that she appreciated those same traits in me. Or so I thought."

"Is this what you were thinking about in Pierre?"

"Yeah. Mostly why something started to feel . . . off. Why she blew me off."

"When?"

"Right away, the day after you found her grandfather. She turned into this nasty snappish bitch, all directed at me. Like I somehow let her down by not saving her grandfather." He laughed bitterly. "At least that's what I thought at the time. She apologized, blamed her reaction on stress, and threw me a bone—literally."

I lit another cigarette.

"Remember the night we went to Dusty's and I said I needed a break from her? That was a lie. She told me she needed time alone."

"Oh." My stomach churned with guilt. I hated he'd been hurt and I hated his male pride made him feel he had to deal with it on his own.

"So, I've had to ask myself: what was it about me that Amery saw as weak and malleable?"

"Kevin—"

"Sex aside, why didn't I see her neediness as manipulation? I would have with any other woman."

"Enough with the self-recrimination. Stick with the facts."

"Which are?"

"You tell me."

He squirmed. "I don't have it all figured out yet."

"Wrong. I'm betting you do. I'm betting you're still dissecting this from every angle so you don't feel like a chump before you knew about the inheritance. Or you're trying to formulate a reasonable excuse as to why Amery acted so cold and calculating. You see the best in people, Kev. I don't. Voicing your honest frustrations won't change how *I* see you."

A flare resembling gratitude briefly shone in his eyes. "Fine. Near as I can figure, Amery hired us as a cover. We proved her worries about Prairie Gardens were founded. Someone on the inside was taking financial advantage of her grandfather and the place had extremely lax security. She could've used both those documented problems to take it to court to file for power of attorney. Initially, I thought that's all she wanted."

"But now?"

"Now that I know about the pile of money? I think she was out to get rid of Vernon all along so she could get her grubby hands on the inheritance. And wasn't it handy she was cozied up with me during the storm, ensuring the perfect alibi?"

"Playing devil's advocate here, but Amery didn't cause the blizzard."

"No, but she used it to her advantage. She left here right after you told her how upset Vernon was, remember? Probably saw it as her chance to confuse him further."

"I'd forgotten that. What time did she show up at your place?"

"Damn near six hours later. Was it a coincidence she 'forgot' her cell phone at the office when she was snowed in with me? And no one could get in touch with her?"

I blew a smoke ring. "Do you think she actually led him out to freeze to death?"

"Yes. With him dead, not only does she inherit, she has a strong lawsuit against the negligent facility. It's twice the windfall. And I handed it to her on a silver fucking platter."

God, this was ugly.

"Say something," Kev demanded.

"So she manipulated you. It happens. People have killed for way less than five million dollars."

"That's it? That's all you have to say?"

"No. But, believe it or not, Amery's not the only one with a motive."

"What the hell are you talking about?"

"Luella Spotted Tail."

"What the fuck? Why would you think Luella had anything to gain, especially since Linderman told you who Sloane's sole beneficiary was? Amery."

"Now, see? This is where I learned my critical thinking skills—from you questioning everything I question. Amery told us after her mother died that none of the financial or legal responsibilities passed on to her. I'm betting the will Prairie Gardens has on file is the original will Sloane submitted when he first went into care three years ago.

"Because Linderman kept saying 'sole surviving heir,' which could mean the will hadn't been changed after Vernon's daughter Susan's death, leaving Amery as the only one left to inherit."

"What're you saying?"

"Just that Luella took Vernon on unsanctioned outings. What if she had convinced him to leave all or part of his estate to Prime Time Friends? Logically, one of the places she'd take him to would be a lawyer's office. But what if she'd known what kind of stink it'd raise if it got out Sloane had another will? Amery

369

would be pissed and could use the instance of 'undue influence' to argue for guardianship."

"Effectively ending any control Luella had over Vernon," Kevin said.

"Bingo. So Luella kept it quiet and continued to care for him like nothing had changed." Something else popped up in my thoughts. "Did Amery talk to Luella at all at the funeral?"

"No. I thought it odd at the time. It was almost as if they were purposely avoiding one another."

Our eyes met in perfect understanding.

"Crap. They might've been in on it together. Amery offers Luella a big chunk of the inheritance if she helps get rid of him?"

"Or Luella approaches Amery and offers her a deal. Instead of the 250K or whatever she's getting for her percentage bequeathed to Prime Time Friends, she suggests Amery forks over a larger amount to keep the old will in play as the only official one."

Even as I said it, the thought made me nauseous. Luella didn't seem manipulative. She genuinely seemed to care for Vernon Sloane. Then again, Kev and I had both bought into Amery's concerned grand-daughter routine, too.

Kevin cocked his head. "This is far-fetched."

"Absolutely."

"Probably we're making it too complicated."

"Maybe. There's one simple way to find out."

"How?"

370

"You pump Amery for information and I'll tackle Luella."

That slimy porn star smile I detested slipped into place on Kevin's face. "We're talking literally, here? Right?"

"Whatever it takes." I pawed through my purse for the scrap of paper with Reva's phone number on it and dialed.

CHAPTER 26

AFTER THE VERNON SLOANE FIASCO, SECURITY HAD tightened considerably at Prairie Gardens. I donned my winter hat/smart girl glasses/wool trench coat disguise and waited in the receptionist's area for Reva to escort me to her apartment.

Reva rolled up, wearing a jumpsuit reminiscent of fish scales: skintight, iridescent, with weird bumps in odd places. She'd clipped a matching bow in her thinning, dyed hair.

I squeezed her frail frame, getting a whiff of butterscotch candy and Emeraude.

"Sweetheart, it's so good to see you again," Reva said loudly. "Come on back. I made your favorite tea."

I couldn't see the TAR's response, but their burning curiosity melted the yarn on my hat as we disappeared down the hallway.

"Did they recognize me?"

"Honey, I almost didn't recognize you."

"That bad, eh?"

"Sydney Bristow always looked better in disguise, not worse."

We didn't speak again until we were in her tiny dining area. "So, what's been going on around here?"

Reva set out the floral teapot, matching cups, and a tin of Walkers shortbread cookies. "Nothing. Feels like we're in lockdown. No roaming the halls."

"Bet that puts a crimp in your spying activities."

"Smarty." She poured two cups of gingerbready smelling tea. "The one good thing to come out of this tragedy is Security is back to the twice daily checks."

"That's encouraging." I sipped the warm liquid and tried not to make a disgusted face. Yuck. This shit always smelled way better than it tasted.

"I know you'd prefer coffee, but I can't stomach it anymore, so you're stuck with Celestial Seasonings." Reva doled us each three cookies. "You didn't come here to talk to me after you found Vernon Sloane. Was it horrible?"

I nodded.

"I'm sorry. What an awful way to die. Are the rumors true, then?"

"What rumors?"

"His mysterious granddaughter is planning to sue this place?"

I nodded again.

"I'm confused. You said you needed to talk to Luella. What does Luella have to do with this mess?"

"I don't know, Reva. That's why I have to ask her a few questions."

"She hasn't been around here much. I had to lay on the loneliness factor super thick or else she wouldn't be coming to see me today."

"I appreciate it."

"Humor me while we're waiting." She bit into a cookie and crumbs dusted her chest. "Tell me something exciting that's happened in your PI life recently."

"Hmm. You mean like when I was stuck doing surveillance during the middle of the night on a meth-head woman after a drug buy? And I took her down at gunpoint and returned her to my client trussed up like a Christmas goose?"

Reva's big eyes blinked rapidly behind her lenses, making her appear even more fishlike. "Really?"

"Yeah."

"Was it fun?"

"Sitting in the cold wasn't fun." Wasn't fun hiding information from my lover either. "Once I knew the suspect wasn't armed, tackling her to the carpet was pretty fun." Right then, I remembered I hadn't read Nyla's notebook. Hell, I'd forgotten I even had it.

Also right then, an ache spread when I thought of Martinez. I missed him. We'd been playing phone tag, and I suspected Big Mike was doing his level best to keep us apart.

Enough. I smiled at Reva. "Excuse me for a second."

"Sure, honey."

I rounded the corner to the bathroom and shut the door. Powdery blue paint coated the walls. A wallpaper border comprised of wispy clouds circled the ceiling. Even though the space seemed fussy, it was surprisingly soothing. I flipped the fan on and flopped on the matching sky blue fluffy rug on the floor. I dialed Martinez's main cell number. It kicked over to voice mail. I tried his private number. No answer. On a whim I dug out the prepaid phone Big Mike gave me and dialed the number in the directory.

Big Mike answered, "What's up?"

"I want to talk to him."

"He's busy. And you know you ain't supposed to be calling me on this phone unless it pertains to—"

"—it pertains to the fact I haven't seen him in two days."

"Julie, he's been busy trying to catch up."

"That's a bullshit excuse and you know it. Where is he right now?"

"Physical therapy."

"How much longer?"

"Twenty minutes, but he's exhausted when it's done and he usually rests."

Made my gut clench to think of him in pain.

"Look. I'll tell him you called."

"When do you think I might expect a call back?"

"I don't know. Later tonight probably."

"Fuck that. I want to talk to him right fucking now. You don't get to decide—"

"Actually, as head of his security team I *do* get to decide and if you push the issue—"

I hung up. I'd made a huge mistake in keeping the situation with Nyla from Tony. Just to be spiteful, I programmed Martinez's private number into Big Mike's secret phone. Oops, what would happen if I got confused and *accidentally* used the wrong phone? The gig would definitely be up, since Martinez's private number was so private only ten people had it. Hah. Then Big Mike's ass would be in a sling, not mine.

An option I wouldn't discount. I called Tony back from my phone and left a rambling message, complete with *I miss you, baby* on both his numbers. If that didn't get his attention nothing would.

I washed my hands and returned to the living room.

Luella's appearance shocked me as much as mine shocked her. She glared at me. "What is she doing here?"

"I want to talk to you."

"I have nothing to say."

"Too bad."

Luella gave Reva a hurt look. "I can't believe you tricked me."

"Don't blame Reva. She didn't trick you. I threatened her. Now I'm threatening you."

"Don't try to run," Reva mock-whispered. "She has a gun in her purse."

I managed to keep a straight face. "Reva? Can you give us a few minutes?"

"Sure. I'll check out the action in the common room. Help yourself to tea and cookies, Lu."

When Reva was out of earshot, Luella snapped, "What's so important you had to threaten a wheel-chair-bound woman?"

"Vernon Sloane."

Luella deflected her gaze to the door.

"Did you have anything to do with that poor old man getting left out in the cold and freezing to death like an unwanted dog?"

No response.

"I found him, remember? Stiff as a board. His eyes were open, like he knew what was going on, not like he'd laid down to take a short ice nap." I paused for effect. "But know the worst thing, Luella?"

"Stop."

"That final, permanent look of sadness and horror on his face."

"Please don't."

"Freezing to death is not peaceful like drowning. It's incredibly painful. The brain is aware of everything since it's the last organ to cease functioning. Have you ever seen anyone who's frozen to death?"

"Stop it. Please."

"Only if you talk."

She nodded.

I pointed to the dining table. "Make yourself comfortable. We aren't leaving until I'm satisfied with your answers."

Luella poured herself tea. Drained the cup—as if in fortification—and poured more.

"Was your relationship with Sloane strictly professional?"

"What are you insinuating?"

"Nothing." I jabbed my finger in the air at her. "And *you* don't get to be snappy and indignant with me. I just don't get why you spent so much time with him. From what I saw of Vernon, he was old. And cranky. And confused. Surely there had to be easier seniors to blow your monthly quota on?"

"No one else wanted him as a client."

"He was just so glad to have a companion that he wrote you checks for thousands of dollars?"

She flushed. "It's not what you think."

"Then explain it to me."

"I switched jobs after the property changed hands and Bradley Boner started the Friends program. I hired the workers. We divided up the residents. From the get-go I knew Vernon teetered on the edge of needing full-time care. We're supposed to report those cases to management."

"Why?"

"Because there's a significant increase in the monthly payment to the facility."

"So it'd be financially beneficial for Prairie Gardens to change his status?"

"Yes. In his moments of lucidity Vernon was adamant he didn't want to move from his apartment because he'd lose even more control."

"Of what?"

"Of everything. His freedom, his environment, his choices. He'd already lost his daughter and his car."

"So instead of reporting him . . ."

Luella's neck turned as bright red as her lipstick. "Instead of reporting him to Admin, I agreed to keep his condition a secret if he offered me a financial incentive to do so."

Jesus. "Do you have agreements like this with other residents?"

"No. And I *was* helping him. Within a month, I had Vernon seeing a new doctor and he was in much better shape, mentally and physically. I believed he'd be okay living on his own."

"Then why didn't you stop spending so much time with him? Because of the money?"

"I didn't only do it for the money."

What a load of shit. "If you were trying to hide the fact Vernon needed full-time care, then you should've tried harder to cover your tracks."

"What do you mean?"

"When I got a hold of the 'volunteer' schedule, it showed you devoting more hours per week to Vernon Sloane than to any other resident. Wouldn't that tip off the front office he needed extra care?"

"It might have if the general manager didn't just sign off on the schedule on a biweekly basis." She sniffed. "The office staff is so overworked they don't care. The senior program is under the direct supervision of the GM. He pays us from a different account than the other employees."

Which rang true with what Bud Linderman had told me. "How well do you know Amery Grayson? Because I distinctly remember, during our first conversation at the doctor's office, you said Vernon didn't have any family."

"She isn't family. She's a vulture. And I tried my best to keep her talons out of him."

"That wasn't your choice to make. Because, like it or not, Amery is Vernon's granddaughter."

Luella glared at me. "I was the one who'd taken care of him. She moves here and decides she cares about poor old Granddad? Baloney."

"Were you jealous of her?"

"No, infuriated by her. Whenever she visited Vernon, always when I wasn't around, he became confused, thinking Amery was her dead mother, Susie. And she let him. She played into his delusion. Then he'd tell me he didn't need me around because his daughter was back. Amery managed to trick him out of twenty thousand dollars, making him think she was Susie. But what could I do about it? Amery snooped through his things, which is why he gave me some of his papers for safekeeping."

Amery was responsible for stealing from her own grandfather?

"Again, she had a right to know, especially if she thought you were taking advantage of him financially." Something didn't fit and I backtracked. "What kind of papers?"

Her eyes glittered. "Let me ask you something. Why did Vernon refuse to give his precious grand-daughter, his only living relative, power of attorney? Knowing he'd been diagnosed with Alzheimer's? With a cooperative client it'd take a lawyer less than a day to get that changed."

My bad feeling intensified.

"Amery didn't have power of attorney because Vernon refused to give it to her. He didn't trust her and told her it'd take a court order. He trusted *me*. I earned every penny he paid me."

"I don't doubt that. But you have to admit it was beneficial for *you* to keep him in the private apartment as long as possible. Not only would you lose the money he paid you every month, but you'd lose the hours you charged to the senior program. How long do you think the GM would keep you on if someone told him about your little kickback scheme?"

Another glare. "You don't have the authority—"

"As a matter of fact, I do. Do you have any idea who I work for?" I lied, "Linderman Properties Limited." At her continued blank stare I prompted,

"LPL? Although they don't write your checks, they own this facility."

That got her attention. "Please. I can't afford to lose this job, especially now that—"

"—your cash cow is dead?"

"No, now that everything is horribly mixed up. It wasn't supposed to be like this! I thought I was helping him. If I would've known he was so far gone that he'd wander outside by himself during a blizzard, I never would've tried to keep him in his own apartment." Luella shifted into total meltdown.

Obviously Luella felt guilty, but she didn't suspect foul play. Which led me to believe she'd been as oblivious to Amery's machinations, besides the outright stealing, as everyone else had.

Or we'd been oblivious to hers. Maybe she was just a really good actress.

As she sobbed, I revamped my strategy. "So you knew that Vernon Sloane was worth five million dollars?"

"Yes."

"You knew about his will?"

She stopped crying mid-hiccup. "What about his will?"

"Just that it doesn't matter if Amery had power of attorney or not because she's set to inherit everything."

"Who told you that?"

I shrugged. "Sorry. I can't reveal my source."

Come on, come on, fall for it.

"Well, your source is wrong."

Bingo. "What?"

Luella abruptly pushed back. "Forget I said anything. I have to go."

I literally threw myself in front of the door. "Luella, talk to me. You can't possibly—"

"I can do whatever I want. Leave me alone."

I had no choice but to tip my hand on our suspicions about Amery. "Please. Listen to me. I don't know what you'd planned to do with this information about Vernon Sloane having a different will. But my partner and I suspect Amery Grayson purposely led her grandfather outside to freeze to death to collect the inheritance she expects."

When she clapped her hand over her trembling mouth, I was certain she had nothing to do with helping Amery.

"You were worried something like this was going to happen to him, weren't you?"

Luella nodded.

"Vernon trusted you?"

"More than anyone else. And I . . . just want to do the right thing by him."

"Then we cannot let that girl get away with killing him. Not only that, she's suing this place for negligence, which would mean even more money for her."

"I don't care about this place anymore. They're all a bunch of vultures, too. Why do you think I didn't tell anyone? I did exactly what they asked me to. It was wrong. I know that now, and I'm sorry. It's not fair that they should benefit either. No one should. That poor, poor man."

I blinked. "Who's 'they,' Luella?"

"Please, let me go," she whispered. "I've said too much. I-I need to clear my head. Let me go."

"On one condition." I searched her teary eyes. "Don't do anything rash. Don't talk to anyone. Especially not to Amery. She's a very dangerous woman." I pulled out a business card. "Think about your options. Anything you tell me is in confidence. I won't say anything to anyone until I hear from you. But if I don't hear from you within two days, Luella, I will track you down." The second I moved she was out the door.

I stared out Reva's small picture window, waiting for her to return.

Poor Vernon Sloane. No one saw him as a man, only dollar signs. I wasn't lucky enough to have had grandparents, or aunts and uncles in my life. Even though I had little experience with old people, I realized I was prejudiced. Calling them geezers. Making fun of the way "white-heads" drove their big cars. Hating to be behind them in line because they were so slow. Bitching about forking a portion of my earnings into Medicare and Social Security.

In other cultures the aged weren't an embarrassment to be locked away. The elderly were looked to for guidance, lauded for their knowledge, and treated with respect as valuable members of society.

The casual disregard with which we treated our elderly in this country made me sick. And I was as goddamned guilty as everyone else in allowing it to happen.

"Julie? You okay?" Reva said behind me.

I jumped. I hadn't heard stealthy girl come in. "Yeah."

"Was Luella able to help you?"

"Some. Not as much as I'd hoped."

"Oh. Anything I can do?"

"Maybe." I continued to gaze out the window because the question I had was wildly inappropriate and completely embarrassing. I didn't know if I could look into Reva's sharp turquoise eyes and ask it. "You told me you don't have any family left. So what happens to your estate when you . . .?"

"Die?" She chuckled. "I had a hard time saying that word at your age, too. I couldn't imagine it. And here I am. Eighty-eight years old."

"You don't look a day over seventy."

"Bah, flatterer, but I'll take it. Anyway, to answer your question, I've left the little money I have to the Campbell County Library System. I know how much it'll be appreciated. That's probably why I'm low on the Prime Time Friends priority list."

"What?"

"That's the other function of the organization, if you hadn't figured it out yet. They try to get residents here to bequeath all or part of their estate to the program."

I let my forehead rest on the icy pane of glass. Why hadn't I asked Reva for this information earlier? Had I automatically discounted her conversation as the ramblings of a lonely old woman? Bitter about her lot in life and her friend dying?

"You mentioned something like that to me, didn't you?"

"Yes, my friend Nettie signed over everything to Prime Time Friends a couple of months before she died. And before you ask, Miz PI, no, I don't think her death was intentional so they could get their hands on the pittance she had. Her death was from neglect, plain and simple."

"That makes me feel even worse for her, Reva."

"Me, too."

I turned around. "So it's the norm for the Friends? To see the residents as dollar signs?"

"That's all we are to most people, Julie. Medicare, Medicaid, funeral planning, free scooters, adjustable beds, wheelchairs, and prescription medicine programs. That's why I like Luella the best of all the volunteers. She never makes me feel like a number."

Yeah, but Luella sure had Vernon Sloane's number. All five million of them. "Well, you're number one in my book. I appreciate all your help."

Reva snorted. "It's not like I have anything else to do."

The slanted jeweled green eyes on her retro cat clock shifted; the long tail twitched back and forth, announcing the top of the hour. I sighed. "I should go. I have a couple of things to finish up at the office before I can call it a day."

"You all done with this case, then?"

"I'm not sure. I definitely need to regroup."

"I wish you luck."

Her shoulders slumped as she cleared the dishes from the little table. Even her sassy hairbow drooped. Guess she thought I'd gotten what I'd needed and wouldn't be back, which made me feel like a heel.

But she's right, isn't she?

Yes, but that didn't mean I couldn't change. I wanted to change. Besides, hadn't I been bitching about having too much free time in my off hours? I genuinely liked Reva and suspected she and I were more alike than either of us knew. God knew I could use a wise woman in my life.

"You kicking me to the curb, Reva? Because I was hoping the next time I stopped by you'd crack that bottle of Jack Daniels instead of serving me that shitty tasting tea."

Her lips quirked. "Such a potty mouth."

"I've heard librarians have seriously creative language once you get them drunk. They start throwing out words like *lugubrious* and *verisimilitude* and get into fistfights about the misuse of the Dewey decimal system. " I fixed her bow. "Let's test that theory. How about a week from Wednesday? Sevenish? You can tell me about your bad boy and I'll tell you about mine?"

"Sounds like a deal."

"Until then, try to stay out of trouble, spy girl. And if you can't be good, have fun being bad."

CHAPTER 27

On the way back across town, I'd come up with a couple different scenarios.

Vernon Sloane had given Luella paperwork for safekeeping. No-brainer what kind of documents he wanted hidden from his snoopy granddaughter. Legal documents, like a new will.

By requiring a copy of a will to be filed on-site, Bradley Boner knew exactly how much each resident was worth. He knew who had heirs and who didn't. It was like a fucking treasure map. Encouraging seniors to gift their entire bank accounts to the Prime Time Friends organization. In exchange for a cheap plaque on the wall in the common area?

I'd hoped Luella wasn't in on it, but courting Vernon Sloane for a five-million-dollar donation to Prime Time Friends would be a huge coup for her.

I smoked, my brain playing ring-around-the-rosy with the possibilities.

Then the truth smacked me upside the head. Luella was hiding the latest will as a bargaining chip. She could blackmail Amery, demanding a large chunk of the five million, or else she'd turn over Vernon's newly inked will, and Amery would get nothing.

If Vernon had written a new will, wouldn't the attorney's office have a copy? Yes. But would a lawyer even let a man with dementia write a new will? Probably not. Which meant Vernon might not have used an attorney. There were plenty of those "create-a-will" kits, and I'd think an old folks' home would be a perfect place to find them, which would also explain why Luella hadn't come forth with the other will yet.

Luella wouldn't be that naïve, threatening a murderer, would she? If Amery killed her grandfather for money, she wouldn't hesitate to kill Luella.

How could I prove it?

I couldn't.

My other get-Amery-to-confess idea was just as lame, but still an option I'd have to fine-tune.

I flipped on my computer and ran a records search on Beth McClanahan, narrowing the age scan to ten years. Then I leaned back in my chair and closed my eyes. A catnap would revive me. Why was I so damn tired all the time? Unfortunately, I hadn't devoted my nighttime hours to sextracurricular activities with Martinez.

My cell phone rang. I was disappointed when TM didn't pop up on the caller ID.

"Hey, Brittney."

"I can't believe you told her!"

"Told who what?"

"My mom. You told her that stuff I said to you in confidence, and now look what you did. I knew I shoulda listened to him about not trusting you."

Him who? Dad probably. At least Trish was trying to rectify her mistakes. I didn't respond, feeling stung she'd automatically jumped in to accuse me of wrongdoing.

Brittney babbled in the awkward silence. "Mom came in my room last night and started asking me all these embarrassing questions about the hired man." Her voice turned churlish. "If he'd touched me in my private parts. That's just gross. What did you tell her? Why would she ask that?"

"Because she was worried about you, Britt."

"That's exactly what she said. So I think you put her up to it."

"No, I didn't. But even if I did, did you tell her the truth?"

Sullen silence.

"I've got plenty of stuff to do besides listen to you sulk on the phone."

Sniff. Sniff.

"Are you crying?"

"No."

Count to ten. "Look. I didn't rat you out, okay? Your mom came to me and all I told her was that she should ask you about it." I paused to let that sink in.

"Really?"

"Really. So why the tears?"

She wailed, "Because right after that my mom and dad had a huge fight. They never fight. Mom was yelling and Dad wouldn't even talk to her and then he took his stuff and slept in the barn."

"Take a deep breath. Parents fight. It's not the end of the world."

"I think they were fighting about you."

I frowned.

"Are you trying to break them up? Because you've been spending time with my mom and if you're telling her the same kinda stories about Dad beating you up that you told me, and then they get a divorce, it'll be your fault."

Why the fuck did I let her—and Dad and Trish—blame me for everything that went wrong in their oh-so-perfect lives? "Again, fighting doesn't mean they're going to get a divorce. The best thing you can do is to stay out of it."

"Really?"

The outer office door slammed. "Really. Anything else I can do for you?"

"Yeah." More snuffling. "I haven't seen you in forever."

More guilt. Big goddamn surprise.

My office door opened. Silver crutches caught the fluorescent light when Martinez paused in the doorway.

Be still, my heart. My blood pulsed, more prominently in some spots than others.

Tony shut the door. And locked it. He stalked me with that look. The look that made me forget my own damn name.

"Julie? You still there?"

"Ah, Britt. I've gotta go. I'll call you tomorrow."

I shut the phone off and closed the distance between us in two steps. "I missed you. Really missed you. Going crazy kind of missing you, Martinez."

"I heard."

"How's your leg?"

"What leg?"

"I'm serious."

"Serious enough to take off my pants and judge for yourself?"

I lunged for him at the same time he lunged for me. The crutches crashed to the floor. We followed in a tangle of tongues, arms, and legs.

When we were both mostly naked, I broke free from a toe-curling kiss to drown in his eyes, losing myself in the look that was mine alone. "You sure—"

"Yes. And I'm tired of you being on top."

He flipped us, then he was on me, in me, and I didn't care about anything else.

Usually after an intense bout of sex, Martinez and I rolled around in bed. Rolling on the cold office floor wasn't an option. We dressed, but he kept me close, kept touching me as if we were still naked.

"How much longer do you have to be on crutches?"

"Been wearing a knee brace the last two days. I left it off after the last PT appointment I just finished."

"Why?"

"Because I knew I was coming here and I didn't want to mess with taking it off and putting it back on again."

"Knew you were gonna get lucky, huh?"

"Yeah."

"I should be insulted."

"You're not. You're wishing we could go at it again."

"True." His backside rested against the front of my desk and I stood between his outstretched legs. I ran my fingers through his hair as he kissed my neck. "You can't stay, can you?"

"No."

"Did you ditch your security team again?"

"I'd like to pretend I did, but they're probably sitting in the hallway waiting for me."

"Do they have a tracking device on you or something?"

Tony's warm mouth brushed my collarbone until his lips reached the necklace. I felt him smile against my throat. "You're wearing it."

"I always wear it."

"I noticed. I'm glad." He kissed the skin beneath the pendant. "I didn't know if you'd like it since you don't wear jewelry. Not even . . ."

The necklace I'd taken back after I'd killed the person who'd killed my brother. Happy as I was to have Ben's prized possession, I had never put it on and I never would. "Not the same."

"I figured. But I wondered if there was another reason."

"No. The reason is simple; I don't have any classy bling. Feel free to shower me with precious gems any time your heart desires, baby. I'm partial to big stones."

He laughed softly. "I know."

"Where'd you get this?"

"It belonged to my mother."

I angled his head back to look in his eyes. "Why didn't you tell me? Dammit, Martinez, you shouldn't trust me with a family heirloom. What if I lose it?"

"You won't."

"But—"

"See? This is the reason I didn't tell you."

"Why? Because you were worried I'd be too para-noid to wear it since it's so valuable?"

"It's not more valuable to me than the person

wearing it, Julie."

Melt my resistance, why don't you. "That's not an answer."

"Yes, it is. I didn't tell you because you'd see it for what it really is."

"What's that?"

"A symbol of permanence."

My heart slammed into my throat.

"You really think I'd give this to you if I thought you'd walk out of my life? Or if I'd walk out of yours?" He curled his hands around my head and his thumbs stroked my cheeks. His eyes were dark, black as molasses, but not hard and cold. "Although it took you long enough to say it the first time, you can tell me you love me more than once."

My cheeks flamed. "Yeah? Maybe I'm waiting for you to say it back to me, asshole."

His right eyebrow winged up. "Asshole?"

"You have to admit it's been pretty one-sided when I've been the only one—"

"*Te quiero mucho.*"

"In English," I snapped. But a strange feeling unfurled in my chest. "Wait a minute. You've been mumbling that to me . . ."

"For months, blondie."

Breathe. In. Out.

"You really need to buy a Spanish-language dictionary."

Martinez had been telling me he loved me. For

months. He understood I'd be too chicken to put myself out there first, so he'd taken the risk upon himself.

Stupid, sweet man.

But, Christ on a Kawasaki, I was also the world's biggest fucking idiot. Why hadn't I seen what everyone else had?

Are you ever going to allow yourself to be happy?

He's crazy fucking in love with you.

Martinez mooning around you all the time.

He's better now that you're here.

Te quiero mucho.

Jesus, Julie. Don't fucking cry.

But if now wasn't the perfect time to shed happy tears, when was?

Four distinctive raps sounded on my office door. An Hombres bodyguard signal.

Martinez muttered, "Never fucking fails." He kissed my forehead and moved me aside. "Later."

He grabbed his crutches and hobbled out the door before I could speak around the lump in my throat.

Took me about four cigarettes to find my focus.

I spun in my office chair and dragged my mouse across the mousepad to get the screen to come back up.

Dumb computer crashed on me. I restarted it,

reentered the information parameters, and hit the online newspapers to see what I'd missed while I waited.

Weather, weather, and more weather. The *Bear Butte County Gazette* only came out once a week so there wasn't any new information on services for Melvin Canter.

On a whim, I looked up the number I'd written down for Marvin Canter and dialed it on the prepaid phone. Hey, Big Mike had paid for minutes; it'd be a shame to waste them.

Three rings and a suspicious "Hello?"

"Marvin Canter, please."

"This is him."

No proper phone grammar in Meade County. "Mr. Canter, I'm the obituary coordinator for the *Rapid City Weekly News*. I was double checking my database and noticed we haven't heard back from your family on service information for Melvin Canter. Do you have a firm date yet?"

"Ask the Bear Butte County sheriff. He ain't released my brother's body, so we can't plan nuthin'."

"Oh. I can see where that'd be a problem."

"It's very frustrating."

"Have you talked to the sheriff? What seems to be the holdup?"

A snort. "He won't say nuthin' besides them bein' behind on autopsies. Flu season's been bad. Guess it shut down the whole staff in Pierre for two weeks, so no one can be spared for the VA. Which don't matter none to me because it ain't gonna make Melvin any less dead. No matter what they find about how he died, it ain't gonna make anyone around these parts more sorry that he's dead neither. I jus' wanna get this whole thing over with. My ma ain't got much time left and she'd sure like to see her son have a proper Christian burial before she passes on herself."

"You have my sympathies, Mr. Canter."

"Thank you."

"I don't know if you're aware of this, but you can demand the body be released and not autopsied on religious grounds."

Heavy pause. "You don't say?"

I wasn't exactly sure how that scenario worked on a suspected homicide case. "It'd be worth a phone call to the sheriff to find out."

"Thanks for the heads-up. What'd you say your name was again?"

"Kate Sawyer." My computer beeped and I hung up.

The search pulled up twenty names. I discarded the first ten and moved on to the next five. Something about number fourteen struck a chord in me. Elizabeth McClanahan. I clicked on the icon for a more in-depth search. Didn't take long.

Elizabeth McClanahan, nee Newman. Born in Alpena, South Dakota. Graduated from high school in Blue Earth, Minnesota. Graduated from secretarial school at Southeastern Vo-Tech in Sioux Falls. Married Michael McClanahan in Luverne, Minnesota. Divorced three years later in the same county.

Wait a second. *Newman.* Wasn't that the name of the preacher whose daughter retracted her accusation of being raped by Melvin Canter? What was the girl's name? Lizzie?

There was that seesaw sensation in my belly again.

I typed the name in and watched the *working* bar fill the screen. The information was identical.

Beth McClanahan was Lizzie Newman.

So little Lizzie Newman had come back. To exact revenge? How long had she been tracking Melvin Canter? I wondered if she'd taken the secretarial job at the church after Melvin Canter returned to Bear Butte County. How could she look him in the eye and not give away her murderous rage? Or had she finally gotten her revenge?

How would I react if I came face to face with my rapist? Could I kill him? Now? Ten years ago? I didn't know. Rape was a hideous experience I survived, but I'd been older than eleven when it'd happened. Painful as it had been, it'd changed my life but hadn't ruined it.

Not like Elizabeth Newman McClanahan's life. Her whole family had pulled up stakes, disappeared, and started over. I'd bet Lizzie dealt with the shame on her own—the shame of the act itself and the lie to cover it up. Did she hold resentment toward her father for turning tail and running? Instead of putting a monster like Melvin Canter behind bars when they'd had the chance?

Could Elizabeth Newman have saved Melvin Canter's other victims if they'd done the right thing all those years ago?

Look who's talking. How do you know the man who raped you didn't rape again and again? Because you didn't do the right thing and report him either.

Jesus.

My feeling of contentment a memory, I shut down the computer, locked up the office, and hauled ass to BD's.

This time I left my manners in the truck, grabbed my Sig, and stormed into the building. BD wasn't alone. A dark-haired woman tapped away at the big desk behind a laptop computer.

"Lizzie Newman?"

They both looked up.

She froze; BD jumped to his feet. "I don't know who you are or what you want, but you can't just come bargin' in here—"

"If you wanna keep people out, BD, lock the god-damn door." I saw Lizzie's fingers sliding across the desktop. I whipped out my gun and sited it on her forehead.

She whimpered.

"Don't move. Hands on the desk, Elizabeth Newman McClanahan."

"Lord, have mercy, what are you doin'?"

"Sit down."

He sat.

I asked her, "Do you have a gun in the drawer?"

She nodded.

Without taking my eyes from hers, I said to BD, "You carrying?"

"No."

"Good. Now, Miz McClanahan, come around the desk slowly and sit next to him."

She did. BD reached for her hand. I let him.

I allowed the gun to dangle by my side. "I have a couple of questions." I directed the first one to BD. "How'd you find out Beth McClanahan was Lizzie Newman? Did you recognize her, since you lived here when she was a girl?"

"No."

"Did you apply for the job at the church before or after you found out Melvin Canter was out of prison and back in this county?"

They exchanged a look.

"After," Beth said softly.

"How long have you been keeping track of him?"

"Five years. Since my divorce. I knew he'd been in prison for sexual assault."

"Did you return to Bear Butte County with the intention of killing the man who'd raped you?"

Beth flinched.

I felt like Attila the Hun, but I repeated, "Did you?"

"I don't know."

BD's eyes flashed angrily. "She wouldn't have.

After she told me who she was . . . well, I started counselin' her on not compoundin' her problems by doin' something rash."

"Murder is pretty rash." Not always entirely unjustified, but that wasn't part of this conversation.

"Beth wouldn't've done it. She's a good Christian woman."

I focused on Beth.

She stared back at me with haunted eyes. "BD's wrong. I would have. Right after I got here, the first chance I saw him alone, I could've pulled my shotgun out and blasted that man in the face and rejoiced in seeing his brains splattered in the snow."

"Beth—"

"It's okay, BD, I can say that now because you helped me get past the bitterness. The angry child inside me is fading away."

"So you came here to face your demons?"

"Yes," she sniffed, "but I'm sure you wouldn't understand."

Like hell I didn't.

"Beth gave her burden over to Jesus Christ," BD added.

Bully for her. I preferred to give Smith and Wesson the first crack at my problems. "Was that before or after the two of you were caught making the beast with two backs over at Sacred Souls?"

Beth cringed.

BD the protector jumped to his feet again. "I told

you what happened. I was tryin' to protect her from all this nastiness. Can you imagine what would've happened if people found out who she was? Then Doug Collins thought he saw something morally wrong, but he was the one who was wrong, and he—"

"—made a big fuss and Beth was fired. Yeah, I know. But isn't it convenient that the body of the man who'd raped her ended up on the land of the man who'd fired her?"

By the collective silence, evidently they hadn't considered that scenario.

"But she din't have nuthin' to do with Canter dyin'!"

Lots of times the most obvious answers were the right ones. But it didn't make sense for Beth to track her prey incognito, kill her prey, set up her fall guy, and then allow her mask to be ripped off to reveal her true identity when she'd all but gotten away with it.

If Beth slit Canter's throat, I would've figured she'd be long gone by now, not in Bear Butte County, falling in love with BD Hoffman.

"Hey. I'm talkin' to you."

My attention snapped back to BD. "I will admit you both make a pretty convincing argument about her innocence. Unfortunately, I'm not the one you need to convince. Sheriff Richards is."

"But—"

"You have a motive, Lizzie, or Beth, or whoever you're calling yourself, a motive much stronger than my father's, as it turns out. And you can bet I will spill every detail about you, your sudden appearance in this county, and your motive to the sheriff. And you can also bet he'll be around to ask you questions, so it'd be a helluva lot smarter for you to go to him first." I pointed at the phone. "Call him. You can be sure I'll be checking to see if you made the right choice."

"Whoa. Wait a durn minute. You said something about your father?" BD demanded. "Who are you?"

"Julie Collins. Doug Collins is my father."

With that embarrassing admission, I slunk out.

I called Big Mike on the secret Batphone. "Any word from Nyla on the whereabouts of Jackal yet?"

"No. And I need you to give this phone back."

"Nah. I kinda like having two. Makes me feel important."

"Great. I've created a monster."

"*Enhanced* a monster."

"Anything else?"

"Nope. Just checking in." I hung up first. Hah.

Then I reached for Nyla's diary. I flipped through the pages, which consisted of bad doodles, snippets of bad song titles, and bad poetry. It was so pathetic and sad I wanted to weep. No personal thoughts or contacts. No secret contacts to decipher. No girlish dreams. Just something to waste the time before she got wasted again.

I felt bad for taking the one thing that had given her joy.

CHAPTER 28

THE NEXT MORNING I FIRED UP MY FORD AND SCRAPED ice from my windshield. Appeared the mercury would hover in the single digits this morning since we were in the midst of an extended cold snap. And yippee! It was snowing again.

Swirling clouds of snow danced across the road. A strange sense of déjà vu enveloped me as I drove out to the ranch. Then again, with the endless white horizon, every time I ventured into the country I experienced that "been here, done that" sensation. Winter wasn't our longest season in South Dakota. It just seemed like it.

I parked in my usual spot. Dad's truck was backed up to the barn. Good. I wouldn't have to go in the house looking for him and drag his ass somewhere for a private conversation. Usually Brittney raced out the door the second I pulled up. Hopefully, Trish would keep her in the house and out of my way. I didn't have the energy to deal with her manipulative behavior when she realized I wasn't here to see her.

The barn itself was frigid, but when I closed in on the far corner, the air warmed up considerably. A bright light shone and voices echoed from the tack room.

I paused in the open doorway. Two old-fashioned Army cots were lined up like soldiers in the space. Dad sat on an overturned plastic bucket, working leather conditioner into an old saddle propped on another bucket in front of him. DJ stood in front of a tall post, twirling a length of rope. I hadn't seen DJ since last summer. The kid hadn't grown a millimeter. He hadn't filled out; he wasn't a skinny, gangly mass of long arms and legs like me. Like Ben. His physique was best described as a little butterball.

DJ said, "I like that other rope better. Has a little more give."

"Don't pay to have a favorite. Gotta be able to make adjustments on the fly with whatever you got handy. Sooner you can make any rope work for you, the better off you'll be."

"Same don't hold true for bull riders, Dad. Them guys get mighty attached to their bull ropes."

Dad snorted. "Bull ridin'. Dumbest thing I ever heard of. I can see bareback and saddle bronc bustin', 'cause breakin' horses is a skill, but climbin' on the back of a bull?" He shook his head. "I raised you to be smarter than that, son."

DJ let loose a low laugh. Whoa. His voice had changed. When he turned and saw me, his smile cracked and dried.

God. DJ's resemblance to our father was uncanny. I expected DJ's usual sneer, his cold glare, followed by a disapproving once-over. But he dropped his gaze to the rope clutched in his big hand, allowing his black felt hat to keep his face in shadow.

"What?" Dad looked up and noticed me. His gaze narrowed. "How long you been standin' there?"

I shrugged.

Without taking his eyes from mine, he said, "DJ, go see if your mother needs more firewood hauled in."

DJ didn't protest. He shrugged into his Carhartt coat, looped the rope over his shoulder, and gave me a wide berth on the way out.

Dad didn't speak until we heard the door creak and slam. "Why're you here?"

"Gee, you used to complain that I never deign to visit the ranch. Now you complain whenever I show up."

"I don't appreciate you bringin' other folks into my business, girlie."

"You mean Don and Dale?"

He glared.

"There are worse things than having friends who want to help you." Another lightbulb moment. "Dale posted bond for you, didn't he?"

More silence.

"Okay, since you won't talk, I will. I found out your hired man was convicted of sexual assault. Not once. Not twice. But three times. None of them here in this state, which means the three-strike rule doesn't apply and he was free to roam around. You and Trish are equally guilty about ignoring BD Hoffman when he tried to tell you about Canter's past."

His mouth hardened.

"But you knew the truth a couple of weeks ago because Dale Pendergrast told you. Trish didn't know until I told her the day before yesterday. My question is: why didn't you tell your wife right after you found out?"

"Because she's the one who hired Canter in the first place without askin' me. What was I supposed to do? Look like an idiot in front of everyone? A man who can't control his own ranch or his own wife? I had to act like it was a joint decision even when she made the stupid mistake all on her own."

"So you punished her by not letting her know Canter was a sexual predator?"

"No, I handled it and kept her out of it. Which is what she should've done—stayed outta my business."

"Why did you and Canter have a fistfight at Chaska's Feed Store?"

"Because he was a filthy liar spewin' filthy lies."

I kept pushing. "Is that why Trish had no clue you'd fired Melvin Canter?"

"That's where you're wrong and she's lyin'. I told

her he wadn't workin' here no more two days before she and the kids left for Denver."

So Trish had lied to me to get me to come out here in the middle of a goddamn blizzard, and continued to lie so I'd help her. What else had she lied about?

"For the past four years you've made it plain you don't want nuthin' to do with me. I won't stand for you comin' in here like a vulture and pickin' at things that're better left alone, things that ain't your concern. Family things that we'll take care of."

Instead of being cowed, I stung back. "Family things? You mean brushing your Indian son under the rug? Like you beating me? Those kind of embarrassing family secrets?"

"You don't know nuthin'."

"Try this secret on for size: yesterday I discovered Beth McClanahan, the secretary you fired from Sacred Souls, used to live here. She knows firsthand what kind of man Canter was because he raped her when she was eleven years old.

"Her father was the preacher and thought he'd do the Christian thing by leaving the 'judgment' to God. So rather than putting him in jail, her family dealt with the thing by ignoring it. By lying about it. By brushing it under the rug and ultimately by running away."

"Sounds to me like that gal had a good reason to want the man dead. Maybe your good buddy the sheriff oughta be lookin' into her motives instead of mine."

411

"Oh, I'm sure he will. Just like I'm sure now he'll have a bigger reason to bring *all* members of the Collins family into the sheriff's office and grill them about what your hired man did when he was alone with your kids."

Scritch scratch of the rag as he worked the saddle.

Ignoring me wouldn't make me go away. "Trish can't stay in the room with Brittney when the sheriff talks to her. You can't either. What about DJ? Maybe he'll shed light on this situation since he spent as much time with Canter as Brittney did. Maybe DJ saw something or knows something he's too afraid to talk about when you or Trish are around."

Dad leapt up so fast the bucket crashed to the ground. "You stay the hell away from my son. He's not talkin' to nobody about nuthin'. Ever. I'll never let you nor the law anywhere near him. You understand?"

Right then all of Doug Collins's motives became apparent. By keeping his mouth shut he hadn't been protecting himself. Or his daughter.

"My God. It never was about Brittney. It was about DJ."

"Shut up."

"Canter tried something with DJ, didn't he?"

Dad got right in my face and snarled. "You shut up. Shut your big stupid mouth."

"No one would—"

"No one will ever know, you hear me? *No one.* You think I want my only son to hafta grow up listenin' to the whispers of everyone in the county? Thinkin' he's weak? Thinkin' he liked what that sick man done to him and DJ couldn't stop it? Thinkin' he's some kinda homosexual freak? He ain't, but that's what folks will believe."

"So instead you're going to allow people to believe *Brittney* was sexually assaulted? How is that different? For Christsake, how can you possibly justify that's somehow *better*?"

"Because she's a girl. Because like you said, people will know Canter done it before with other little girls. She'll get sympathy. DJ wouldn't. That boy'd never be able to hold his head up in this county again, and I ain't gonna allow that to happen."

"Does Trish know any of this?"

"No. What do you think, I'm stupid? That woman is just like every other woman, can't keep her big mouth shut to save her life. Or in this case the life of her son."

I stared at him, absolutely speechless.

"So help me God, if you breathe a word of this to another livin' soul I will make you pay. Everyone knows about your vindictive streak. You killed the woman who killed your precious brother Ben. Now you're usin' DJ to get back at me because you're jealous of my new family. DJ don't want nuthin' to do with you, unlike your sainted injun brother."

"No one will believe you."

"If it comes to it, I'll tell Sheriff Richards I killed that sumbitch. I will go to jail to protect my son. Trish

413

will hafta sell the ranch." His eyes were angry blue flames. "Bottom line is my family will have nuthin'. And every bit of it'll be on your foolish head, girlie."

His nostrils flared rage as he leaned over me, his stale breath hot with fury. His fists closed tight in readiness to meet my face. Instinctively, I shrank inside myself in remembrance of other times I'd faced his wrath.

Hooves connected with the slats in the stall, making a loud clatter, breaking the moment.

Dad retreated. "Get out. And stay out of this, you hear me?" He spun on his boot heel and I heard the door slam.

I'd made it to the door when DJ oozed from the shadows. I jumped back. "Oh. DJ. You scared me."

"I oughta scare you good."

Everything inside me went on high alert.

"My dad better not end up in jail because of you and your big mouth. He's right. None of us want you here. No one would care if you never came back."

"Brittney would care," I whispered.

He laughed. "You think she really *likes* you? Wrong. She's usin' you to hurt Mom's feelin's. Always tellin' Mom how much cooler you are than her. How you'll let her do whatever she wants whenever she's with you. Brittney is a spoiled baby. Don't think it'll take much for me to turn her against you, 'cause I will do it. Leave us alone."

Sick of his intimidation, I tried another tactic.

"What did Melvin Canter do to you, DJ?"

"None of your fuckin' business."

"Whatever it was, it's not your fault. *You* did nothing wrong. You don't have to deal with it Dad's way."

"Back off or I'll show *you* exactly how *I* deal with people talkin' shit 'bout me and makin' me do stuff I don't wanna do."

Holy fucking Christ. Looking in his hate-filled eyes, I knew the truth: somehow, someway he'd killed Melvin Canter.

Losing battle here, Julie. Let it go.

I shouldered past him out of the dark barn into blinding white. Snowflakes pelted me, sticking to my burning face. A blast of cold air shot out of the vents when I cranked the ignition. Everything cooled down fast in these frigid temps.

I was numb. Frozen to the marrow of my bones.

Trish waved me down when I bumped past the house. Just made me increase my speed.

At least Brittney hadn't sought my attention. If it came down to it, the poor kid would be a sacrifice to her brother's worthless honor. Maybe Dad hitting me was better than the false sense of security he gave her. I'd never been delusional about how Dad felt about me.

Although it appeared I'd been delusional about my relationship with Brittney.

When I hit the gravel road, I hung a left rather than returning to the main highway, deciding to take the long way home. It'd allow me time to think about

415

why I ever thought my dad would change, except from bad to worse. Or about why I thought *I* should change. Kim had been right. Doug Collins was a cancer I needed to cut from my life. Now.

The words kept repeating on a never-ending loop, *DJ killed Melvin and your father covered it up.*

For the first time in a long time, I had no idea what was the right thing to do. Ignore it? Turn them in?

I fished inside my purse for the disposable phone. I could make an anonymous call to the sheriff.

And say what? *This is no one you know, but my fourteen-year-old brother just basically confessed to killing their hired man, whose initials are MC and it is an open case in the county.*

Right. I threw the phone in the seat.

Confused, angry, heartsick, I cracked the window. The cab resembled a meat locker but the cold did the trick and kept me from crying.

As I fought for control, the idiot warning buzzed in my head because the snow was falling so furiously I couldn't see five feet past my front grill. In my fit of pique, I'd taken the road less traveled.

Great plan in a snowstorm, Einstein.

I slowed down. Had I missed the turnoff? Within thirty seconds of dropping my speed, something rammed into the back end. My truck sailed forward; my seat belt jerked me back.

Damn. I touched the brakes and kept the pickup on the road.

The vehicle probably hadn't seen me until they were right up on my taillights. I pulled over to see if the driver of the other car was all right, when I was rear-ended again. Harder.

Snow flew, covering the windshield completely as I nose-dived through the ridge left by the snowplows.

I hit the gas and jerked the wheel to the left. No way was I going to get high centered or stuck in the goddamn ditch again and have to walk back to the ranch and ask my dad or DJ for help. No freakin' way.

I bounced off the embankment, busted through another ridge of snow, and came to a dead stop. I slammed the truck in park, unbuckled, and threw open the door, ready to give this asshole a piece of my mind. My feet hit the ground and I stalked back to where I saw a faint glimmer of headlights.

"What is the matter with you?"

No answer.

When I reached the Blazer, sitting crossways in the road, I realized the driver's side door was wide open. What the hell? Where was the driver?

"Hello?" I heard the crunch of snow behind me and I twirled around.

Right into the barrel of a gun.

I looked up.

Jackal stared back.

Then he backhanded me.

I tasted blood before everything went black.

CHAPTER 29

I CAME TO LYING IN THE MIDDLE OF THE ROAD. THE side of my face dug into the gravel and ice. Someone was slapping my other cheek. Cold liquid pooled in the corner of my mouth.

"Wake up. Jesus. I didn't hit you that fuckin' hard."

I flinched. Shivered. Blinked. Didn't help. I saw nothing but white spots.

"Ain't as tough as everyone claims, are you, bitch?"

When I didn't respond, a hiking boot connected with my ribs. I curled into a ball and tried to protect my head.

"Get her up. Didja get her cell phone out of her truck?"

"Right here."

The female voice sounded familiar. Somehow I managed to open my eyes and breathe through the bone-chilling fear.

Jackal loomed over me. "Get up. I ain't got all goddamn day."

I pushed into a sitting position. The cheek that'd been pressed to the road burned. The other cheek where Jackal smacked me smarted. I wasn't wearing gloves so my hands were red and stung like a million needles were jabbing them. I turned my head and spit a mixture of blood and saliva on the snowy ground. Not teeth, though.

"You sure ain't as mouthy when Martinez ain't around to protect you."

"It's a little hard for me to talk when I'm knocked out cold."

He laughed. "True. You scared?"

I nodded. My life meant nothing to him and he wouldn't hesitate to end it.

"Good." Jackal laughed again. "On your knees."

I rolled up, concentrating on the pain of the rocks from the gravel road digging into my kneecaps and not the fear causing my whole body to shake.

"Let's do something fun." To the unseen woman off to the left Jackal said, "Is there a camera on her phone?"

"Yep."

I didn't have a camera on my phone. Wait. The phone Big Mike gave me did. She hadn't grabbed my

419

phone. She'd grabbed the one I'd tossed in the seat.

"Figure out how to work it." Jackal hunkered down in front of me. "Which number is his? Don't lie to me, it'll just make it that much worse on you."

"Listed as TM." Jackal's stench, pot smoke, greasy skin, dirty hair, surrounded me, but I didn't look at him.

Until he bunched my ponytail in his fist and jerked my head up, holding the gun to my temple.

"Pay attention."

"What do you want?"

"See, your old man took something that don't belong to him. I want it back. And you're gonna help me get it."

"I don't know what you're talking about."

Jackal yanked me closer by the hair and the gun gouged my skin. "I'm sure you don't, 'cause he keeps you outta his business. But Mr. Big Shot is fuckin' around with me. So now, I'm gonna fuck around with him." He didn't bother to turn his head when he yelled at the woman, treating me to a sour blast of his booze and garlic-laced breath. "Got that camera figured out yet?"

"Yeah. Snapped a nice shot of you pulling her hair. Want me to send it?"

"He does have a thing for your hair, don't he, *blondie*? Maybe afterward I oughta scalp you as a souvenir for him. So he'll never forget you."

Oh, Jesus. Jackal was going to kill me and take pictures of it and send them to Martinez. Tony would go berserk. Not only because he couldn't save me, but because no one else could save me either. No knights riding to my rescue this time since I'd made Big Mike call off my security detail.

Three days ago.

Was this about Nyla? The something Martinez supposedly took? Tony knew nothing about that. If I told Jackal the truth would it buy me time?

Doesn't matter. You're dead or worse anyway.

"Hands behind your back. Like you're gonna bob for apples. 'Cept it ain't apples you're gonna be bobbing on."

The woman neighed like a horse.

My throat tightened against nausea.

Jackal rose to his feet, still holding my hair. "Come here, bitch, close as you can get." He yanked my head and smashed my face into his crotch, keeping the gun aimed at my temple.

I gagged. Tears poured from my eyes.

Wake up wake up wake up.

He ground the bulge behind his zipper across my mouth. "Take the fuckin' picture. Another. Get a close-up of my face so he knows how much I'm enjoying this."

I pulled my lips inside against my teeth, hating to have any part of me touching this piece of filth.

"Got 'em. Which one should I send first?"

"Send them all to him. We'll see which one he likes best."

I quit breathing. Maybe I could make myself pass

out. Maybe it'd take away some of Jackal's fun.

He flung me away like a used blow-up doll.

I fell, turning my head until my lips brushed the dirty snow, and retched. My stomach was empty, but I couldn't stop the dry heaves.

Triggering my gag reflex pissed Jackal off. He kicked me again. This time in the middle of my back. I gasped. Snow snakes drifted into my mouth.

"Keep it up, cunt, and the next picture I take of you blowing me *won't* be fake."

I gritted my teeth, focusing on the pain in my spine.

"This is a cool cell phone, Jack. You should buy me one like this. I could send you naughty pictures of me."

"Shut up, Trina, and give me the goddamn phone."

Trina. No wonder her voice sounded familiar. I'd worked with her at Bare Assets a few months back. In addition to being a shitty cocktail waitress, Trina was a drug addict. But I never would've guessed she'd thrown in with Jackal, especially after he'd set her up to take the fall if a drug bust would've gone down in Bare Assets during my short stint.

Maybe she didn't know. If I told her would it make her turn on Jackal so I could get away?

No.

Something else occurred to me. Big Mike said they'd figured out who the shooter was and how the shooter had been able to get to Martinez so quickly. Shame on me. I'd assumed it'd been a man.

I lifted my head and looked at her. "Did you shoot Martinez?"

"Fucker deserved it for what he did to Jack. I wish Jack would've let me kill him instead of just wounding him."

The cell phone rang and my heart rate doubled.

Jackal answered: "Like the pictures? No? Trina is crushed you don't appreciate her artistic ability. Does that mean you want us to redo them? With a little more realism this time?"

My gag reflex threatened again.

"No? Your loss." Jackal trained his gun at me as Martinez talked. "Why? Not a death wish. You have something of mine; now I have something of yours. Sure. I'm willing to trade." He jerked his head at Trina and she sauntered over to me. He made the "get her on her feet" gesture with the gun. "No dice. Because you'll fuck me over if I don't retain a little leverage. No. She ain't worth it."

Leverage? An even exchange. Me for Nyla? I shuddered to think which one of us wasn't worth leveraging.

"You listen to me. Here's the deal: I'll give you one, but not both. You knew she did it, huh? Well, get whatcha pay for." Jackal beckoned Trina forward.

I willed the blood to stop whooshing in my ears so I could hear Tony's voice one last time.

"Now ain't the time to threaten retribution." Jackal took two steps. "Really? I'm shocked. But not so fuckin' shocked that I'll let you choose. No, I get to play God today, *hombre*."

Jackal lifted the gun and sited my forehead. I'd been shot before so I knew it'd hurt. But I wouldn't give this fucker the satisfaction of squeezing my eyes shut.

Then he swung the gun at Trina and pulled the trigger six times.

She screamed.

I screamed. Her blood sprayed across my face before she crumpled to the earth at my feet and I tasted her blood on my lips.

Jackal pointed the gun at me again and made the "quiet" signal with his finger across his lips, his crazy eyes locked to mine.

I didn't make another sound.

"Shut the fuck up, Martinez. I'm givin' you a chance. Find the one who's alive. I'll leave them both here. For shits and giggles, I'm taking the coats. Since you're a college boy, good with numbers, try to figure out how long the survivor will last with the windchill. Don't try tracking this phone because I'm taking it with me and ditching it first chance I get. I'll be in touch."

Jackal hung up. He shoved the cell in the pocket of his filthy cargo pants and eliminated the distance between us.

I didn't have the energy to cringe. My ears rang

from close-range gunfire. I was absolutely fucking numb with fear. This man redefined *monster*. I just wished I would be around to see what torture Tony inflicted before he allowed Jackal to die.

I couldn't help but look at Trina. Her eyes were open. Her mouth was slack with death. Blood spread across her chest like her heart exploded upon impact. Looked like wild animals had torn out her throat. How had she managed to scream?

"Why did you kill her?"

"She was as good as dead anyway." Jackal pressed his nose to mine, and again the sour odor of his mouth and skin and soul made my flesh shrivel with revulsion. "What do you think the Hombres would've done with her once they found her, huh? Let her go? Trust me, they would've found her eventually. No matter what."

I didn't move.

"Do you think they woulda talked to her? Asked her why she had anger issues? Do you think they'd understand why she opened fire on their leader? No. The Hombres don't talk; they act. They'd rape her, then beat her, then rape her some more before they started torturing her. I've seen it before. Hell, I've *done* it."

My throat hurt with the need to swallow, but I couldn't.

"No way would they've let her live. She signed her own death certificate when she shot at Martinez.

Trina served her purpose. Me killin' her fast like that was the least I could do for her. It was the . . . humane thing to do."

Humane? Fucked-up logic for sure, but I didn't dispute his rambling.

He grinned nastily. "And blowin' holes in her was worth hearing calm, cool, and collected El Presidente lose his fuckin' mind when he heard the shots. That's just a personal bonus for me, with him thinkin' I killed you. With him freakin' out about what he'll find when he does eventually find you out here in the middle of fuckin' nowhere. You're dead, too. You know that, right?"

I nodded.

Jackal dangled a pair of handcuffs. "Take off your coat. Get on your knees."

I threw my wool coat on the ground. "Are you gonna kill me?"

"Not with the gun. But if I stuck around you'd probably beg me to shoot you. Ain't gonna be fun freezin' to death, which is why I didn't shoot you. I want you to endure pain. I want you in agony before you finally die. I want Martinez to see how you suffered and to have to live with the fact he didn't get to you in time."

I thought of Vernon Sloane for the millionth time. Dying alone. Did he wonder who'd find him? I knew who'd eventually find me.

"Get on your knees down by the trailer hitch.

Hold out your right arm."

I did.

Jackal snapped one cuff around my wrist and the other one around the ball hitch. He tugged hard. Satisfied I couldn't get loose, he straightened and grinned maniacally. "It'd almost be worth it to see Martinez's face when he sees you as you really are: a frigid fuckin' blonde with ice in her veins."

I shivered so hard the chain on the cuffs clattered. I heard his footsteps fading, half-afraid he was taunting me and planned on shooting me in the back of the head at the last minute. My whole body convulsed and didn't stop even after he'd climbed in his Blazer and sped away.

Don't look at her.

But I knew if I closed my eyes I'd fall asleep or drift off into that dreamy state of cold nothingness like I'd been in when I'd stumbled through the blizzard at the ranch.

Guess Dad wouldn't have to worry about me spilling DJ's secret.

Guess Kim wouldn't have to worry about me ruining her wedding day.

Guess Tony was right. I needed a goddamn

bodyguard.

I had no illusions about how this scenario would play out. No chance for rescue. I'd made sure of that by insisting I didn't need help, coddling, or protection. It was too late to admit to Tony, or to anyone else, that I did need protection. Mostly from myself and my own stupid pride.

Jesus. I never learned from my mistakes.

Yes, you learned one thing. You told Martinez how you felt about him.

It'd be cold comfort when he stared at my lifeless body.

God. It would ruin him. I knew that. If the situation were reversed it would destroy me.

I started to cry. I didn't want to die. Not like this. At least when I'd had the showdown with Leticia at Bear Butte, my death would've had meaning. A sense of purpose. A twisted nobility. Vengeance served cold.

Right now I had nothing but a truckload of regrets.

Sobs racked my body with such violence I felt I was being electrocuted. Tears froze on my face. I jerked and tugged on the handcuffs trying to get free. Maybe if I twisted it I could make the metal edge sharp enough to cut my hand off. Better to live with one hand than to die with both.

I screamed until my throat was raw. The cries mixed with the shrieking wind and vanished into the white sea of barrenness.

Not fair. Not fair. Not fucking fair!

I wished I had a do-over. I wished I would've turned right after leaving the ranch. I wished I would've stayed and talked to Trish. Or to Brittney. I wished I would've called Martinez, Kevin, Jimmer, the sheriff, anyone, so someone knew where the hell I was.

Might as well wish for a pair of bolt cutters while you're at it.

I went utterly still.

Whoa. Wait a second.

I slowly lifted my head. Icy wind rippled through my hair. I squinted at the lumps in the snow-covered truck bed.

Jimmer's voice: *Don't you ever clean this shit out?*

My answer: *You never know when you might need something.*

Like bolt cutters.

I quit breathing. I had a pair of bolt cutters. Recently. But when?

Never. This is an illusion.

No. I used them for something.

What?

I don't remember.

That's because it was in a dream. Wishful thinking.

No, it's not. Focus.

Snow pelted me in the face. I shook my head to clear the fuzzy thoughts. Was this a mind trick? A reason to give me false hope?

No. Think, Julie. When was the last time you had them?

With Dad on the ranch when we were calving? No.

429

Those were chains and clamps.

With Jimmer? No.

Don and Dale had used their rusted-out, old-fashioned pair of bolt cutters to hack through the barbed-wire fence at the ranch, not mine.

That wasn't it.

Think. Come on. Picture your bolt cutters in your mind. Big wooden handles. Rusty spot near the spring.

It clicked.

I'd used my bolt cutters to sever the chain to Nyla's motel room.

I stood so fast I nearly tore my arm from the socket. My feet lost traction on the ice and I crashed, smacking my tailbone into the ground, jerking my arm again.

Unless someone stole them out of my truck bed, they should be there. Right there up near the passenger's side door.

I stretched my left arm out as far as I could reach. My frozen fingers frantically pawed through the snow. I wasn't even fucking close to the other side of the truck bed.

Maybe I could reach it with my feet. I swung around and crawled into the back of the pickup. Lying on my back, my body stayed at a funky angle since my right wrist was attached to the ball hitch outside the truck bed. But I was goddamn glad I'd opted for a cargo net instead of the traditional tailgate.

My breath came hard and fast. Forcing myself to go slow, I swept my legs from side to side to clear away the crusted snow. *Clunk.* I made the same movement again. *Clunk.* Metal striking metal.

Bingo. I'd found it.

I felt the lump beneath the toe of my right boot. I slid up and dropped my boot heel down, using it to drag the long wooden handle close enough to grasp it. My fingers were stiff and practically useless, but somehow I managed to wrap them around the handle. I dragged it closer only to realize I'd grabbed the shovel. I tried again. Three attempts later and I had the smooth handles in my icy hand. Immediately I burst into a mix of laughter and tears.

Don't get cocky. Your hand is still cuffed and you've lost fine motor skills.

I forced three more deep breaths into my lungs, never letting go of my precious tool as I stared up at the white sky. Then I scooted back to the tailgate. Snow went down my pants and up my shirt but I didn't care.

Putting the sharp tip of the bolt cutters around the chain links one-handed was like threading a needle. My strength was totally zapped. I'd already used every drop of adrenaline.

Wind stung my cheeks. I licked my lips, tasting salt and blood but feeling nothing because my face was encased in ice.

After two misses, I decided to use my upper body for balance and momentum. I braced the handle against the bottom of the tailgate and rocked into it.

Nothing.

431

I didn't have voice enough to swear.

Deep breaths. In. Out. Patience.

Seemed a hundred pushes before the link gave way, separating me from the hitch. Half of the set of handcuffs circled my wrist like the world's ugliest bracelet. Weird. Even though the silver ring hadn't been tight, I couldn't feel my hand. I tried to squeeze the fingers of my right hand into a fist. Even weirder. The bolt cutters in my left hand crashed to the ground.

Everything swirled in slow, dense fog. Snow eddied around me and I was mesmerized by the shifting and floating white forms. Shapes like ghostly fingers beckoned, sibilant whispers taunted, a hiss of temptation—no words—existing only as pure sound.

The high tinkling tones of *The Dance of the Sugar Plum Fairy* trilled on the wind.

Ooh. Pretty. I loved that song. I swayed back and forth, humming along.

Get out of the fucking cold, you idiot.

The voice of reason snapped me to attention.

I backed up and fell right on top of Trina. Her rib cage cracked beneath my weight and blood or something wet and sticky soaked into the seat of my pants.

Eww. A hoarse squeak burst from my mouth. I attempted to scramble away, but the grommet on my boot hooked Trina's coat, dragging her bloody bag of skin and bones along as I literally tried to escape her deadweight.

Reach down and unhook it.

I shook my head.

Don't be stupid. Unhook it.

No. Shut up. I'll do it my own way.

My heart rate remained sluggish as I kicked, flailing my leg without touching Trina. Finally the metal tab ripped free on its own. I crawled the last few feet to the driver's side door, opened it, and climbed inside.

Needed to get warm. Needed keys.

Where were my keys? Not in the ignition where I'd left them because I'd left my truck running when I'd initially jumped out. Had Jackal stolen them when he'd turned it off?

Frustrated, I whimpered. So close. So goddamn close, just to fail at the final buzzer. I was so tired. So fucking cold. So tired of being so fucking cold all the time. Maybe if I lay down I'd warm up. Body shaking, I flopped sideways on the bench seat.

Something sharp jabbed me in the cheek.

Slowly I turned my head. My keys. Lodged in the seat crack.

An illusion.

I moved and they jangled. Hah. Not an illusion.

Somehow I made my fingers bend. Somehow I hooked the key ring on my index finger. After dropping the keys to the floor mat four times, I started my truck, cranked the heat, and passed out to the strains of *It Won't Hurt*.

CHAPTER 30

THE AROMA OF LEATHER ROUSED ME.

My voice scratched out, "Tony?"

"I'm here."

"I know. I smelled you."

"You saying I smell bad? No. Don't answer that, blondie, just hang on."

The music faded as my body was lifted from the bench seat. Icy wind swept over me. I was so cold. I shivered. The arms around me tightened. Doors slammed. Then softness and heat. Leather. Sweat. Him.

Spanish gibberish filled my ear.

Everything went dark again. I didn't mind. Better than being lost in the white void.

I was hot. Too hot. I attempted to sit up but couldn't with a thousand blankets piled on top of me.

I focused on the male voices by my feet.

"Frostbite. Dehydration. Exhaustion."

"Which means?"

"She oughta go to the hospital and get checked out."

"No fucking way. I can't protect her there."

"Thought you might say that." A sigh. "Truth is, she should be fine if you keep her warm. Keep her hydrated. Make her rest. And, for Christsake, feed her. She's goddamn lucky you saved her."

"I didn't save her," Martinez snapped. "She saved herself."

Ooh, and didn't he just sound plumb tickled about that?

I tried to roll my shoulders and couldn't. Had I been mummified? Jesus. Was I wearing a fucking *hat*? I wanted to scream but I couldn't breathe. I settled for kicking my feet, which were trapped in four hundred pairs of wool socks.

"She's awake. Call me if you need anything."

I heard the door click as the Hombres' doctor left. Then the cotton sheet was removed from my face. I stared into Tony's eyes.

He said, "Don't talk."

"Bet you'd like that." Whispering was as close as I'd get to talking after screaming like a banshee in the snowstorm. "Take off this goddamn hat. I'm thirsty. Help me up."

435

"Hang on, blondie. One thing at a time."

The layers of covers were peeled back. Once my hands were freed I realized I was wearing gloves. Two pairs. I whipped them off and saw I had on my favorite flannel pajamas. No wonder I'd been so toasty. I scooted into the pillows piled on my side of the bed.

Martinez opened the bottled water before handing it to me. I drank the whole thing.

"You want another?"

I shook my head, letting it fall back, hoping I wouldn't barf up the liquid sloshing in my stomach.

He didn't speak. Even though I'd closed my eyes, I felt him watching me. Worrying. Feeling guilty. Feeling relieved. Probably feeling déjà vu.

I didn't know what to say to offer him solace. So I merely held out my hand to where he'd perched on a folding chair. The second that warm, rough palm covered mine, I sighed.

All the encouragement he needed. He crawled next to me, pulled me into his arms, and became my comfort, my pillow, my blanket, my heat, my light . . . my everything. And I wouldn't be scared to admit it to him or anyone else. Not ever again.

He whispered, "Jesus, Julie. I'm so sorry."

"I know." I repositioned my sore cheek so I could hear his heart beating. "How did you find me?"

No answer.

"Divine intervention?"

"No. GPS."

"What?"

"I put a tracker on your truck."

I lifted my head. "When?"

"Right after the blizzard when you were missing for two days. Drove me insane. Jackal was on the loose and I figured it'd piss you off if you knew I knew where you were at all times so I didn't tell you."

"That's how you knew I was at Dusty's? And at the Road Kill Café? And out in the middle of nowhere?" I couldn't exactly be indignant about it so I didn't pretend to be.

"Yeah. You made it clear you hated my security team following you. I had to do something."

"But you still had your goons following me after that."

"Better safe than sorry. You have no idea how fucking sorry I am."

I wondered if he knew . . .

"If you hadn't convinced Big Mike to call off your tail without my permission, I would've been there sooner. Might've gotten to Jackal before he got to you." Martinez's angry breath pulsed across the top of my head. "When he sent those pictures from that phone . . ."

"Tony—"

"And then I heard the gunshots. Christ. If Bucket would've had a tranq gun, he would've used it on me. I fucking lost it, Julie, like I've never lost it . . . I didn't know what I'd find when I got to you . . . how I'd ever

. . . if you weren't . . ."

I cried. Mostly to keep him from breaking down.

It worked. He used his fears to calm mine. "Ssh. Baby. It's okay. I'm here."

"Don't go. Promise you won't leave? Even if I fall back asleep?"

"I promise."

"I thought I was a goner."

He said nothing, just kept soothing me with long sweeping caresses down my spine.

"What happened to the handcuff around my wrist?"

"I cut it off."

"I don't remember that."

"Good."

"I do remember Trina admitting she shot you. Did you know?"

"Yeah."

"Jackal said he killed her because the Hombres would've done worse, torturing her and raping her before letting her die."

Tony didn't deny it; I hadn't expected him to.

"I know that's what the Hombres do to keep order. I don't understand. I sure as hell don't wanna know the details—ever—but at the same time, I'm not sorry Trina is dead. Just sorry I had to see it." I waited a beat. "Does that make me callous?"

"No."

Does that make me like you?

My dad's voice chimed in. *Gets easier to kill, don't it?*

If I had to choose, I'd rather be like Tony Martinez than Doug Collins.

And again, I did my ostrich imitation and yanked the covers over my head when I realized the truth of how far removed I was.

Tony gently peeled them back. "Don't hide, especially not from me, blondie. I couldn't stand it."

"I'm not. I'm just cold." I burrowed into him. After a while I said, "And Jackal?"

"Is a fucking dead man soon as we find him." Martinez twirled a hank of hair around his finger. "After I discovered my Wonder Woman had escaped on her own again, and she was sacked out in her truck listening to that goat-yodeling shit—"

"Watch what you say about my boy Dwight."

"I wanted to hide you at my place. Throw you in the hot tub, prop you by the fireplace, wrap you up, hell, *tie* you up, but it was too far, so I had to settle for putting you in the shower here."

"I don't remember that either. How long has it been since you . . ."

"Eight hours."

"Were you in there with me?"

"Someone needed to hold you up."

"Getting tired of that yet, Martinez?"

"Never." He brought his mouth to mine and kissed me with all the seductive sweetness I craved.

439

My stomach rumbled.

He smiled against my mouth. "Hungry?"

"Yeah. Can any of those guys out there cook?"

"No. I'll send someone for food. What do you want?"

"Steak. Fries. Bread. Brownies."

"Done." He whipped out his cell and sent a text message to the next room. Closed it and pulled me across his body. "Try to rest, okay? Food'll be here when you wake up."

Martinez probably had a million things to do, but he didn't leave me. Not for a single second. I finally accepted he never would.

I scarcely had enough energy to eat and return to bed. Even the next morning I felt nowhere near normal. Martinez coddled me. I let him. Something had changed significantly between us once again. Two near-death experiences in a week will do that.

Later in the afternoon, Big Mike knocked on the bedroom door. "There's a kid here to see Julie. Claims she's Julie's sister?"

"Frizzy hair? Polite, but a little geeky?"

I whacked Martinez on the arm.

Big Mike nodded.

"Yeah, that's Brittney. Tell her to hang out for a sec." Tony pecked me on the forehead and slid off the bed. "Want me to stick around?"

"To protect me from an eleven-year-old girl?"

"Smart-ass. But you're kidding yourself if you pretend she doesn't have the power to hurt you."

His insight made me squirm. "Thanks, but I'll be okay."

He opened the door. Brittney looked up at him and said, "*Hola, Señor Martinez.*"

"*Hola, Señorita Collins. Como estas?*"

"*Bueno.*"

"I'll be out here if you need anything, Julie."

"Thanks."

Brittney gave me a once-over. "Wow. Must be nice to sleep in all day."

Yeah, that was me, lazing around like a slug all the time.

She balanced on the edge of the mattress. "Something wrong with you?"

"Got a little chilled yesterday. Better to be safe than sorry. How'd you get here?"

"The bus driver dropped me off like last time."

"Ah. What's up?"

"I wanted to give you the souvenir I bought in Denver." She passed me a small item packaged in newspaper.

I unwrapped a shot glass. With the Denver skyline etched on one side, and *Colorful Colorado!* on the other. "Thanks, Britt."

"I know you'll use it since you drink all the time. Most of them had Denver Broncos or Denver Nuggets, or Colorado Rockies or Colorado Avalanche emblems on the sides. Couldn't find any with bull riders."

She had such a high opinion of me and I felt myself bristle.

"I came out to the barn to surprise you with it yesterday."

My gaze caught hers. "When?"

"Right after you got there. I snuck in the side door, and I heard . . ."

"What?"

"Everything."

Shit. "And that's why you're here?"

"Yes. You always say I can ask you anything. I'm asking you: don't call the sheriff on DJ and turn him in for what he done."

Not what I'd expected. "If you heard it all maybe you should understand—"

"Understand what? That man was a bad, bad man and I'm glad he's dead. I wish I woulda done it." Angrily, she wiped the tears glistening on her lashes. "Daddy is right. My mom shoulda never hired him and it's not fair to make DJ pay for Mom's mistake."

"Your mom did not kill Melvin Canter, so she *didn't* make that fatal mistake."

"But if she wasn't so stupid to hire him without talking to Daddy about it first, then none of this would've happened!"

Why was she sticking up for him? "Does Dad know you're here?"

She shook her head.

"Did you hear all of what he said yesterday? That he'd rather let people think Melvin sexually molested *you*, rather than DJ?"

"I don't care. *You're* the one who's always telling me it doesn't matter what people think. They can think whatever they want just as long as they don't send my brother away."

"He killed someone."

"So did you. You told me it was self-defense. So it's no different."

Stung, I snapped, "That is not for you to decide. That's why there are cops and lawyers and a legal system."

"It's not for you to decide either," she retorted. "DJ is my only brother and you don't have the right to try to take him away from me just because your brother is dead!"

My heart actually stopped.

"How can you love Ben so much and hate DJ? He's as much your brother as Ben ever was. Is it because you think Ben was more special because he was Indian?"

"Brittney—"

"DJ is the only brother I'll ever have and I'll do anything to save him. I *will* tell people *I* killed that bad guy because he was touching me and stuff . . . and they'll believe me when I tell them I had the tractor out because I was trying to hide his body."

Why hadn't I considered she'd have the same unwavering love and devotion for her brother that I had for mine? Just because I didn't feel that way about DJ didn't mean she didn't.

Brittney's hazel eyes burned with a mean glint I'd never seen on her sweet face. But I recognized the look; she'd learned it from our father.

I realized she was far more our father's daughter than I ever was. I'd tried to ignore all her smarmy comments, her backhanded compliments, the overwhelming guilt she loaded on me. I'd brushed aside her behavior, conveniently blaming it on her age, not her genetics.

I was such a fool. DJ had been right; so had Kim. Brittney didn't care about me. She used me as leverage with both her mother and father. Why hadn't I seen it?

In that moment the tiny crack between us splintered into a full-blown fissure and I tumbled into the abyss of dark truth. I hit rock bottom with the realization my relationship with her was as fractured as my reasoning for it.

Last year I'd told Sheriff Richards that Brittney and I might share the same blood, but we did not share the same father. I'd always believed it, abided by it, used it as a protective shield. As my friend, Richards made me question that rigid stance, and he'd been sincere in bringing it up, making me wonder if I had been wrong.

Turns out I'd been right all along.

Ben's ghostly familial advice from the great beyond notwithstanding, I finally saw it for what it'd been: my hallucinogenic grasp at straws. Nothing would fill the void of losing Ben. I didn't want or need a replacement sibling. I'd been an idiot to try to forge a connection with Brittney where there wasn't one. Where—if I was totally honest with myself—I didn't want one. Ben had tried to forge a new family bond with his sister Leticia and look where it'd gotten him. She'd slit his throat and left him to die.

Just like DJ had done with Melvin Canter. Wasn't it ironic they both thought their actions were justified?

Brittney and I would never come to terms on our father, what he'd done to me, as opposed to how she saw him. If by some miracle when she was older and she'd gained a different perspective, it'd be too late. For both of us.

Another wave of sadness and loss washed over me, but I managed to suck it up.

"Do you have a ride home?"

"No."

"Tony?" I called, a little louder than necessary, a little more desperate than necessary.

The door opened. Big Mike popped his head in and said, "Whaddya need?"

"Call Brittney's mom to come and get her."

"No problem. Come on, kid. You can wait out here. Julie needs to rest."

445

Brittney made it to the door before she turned back. "You won't tell on him?"

I shook my head. What she didn't realize was this might be beyond the control of either of us.

"Thanks. See ya, sis."

And I couldn't snap back my usual, "Not if I see you first," response, because this time, it wasn't a joke. From now on, I'd go out of my way to stay out of her life. Not out of spite; out of self-protection. The kid could destroy me and she knew it. And I'd almost let it happen out of some misplaced sense of family loyalty. A family who had never wanted anything to do with me anyway.

When the door closed, I pulled the quilt over my head and hid from the world.

CHAPTER 31

Less than thirty minutes later the door opened and the mattress dipped. "You're gonna smother under there, sugar, regardless if you had hypothermia yesterday or not."

Kim.

The covers were stripped back. Her cool hand soothed my tear-dampened face. But I couldn't look at her.

"Okay, so let's bust this little tiff we had last week wide open. You pissed me off. So to be contrary and mean, I downloaded that Winnie the Pooh song into my iPod. You know, the one about being the little black rain cloud? I planned to make you listen to it over and over, but the second I heard it . . . Lawd almighty, I was weepin' like a willow tree."

I snorted. "You cry at the drop of a hat. Or a baby

bootie. Or a Bud Light commercial."

"I've been acting like grumpy old Eeyore, too."

"The jackass comparison works for me."

"Can I blame my shitty behavior to you on pregnancy hormones?"

"No."

"Gonna make me grovel, aren't you?"

"Maybe." Her throaty laughter made me smile. I opened my eyes. "Why're you really here, Kim?"

"To say I'm sorry."

"And?"

"To say I missed you and I had the strangest feeling things weren't right with you, Jules."

"Martinez called you, didn't he?"

"No. Actually I called him."

A tiny sense of relief surfaced that she'd chosen to be here on her own, not grudgingly shown up at my lover's request. "Why?"

"Because you haven't been in the office. Kevin seemed clueless and preoccupied after I asked him where you were. No answer on your cell. When I reached Tony today, he said you were taking some downtime. I called bullshit on his explanation on how you ended up with a case of hypothermia, especially not with four of his armed bodyguards holed up in your house." She scrutinized the marks on my face. "Can you tell me what's been going on?"

"No." My eyes filled. "But I can tell you I'm glad you're here, Kim. So goddamn glad."

"Hey." She crawled on the bed and lay down, facing me. "Stop bawling or I'll start."

"Okay." The stupid tears kept coming.

"You're really upset, huh?"

I nodded.

"Talk to me. There's not a damn thing you can tell me that will make me run out of here screaming. Sometimes I don't like what you do, but that doesn't mean I don't like *you*. We're buddies, pals, BFF, no matter what."

The silence lingered, not unwieldy, just there.

I sighed. "You know why I like you?"

"There are so many reasons I don't believe you'll have time to list them all before I have to go home," she teased.

"Ha ha. Seriously, I like you because I don't *have* to like you. Makes it my choice, rather than something I feel I have to do."

"Is this about Brittney?"

"Yes." One simple word. No simple answers.

"Let it out, darlin', I'm here."

"You were right. I thought it could be different for me than it was for you. I felt a little smug, if you want to know the truth, that maybe I could overcome my past with my father in a way you couldn't with yours. But the truth is, I can't be around him, because he *is* poison. And being around Brittney means being around him, so in a strange way, she's poison, too. Why didn't I see her manipulation of me?"

"Because you didn't listen to your gut. Because you wanted what you had with Ben, sugar."

"Ironically, she's the same age I was when Ben showed up. I can't imagine what hell my life would've been if he hadn't bulled his way into it."

"I sense a 'but.'"

"But Ben and I held a similar view of Doug Collins. It bugs the shit out of me that Brittney doesn't see him for what he is."

"Honey, she won't. Not unless he reverts to how he was to you."

"As glad as I am that he isn't beating on her, at least his apathy and hatred toward me and Ben were overt, not covert. It doesn't bother her that Dad would throw her to the wolves to save DJ."

Kim didn't respond right away. "It hurts. I'm sorry. Other people would tell you to try to work it out, she's family, and it matters. But you *are* doing the right thing by letting it go, by letting her go. This has to do with *your* mental well-being, not what other people think. Including me.

"There's lots of good people in your life who love you as you are, Jules. Martinez. Kevin. Jimmer. Me. We are your family by choice. I might get pissy with you, and pick out the ugliest bridesmaid's dress on the planet for you to wear at my wedding, but, face it: I need you as much as you need me."

"You say that now, Kim, as I'm lying here bawling my eyes out, but you haven't needed me." I forced myself to look at her even when I was afraid of what I'd see. "In fact, it seems like you've been trying to cut me out of your life."

A soft sigh. "Maybe I was. I'm flying without a net, getting married and figuring out what this pregnancy and baby business is all about. You were right when you said you hadn't changed. You drink. You smoke. You swear. You have a dangerous job at times. The man in your bed and in your life is one of the most feared men in five states. It's never bothered me before. But now? I wondered if that was the kind of friend I wanted my baby to be around."

I bit the inside of my cheek to stop a cry from erupting at another loss in my life.

"Then I realized I don't need you to be the baby's friend; I need you to be my friend."

"That's sweet, but you've still been preg-zilla and now you're trying to make me shed happy tears so you don't feel so mean."

"Have you ever known me to throw out a mercy compliment?" Kim laughed. "Just so you don't think I've gone too nice, you definitely need a haircut, girl-friend." She gasped softly.

"What? You okay?"

Instead of answering, she grabbed my hand and placed it on the front swell of her stomach. "Feel that?"

I waited. Then something booted my palm. Hard. My hand snapped back. "Holy shit."

Kim snagged my hand and put it back on her baby bump. "Isn't that wild?"

"Freakishly bizarre." I poked her stomach. The skin was taut, not squishy. "What's it feel like from the inside?"

"Hard to explain. I'm gonna ask you the same question when you're pregnant."

And things'd been going so well. "Will you retract the BFF statement if I tell you I don't want to have kids? Ever."

"No. But you don't know—"

"Yes, actually I do."

"You and Tony have discussed it?"

I couldn't tell her about Tony's son or the regret he carried about giving him up to the boy's mother. I didn't want to talk about my miscarriage or why it seemed every child in my life broke my heart. "We don't have to talk about it."

"Meaning what?"

"Meaning we've chosen this lifestyle. Neither of us wants to subject a child to it." I softened my tone. "Being with Martinez is more happiness than I thought I'd ever find, Kim, and that's enough for me."

"It should be. Okay, okay, sorry. I'll stop trying to push my life off on you." She drew my hand across her belly as the kicks grew more intense. "She is gonna be a great soccer player."

"Or he's gonna be an excellent kickboxer."

"She for sure. We found out last week it's a girl."

I grinned. "I am so happy for you."

"That, I never doubted. So . . . come to Vegas? Please? I want you to stand up there with me when I get hitched."

"Just as long as you were kidding about the ugly dress."

"Nope. It's lilac satin with pink ruffles and bows, yellow lace, and a matching parasol. Ooh, and satin pumps with itty-bitty rose buds glued on. Dyed lilac, naturally."

"Naturally."

Kim sat up. "I don't care what you wear. Just as long as it's not black. Or white. Have Tony pick something out for you. He has good taste."

"In all things," he said from the doorway.

I jumped.

"Did you get Brittney home okay?" Kim asked.

"You took her home? Personally?"

He nodded.

"Call me if you need anything, Jules." She whirled on Tony and chattered a Spanish phrase that made him grin.

After Kim left, he closed the door. "Before you chew my ass, let me say it was time I met your father."

I didn't ask him what he thought of Doug Collins, because I didn't want to know. "Is he still alive?"

"Yes, unfortunately."

"What did you do?"

"Honestly? Nothing. I imagined a lot of painful

things I could do. But unless he lays a hand on you now, I don't give two shits about him." Those black eyes bored into me. "I heard what Brittney said."

"All of it?"

"Yes. I've seen you struggling with this relationship with her in the last few months. Obviously, any continued contact with your family is your choice, Julie, but I'm not gonna pretend I understand why you'd want it."

"Me either."

"So, what now?"

"Now I say thank you."

"For?"

"Saving me."

Martinez shook his head. "Like I told the doc. You saved yourself yesterday."

"I'm not talking about yesterday, Tony. I'm talking about every other day since we've been together. Being with you has saved me."

We stared at each other, aware another boundary between us had disappeared.

He softly said, "Same goes." Then he locked the door and came to bed.

CHAPTER 32

THEN NEXT MORNING I COMPLAINED, "WHY DON'T I get to choose?"

Martinez sighed. "Because I know who you'll pick."

I batted my eyelashes at him. "But, sugar-sweetie-pie-honey-bun, you know I'd choose you every time."

No-neck, Cal (God, I had to stop calling him No-neck), and Buzz grinned. Their mirth disappeared the second bossman glared at them.

"No, you'll pick Big Mike. Since the two of you decided to handle things without my consent, or approval, you know you can get around him, and that ain't happening again."

Big Mike glanced at me from beneath blackened eyes. The balloonish swells on his face deflated some, although his mouth was still puffy, like a Botox experiment gone awry.

I didn't break eye contact. It was the least I could do; acknowledge his sacrifice, since he'd borne the pain of our joint decision to circumvent Tony.

When Martinez discovered Big Mike's idea to smoke out Jackal, my solo excursion with Nyla, and the fact we'd kept our nefarious plans a secret from the all-powerful El Presidente . . . well, El Presidente blustered into *El Niño* and showed his wrath big time. With his fists. The other Hombres security goons did nothing to stop it; Big Mike did nothing to defend himself.

I hadn't known about the disciplinary act until after the fact. I wouldn't have interfered because Big Mike had chosen the Hombres lifestyle. He knew the penalty for disobeying a direct order. The other bodyguards considered Big Mike's punishment fair. Just. Swift.

Big Mike aimed his focus on Martinez. "With all due respect, sir, I'm probably the first one you should trust with Miz Collins's safety since I have the most to lose if anything happens to her."

Martinez leveled a tough guy glower on all three men. "True. But I'm giving the headache to Buzz today."

I opened my mouth to protest the *headache* moniker, but it snapped shut when Tony growled, "Out," and everyone scattered.

He stalked me, and damn if I didn't retreat until my back hit the wall. "Quit bullying me."

"I haven't even started bullying you, so don't

fucking push me. Three rules today, in order for you to walk out of this house with Jackal still on the loose. One—You will not go anywhere without Buzz. Two— You will listen to Buzz. Three—You will not ditch Buzz. If you break any of these three simple rules, I will lock you upstairs in Bare Assets and leave your buddy Charity as your caretaker. Is that clear?"

"You are a cold, mean bastard, Martinez."

"And your point is?"

I looked down at my hands. "Does Kevin know?"

"That I've assigned you a temporary bodyguard? Yes. Specifically why? No." His warm fingers lifted my chin. "He knows I'll go to extremes to keep you safe. Once Jackal is gone, things will return to normal."

"Promise?"

"Yes. Sure you're up to going into the office today?"

"I have to do something . . . normal."

"I understand. At least Buzz won't bitch about the music in your truck. He loves that caterwauling crap you've been listening to lately."

"If you're done insulting me, can I go?"

He gifted me with a steamy tie-my-insides-in-knots grin. "Uh huh. Just as soon as you say it."

"Sadistic fucker."

"Such a sweet talker." Martinez nuzzled my ear and whispered, "You know what I want."

Perverse of me to withhold it? Yes. But dammit, I liked that he was as greedy to hear it from me, as I was to hear it from him.

"I'm waiting, blondie."

"Fine. I love you, okay?"

"Mmm." His teeth nipped my earlobe and he backed off.

"Forgetting something?"

"Fine. *Te amo*, okay?"

"That wasn't I love you."

"Yes, it was. As heartfelt as you said to me." He kissed my forehead. "Later." And he was gone.

Buzz let me drive. He wasn't chatty, but he wasn't as scary/stoic as Bucket. He didn't bitch when I sang along to *Crazy Ex-Girlfriend*.

I wondered if he'd just sit in the reception area all day staring into space. Or if he'd brought a book. Or guns to clean. Or knives to sharpen.

Kevin gave Buzz a once-over before beckoning me in his office. He even shut the door. I was really in for it.

I moved to the comfy chairs across from the desk, but Kevin stopped me cold.

He whispered, "I want to know every fucking thing that's going on, right now. You may have loyalties to Martinez, but you also have loyalties to *me*.

And if you don't think you can trust me, Jules, when we've been friends since we were twelve, then walk out that fucking door and don't come back."

Kevin's ultimatum pissed me off, yet I knew he was right. So I gave him the abbreviated version of my current saga.

Afterward, he paced. When he stopped and faced me, I recognized his hard expression, and I braced myself for another make-or-break moment in another relationship in my life.

"Is this the life you want, Jules? A bodyguard? People gunning for you because you're with him?"

"I know you don't understand—"

"I don't. Not at all." Kevin's hands cupped my shoulders. "What about down the road? Will you be swilling tequila in a biker bar, dodging bullets and rival drug dealers in ten years? Twenty? Don't you want a family? Kids?"

"And a house with a picket fence, a nine-to-five job, a husband puttering around on weekends? No. I'd make a lousy fucking parent, Kev, and not just because of my childhood traumas. I don't want the life everyone else leads. Not because I'm cool, or a rebel, but because I *like* the way I live. I like my job and my friends. I've done some stupid things, some dangerous things, made some serious mistakes, but falling in love with Tony Martinez was not one of them."

"You deserve better."

Count to ten. To twenty. To one hundred. As high as

it takes to stay calm and keep this in perspective.

"I'm gonna say this one time. He is a permanent part of my life. Period. If you can't handle that, then I will leave. But don't make me choose. Please. Don't make me choose."

Those thoughtful green eyes bored into me: heart, body, and soul. A lump lodged in my throat when I considered I might not be the type of friend or business partner he wanted anymore. I understood, even when I wished I didn't.

We stared at each other for a long time.

Then Kevin used the charming grin that'd won me over in Mrs. Swigart's seventh grade English class. "It sort of sucks."

"What?"

"That I'm jealous as hell. You've found a man who takes you as you are, on your terms. Much as I love you, Jules, and harbored this crazy idea you and I would eventually end up together?" He shook his head. "I'd try to change you. Hell, I try to do it right now—even when you don't need it. And you, my friend, have always deserved better." He kissed my forehead. "Now get your ass to work and file something."

I turned away so he didn't see the moisture in my eyes.

There really wasn't much for me to do. I hid in my office and smoked, trying to piece together my recent life events.

My father had either helped commit murder or covered it up.

What purpose would jail time serve for him or DJ? Besides to allow Melvin Canter's actions to ruin yet another family? I vehemently disagreed with Dad's reasoning and willingness to sacrifice Brittney's emotional well-being to save DJ's, but he was a hundred percent correct that if he went to jail, Trish and the kids would lose the ranch.

Truth was, Melvin Canter was a piece of human filth. The world was better off without him because the justice system hadn't worked—numerous times.

So, once again, I was dealing with issues of vigilante justice. Once again, I was turning a blind eye to the outcome. And I'd become well versed in keeping secrets about orchestrated endings:

Bobby Adair.

Maurice Ashcroft.

Roland Hawk.

Melvin Canter.

All dead, none by my hand, but all deaths well deserved, and none mourned.

Was I becoming what I'd once loathed? Passing judgment only when it suited *my* parameters and ideals? Acting indignant when it didn't?

If I had the chance to kill Jackal, would I do it? I had an up close and personal view of his "humane" execution of Trina. He'd left me to die. Jackal would happily destroy Martinez if given the opportunity.

Losing Martinez would destroy me. I'd finally begun to heal from losing Ben.

I'd convinced myself killing the person who'd killed my brother would be easy. It hadn't turned out that way. I still suffered from nightmares.

But not from guilt.

So why did I see Amery Grayson's murderous actions as wrong? How was what she'd done somehow worse? Even when I wouldn't feel any differently if I knew she'd whipped out a gun and shot her grandfather rather than leaving him to freeze to death alone? Were her motives less pure because of the vast amounts of money involved?

Was honor or revenge a more acceptable reason for murder than a financial windfall?

Yes. I don't know how I'd come to that realization, but it worked for me. I'd colored it another shade of gray. If God, or Buddha, or Allah judged me harshly, so be it.

That didn't mean I wouldn't allow the legal system to judge Amery Grayson given the chance.

As I was getting ready to leave, the intercom rang. "Julie. Luella's here to see you. Buzz won't let her in."

I stormed out my door and glared at my bodyguard. "She's fine. Let her pass."

Buzz shrugged and stepped aside.

"Hi, Luella, come on in." To Buzz I said, "I'm not leaving the door open, so don't even ask."

"Coffee?" I asked politely.

"That'd be great. Black."

When I returned with the cups, she was looking at the picture of Ben and me, taken the summer after I'd turned eighteen. We were both laughing. Happy. Young. Cool. It was my favorite picture because it reminded me we had lots of good times before his murder. I'd placed it next to a picture of my mother and me mugging for the camera the summer before she died.

"Is this your brother?"

"Yeah."

"Handsome. What was his name?"

"Ben Standing Elk." I braced myself for a gasp of surprise. Leticia's death had caused huge ripples on the White Plain Reservation, and I'd found myself sucked into the riptide and spit out. I chanced asking, "Do you know the Standing Elk Family?"

"No. I'm from Eagle Butte. And I won't snap at you and assume you meant because I'm Indian I should somehow know all the other Indians in the state."

"You know what I meant."

"Sorry. I'm just a little sensitive about that."

"I can imagine."

She took the coffee and dropped her coat on the chair, and I fished out my cigarettes, giving her time to settle. "What I tell you is confidential, right?"

Ethical dilemma.

No. It's only a dilemma if she tells you what you don't want to hear.

My thoughts teetered between serving my conscience and serving hers. I sighed. "Yes. It's confidential."

"I've been thinking a lot about what you said and I still don't know what to do." Pause. "I'm sure you figured out Vernon made another will just a couple weeks ago."

"Yeah, I did. I guess I wondered how it happened. Did he ask you to take him to a lawyer's office?"

"No. He hated to leave the facility. We had a group seminar geared for the new residents, dealing with updating their wills, and Vernon showed up. I helped him fill out the paperwork, never expecting he was serious. The only reason he willingly hung around other residents was when I was there to act as a buffer." She cleared her throat. "It's not what you think. We were just friends. Vernon hated group activity weeks because I usually did Admin that week and spent less time with him. Anyway, the will kit was a simple 'do it yourself' jobber we use at the retirement center as a template. I didn't notice he had it notarized until we were back in his room."

I had guessed right about the will not being on file in some legal office. "Where is the will now?"

"At my house. And if your next question is if there

are copies elsewhere, the answer is no. I have the only copy."

"What did Vernon change?"

She shifted. "Everything. He cut Amery out of it completely."

"Who gets the estate?" Luella hesitated a beat too long and a sensation like I'd swallowed ground glass spun in the pit of my stomach. "You?"

"No. Worse. Prime Time Friends."

Another ugly pause.

"Ironically enough, when I was put in charge of the program I was under orders from Mr. Boner to convince Vernon Sloane to gift some of his money to us. That was the initial reason I'd insinuated myself into his life. Horrible, isn't it?"

The pain in her voice made me cringe.

"But the plan backfired on me." She made dents in the top of her Styrofoam cup with her fingernails. "The more I got to know Vernon the sorrier I felt for him and the more I wanted to protect him. Everybody wanted a piece of him, and no one saw what a sad, lonely little man he was. I did."

"So by playing on his sympathies, you got him to sign over everything anyway?"

Her skin became a deeper shade of scarlet. "It might seem that way. I did feel guilty, which is why I initially never told anyone about the new will. He gave it to me because he said he didn't want it around, but I don't know if he meant for me to hide it or destroy it.

So I don't know what to do."

"Your option seems pretty cut-and-dried to me. You turn in the will, get to be the big hero to Prime Time Friends, and Amery gets nothing. I doubt we can prove she killed him—"

"But what if she *didn't* kill him?" Luella's eyes finally met mine. "Like you said, there's no proof."

"Now you think it was an unfortunate accident?"

"I hate to say this, but Vernon had been known to wander. Out looking for his car. Waiting for his daughter to pick him up even though she's been dead a while. One time last fall I found him in the drainage ditch."

"Why are you waffling on this, Luella?"

"Because I don't know which one is worse. Amery getting the money or PTF."

"But wouldn't you get five percent of the five million as a finder's fee?"

Another bout of silence.

"I don't want it."

"Why not? That's like . . . a lifetime supply of cash."

"It's blood money. Do you really think Bradley Boner is just gonna hand it over?" She shook her head. "He's been trying to get rid of me since he took over. He's racist. He thinks I'm too old. Mark my words, he'll find some way to keep every penny and make me look bad and where will I be?"

Was her paranoia justified? Was that why she

hadn't told Boner?"

"Doesn't matter if Amery or a staff member killed Vernon; it doesn't change the fact I'm benefiting from a man's death, when the man shouldn't be dead. When I should've been more vigilant about protecting him."

"Luella. It's not your fault. But I missed something when you said a staff member might've killed him. Why?"

"What if Vernon told someone else who works at Prairie Gardens besides me about changing his will? That would give Prime Time Friends the exact same motive as his granddaughter. And when I really think about it, it'd be easier for someone who's there all the time to lead him astray. If Amery did it, why didn't anyone see her?"

I hadn't thought of that. Sharp-eyed Reva hadn't seen Amery at all in the last few months, and if anyone knew the goings on at Prairie Gardens, it was Reva.

I didn't see Boner trusting any of his shitty staff to do the job and keep their mouth shut. Nor did I see him doing the dirty work himself. Leading me back to square one: Amery.

Again, I listened to my gut instincts. Amery was responsible for Vernon Sloane winding up dead. She flat out admitted the cold and snow didn't bother her. No one would've noticed her in the middle of a blizzard, with her back against the brick wall as she watched her grandfather die.

Like you knew in your gut your father had nothing to

467

do with Melvin Canter winding up dead?

What a fucked-up mess.

"I don't know what to tell you, Luella, besides the five million will make lots of older, lonely people like Vernon happy. In Amery's case, it'll make one person happy. Sloane left the responsibility to you because he trusted you to do the right thing. I think you know what the answer is." I didn't need to pander and remind her of the Lakota philosophy, which, in a nutshell, was "share and share alike," nor did I interrupt her internal struggle.

Luella sighed. "You're right. What do I do now?"

I glanced down at the long silvery ash in the ashtray. Another cigarette burned to nothing. "I think you should talk to Bud Linderman, CEO of Linderman Properties Limited, before you approach Boner. Do you know him?"

"I've met him a couple of times. He hangs around the offices some nights." She looked at me expectantly. "Since you know him, will you come with me?"

Not with a bodyguard dogging my every move. "I can't. But I'll call him. I'll send my partner, Kevin, along with you."

Her silence was weighted between fear and anger.

"Trust me. He's the best choice. Hang on." I dialed Kevin's office and he scooted right in. I smoked and listened to Kevin's quiet assurance and Luella's acceptance of it and him.

Kevin said, "Call Linderman. Give him my cell

phone number."

After a very brief conversation with Linderman, and Kevin and Luella's departure, I was back to staring at four walls, feeling distracted and . . . disappointed?

Why? Had I figured there'd be a bloody end to this case? Amery and I wrestling in a snowbank in frigid temps before I attempted to rescue a bound and gagged Luella from certain death? Amery laughing and balling up the only copy of the will and tossing it into the creek? Me diving into the icy water to save it? Managing to retrieve it, fighting with Amery and knocking her unconscious, trussing her up like a turkey until the cops came, after I'd saved Luella to boot?

Right. Most cases ended with a whimper, not a bang.

Some semblance of justice had been served. It was done. Over. *Finito*. I could leave this case. Walk away. Move on.

Or not.

CHAPTER 33

Buzz and I ate lunch at Southside McDonalds. The Kinsey Millhone hangover special for me. Four double-cheeseburgers and a yogurt parfait for him.

A few blocks down Mt. Rushmore Road I smoked the tail end of my cigarette and studied the travel agency, nestled in a remodeled 1940s ranch house. Why people didn't buy airline tickets, cruises, and getaway specials online boggled my mind.

"What're we doin' here?" Buzz asked.

I'd called ahead to make sure Amery was working. "Kim is getting married in Vegas in a few weeks. I need to check on ticket prices for me and Martinez."

"Bossman know about this trip?"

"Ah. It's a surprise."

"He don't like surprises."

"Well, I wouldn't just spring it on him, which is

why I want to look at all the options before I bring it up. The different hotels. Suite sizes. Entertainment packages. You know what I mean." I shouldered my purse and paused. "You coming in to help me?"

The pained look on his mug told me how much the option appealed to him.

"No? That's okay. I promise I won't be more than five minutes."

"Julie—"

"Listen. I'm not gonna ditch you. I'll be in and out." I pointed at the office drones working in front of the big windows. "You can even see me. I'll stay in sight."

"Five minutes or I'm comin' in."

Heeding his warning, I scooted inside and plopped right down in front of Amery's terminal.

She blinked and glanced around. "Julie. This is a surprise."

"Not as much of a surprise as it is for me to see you still playing the part of a working girl."

"Excuse me?"

"God knows I wouldn't be shilling cut-rate senior bus tours to Branson, Missouri, if I stood to inherit five million smackers. And that's not counting the multimillion-dollar lawsuit you have brewing on the side."

Her expression changed not one iota. "What do you mean?"

I leaned forward. "Cut the shit. The grieving granddaughter routine only goes so far, and you've

471

stretched it to the limits of believability with me."

"I really—"

"—didn't think we'd find out how much old Vern was worth? For Christsake, Amery, we *are* professional investigators."

She bit her lip, but I didn't buy her pitiful little-girl act. "Does Kevin know you're here?"

"No. Kevin and I don't see eye to eye where you're concerned. He sees you through a fog of lust. I see you taking advantage of his trust."

She permitted a tiny simpering smile. "Maybe you should talk to your partner first before you try to intimidate me and ramble on when you don't know the score. Because it sure didn't seem like I was taking advantage of his trust when he was in my bed last night."

Kevin, you randy dog. You literally did pump her. Not for info, but for revenge sex. I was impressed.

"Is that it? Came here to warn me off?"

"No, I'm here as a public service." I leaned close. "I'm onto you, doll. Every cold-blooded move you've made. Hiring Kevin to uncover the terrible things that *could* happen at your beloved Pop-Pop's retirement home. Skipping off to his condo during a blizzard, right after you left your grandfather to fucking die alone like an unwanted dog. Then conveniently 'forgetting' your cell phone, so you're out of touch. Jetting off to Vegas only to be called back to face the very tragedy you feared."

Amery cocked her head prettily, like a beribboned cocker spaniel.

"Then, horrors! Everything you fretted about came true. But you forgot two teeny things. One— you shouldn't have dumped Kevin so soon after your potential cash windfall. He's a guy. He's gonna take the piece of ass if you shake it in front of him. If sex is throw-off-your-inhibitions-in-the-middle-of-the-work-day-and-screw-on-the-conference-table fantastic then he's gonna expect more of it.

"So, when you suddenly yank the hot sex away, not even attempting to replace it with the old standby of preferring cuddling time, he'll get suspicious. Like you were . . . *using* him for something besides sex. And being the snoopy sort, he'll start digging for answers.

"And because I'm the suspicious sort, I'll start digging, too. We'll compare notes. And because we are professional snoops, people who have a vested interest in the outcomes of certain legal grievances come to us with all sorts of theories. Paperwork that brings up more questions than answers."

She didn't take long to mull it over. "Fascinating theory. How is it that Kevin came crawling back for some of that hot sex last night if he's so suspicious of my motives?"

I mock-whispered, "You think you're the only one who can use sex to get what they want? He was in your bed last night? Interesting. I sure hope you didn't fall asleep too hard and leave him unattended in your house."

Little girl lost morphed into the "old soul" Kevin mentioned, but I just saw her as a cunning monster who'd led a man to an icy grave.

"I'm sure those unnamed 'people with a vested interest' won't question your theories at all. Because you'd *never* drag your agency through the press, just for the press. Things've been awful slow without new cases coming in. Gee, it's been months since you've been the lead story.

"And you've personally killed, what, *two* people in the last year? Now you're going after a grieving woman whose only living relative was found frozen to death? After *your* agency was snooping around the very facility where he was found? A few days later *you* just happened to stumble upon the victim? Maybe you could've prevented the tragedy if you'd done your job. And, oddly enough, I heard that from your . . . partner. It's such a shame when miscommunications and legal matters break up partnerships and friendships, isn't it? And there's nothing you can do about it?"

Conniving bitch. She'd had this all planned from the beginning. Picking our small agency. Playing Kevin. Playing me against him. Using the storm. Finding her grandfather was just sheer bad luck on my part, and yet she'd discovered a way to spin it.

Her crafty grin alerted me to the idea she thought she'd won.

Wrong.

Amery checked her watch. "Like I said. Fascinating

theory. But I am running behind. So if you'll excuse me—"

"Sure. But you forgot the other teensy thing. I mentioned two, remember?" I inched on my left leather glove a finger at a time. "Better hope that lawsuit lottery holds up, because according to my sources, Grandpa dearest wrote a new will, and you ain't in it. At all." I locked my gaze to hers. "Oh, and that's not just a fascinating theory; that's a fact."

I waved at Buzz through the window to let him know I was done before I waltzed out.

CHAPTER 34

Jimmer called my cell while I was leaving a message for Martinez. I clicked over and heard, "Lemme talk to Buzz."

"One of these days, Jimmer, you are gonna call just to talk to me, right?"

He snorted. I passed the phone to Buzz.

"You're sure?" Buzz shot me a sideways glance. "With her along? No fuckin' way."

Not good.

"Don't matter 'cause I ain't gonna ask her."

"Ask me what?"

"Fine. Jimmer wants to know if you've got your gun with you."

"Uh, yeah."

Buzz sighed. "Five minutes. But if he—" He closed the phone and clutched it in a fist the size of an Easter ham. "Shit. Get to Highway 44. Fast."

"What's going on?"

"Jimmer's got a lead on Jackal."

"Jimmer? Since when did he turn into a divining rod?"

He shot me a look. "You're fuckin' kidding, right?"

I shook my head. Switched lanes when I saw the Blue Lantern Lounge. Waited for the light to change, and turned right on the ramp merging onto Highway 44 South. "Jimmer's a hunting guide."

"Tracking people is the same as tracking animals. Except people leave better trails."

I Hate Myself for Loving You blasted out of my cell phone and I smiled. During the hours I'd spent attached to my cell, I'd programmed ring tones for my frequent callers: Joan Jett for Martinez, Aerosmith's *Janie's Got a Gun* for Jimmer, *Mamma Mia* by ABBA for Kim.

Once I started, I couldn't stop, pegging *Private Eyes* by Hall & Oates for Kevin. Yeah, I was pretty pleased with myself when I decided Ben's special tone would've been *Half Breed* by Cher.

However, Buzz wasn't amused when I said, "It's your boss."

"Fuck." He flipped the cover open. "Hello? Yessir. No. Everything is fine. We're just getting a snack."

A lie? Interesting.

"It's a bad connection because we're in the fuckin' Sonic drive-thru. She wanted a banana shake. Yes, I'm paying. Hang on. She says she'll call you back."

Click. He said, "Fuckin' A."

"What? Should I be worried?"

He grunted.

"You lied to your leader, Buzz."

"Don't fuckin' remind me. I saw what Big Mike looked like, all right?"

"Martinez doesn't know about us meeting Jimmer?"

"Nobody's supposed to fuckin' know. Especially not you. Turn left here."

I bumped over the railroad tracks and slowed because the pavement ended. "Where to?"

"Straight up the hill and down the other side."

Good thing I had four-wheel drive.

But the area at the bottom of the hill surprised me because it wasn't out in the boondocks; it was its own mini-industrial region. An abandoned-looking section of town I'd never seen. With a junkyard. Metal buildings were scattered at odd intervals. We took another sharp right and stopped in the gravel parking lot between two buildings, where Jimmer stood in full winter camo. Whoa. No shotgun resting on his shoulder? No sign of Jimmer's beloved Hummer either? Just a Bobcat and the backside of the salvage dump.

Buzz climbed out first. After the door slammed I shoved my gun in my jacket pocket and jumped out. Goddamn, it was cold out here. Spooky, too.

Jimmer ambled up and said to Buzz, "We ain't got a lot of time. Give me a breakdown."

"Jackal hired an employee to take a shot at bossman

at his own place of business."

"Ballsy, but stupid."

"You heard what he did to her?"

"Why the fuck do you think I'm here? He oughta fuckin' die for that alone," Jimmer said.

Should I remind them I'd handled that situation on my own?

"You know what he done to his guard?"

"Yeah. The eyeball-slicing thing sounds nasty. So, if this is about retribution, I'm cool with helping out." Jimmer's face became placid, but his voice was pure steel. "But if it has to do with the missing product I've been hearing about, I ain't gonna get involved. I'm a fence sitter, dig?"

Buzz nodded. "Bossman wants to be the trigger-man, which is exactly why he shouldn't be. Big Mike, Cal, Bucket, me, we're all in agreement on this one."

"You got a death wish?" Jimmer pushed closer to Buzz. "You're going behind Martinez's back? I never would've offered my help if I would've known he wasn't in on it. What the fuck happens when he catches wind of it? He's gonna go ballistic."

They argued and circled each other, herding me against the truck behind them as they snapped and snarled like junkyard dogs.

"You're safe. You don't gotta follow the same rules as we do, Jimmer."

"Neither do I," I offered.

Buzz looked at me like I'd spoken Farsi.

Jimmer snapped, "Jesus Christ, Jules, get in the fuckin' truck. Tony'll castrate me if he finds out you were here."

"The last thing bossman needs is to look weak. I get that, okay? He's gonna be on the warpath when he finds out what we done," Buzz said. "But he don't need to take chances just because he can. Nobody wants him in jail."

They eyeballed each other.

The low rent industrial ghost town gave me the creeps. I half-expected the weird old cars to morph into some giant robotic monsters and chase us off. My breath puffed out as I fought off an unexpected surge of panic. This felt wrong. Really wrong. A little voice was telling me to get in my truck and gun it back to civilization.

Before I could voice my paranoid thoughts, Martinez's Escalade barreled around the corner. I hadn't heard him coming. Jimmer and Buzz said "fuck" simultaneously and stepped in front of me.

Martinez eased out the driver's side, wearing his leg brace, Big Mike hot on his heels. Tony was mad as hell.

Double fuck.

"Did I miss the invite to the Julie Collins fan club meeting?"

"It's not—"

"Because that's the only reason I can fathom you'd fucking *lie* to me about where you were going, Buzz."

Buzz remained mute.

"Where's the rest of my security team? Buying balloons and party favors?"

The air outside wasn't nearly as cold as the glare he

aimed at Jimmer. "You in on this, too?"

"I have a stake in making sure you don't do nuthin' stupid, Tony. Buzz and I were discussing some options."

The wind blew an icy blast across my face, but I didn't dare look away.

"Last I knew, I headed the Hombres. You should be talking to *me*, Jimmer, nobody else."

"And now I am."

Gunshots rent the air, pinging off metal. I didn't know if bullets hit my truck or Martinez's vehicle or the building behind me or the Bobcat. I didn't stick around to match paint chips; I ran for the biggest protective structure, and that sure as hell wasn't a man.

No way would I hide out in a junkyard, which left two other choices. I made tracks for the building behind me, the one closest to the road.

Buzz and Big Mike's priority would be Martinez. Jimmer would go after the shooter. I'd be on my own. Again.

As I picked my way through the snow along the north side, gun in hand, I heard more shots. I couldn't tell where they were coming from. Or where they'd hit. I didn't dare stop moving.

I doubted the shooter was around the side facing the street, so that'd probably be the safest place for me to hide. I stayed low, even when my black coat was a bull's-eye against the mint green metal siding and the white snow.

The effects of my hypothermia came back full force in an instant. My teeth chattered. My limbs shook. I couldn't catch my breath. The latter was probably from fear, not forced exercise. Sad, that I was beginning to recognize the difference between terror and smoker's overexertion.

My knees locked. Each boot step through the caked snow seemed thunderous in the deadly stillness. I counted steps. One, two, three. At twelve I reached the end of the boxy structure.

Deep breath, Julie. Probably nothing around the corner but an air conditioner unit and a Dumpster. Either would make a fine hiding place.

What was safety protocol? Did I poke my head around first? Or lead with the gun? I'd seen enough old PI and cop TV shows; I should remember. As I contemplated how Remington Steele would've done it, I tripped over an extended downspout and face planted into a hard pile of snow. My fingers were stiff as frozen fish sticks and I couldn't keep the grip on the Sig. It skidded out of sight.

Took every ounce of restraint not to yell, FUCK!

Freezing, scared, and unarmed. Great. Could this get worse? I pushed to my knees, sat back on my heels, and swiped the dirty snow from my face.

When I looked up, Jackal's "gotcha" grin swam into view. Along with the muzzle of the gun he'd aimed at me.

My survival instincts scrambled for dominance, but my body remained inert.

Jackal made a single step my direction and a barrage of gunfire echoed around us. Jackal's cruel mouth did a twisty thing and half his head exploded as he jerked and twitched. Before I saw anything else, a flying tackle broadsided me, forcing the air from my lungs while my face slammed into the snowdrift.

I didn't complain. I didn't move. Actually, I couldn't move with Buzz on top of me. I heard Jimmer's voice.

"She all right?"

"Knocked the wind out of her."

"How's Martinez?"

"I knocked the wind out of him, too."

"Why? How the fuck did that happen?"

Buzz pushed up and muttered, "He was ignoring protocol, trying to get to her."

Oh crap. That wasn't good.

"Let's worry about protocol with this asswipe."

"He finally dead?"

"Yeah. Seems a waste of bullets even now."

No more Jackal. I slumped with a sick sense of complete relief.

"Where we dumpin' him?"

Mumbled male voices gave instructions I didn't care to hear.

More footsteps. I lifted my head slightly and surveyed the scene. Cal and Bucket stood in front of Jackal's body, each holding a shovel. An arc of blood sprayed across the snow. Not pretty like red sugar crystals on vanilla cookie dough, but ugly; the bloody finality of death. Jimmer pointed to the Bobcat, the junkyard, then at a can of gasoline.

Buzz helped me to my feet. "Bossman is waiting for you with Big Mike." I attempted to turn around, but Buzz's hands clamped on my shoulders. "Nuthin' you need to see back there."

"But, I need—"

"What?"

"My gun. I, ah, dropped it."

Jimmer snorted. "I'll find it."

Buzz directed my hobble to the front of the building. I shook like a wet cat. Odd, now that I really thought about it. Where had the Hombres security guys come from? No other vehicles circled the Escalade. The passenger's door to the luxury SUV opened. Big Mike lumbered out.

Had the Trifecta of Terror locked El Presidente in his Caddy during the shootout? Don't know why I found that so funny. I bit my lip to keep from laughing uncontrollably.

Maybe I was in shock. Or perhaps simply relieved my lover hadn't murdered the man who'd fallen ten feet in front of me. Then again, this hadn't been a random—*oh, look who showed up, let's get him* situation.

This'd been a setup.

"Finally. He 'bout killed me he's so goddamn anxious."

"Tough." I slapped my hand on Big Mike's chest, stopping his flight. "What the fuck just happened?"

"Jesus. You sound exactly like him."

"Start talking."

His gaze cut to the driver's side; his voice dropped. "We knew once Jackal found out he'd try for you again."

"Found out what? I'd escaped?"

"That, among other things."

"Define 'other things,' Big Mike."

"Things like Nyla."

"What about Nyla?"

"She OD'd." He held up his hand. "Not our fault. She didn't tell us shit about Jackal, we let her go after the situation with you, and she went on a binge. Maids at that motel found her yesterday."

I stared at him. Had Nyla chosen to die by drugs rather than Jackal's hand? "What else?"

"Jimmer heard what happened with you and Jackal. He called last night to talk to bossman, to offer to help, because he thinks Tony sucks at keeping you safe. I intercepted the call because you guys were otherwise occupied. I told him to stay out of it."

Whoa.

"Jimmer, being Jimmer, didn't listen. He took it upon himself to follow you and Buzz this morning to see if anyone followed you."

"And did anyone?"

"Jackal did. Personally. Jimmer was mad as hell when he called and said Jackal tracked you to both your office and the travel agency and you only had one guard. He said he was sick of pissing around with our lax security. Then he demanded Cal and Bucket get into position out here, knowing Jackal wouldn't pass up an opportunity to go after you in a remote location. Buzz didn't want to do it."

My mouth dropped open. "You let Jimmer call the shots? This is Tony's organization. Isn't that like breaking a million Hombres 'no outsiders' rules?"

"Yes." Big Mike pointed to his bruised face. "You think I want to get the fuck beat out of me again? You think any of us like ignoring a direct order? No. Jackal's had the upper hand for weeks. We've all been frustrated. It doesn't help Tony hasn't been at one hundred percent, and his worry about you is clouding his judgment. And no, this isn't a power play from me, or Cal, or anyone else. Martinez is our leader. Period. We're all prepared to deal with the fallout."

"Where was Martinez when this was going down?"

"At physical therapy."

"By *himself*?"

Big Mike scowled. "No. With me."

"Just you? Just one goddamn bodyguard?"

"You surprised he's a real fuckin' dickhead about not wantin' no one around when he's doin' that painful shit?"

I shook my head.

"Anyway, he knew something was up. He's got some sixth sense about that. Some comment Buzz made to him when he answered your phone struck Martinez wrong."

What? Oh. The ice cream. Buzz had said I was getting banana ice cream. Tony knew I hated anything banana flavored.

"We were on our way back to the clubhouse when he made me pull over so he could drive, and he followed the tracker on your truck."

"Did Buzz know about this plan?"

"Not until the last minute when Jimmer called

him with specifics."

"So, I was fucking bait?"

"Yep." Big Mike grimaced. "And we're all gonna get our asses beat because that's twice he'll believe we've put you in danger on purpose. Jimmer left us no choice. Might be worth it now that it's over and things can get back to normal."

"Over?" I gestured to the surrounding area. "What about the cops? Someone heard gunfire. It's only a matter of time before it's reported."

"These buildings are abandoned. Jimmer uses this area as a training facility for urban warfare tactics. Anyone asks questions, or says they saw something, he'll claim it was just another training session."

Not implausible, knowing Jimmer, the mysterious contracts within his pawnshop business, and his purported shady dealings with off-the-books government agencies like Blackwater. No wonder Hombres security didn't argue with him—against protocol or not—when he came up with a plan.

"Get in the car before Martinez has an aneurysm."

By the time I opened the door, my body vibrated like an opera singer's voice box.

Martinez said, "Where are your keys?"

"In my truck."

He threw the SUV in reverse and we took off.

"Hey, my purse—"

"—has an electric blanket tucked inside it?"

"No."

"Then I don't care. I'm taking you home to warm you up. *Again*. Stupid motherfuckers. I oughta kill every goddamn one of them for putting you in the line of fire. As it is I'm gonna have to remind them just who the fuck is in charge of this club." He ranted and I tuned him out.

He noticed I hadn't said boo before he saw the pinched look on my face.

"What's wrong?"

"Are you fucking serious?"

"Are you hurt?"

"No."

"Then what?"

"I'm supposed to be *used* to people getting their brains blown out in front of me? That's twice in three days! I'm just supposed to go 'oh well, another one bites the dust'?"

"You telling me you're upset that Jackal is finally dead?"

"No."

His eyes bored into me. "I don't understand what's going with you."

"I know you don't. So forget it, okay?"

"Julie—"

"Drop it, Tony. Just leave it alone."

He sighed.

The trip to my house was made in silence. I didn't have my cigarettes, my cell phone, or my keys. Had to wait for Martinez to unlock my front door before I could get into my own damn house.

His phone rang—big surprise—I grabbed the Don

Julio and retreated to the bathroom. I knocked three slugs straight from the bottle while peeling off my clothes.

The heat from the water warmed me. I blow-dried my hair and stayed in the humidity until I was calm enough to deal with him.

But Martinez was still on the phone.

As I dressed in my pj's, I heard the shower kick on. Mentally exhausted, I crawled in bed and willed sleep to come fast. When had it become so easy to nap during the day?

After you killed someone.

Stop. Dammit. I was tired of that single incident being the first excuse that popped into my head every time something went wrong.

The bedroom door banged open. "We need a bigger water heater. I'm sick of cold showers."

The old me would've said, "So take a shower at your place if you don't like it." The new, mooning-around-in-love me felt guilty and said, "Sorry."

The bed shifted and he slid under the covers, wrapping himself around me like a cocoon.

Maybe it was selfish, but I wanted to hide under the covers with him and pretend everything was hunky-dory. No dead bodies, no business secrets between us. Just us. Just for a little while.

Finally, Martinez sighed. "I am trying."

"Try harder."

His soft laughter was the last thing I heard before I drifted off.

CHAPTER 35

TWO HOURS LATER THE BEDSIDE PHONE RANG. SHERIFF Richards was on his way over to talk to me. He didn't mention about what.

Martinez wasn't happy. Neither was the Hombres security team. They opted to chill in the bedroom. Tony refused.

When the sheriff arrived, he shook Martinez's hand, which shocked the hell out of me. Then I remembered they'd worked together last fall to track me down at Bear Butte. I filled cups and pretended a coffee klatch with my former cop boss and my current criminal lover was an everyday occurrence.

Tony and I sat side by side on the couch. He kept his hand on my thigh.

Sheriff Richards scrutinized me from the easy chair. "Collins, you look terrible. What happened to you?"

"Skiing accident."

He frowned. "Since when do you ski?"

"I don't. I'm learning. Cross-country. Not down-hill." I pointed to Martinez's leg brace. "I fell, then he fell, and we ended up spending more time out in the elements than we'd expected."

"Gotta be careful. Hypothermia is dangerous stuff." He rested his forearms on his knees and studied Martinez, then me. "You have an inkling about why I'm here?"

"I'm not being flip when I say not a clue."

He gave us that back-and-forth squinty, hard cop eye. Made me wonder who'd win in a stare down between him and Martinez.

"I'm here because BD Hoffman and Beth McClanahan came to see me yesterday and told me everything. I've gotta say I'm impressed you dug that connection up, because I missed it."

I waited.

"But it's a dead end."

"What do you mean?"

"DCI in Pierre called me this morning. They've been behind because of a flu epidemic and haven't gotten to Melvin Canter's case. Now Canter's family is making a big stink about refusing an autopsy and wanting the body returned for burial."

I wondered if I'd averted my eyes and started whistling would my part in that be too obvious.

"With the excessive postmortem wounds, including chunks getting chopped out of the corpse by the tractor, and the obscenely large amounts of alcohol in the blood system, the docs at the VA can't determine manner of death for Melvin Canter."

"Really?"

"Really."

"Never heard of this before. Never had this happen in all my years of law enforcement. They've closed the file as an accidental agricultural death, and the body is en route to the funeral home as we speak." He sipped his coffee, staring at me. "Do you have anything you'd like to add to their official observations?"

Yeah. My half brother killed Melvin Canter, and he and my father worked together to cover it up.

Putting my father or DJ in jail wouldn't help anyone. I didn't like it. But I liked it even less that the justice system had failed so many other times with children and there were multiple victims of Melvin Canter's sexual assaults.

But . . . what if not addressing DJ's problem or his violent reaction caused him to become a sociopath? Or a predator? Or allowed him to think he was above the law?

"Julie?" Martinez prompted.

I shook my head and said nothing.

"Case is closed then. Look. I don't normally do this, nor do I let people wait this long to file after an incident has occurred, especially when it didn't raise flags at the DA's office, but I wanted to let you know that BD Hoffman pressed assault charges against Doug Collins when he was in yesterday."

"What?"

"For the incident in Bevel's Hardware last week. I know Deputy John encouraged BD to drop it, but Beth McClanahan urged BD to follow through. Said she wishes she would've followed through years ago. She wondered how many kids she could've saved from humiliation and heartache if she would've done the right thing.

"So, I've asked Doug to turn himself in. Since he doesn't have a record he probably won't do much, if any, time in jail. Probably have to attend anger management classes. Seems fitting after all these years, don't it?"

I nodded, even when I suspected it'd be too little too late.

Sheriff Richards stood. "Thanks for your help. I ain't kidding when I say I hope it's a long time before I see you in an official capacity again, Collins."

"Likewise, Sheriff."

I walked him to the door and watched him pull away in a Bear Butte County patrol car.

Martinez sent his bodyguards for pizza and wrapped his arms around my midsection. "You okay?"

"Were you worried? That he'd found out what'd gone down with Jackal and Trina and he'd come here to ask questions?"

"I wondered. Nothing is foolproof."

"Nothing meaning covering up a murder?"

"Nothing meaning you didn't kill Trina and neither did I. The guy who did was on the loose. You think if I couldn't catch him that the sheriff could?"

493

"I don't know. You pissed off about Jimmer overstepping his bounds?"

"Some. I'll have to keep an iron fist on the members so they don't get any ideas about taking matters into their own hands or taking them to someone else. Jimmer won't stomp on my toes again, but I am grateful the problem is solved.

"Bottom line is Jackal killed three people in the last two weeks. He tried to kill three more. That says defective human. Like Melvin Canter, Jackal couldn't be rehabilitated. Goddammit, I tried. And look where it got me. I almost lost you. I won't be forgetting that anytime soon."

"So, Jackal usurped your authority, turned your employees against you, killed an Hombres guard, killed Trina, tried to kill you, tried to kill me—does that mean his death was a business-related hit?"

"As far as my business associates know? Yes. But in my mind, it was personal. I won't apologize for it."

"I don't expect you to." My fingers traced the lacy ice pattern on the glass. "Jackal said you took something that belonged to him and he wanted it back. What was it?"

Martinez didn't answer right away. "If I tell you, things will change between us."

"Why?"

"Because even though it might not seem like it, you are the one thing in my life that doesn't have anything to do with Hombres business. I'd like to keep it that way." He feathered kisses by my ear. "You know I don't sell puppies, blondie."

"I pretend you do."

He chuckled.

"Dealing with law enforcement is part of my business. Will that be an issue for you?"

"Not unless you're meeting with them to turn me in."

"I'd never do that."

"I know." He buried his mouth in my hair. "What's really on your mind?"

"I've been thinking. You talked about permanence. I want that. I'm tired of living apart. I want to exist in the same space, all the time, not just three nights out of seven."

Silence.

Way to throw your needy self out there, Julie.

"Say something, dammit."

"It's about fucking time."

I smiled. "There's no reason for me to live here anymore. I don't work for the county. I'm making a permanent break with the Collins family. I'm tired of the drive. You and all my friends live in Rapid." I turned my head to look at him. "I don't suppose we can live at Casa Martinez full-time?"

"Not possible. It's gotta stay off the radar, because it's the one place I feel completely safe. It's the one place I feel I can keep you safe. It's the one place where we can truly be alone."

"So I guess I'll live above the goddamn strip bar if it's an issue of your safety and if you're concerned about mine."

"A temporary fix, I promise. We'll find someplace in town that's ours. That'll work for both of us. Might take a few months."

"I'm okay with that."

As I leaned into Martinez, I saw the sky was clear. No snow, giving me the perfect view of Bear Butte. It was funny, how long I'd hated that chunk of rock. How long I'd lived in its shadow. Now that I'd finally made peace with it, I'd be moving away from it. For good.

I deserved a fresh start. And I'd go into it with my eyes wide open.

Three weeks later . . .

Page 29   *The Senior Citizen News*

(Rapid City)—Prime Time Friends COO Bradley Boner, and Rory Linderman, CEO of Linderman Properties Limited, announced the appointment of Amery Grayson as the new executive director of the senior volunteer organization. This is following the dismissal of Luella Spotted Tail, former director, who was released from her duties last week, amidst (unconfirmed) rumors of financial mismanagement.

In her first official statement, Ms. Grayson confirmed her grandfather, the late Vernon Sloane, had left five million dollars to the organization "for the betterment of all seniors." Ms. Grayson has stated her intention to create a friendlier senior volunteer organization, dedicated to the mental health and safety of the elderly, especially those afflicted with Alzheimer's, after the tragedy in February that claimed her grandfather's life.

The newly minted director hopes to expand Prime Time Friends, a not-for-profit organization, beyond the current facility, Prairie Gardens Assisted Living Center, and other LPL properties, into every elderly healthcare facility in town, and eventually across the state.

For more information
about other great titles from
Medallion Press, visit

www.medallionpress.com